CATASTROPHE

Ian Sutherland
CATASTROPHE

Vindigo
PRESS

Published in 2022 by Vindigo Press
Cape Town, South Africa
vindigo.press@gmail.com

ISBN: 978-0-6397-2520-8 (print)
ISBN: 978-0-6397-2521-5 (ebook)

Front cover photographs by Unsplash: Mick de Paola,
Nicola de Poli and Saad Chaudry; iStockphoto: AYakovlev
Back cover photograph by Unsplash: Aaron Burden
Cover design and typesetting by Monique Cleghorn
Set in Minion

Printed and bound by Novus Cape Town

To my mother, Charmian

Author's Note

This novel is principally a work of fiction. However, I have gone to considerable lengths to ensure that the historical, political, and geographical landscapes are as accurate as possible within the confines of the story.

At 01:23:58 on the 26th of April 1986, an explosion destroyed Reactor Number Four of the Chernobyl Nuclear Power Plant, situated roughly 180 km north of Kiev (now Kyiv), then capital of the Ukrainian Soviet Socialist Republic. At first, the Soviet authorities covered up the accident, only admitting to it after Swedish scientists at Forsmark, 1,100 km away, detected heightened levels of radiation. Even then, they delayed informing their own citizens of the dangers, allowing the open-air May Day parades to proceed, despite being aware that a vast cloud of radioactivity was spreading overhead.

Within days, over 100,000 residents of Chernobyl, Pripyat and surrounding villages were evacuated from a 30 km 'exclusion zone' about the plant – in what became a permanent exile. The exact dates and sequence of these events vary considerably by source. I chose to be guided by the official timeline represented by the Ukrainian National Chernobyl (now Chornobyl) Museum. Note that many residents were initially taken to remote locations outside the exclusion zone, and Lena's bus ride to Kiev in this story is my construct.

The exact causes of the accident were fiercely contested in the International Atomic Energy Agency in Vienna by scientists from the USSR and the West. Consensus points to design deficiencies, human error and the overall safety and control environment. The reasons hinted at in this story are plausible but speculative.

Many historians, as well as General Secretary Gorbachev, the architect of the glasnost and perestroika reforms underway at the time, contend that the Chernobyl disaster hastened the break-up of the Soviet Union. The fallout also had a devastating effect on the natural environment of vast swathes of what is today Ukraine, Belarus and the Russian Federation – and on the lives of hundreds of thousands of people.

The main characters in this story are ethnic Russians. For the most part, the language reflects this, for example the transliteration of the capital city of Ukraine from Russian to English as Kiev. The few exceptions include the Ukrainian spelling of street names in the capital as they appear in modern times.

Russians who know each other well like to address each other using nicknames, often in the diminutive, such as Sasha for Alexander and Lenochka for Lena. The more formal approach uses the prefix comrade or the first name + patronymic (middle name). A female child is given a patronymic after her father. Lena's full name, Lena Sergeyevna Chizhikova, implies that her father's first name was Sergey.

Finally, it should be noted that I had written several complete drafts of this novel prior to the release of the HBO television series *Chernobyl* in 2019 and the Russian invasion of Ukraine on the 24th February 2022.

Prologue

Know this, my little dove, a mother's heart never stops beating for her daughter. Nor hoping. And I've held this moment in my mind's eye every waking hour of the four years and three months since you put the phone down on me. But please, promise me you won't start to hate me again.

Your words exactly. Someday you'll understand how that pierces a mother's heart. But the past is another country. All that matters is that we've reconnected at last, and that cheers me.

So here we are! Talking again, at last.

Thank you!

For everything. Mainly, for being your beautiful, precious self. And so generous!

Yes, I know it's you and – Bob is it? – who've been paying for this surprise upgrade to a private room. Did you really expect it would stay anonymous? No chance. The staff here are such delightful gossips.

Look at this place! You'd think I was in a luxury hotel: three good meals a day, a choice of mains and a sweet treat. Last night they brought me chocolate mousse in a little plastic container, just like you get from Dean & DeLuca. Funny, I used to fantasise about breakfast in bed, and just look at me now! Nurses doing pirouettes around me, fresh linen daily and a million-dollar view of the Upper East Side, all the way to the Queensboro Bridge. And all these flowers! Roses, red like they were in Pripyat. You'd think I was already dead.

But tell me, how did you know I was in hospital?

Oh of course! The ladies at the Russian Club. I should have guessed.

Yes, it's thyroid cancer. It got to me eventually. Like so many thousands of others from Chernobyl. Can you believe it happened over thirty years ago? The night my life started falling to pieces, and the whole rotten system with it.

Remember how you used to beg me to tell you more about my past? You obviously sensed something amiss, that my life here was built on a lie. No wonder we fought. But I couldn't reveal anything... Not until you were an adult. And by then you didn't want to know.

Now time's running out.

Of course there's always hope, but I'm stage four already; things could go either way, and fast. So, make yourself comfortable. I'll just make sure this microphone is at the right distance. Okay, let's pretend I'm telling you a bedtime story. Never mind that it's me in the bed this time!

Ah, but where do we begin? Unfortunately, there isn't time for my childhood and how I became a dancer. Let's rather go straight to talking about your real father.

Yuri was his name. Which means 'farmer', though nothing could be further from his role in life.

Okay, take a deep breath, my darling. The rest of this isn't going to be easy to hear. But bear with me, you'll soon understand. How much I loved him and he you – even before you were born. And why I left Sovetsky Soyuz without him.

One

It was a Friday evening on April 25th, 1986, the year after Gorbachev came to power and started his glasnost and perestroika, pretending to save the world. Yuri and I had been living in Pripyat for about a year since his transfer to Chernobyl.

Oh, what an evening! It was unseasonably warm, and the air was alive with pollen and dandelion snowflakes. It felt surreal, like we were inside one of those snow globes you shake up. Lovely; at that moment, everything was lovely.

Your father and I were on our evening stroll through the greenbelt behind the city centre. As usual, we paused at the construction site of the long-promised amusement park where he loved to indulge his obsession with the Ferris wheel. Day after day he'd marvel at its intricate hub-and-spoke design and the giraffe-like columns of the cranes. I'd have to listen as he explained – yet again – how a girder's span influences its moment of force. It was a wonder he hadn't settled for structural engineering rather than nuclear physics.

I still picture us standing there together that last day, under the chestnut tree, his leg pressing through the folds of my dress, and his hand in mine.

'What's wrong, Lenochka?' he asked.

'What?'

'You're crushing my hand.'

'Oh,' I said, relaxing my grip. 'It's just… it's him, there.'

Yuri's nemesis, Vladimir Semonovich Yavlinsky, stood slouched against a lamppost not far ahead of us, smoking. His official title was Chief of Personnel, Reactor Number Four. But in truth he was KGB, and his role was to ensure people thought 'correctly' – in other words, toed the Party line.

'I see,' Yuri said, tugging my hand, 'Okay, let's move on.'

But instead he paused, gazing in the direction of the merry-go-round, directly opposite Yavlinsky. There was Yavlinsky's wife Sonya on a park bench, her long, sculpted legs splayed to soak up what remained of the sun before it sank into the forest. After those harsh, dreary winters we all embraced spring like a prodigal daughter.

I stole a glance at Yuri. Sure enough, he was gazing at Sonya. But before I could stew on that, a movement caught my attention from the direction of the bumper car enclosure.

The Yavlinskys' five-year-old son was climbing the barricade. Somehow he'd managed to get a toe hold near the top of the fencing. I watched spellbound as he heaved himself up and steadied himself with both hands on the railing. Then he straightened, arms free, and tilted forward as if about to dive. To my eternal shame, I did nothing. Even now with the perspective of three decades, I don't know why I didn't shout out a warning. I just stood in the shade of that *kashtan* tree and watched him teeter on a knife edge – entranced at how instinctively he extended his leg behind him for counterweight and reached his hands toward the bumper car's shiny red bonnet. *Blin,* I had sacrificed my entire childhood at the barre to approach such elegance, and here this young child, by sheer chance, achieved an *arabesque allongée.*

To my great relief, the boy managed to right himself, rocking gently to and fro. He was fine, I reasoned; no more than a metre and a half above the ground, and clearly agile. Like a true Soyuz citizen, I persuaded myself that all would be well, rationalising my complicity when things were so obviously off kilter.

Gradually the boy began to teeter again, and then topple, until it was irrevocable. 'NO!' I silently screamed as he fell. I even tried to point; but my hands seemed glued to my stomach. I heard the boy hit the paving with a dull thud. He gave just one cry, but it was enough to rouse his mother. Sonya leaped off her bench. 'Sasha, Sasha, no!' Effortlessly, she swung one slender leg after the other across the barricade and dropped to her haunches, cradling her son's cheeks.

'Oh, my darling. Are you all right?' she fussed. 'Look at me – here, in my eyes, focus. Oh, thank God.' Her shoulders visibly relaxed.

Still, I couldn't move. Yuri, as usual, had reacted first and surged forward.

Finally, my feet responded and followed him. But I stopped halfway. Being six foot one, Yuri had scaled the barricade with ease and was at Sonya's side before I could blink.

Sonya was running her fingers over Sasha's forehead and through his blonde curls. From where I stood, there was no sign of blood. But his body was motionless, his mouth open like a goldfish. My first thought, in my shock, was that he was dead.

Sensing a presence, Sonya turned her head toward Yuri. At first, she looked like a deer in the headlights. Then, I could have sworn I saw her blush.

'Can I help?' Yuri asked with a kindly smile.

'Thanks, but...' She glanced nervously across the paving toward her husband.

Yavlinsky continued to smoke, apparently oblivious. He took a drag of his ill-gotten Marlboro, then shifted his weight languidly from one foot to the other.

Sonya stood up to full height, her sleek fingers on her hips. 'Volodya!' she shouted. 'Come!'

'What is it?' He puckered a smoke ring and watched it dissipate.

'It's Sasha; he fell.'

'Okay.' Yavlinsky slowly straightened his shirt collar, extinguished his cigarette underfoot and started lumbering across the paving.

Yuri, meanwhile, was on his haunches gently examining the boy's head. 'Are you okay, Sasha?' he said. 'Let's see here at the back. Oh dear, look, a bump coming up already. Is it painful? Don't worry, by tomorrow you should be fine.'

Hearing these assurances put me at ease.

I backed off a couple of paces and waited. Now I had a perfect opportunity to watch Yuri and Sonya interact. I had suspicions. They practically worked on top of each other, she being a secretary in the control room of Reactor Number Four, where Yuri worked off and on. A couple of times Yuri had come home an hour or more after the shift change with a dishevelled shirt and fresh deodorant. Admittedly, the deodorant proved nothing. He'd use it several times a day – a French brand only available from the Special Shop. An oddity, I know, for an otherwise staid scientist to be such a dandy.

Sonya bent over the boy again. 'Oh, my darling,' I heard her exclaim, 'you *are* bleeding, under your hair. Let's wipe it for you.' She rummaged through her purse.

'Here.' Yuri offered his handkerchief.

She hesitated, glancing toward her husband, who was taking his time, looking the other way.

'Thanks,' she smiled at Yuri, taking the cloth and dabbing the child's head.

When Yavlinsky finally arrived, Yuri stepped back.

'What's the damage?' he said, wheezing.

Sonya looked intently at her husband. 'You said you would watch him.'

He mopped his brow. 'Enough… it won't help to blame each other.' He edged her aside. 'Let's see…' He lifted the boy's head. 'So, you had a little stumble.' He slapped his son's cheek. 'Wake up.'

A deathly silence followed. The only sounds were the lilting melody of nightingales from the birch trees nearby. The boy remained limp.

I began to fear the worst, as usual. I was always on edge back then.

At last, the boy stirred.

'Sasha!' Sonya cooed, stroking him.

As Yavlinsky bent further to inspect his son, I could clearly see his look of disdain. 'What's all this drama?' he said, 'The boy's fine. Just a little knock to the head.' He poked down at his son's chest. 'Stop this acting.'

The child struggled to lift his head, and then slumped. And again. Finally, he managed to squirm to a half-seated position. But his stare was expressionless.

For the first time, Yavlinsky looked uncomfortable. He ran his finger between his neck and collar. His skin showed a film of sweat in the sun's angled rays. 'So,' he said, fixing on his wife, 'why all the fuss?'

Sonya brushed him aside and helped her son to his feet. The boy's body was rigid and his face expressionless, but he started to totter. She steadied him at the elbow. 'Here, come with Mama. Let's go home. I'll make some tea.'

Yavlinsky shook his head. 'Softy,' he muttered, and lit another Marlboro.

Mother and son hobbled off in the direction of the sun which was settling on the tops of the trees, past a pair of *stariki* playing chess at a marble table. Despite official denials, street tramps were a common presence in Sovetsky Soyuz.

The old men stopped and watched Sonya pass.

I glanced at Yuri. He too seemed to be admiring the sway of her hips.

Okay, I admit, I was jealous. She was tall and slender with the perfect figure despite having had a child. And she'd never darkened the door of the gym.

To my surprise, instead of taking his leave, Yuri turned to Yavlinsky, having apparently forgotten I was there.

'He's going to feel his head tonight, poor child,' Yuri said, stroking his moustache.

Facial hair was in fashion then and Yuri did nothing in half-measures. He had one of those full broom-heads like Tom Selleck. Remember Magnum PI, your first crush? Ha, you used to scream blue murder if I wouldn't let you watch an episode. As if you knew...

Yavlinsky continued to smoke in silence. Yuri wandered up to the red bumper car, ran his hand over its bonnet.

'Such temptation for a small child,' he said. 'Forbidden fruit in the Garden of Eden.'

'Don't tell me you believe those fairy tales,' Yavlinsky sneered.

'Of course not. But a fiction told well can trump the truth.'

Yavlinsky chuckled approvingly.

'You should give your boy a break,' Yuri said. 'He's had to wait months for this park to open.'

'That's no lie. It's taken forever. Engineers... bloody perfectionists.'

9

'Have you considered it might be because you put a bureaucrat in charge of a construction project?'

Yavlinsky dropped his cigarette butt and ground it under his heel. 'Lucky for you, comrade Chizhikov, I'm in a good mood today, so I'll ignore that.'

Yuri removed his glasses. 'Tell me: were you in the control room this afternoon?'

'Where else do you think? Unlike you, I have a real job, with responsibilities.'

'Ha!' Yuri swallowed a chuckle. 'Let me think, you had to be at a business lunch; *napitsya* again.' That's one of a hundred ways to describe getting drunk in Russian.

'What's it to you, where I am over lunch?' Yavlinsky snapped. Clearly, Yuri was getting under his skin. Why he did that so brazenly, I don't know. It was as though he was looking for trouble. 'And why do you care if I was in the control room or not?'

'Surely you know,' Yuri replied.

'Ah, your baby, the turbine test. Such a waste of production time. Tell me, why is it such a big deal to you?'

'I've taken pains to explain the technical arguments. As have my bosses, for years.'

Yavlinsky eyed him. 'Yes, but there's something more; you're always sneaking around. What are you hiding?'

"Hah! If anyone's hiding something...' Yuri shifted on his feet. He was about to say more but paused. He rubbed his glasses with his other handkerchief. Then he said, 'do you know if they've tapered the power yet?'

Yavlinsky averted his eyes. 'You didn't hear?'

'Difficult when I'm sleeping.'

'Of course, you're on night shift; the second team. I forgot.'

'So, what happened with the test?'

'Postponed.'

'Please tell me you're joking.'

'Do I look like the village clown?'

'*Blyad*!' Yuri swore. But there was something forced about the way he said it.

'Relax, Chizhikov, things happen.'

'Which is a bureaucrat's way of saying someone higher up the chain made a mistake.'

'You must watch your cynicism, comrade. It'll get you into trouble one day.'

Yuri never flinched. I'd rarely seen him afraid or rattled in public. Fortunately for me, his kindness and intelligence more than compensated for his reserve. But his attitude toward Yavlinsky was typical of a genius like Yuri: he thought he was untouchable. And for good reason: his credentials were impeccable. A Little Octobrist from the age of seven, he'd been active in the Young Pioneers, a Komsomol leader at Moscow State, earned a PhD with honours from the Moscow Engineering and Physics Institute, and been admitted to the Party soon after graduation.

So, instead of showing fear, Yuri casually replaced his glasses and said, 'What exactly was the problem?'

Yavlinsky shook another Marlboro from his pack. 'Until this morning the test was on track. Then at lunch the controller in Kiev Oblast called to say another station on the grid was down for repairs and they need all the power they can get for the evening peak.'

Yuri barely blinked. It was as if he was half expecting it. 'But the directive was clear,' he said calmly.

'Yes, but Brukanov countermanded it, I'm told.'

'I'm sure he never lost sleep over that decision,' Yuri said. 'Didn't have to manufacture another excuse to delay.'

Yavlinsky's face reddened. 'Your disrespect for our Director will be duly noted in your file, comrade Chizhikov.

I was terrified. To spar with the KGB's local representative was one thing, but to openly question Plant Director Brukanov – Hero of Socialist Labour and Order of Lenin – who oversaw the construction of Chernobyl from virgin forest? It was like railing against God.

Yuri swallowed. 'No disrespect intended. You know how passionate I am about the safety of our nuclear programme.'

11

I exhaled.

Yavlinsky looked somewhat appeased. 'You can rest assured, comrade Asimov gave the night shift operators a thorough briefing.'

'Asimov is a lightweight.'

'Everyone's simple to a clever Dick like you.'

'No, only people who confuse political savvy with competence.'

Yavlinsky's eyes retreated into their sockets. 'Why do we need this test at all? Our engineers say they know exactly how these reactors behave with a break in electricity. Workhorses, designed to refuel without stopping; and safe as houses.'

'Did they tell you what happened in Leningrad in '79?' Yuri said.

'One swallow doesn't make a summer.'

'There've been other accidents.'

'Mere speculation,' Yavlinsky tut-tutted. 'Paranoia… You must be careful what you feed your mind, comrade. And by the way, why the sudden urgency? These malicious rumours have been doing the rounds for years.'

Yuri seemed momentarily flustered.

Clearly, Yavlinsky noticed. 'See, you admit it's hot air,' he said. 'We were doing just fine before you came along from that so-called elite military establishment and started meddling. Hell, we'd broken the Soyuz record for time to construction, made our annual targets every year...'

'Really?' Yuri responded. 'You think all is well just because an acolyte who fears his fingernails will be pulled feeds you the production numbers you want?'

Yavlinsky laughed. 'You have a vivid imagination. Yes, enforcement is a horrible business, but someone has to ensure you technical people stay focussed.'

'Is that also why you give us all those unnecessary forms to fill in? It's a wonder we get to produce anything.'

'We – a loose cannon like you pretending to be a team player? Imagine if you spent just half your overpaid hours helping our engineers raise productivity instead of tinkering about all night at state expense.'

'It's pointless improving a process that's fundamentally flawed.'

'And whose fault would that be, these so-called problems with the design that you've sucked out of thin air? Wasn't your doctoral super-visor – your so-called 'substitute father' – the lead scientist on the RMBK-1000 reactor development team?'

'I'm impressed; you've learned your acronyms.'

'I'll take that as a compliment. But it was hard not to pick up some knowledge with all that coverage at the last Party congress. What did comrade Alexandrov say then? That they're as safe as samovars brewing on Red Square. So what's the problem and why these tests?'

Yuri shook his head. 'He's more a politician than a scientist. Did anyone think to ask him what happens if these reactors are neutron poisoned? What's wrong? Oh, sorry, you wouldn't know what that means; you're a people's person. And you call the shots? God help us.'

Yavlinsky's cheeks flushed. He scanned his surroundings. Then he leaned further into Yuri's personal space and said, 'So, Yuri Petrovich: what exactly is it you do, prowling about the reactor all by yourself, night after night?'

'Sorry, I'm bound by the Secrecy Act.'

'Hah, how convenient; he claims confidentiality.' Yavlinsky drew on his cigarette. 'You think you're untouchable because you report to the Ministry of Medium Machine Building?'

Yes, don't Russians just love their grandiose designations! Sredmash, as the MMMB was also known, oversaw all military research installa-tions. They developed Tsar Bomba, for example, the world's biggest hydrogen bomb, in '61. All the greatest minds in nuclear science – Yuri included – cut their teeth there. Top secret doesn't describe them. They established the so-called 'closed cities' in the remotest parts of Sovetsky Soyuz, which weren't even on the map. Workers were forbidden to talk of them on pain of the Gulag. Pripyat was a good example: a city of forty thousand, built to house the workers of the largest nuclear power complex in the world. Yet the residents of Kiev, just a hundred and eighty kilometres south, weren't even aware of its existence. But strangely, Chernobyl – also known as the Vladimir Ilyich Lenin Power Station – officially fell under a civilian authority, the Ministry of Energy. Which meant there were two camps at Chernobyl: Yuri in the one and Yavlinsky in the other.

I was getting increasingly uncomfortable as they went on baiting each other. I was desperately hoping Yuri would leave and we could resume our walk, but he seemed to have completely forgotten about it. The matter of the test was clearly important to him. I backed off further to the *kashtan* and waited.

'We're onto you, comrade,' Yavlinsky said, 'And we're closer than you think.'

Yuri seemed unfazed. 'So, what was the reactor power when you left?'

'Let me think... Does fifty per cent of maximum sound correct?'

Yuri shook his head.

'Relax. Senior Engineer Medvedev said he expects it to reach 1600 megawatts by sunset.'

Yuri rolled his eyes. 'Those youngsters have no idea how the RMBK-1000s will react. Did anyone mention void coefficients? Thought not.'

'If you're so concerned, why have you been insisting that the test go ahead this week or next? Don't pretend you weren't the mastermind behind this madness.'

'There's nothing to fear – the contrary – if it's done right.'

Yavlinsky flicked ash. 'Your way, you mean, with no-one to hold you to account, so you can pursue your nefarious agenda – whatever that is.'

'Hah, if I was up to something, why would I have advised that the day shift perform the test?'

'Because you're a devious bastard.'

'Oh, how so?'

'You devise an overly risky procedure and let another sucker take responsibility. Clever: you can claim credit if it works and have a scapegoat if it's a fuckup.'

Yuri was clearly fuming. 'Don't you go projecting your conniving mind onto mine.'

Yavlinsky stepped closer.

My anxiety skyrocketed. Yuri hated it when someone invaded his personal space – a thoroughly un-Soviet trait. With the acute housing shortage we were accustomed to living on top of each other, extended families all in one apartment with communal ablutions. Perhaps it was Yuri's smalltown upbringing, but I suspect it was his temperament. The way of the genius is a lonely way. Apart from Sergey, who he'd known since childhood, Yuri didn't seem to have close friends. Even to me his heart seemed impenetrable.

Yavlinsky bristled. 'I'd retract that if I were you.'

'And if I don't?'

His face reddened. 'We know more than you think, comrade.'

'Like?'

'Your skulduggery at Arzamas.'

The most secretive 'closed city' whose existence even Gorbachev didn't acknowledge, despite all his talk of openness and disarmament.

'The whole damn place is skulduggery,' Yuri retorted.

Yavlinsky's scowl darkened, but he remained calm. 'Don't think you're untouchable because you have letters behind your name and powerful connections in Moscow.' In Yuri's case, this was someone on the Plenary – the body just one level below the Central Committee – who was also in Sredmash.

Yuri just smiled. 'I don't *think* I'm untouchable,' he said, 'I *know* it.'

'Hah, you'll slip up, eventually,' Yavlinsky said. 'Everyone does. And I'll be right there to kick your butt all the way to Vladivostok.'

A bleaker place than Vladivostok you could hardly imagine, my little dove. I once danced in their awful little state theatre on a tour of the east when I'd just graduated. 'Vladivostok' means ruler of the east, from 'Vladimir', ruler of the world. Enough to make my hair stand on end thinking about it today.

Okay, my girl, I'd better stop there, I'm feeling awfully tired. Perhaps you are too, after a full day's work in that impressive new midtown office of yours.

Yes, I follow your progress. How they moved you there from Jersey after your promotion. Goodness, I'm so proud of you, girl – you've taken full advantage of the opportunities you've been given here in America. Your father would be thrilled.

15

Two

rivet – Katyusha! Here we are talking again. How happy it makes me! I've just been enjoying the view from my window. The fan-shaped ruffles on the river are from the breeze. If not for the current surging about that pylon, you'd swear the river was flowing the other way! And that's Roosevelt Island below all the way to the Queensboro Bridge. I look at the long, cantilevered trusses and think how they would have impressed Yuri. If I lean right over this oil heater here I can watch ordinary people going about their business: lovers strolling hand in hand, harried commuters jostling for a taxi, a mother pushing a stroller. Oh, she's stopped to buy an ice cream. Funny how it's the simple things we miss the most.

Ah, and down there, leaves are budding on the trees all along the river.

Sorry, the effort of stretching has exhausted me. Let me return to the bed so we can continue.

That's better.

The unusual midsummer heat in Pripyat that evening before the catastrophe was rather uncomfortable, and more so for me because I was pregnant. Yes, my darling, with you! I was about four months along by then.

So with the drama of the boy's fall and Yuri's argument with Yavlinsky, I'd begun to feel lightheaded and feared I might throw up. I sank to my haunches against the tree trunk, closed my eyes and breathed until I felt steady again. Then I slipped quietly away. They were still talking as I left, and neither seemed to notice my disappearance.

But I wasn't ready to go home. I was rattled and trying to make sense of the confrontation I'd just overheard. So I walked slowly toward the city park, seeking solace in nature. The gate of the Avanhard Sports Stadium was open and I wandered onto the field. The grass was thick and soft under my shoes as I followed the touch line. The stands alongside were empty but for the twittering of swallows under the canopy. Deep in thought, I was at the centreline before I noticed a huddle of players near the goals.

I was surprised they were practising at the start of the weekend. But then I remembered that it was World Cup fever. Mexico, if I recall. One of the players turned my way and seemed to recognise me. But instead of waving, he turned to a teammate and mumbled something. Then he poked him in the ribs and raucous laughter spread among them. I was clearly the butt of the joke. Trying to ignore the sting of their gawks and giggles, I marched stony-faced toward a copse of trees beyond the far spectator exit.

Unfortunately, the chattering classes of Pripyat considered me strange, and not just because I was a moderately famous dancer. Having mixed in bohemian circles in Moscow, I must have seemed unfathomably otherwise to the conservative folk in that backwater. Some even referred to me as a mad-woman and a sorcerer. The women in particular ostracised me, and my tendency to flirt probably didn't help. But as a performer I thrived on attention and flattery, and I was lonely with Yuri on nightshift and asleep all day. Not that I had any interest in starting an affair. The men of Pripyat certainly paid me attention, but they were a dull lot, and I was a newlywed very much in love with my husband.

Thankfully I at least had Olga. Olga was like the sister I'd never had. It was hard to imagine we'd known each other for barely a year. We'd met by chance, or so I thought, in the teachers' canteen of School Number Four after my third week as the school's resident ballet teacher. I'd begun to fear I was doomed to eat alone forever. Olga taught Physical Education, but her passion was coaching the swim squad at the Azure after hours. We had a lot in common. She'd been selected for the Moscow Olympics in '80 and the Los Angeles Olympics in '84 but couldn't participate because of the boycott by the Americans. Think how it must have gutted someone like her who had sacrificed so much – her adolescence, her family – only to be robbed. Ask me. Perhaps that's why we clicked from day one.

I passed through the turnstile to exit the stadium and ambled on through the luxurious flower beds on either side of me, leaving footprints in the fine yellow dusting on the path. The sun by now was bloated and orange, a thumb's length from the horizon.

With every step I took along that wooded path I began to feel a little calmer, until I reached a clearing between the trees. A stone's throw to my left, and there was my swing-chair. Not literally mine – I had no idea who'd built it, but I thanked him every time I went there. I leaned back against the still-warm iron of the seat and swayed gently, soothingly. But I wasn't finding it easy to relax.

The altercation I'd just witnessed at the funfair had stirred a deep sense of dread. I'd heard the menace in Yavlinsky's voice, and I was struggling to erase that odious, fat-faced portrait of turpitude from my mind. Not that my Yuriok couldn't look after himself. He'd volunteered for Afghanistan – imagine! – and served with distinction. Sergey had told me that hardened veterans marvelled at his composure under fire. And he'd know – Sergey had made the air force his career, fully expecting to be posted to Afghanistan. He'd trained as an officer and become one of those special force action men who fly helicopters and even jump from them.

But courageous or not, for Yuri to pick a fight with a man like Yavlinsky could be tantamount to suicide – especially at the end of the plan year. Thanks to Stalin, every organisation in Sovetsky Soyuz was subject to an annual quota. For a factory it could be tons of steel, for a power plant, megawatts. But the KGB quota was the number of people interrogated, imprisoned and executed.

The thought made my nausea rise again. I moved on through the park, longing now for the soothing serenity of the forest, which was thankfully only a few blocks beyond the road. In a planned city like Pripyat, the urban edge could be as sharp as a fence wire or narrow lane, and within moments, I found myself alone in a pristine forest so vast, dense and verdant that it felt like I had been swallowed whole.

I could literally feel the trees growing, already packed so close that I could barely slip between them as my feet padded over last year's leaves, still damp and spongy from the snow melt. I picked my way over fallen

18

branches speckled with lichen and mushrooms, seeking out a log just high and broad enough to perch on. Gripping the rough bark with my hands, I hoisted myself up, swivelled about and sat with my feet dangling freely. Then I closed my eyes and inhaled: musty peat, a hint of blossom and the freshness of new leaf growth. Soon the birdsong paused and that sudden mysterious hush descended, as profoundly silent as only the forests of Polesia can be in those minutes while the sun rests its chin on the horizon. And, for a few blessed moments, my mind was stilled, and all thought ceased beyond a heightened awareness of the forest around me.

Feeling restored, I slid off my branch and headed homewards. As I approached the urban boundary the leaves were momentarily backlit, glowing so bright they seemed luminous, then mellowing to gold in the twilight. And as the light gradually faded, the mosquitoes arrived – whirring in swarms so dense they hastened the dusk.

Soon afterwards I was back at home.

'Oh, there you are,' Yuri said. 'Where've you been?'

'For a stroll. Why?'

'You disappeared from the park without a word. Next thing I looked you were gone.'

'That's not surprising, considering how engrossed you were with Sonya and that… husband of hers.'

Yuri seemed about to say something and then changed his mind. 'Whatever,' he said. 'Glad to have you back. He kissed me on the forehead. 'Come,' he said, 'let's have a drink before it's too late.'

From our fourth-floor balcony we could look out at the city's urban edge and over the parapets of the opposite apartment buildings to the dense, dark forest encircling the city. Normally, it would have been clear enough to see the power plant in the distance, but the breathless warmth that day had created an inversion of smog. In the advancing dusk, the tops of the reactor buildings and cooling towers were a blur.

Sharing sundowners on the balcony was our favourite evening ritual, enveloped in the softness of our Moravian sofa – a wedding present from Yuri's uncle.

As always, we were accompanied by our elderly cat Matrushka, who curled up at my ankles. Matrushka had been abandoned by the previous tenants, and a more loyal friend I'd never had. Well-mannered too; she never helped herself to our precious *salo* – cured slabs of cold pig fat usually eaten with vodka. A luxury a construction manager at Reactors Five and Six would slip Yuri some of every week. That was my husband. Exchanging favours. Never mind that it wasn't legal.

We lived on Lelina Prospekt – a double-lane avenue separated by an island – a third of the way from Gorkom Square in the city centre toward the bridge that crossed the Pripyat River at the edge of the city. Half a kilometre beyond the bridge you could turn left to the power station or continue another ten kilometres to Chernobyl town, capital of the region.

The sidewalks of our street were dotted with freshly planted saplings and neat, rectangular flower beds hemmed by knee-height cast iron fences. In late summer, the whole of Pripyat would be strewn with rose petals like confetti after a wedding. And, typical of the hour about sunset, the citizens of Pripyat would be out in droves, strolling and chatting – Georgians, Armenians, Kazakhs and Russians drawn from Vladivostok to the Crimea.

There we sat like two peas in a pod, sipping our vodkas. Yuri drained his first glass and went inside to fetch the bottle. I heard the sliding door rattle and then... *smack.*

'*Blyad!*'

'What's it, Yurochka?'

'Shoddy workmanship everywhere.'

I turned to see a smattering of plaster where the doorframe met the floor and Yuri trying to manoeuvre the door back onto its track. 'You were going to fix it last week,' I said.

'And where am I supposed to find the time?'

'It's been two months. Why don't we get a *tolkach*?' That was slang for a handyman who moonlighted.

'At three times the cost?

'At least they get things done.'

Yuri reappeared, bottle of Stolichnaya in hand. He poured a thumb into each of our glasses and sank into the sofa beside me. 'Give me enough time and I'll move the world.'

'You make time for what you value,' I retorted.

'How many times must I explain,' he said. 'I'm a scientist, not an engineer.'

'Don't worry,' I patted his thigh. 'You're dexterous where it counts.'

'Hah, hah. Here…' He took my hand and slid it under his shirt.

'Ooh…'

'You're pretty handy too,' he said, 'for someone who works with her feet.' And then he started unbuttoning my blouse.

I withdrew. 'No. Later.'

'Ah, you tease!'

My body felt rigid, yet my resistance was melting.

Yuri's hands slid gently up my leg.

But I stood.

'Where're you going?' he moaned.

'To make dinner.'

He grabbed my hand and looked up, imploring me.

'Sorry, I'm not in the right frame of mind.'

'Don't say that.'

'Have some grace.'

'Hell,' he muttered, and whipped the top off the Stolichnaya. 'I'll have to drink then.'

'But we agreed to no more than two tots in an evening.'

'Hah, don't be a killjoy.' He poured himself a shot and raised his glass. 'You sure?' he said, eyeing me through the clear liquid. 'Okay. *Za Lyubov.*' He drained the glass. 'Ah…' He refilled it, then half of mine.

I'd reduced my intake. The doctor had told me that alcohol aggravates melancholy. And as a ballerina I had a will of iron; I knew that even the tiniest concession was a slippery slope. It was hard on Yuri – Russian men aren't known for temperance – but he understood. He really did love me! Still, that night… how could I refuse his rakish grin?

21

Westerners think Russians never smile; we did, often, but only among family, friends and colleagues. In Russia only a con artist or an idiot would grin at a stranger.

Anyway, I'm eternally grateful that I accepted his drink that night.

I raised my glass and made a toast to the dregs of the setting sun.

'*Za zakhod solntsa,*' Yuri chimed.

I swallowed, letting the burn slide down my throat, and enjoyed the glorious afterglow the vodka left in my stomach and the way it soon made my head swim.

Yuri reclined further. 'So,' he drawled, 'Earlier, at the amusement park…'

Typical of him to suddenly change the subject. In the beginning it used to unnerve me; I thought he found me boring, but that was how his mind worked – three steps ahead, considering a matter's indirect consequences when others still dwelt on the apparent. But not flighty – deliberate, like a bull terrier with a bone.

'You were listening,' he continued.

Instantly, my heart was fluttering in my throat.

'I was waiting for you. You were supposedly on a walk with me,' I said indignantly.

He took another sip of vodka. 'How much did you hear? It's important I know.'

I shrugged. 'Snippets. Enough to make my hair stand on end. You should be more careful.'

'Why?'

'Yavlinsky—'

'That fool has an inflated sense of his own importance.'

'Yes, but he's Chief of the Personnel Section.'

'Titles don't scare me.'

'And the stories?'

'Like?'

'How about Abramovich?'

'Hah. Don't believe all the chatter about the KGB, Lenochka; it's not all bad.'

Yuri was an unabashed conservative; old school at the tender age of twenty-nine. I'd be lying if I said I wasn't sympathetic to his views back then, but I had a role to play, so we had countless arguments, which I tended to lose. Even while acting, logic was my weak suit. His views weren't uncommon, mind: that the security complex was a necessary evil to root out subversive elements, despite its own bad apples and excesses. It stood as a bulwark between us poor, misunderstood Russians and another Time of Troubles or invasion. It takes my breath away to think how easily a whole society can be deceived. Babushka told me that ordinary, hardworking citizens broke down and wept when Stalin died, no matter how many loved ones they'd lost in the Terror.

But that night I wasn't going to let up. 'You didn't answer my question, Yuri,' I insisted, 'about what happened to Abramovich.'

'That snitch had it coming,' he said.

Abramovich was a shift manager at the rubber plant who couldn't refrain from making jokes critical of Gorbachev and perestroika. He thought he'd earned immunity by blowing the whistle on his boss for accepting a bribe from a *kolchak*. But instead of a pat on the back, he had thugs pounding on his door at three in the morning. When he returned to work three days later his face was so badly smashed he could barely see. So, naturally, I was frightened for Yuri after the argument. 'Can't you just keep your head down like everyone else?' I pleaded.

'You mean compromise?' Yuri responded. But after an awkward silence he changed the subject again. 'So, what did you get up to when you left the amusement park then?'

'I could ask you the same question.'

'You first.'

'I went for a walk in the forest.'

He smiled. 'I should have guessed. My little sylph, frolicking among the trees.'

We sat there in a measure of peace, side by side on the sofa, but without speaking. The crickets had started chirping. Then, at length, I smiled; and, for the first time in weeks, I felt happy.

'What are you thinking about?' Yuri eventually asked.

'Sparrow Hill.' The suburb of Moscow we had lived in where the State University is situated. Our apartment was on the twelfth floor of the ice cream cake, one of the tiered skyscrapers built by Stalin. We had a spectacular view of the river snaking toward the city skyline. Professor Ginzburg – Yuri's supervisor, full member of the Academy and multiple prize winner – had used it, in part, to lure Yuri back from Arzamas. Why Yuri would need extra encouragement to move from a place that officially didn't exist to the centre of Moscow eluded me. Moscow was like New York in that way: after a few years, you start to believe that the world revolves around you, and to move away would be an admission of failure. But this attitude of mine infuriated Yuri.

'Not again,' he said, rolling his eyes.

'Stop patronising me! Why don't you tell me the real reason we had to come to this dump?'

'What's so wrong with Pripyat?'

Suddenly, I felt exhausted by the conflict. I shrugged and gestured at the view. 'I suppose it does have its own beauty if you block out the eyesores, but my God it's dull.'

He took some *salo*. 'What does Moscow have that we can't get here?'

'Friends, for one thing.'

'What's Olga then?'

'I mean a social life.'

'Give it time.'

'Hah, with you on night shift?'

'For now; the testing's almost done.'

'You've been saying that since New Year.'

'That's only three months.'

'Four.'

'Whatever.'

I felt a spike of anxiety. 'Yurochka, do you really have to do the test?'

He placed his hand on my shoulder. 'You mustn't heed the rumours.'

My heart was thumping. 'I… you… you told me yourself you were worried – last weekend at the picnic.'

Yuri simply shrugged. 'I must have been drunk,' he said.

'Nonsense,' I replied, 'I know you're concerned.'

He tensed. 'How? Have you been snooping?'

I closed my eyes, inhaled, and summoned all my theatrical skills to feign offence. If Yuri realised I was acting, he never showed it. Instead, he embraced me. 'Ah, come here, my darling,' he whispered.

I felt his gentle arms of steel tighten. Instantly I yielded, my cheek on his chest until I could hear his heartbeat, even and assured, like I used to feel with certain danseurs. The certainty that they're in control, masters of themselves with the competence and strength to take me through the most complex progressions, allowing me to relax and focus on the sequence.

'M-my darling,' I sobbed into his shirt. 'What's become of us, and in so short a time? Remember how, on those strolls through Gorky Park, we'd share our most intimate dreams, attend the theatre, enjoy a party every other night and fall asleep holding hands? We called our relation-ship a mighty warship, watertight and safe. Don't let it flounder or be dashed on these reefs of suspicion. Let's leave before it's too late, run away if needs be.'

Yuri ran a fingertip across my cheek and then used it to tuck a strand of hair behind my earlobe. 'I made you a promise, Lenochka.'

'Repeat it.'

I glimpsed his chevrons, those angled creases about his lips when he smiled.

'All right.' He took my hand and gently massaged my wedding ring. 'I, Yuri Petrovich Chizhikov, do hereby solemnly…'

'Don't be silly.' I wriggled my finger free.

'Seriously.' He took my hand again. 'I promise that once you've completed your rehabilitation and passed the Kiev Company's fitness audition, we'll either move there or one of us will commute. Unless…'

His eyes, wistful, drifted to my stomach – and everything changed.

'Unless what?'

'You come to your senses.'

I yanked my hand away. 'It's my body; I'll deal with it.'

'Him or her, you mean.'

'Stop!'

'But…'

'No!'

'But why can't you see sense? Some famous dancers have had a child and…'

'Name them.'

He hesitated.

'See!'

'No… there's what's-her-name. I read it in Nedelya, I…'

'Bet you can't name three ballerinas, period. You haven't a clue about my world. All you care about it that bloody "research" you do all night.'

'Lenochka…'

'No. It's time I spoke my mind. How often have *you* accompanied *me* to a work function? Twice. Yes, and only to the ballets you wanted to watch because you have a crush on that… daddy-long-legs bitch!'

'That's not fair. By the time we met, you'd all but left the company…'

'Don't you dare…'

'Come on, Lena, when are you going to get over what happened? It was an accident.'

'Get over it? Easy for you, who happily sets off to work every night, all busy and important, to pursue his dream. You haven't had to give up your life.'

'It's hardly like you had a choice.'

'Of course, I did. They offered me a leave of absence.'

'*Bah* – we all know what that means.'

I felt like I'd been punched in the gut without the energy to counter. And then came the cocktail of anger, fear and guilt, and as always in the end, the *grust* – that visitation of sadness, something between a lingering moroseness and depression to which every artist is prone, which, if permitted to settle, inhabits her soul. Yes, a ballerina is as much an artist as a painter, obsessed with mastering every component of the dance and the body – an impossible task, which is why we're neurotic. The superhuman self-discipline required for the countless hours of practice masks our deep insecurity. We're brittle as glass. The tiniest misstep – one an

26

audience doesn't blink at – can shatter our confidence and take months to overcome. As for a full-blown fall…

Anyway, after Yuri said that, I felt real tears welling. I averted my eyes from him to the haze beyond the balustrade, where the forests surrounding Pripyat were now dark and foreboding. I shivered. Then I stood. 'I'd better get dinner going.' I fumbled for the handle of the sliding door. As I drew it shut behind me there was a *douff* and more plaster fell. But I didn't care. My shame was so great, I wouldn't have minded had the whole building collapsed and buried me under the rubble.

And can you believe, Katyusha, after all these years, the memory of my fall still stings.

But enough of my burdens. Silly me; I can be so self-absorbed. You must be reeling from all these revelations. Especially that I wasn't planning to go through with the pregnancy at first.

My darling… please understand. It was early days then; I was hardly showing. Nor had I conceptualised what was happening as a real live person growing inside me. Remember, in Sovetsky Soyuz we'd been taught that a baby was only alive once it had taken its first breath. Abortion was as common as having a tooth pulled. And I simply could not imagine myself as anything but a ballerina.

I'd been an orphan from the age of seven and sent by Babushka to the Bolshoi in Moscow all alone at ten: I didn't feel I belonged anywhere. The only place I knew any self-worth was on stage. And I'd dedicated my whole childhood to it. I had no other skills or identity beyond ballet. On top of that, my accident had dealt a devastating blow to my career and identity, and I was desperate to recover. I couldn't see any other way forward.

But by the grace of God, I have you after all, and I'm thankful every day for that. And that we're speaking, regardless of whether we ever fully reconcile in what time I have left in this life.

Oh, my darling, please don't be upset. Yes, I'm ill. Cancer isn't for the faint hearted. But thanks to you and Bob, I have all the creature comforts I could wish for and the very best care.

Three

My dear Katyusha… I was worried you'd taken that bit about my pregnancy badly. No doubt you'll need time to process it properly. But the important thing is that we keep talking. Even if it's fractious. Like your college years before you went to Columbia for your post-grad studies and met those political hotheads who got you so wound up you put the phone down on me. I'm not sure I can bear… Promise you'll never shut me out again. Please.

So, where had we got to last night? Yes, Yuri's dig at me, reminding me of my accident.

It was one of those freak events that only ever happen to others.

Sorry, it's still so painful to think about.

Okay. Deep breath…

It was my first year as a soloist, and we were performing Giselle at the Bolshoi Theatre. Gorbachev himself was in the Tsar's box that night, one of the most powerful men in the world, even though he wasn't yet the General Secretary. He was sitting directly opposite, watching my every move. I'd got through the first act to great applause, and the curtains had opened for Act Two. No nerves. I was soon in full flow as Myrtha, Queen of the Wilis, serene and commanding, feeding off the energy of a packed house. Round and round Albrecht I danced with my bevy of vengeful maidens… Then a fleeting distraction, and I sensed something amiss in my timing: fractional, the audience wouldn't have noticed. Perhaps my ankle was a few degrees out, I'll never truly know, it happened so quickly. All I felt was a sudden blinding pain in my left knee as it gave way under my weight.

Oh, the horror, the mortification! I had to be carried off the stage. I'd torn my cruciate ligament, it turned out, and with that, my dreams.

Sorry, my darling, the pain is still almost physical. Give me a moment while I just reach under the bed...

Bingo. Look what we have here: a half jack of Stolichnaya! Just a little drink to settle my nerves. Come, join me! Let's celebrate our reconnection and treasure every second of our time together. Truth is, none of us have any idea how long till our time is up. I wish I could have known my own mother as an adult. I wonder if I'd have liked her... as a friend, I mean. My memories of her are so faint. First they took Papa. She was never herself after that. Imagine not hearing from your husband for months, then being told he's lost his mind – a man famed for his intellect – followed by reports of shock therapy. A year later and she too was gone. At seven I was too young to understand, but I've never stopped mourning her. I suppose I must have cried, I don't remember. But an orphan soon realises that tears don't help; no one's listening. So that part of my brain shut down.

Mmm... Delicious. I think I can take up the story again now.

Instead of expressing my hurt that evening, after Yuri insinuated that I'd been dismissed by the Bolshoi Company, I bustled about the apartment – straightening a portrait, packing away dishes, scrubbing the countertop – anything to keep busy. To no effect. So, I turned to my music collection.

We had a whole bookshelf of LPs. And nothing beats vinyl for richness of sound. I rifled through looking for anything but a ballet score, until my eye caught Mussorgsky's *Pictures at an Exhibition*, a live recording by the Ukrainian National Orchestra. I slid the record from its sleeve, wiped it and placed it on the turntable. Then I positioned the stylus above the fifth movement and wandered into the kitchen to the strains of the *Ballet of the Unhatched Chicks*. I opened and shut cupboard doors at random until I remembered I was there to prepare dinner. From the fridge I hauled spinach, a bunch of carrots and last night's chicken.

I tossed the carrots and spinach into the sink, sank my hands into the water and started rinsing and scrubbing like a demon. But nothing could shrug off that desperate, plunging feeling and the tears misting my eyes.

I stopped washing, hands still in the water, not needing to turn to know Yuri was sitting at the table. A man loves to watch a woman cook. It's primal.

Ignoring him, I drained and diced the vegetables and flicked the oven's 'on' switch. And again.

'Broken,' Yuri muttered. 'What's new?'

I scooped some cooking oil into a saucepan.

'I suppose we should be thankful the stove works,' he said. 'Mediocrity is like a cancer in this country. And what does the new leadership do? Blow hot air up our arses.'

When it came to griping, Yuri was like a stuck record.

'At least Gorbachev's trying to reform,' I ventured.

'Huh! This perestroika nonsense is messing with people's brains.'

'Shh.' I rolled my eyes to myself. 'The Khachishvillis are home.'

'To hell with them, I'll talk in my kitchen if I want to.'

The kitchen was where people felt free to speak their minds. Generally, it was at the geographic centre of the apartment with the most ambient noise to neutralise our words. Still, we had to lower our voices; the walls were thin and had ears. Our problem was Pyotr Pavlovich and his wife Martina – Georgians, like Stalin. Also, in the kitchen we'd have the *radio-tochki* spewing the *Sovetsky* anthem and *Radio Moscow*. Which at least was one-way traffic, and you could turn it off.

That night I may have been sad but I wasn't about to take Yuri's nonsense. I put down the dish, turned to face him, and said, 'At least Gorbachev is frank enough to admit the system needs fixing. "Identify the problem and you're halfway to solving it," as you engineers say.'

'I'm a scientist, dammit.'

'A rose by any other name,' I said.

'Names matter,' Yuri snapped. 'What if I called a proton a neutron?'

I realised I was getting nowhere, so I picked up our copy of *Pravda* and handed it to him. 'You should read the op-ed retrospective on the 27th Party Congress,' I said. 'How they're revising the plan fulfilment criteria.'

'Hot air,' he said, dropping it on the counter.

30

'It's already happening. Last night on *Vremya* they interviewed the director of an iron smelter in—'

'Nonsense! The Black Sea will ice over before it happens in Chernobyl. You heard Yavlinsky earlier.'

I waited.

Yuri gave me his blank expression. Just like an interrogator, he was trying to get me to speak to fill the silence. To learn how much of the conversation I'd overheard.

Determined not to fall into Yuri's trap, I said, 'What about Gorbachev's new industrial policies, like incentive schemes, or devolving decision-making to factory workers? I read an article today about a fitter and turner from the rubber plant who was rewarded for a suggestion to reduce waste.'

Yuri stared like he was X-raying my mind. Then he shook his head. 'That man is a danger to society,' he scoffed, 'a wolf in sheep's clothing. When you strip away the socialist jargon, he's for the free market.'

Yes, believe it or not, back in '86 the average Sovetsky citizen equated capitalism with unemployment, inequality and exploitation.

'But Gorbachev espouses a return to Lenin's teachings on benign socialism, just a better, more effective form to fit the times.'

'The fool loves the sound of his own voice, blabbering on about the dire state our nation. Imagine how such public self-abasement emboldens our enemies.'

'Don't be silly,' I said, 'he's doing it to discredit his enemies *inside* the Party, painting such a bleak picture that no one will complain when heads roll. Plus, an emergency spurs people to action. Besides, the state of our economy is hardly a secret; the CIA probably knows more than the Politburo.'

I saw a flicker of uncertainty in Yuri as he eyed me. 'What was wrong with Andropov's approach? Good old-fashioned discipline and hard work is how we'll make Russia great again.'

'Oh, please! Russia this, Russia that; more missiles, bigger bombs – America does likewise and round and round we go until someone makes a mistake or we all go bankrupt.'

Yuri frowned. 'Who told you that?'

'A newspaper, talk in the teacher's room, what does it matter?'

'Gorbachev is Reagan's lapdog,' he scoffed.

'What about keeping your friends close and your enemies closer?' I said, 'Give him credit: he was your hero's understudy.'

Yuri scowled, 'Andropov would never have let that failed American actor lecture us on human rights. And now we must free Sakharov? From what? So-called internal exile. Remember that documentary we watched: they're living the life in Gorky; their apartment is twice this size and they have all day to wander in the forest.'

'Come now, Yuriok. It can't be much fun being banished to a remote city. Imagine being kept from your family and friends, the travel restrictions, your life's work on hold.'

'Work? *Hah*! He's done nothing worthwhile since *Kuzkina Mat*.' That was code for 'we'll show you', as in the middle finger, which is exactly what that famous Ukrainian Khrushchev promised to give the Americans in 1960; and then did a year later by testing the biggest hydrogen bomb ever – the Tsar Bomba.

'Well, you'd think that in itself was a huge achievement for a scientist in one lifetime,' I said.

Yuri sighed. 'Lavrentiev developed the concept and another scientist got it working. Trust Sakharov to claim credit, the leech.' Sakharov was Jewish, and sadly anti-Semitic slurs were par for the course back then. His family had probably changed their name at some point to survive.

'Didn't Sakharov also invent the *tokamak*?' I said.

Yuri froze. 'Who told you about that?' he snapped.

'Relax, I'm not a criminal, dammit,' I retorted, playing the victim. 'I'm your wife!'

'Still, how did you hear about it?'

I had to think quickly. 'From you.'

'Really?'

I nodded. 'I think you were a bit drunk. You just said something about how foundational it was to your line of research. Can't you at least give me the basics. I'm your wife. How can such a huge part of your life be off limits?'

Yuri's scowl softened. He seemed to be wavering. In the background, the Ukrainian National Orchestra's rendition of *The Catacombs* built to a crescendo.

'Please?' I urged.

He looked at his feet.

I worried I'd gone too far too fast. Whenever our conversation strayed to his job he'd clam up. When we were dating, I ascribed it to self-effacement and assumed he'd relax when we became more intimate. I first asked him the night before we signed our marriage papers. To grease his vocals, I'd brought along a precious Bulgarian red, given to me backstage by an aide to Andropov after a performance of *Sleeping Beauty*. To no avail. I gave him my hurt expression and asked how I was supposed to commit to a man without knowing what he did for a living. All he volunteered was that he was a physicist with a PhD in Nuclear Physics which he'd completed in a record two-and-a-half years. He wouldn't even say where his first job was, claiming it was a state secret.

Anyway, by then I didn't strictly need to find out. But old habits die hard, and besides, I was genuinely interested. A woman wants to know what her husband really does for a living.

When he finally looked up, his expression was sad.

Regardless of my motives, I felt overcome with guilt. Still, I waited.

Eventually, he sighed. 'Okay; I suppose the *tokamak* itself is fairly outdated now. I'll give you the general idea. If you promise never to breathe a word. I'd lose my job, if not go to prison.'

My heart fluttered. But to appear disinterested, I broke bread.

His voice was even and matter of fact. 'It's shaped like a doughnut; just much bigger and more dangerous, and it generates thermonuclear power.' He paused while a bus on the street outside shuddered noisily past. 'Instead of an explosion, like from a bomb; it's a controlled process with a magnetic field powerful enough to keep plasma at a hundred and fifty million degrees Celsius, to fuse hydrogen and helium atoms. The conditions in our sun.'

I sprinkled flour and crumbs on the countertop, unpacked the chicken pieces, and said, 'For what?'

'Energy,' he responded. 'It's almost limitless. And the only by-product of fusion is water. Imagine the potential for electricity generation.'

'Doesn't that happen already here in Chernobyl?'

'No; that's fission – splitting atoms – which we've mastered. Fusion's another story, the holy grail of science. We've proven it's possible, but not yet on an industrial scale.'

I furrowed my brow, feigning ignorance. 'What's wrong with fission?'

'Spent uranium. Guess what that stuff's half-life is?'

I shrugged and took another piece of chicken.

'Hundreds of thousands of years!' There was an intensity in his voice that made me turn and pay full attention. 'If enough of those heavy isotopes get into the food chain, life as we know it is over. And all it takes is a leak from one of these reactors in, say, a runaway reaction...' He shuddered. 'It's happened before, you know, several times with these RMBK-1000s; which is why tonight's test...' He stopped. 'Sorry,' he said, his voice changed. 'That's enough; I need the bathroom...'

And then he was gone, leaving me with the chicken in my hand and my heart missing every third beat. He'd taken a 'circuit breaker' or calculated pause, common practice in a negotiation or interrogation to calm down and gather one's thoughts. Not that he did it consciously or suspected me, or so I thought.

When he returned, I'd recovered. 'I thought you looked up to Sakharov. What happened?'

He nodded sagely, choosing his words. 'He was my idol until I got to university and learned how he'd stolen Lavrentiev and Tamm's thunder. Still, I had to admire such intellect. But when he started writing nonsense like *The Danger of Thermonuclear War...*'

'What's the matter with—?'

'Ah,' he was half smiling, 'so you've read it!'

My God, Yuri was clever. Instantly, he'd turned the tables and he was probing me; the essay he was referring to was *tamizdat*, meaning 'published abroad'. A person could be imprisoned for reading let alone

34

distributing such material. Nevertheless, by the '80s it was widespread, and the authorities usually turned a blind eye if you remained discreet.

'What did you think of it?' Yuri said, keeping the pressure on me.

Instinctively, I glanced about and lowered my voice. 'I don't know. He said something about a nuclear winter if I recall.'

'What nonsense! Does he expect us to beat our swords into ploughshares? Fine, if all sides do so simultaneously. But we've tried before, you know. Tsar Alexander Pavlovich told us not to worry about the threat from the West. "We're fellow believers," he said, "if we become more European, we can all live together... Napoleon's our friend... we have a treaty..." And then we blinked and the bloody Frenchman and his *Grande Armée* were in Moscow by the fall. A hundred something years later, Hitler tried to exterminate or enslave every Slav on the planet, and got within a binocular's view of the Kremlin in the process. No! Mutually assured destruction is our only insurance, and Sakharov undermines it.'

'Mmm,' I replied, 'Have you ever considered it's the opposite: that he wrote it to make our enemies go soft?'

'Hah, the West seduced him. "Genius," they shout, "great man," and it goes to his head. Selfish bastard went on hunger strike so his wife – what's her name – Elena Bonner; she wouldn't even change her name – could go and visit her relatives who'd fled to America.'

My husband had finally hit a hot button. 'That was for medical treatment, damn it,' I almost shouted. 'She's got a weak heart.'

'Nonsense. She's a drama queen.'

I could have strangled him.

He turned his cheek to me. 'Go ahead,' he said, touching it with his forefinger. 'Slap me. I can see how badly you want to. Come on: what's wrong with my little prima donna tonight?'

In truth I had used the flat of my hand with Yuri before – only once or twice, mind. But show me a great performer without a great temper. Besides, it was harmless enough; I was a waif. Though lack of effect doesn't justify an action.

35

With hands on hips, I fixed him with one of my stares. 'What happened to the Yuri I married?' I said, 'You… you were the kindest man I'd ever known. It's what endeared me to you: your compassion, your love, and your courage to express it. You were the ultimate romantic. Yes, you – macho scientist!'

And he was! No red roses or chocolate on Valentine's Day – that schmaltzy construct of the consumer society. But how many men in this world could quote Pushkin and Yesenin, hold my hand in public and accept me with all my failings? And keep loving me to the end, even knowing what I did to him?

He was looking at me with that puppy dog expression of remorse. 'I was just making the point that travelling abroad for medical treatment is an indulgence,' he said. 'We have world class specialists here in Sovetsky Soyuz.'

The best scientists, the best farmers, the best doctors: most of us believed that, though our society might be fraying at the edges – stagnating even – we were still, in every way that mattered, superior to the West. Also, most of us thought Bonner was nothing more than a querulous spirit or, worse, unhinged. Remember, the Nureyev saga was still fresh in our minds. We considered him a traitor with no moral fibre who'd run away for fame. That's how we viewed anyone who expressed a desire to live in the West. Capitalist countries were portrayed as cold and heartless places beset by unemployment, where the homeless slept on the streets and the poor were denied hospital care. We were all brainwashed, and neither the intelligent nor the well-meaning were immune. We were all sympathetic to the cause to a lesser or greater degree. But then the tide turned, and a few years later it was rare for a Russian to admit having believed in communism.

'And what about the Yavlinsky woman?' I demanded. 'Where did she go in December?' I pressed on. 'Italy! Don't look at me like that. I know things. Chest infection? *Hah*! Boob surgery, more like it.'

'Stop it, Lena. The antibiotics the doctors prescribed her weren't working.'

'Oh? And we're supposed to believe a Yavlinsky but not a Bonner?'

'Keep Sonya out of this.'

'Oh, so now it's "Sonya"?'

'Don't be silly.'

'I'm not being silly. So, where did you go after the playground?'

Clearly, he was off guard. 'Yavlinsky and I carried on the conversation and then went back to our own homes,' he said guardedly. 'What are you implying?' His cheeks were flushed, and not just from the vodka or the sun.

'I see the way you look at each other, Yuri.'

'Don't be ridiculous.'

'You're infatuated, aren't you? Understandable, I suppose – she's blonde, long-legged, busty, ditsy – everything I'm not; and you sure as hell have the opportunity.'

He threw his head back and rolled his eyes. He usually did that when he was wracking his brains. But slowly a smile appeared, and soon he was laughing, and from the belly. 'An affair with Sonya? You think I've got a death wish?'

I swallowed to stop the tears. I was starting to feel like a fool.

'My darling,' he said soothingly, 'so, that's what's been bothering you.'

I turned my back to him and smoothed the surface of the chicken pieces. But I heard him pad up behind me and then I felt his hands, firm yet light on my shoulders. He ran his fingers through my hair. 'How can you think such a thing?'

Tears began to flow down my cheeks. It was as if all the suspicions and imagined hurts I'd stored up over the past few months had finally found an outlet.

He put his arms about me.

'Stop!' I cried, and squirmed free of his embrace. I lit the stove, took the saucepan, threw in the chicken pieces and stirred. 'Do you think I haven't noticed how late you've sometimes come home after your shift, and with deodorant to cover it up? You've never offered a proper reason. *Blyad*, Yuri, just because I make my living from my body doesn't mean I can't think.'

He wrapped his arms about me again. I felt a stirring in me, but I was still mad, so I threw his arms off and shifted to the sink. I tossed the dirty breakfast plates into the cold water, added dishwashing liquid and scrubbed for my life. Then I stacked the plates on the drying rack. Finished, I thrust my hands back into the cold, soapy water and rattled the remaining cutlery.

Yuri coughed. 'Okay, slap me if you must: I'll admit she isn't sore on the eyes. I even... like her. We get on, okay. But an affair? That's a joke!'

It didn't need much acting to coax a tear from the corner of my eye. Still, I couldn't bring myself to turn. I wasn't ready to concede. 'When did you learn to flirt, Yuri? I thought you were an all-in-or-out kind of guy.'

'Well, I am. I'm all in, with you.'

'Hah!' I lifted the cutlery from the sink and dumped it in the drying rack. 'I've had it with your duplicity, Yuri.'

Behind us, the orchestra was transitioning to *Baba Yaga* – the witch – and the record hissed static. My tear dropped into the water, and as I finally forced myself to face him, the sorrow and sincerity in his eyes disarmed me. What an emotional idiot I was, I thought. Here stands my soulmate – the one I dreamed of as a little girl, my prince – contrite before me. And what if I'm wrong? There's no proof. He could have been doing any number of things at the reactor: research, playing cards, drinking with colleagues. Every impulse in me wanted to forgive and forget and be forgiven, and to hold him to my bosom forever. But I was too proud.

'So, now I'm a liar too?' Yuri said. 'Fine, but first show your eyes if you're going to be my accuser.'

I picked up a plate. Tears were flowing – real ones.

'Come here.' He took my hand from behind and tugged. 'Come, let's call her. You'll have the element of surprise.'

'Don't be silly.' I gave the pan a shake to loosen the pieces. By then the music was filling the room as the orchestra built to the climax of The *Great Gate of Kiev*. I was doubting myself again. What if he was telling the truth? Soon my anger morphed into guilt and shame. I knew Yuri was behind me now; I could feel his breath on my neck. There was no question of me offering more than token resistance. I'd forgotten and forgiven all things, and every part of me wanted him more than life itself. But I pretended not to notice him, even as waves of anticipation flooded me. I reached to switch off the stove, my hands dripping. Then I felt a tug and my dress slid down, turning my shoulders to gooseflesh, while his fingers fiddled with my bra… next thing I was so hot I could burst into flames, yet frozen to the spot. He worked his belt loose and I heard a flop on the floor and then felt his breath on my neck again… His arms curled around and clasped my belly, and as he tightened, his body pressed into me from behind. But he was tentative at first, as if asking permission. My Yuri was the truest gentleman I've ever known.

I continued through the motions of drying a bowl but as he pressed my knees gave way and the bowl clattered into the sink. I wouldn't have cared if it was the Tsar's china. By then he was nibbling my earlobe, whispering about my beauty, how I was all he ever dreamed of, his prima, his porcelain doll and…

I moaned as his hands caressed me and inwardly begged him to take it further. Knowing what I liked, he let me pull free and turn to face him, my breathing short and shallow. Then he knelt before me, lifting his head in supplication, and gently stroked my outer thighs as I closed my eyes. My legs were slim and firm and smooth, and I knew they turned him on. Even now, I shudder at the memory of his touch…

Strains of the *Bogatyr Gates* (Mussorgsky's final movement) filled the apartment as Yuri, strong and graceful as a danseur, whipped me off my feet. Cradling me in his arms, he talked naughty in my ear and I giggled like a little girl as he carried me through to the bedroom. The Russian language may sound harsh and staccato to some, but it was the perfect language for such a moment! He set me down on the mattress, where I sank immediately, it being a cheap one without springs that Yuri had bought for a bottle of vodka. Although the window was open, and we were naked, we didn't feel the slightest chill.

Fortunately, Yuri wasn't one to rush things. Sometimes we'd spend ages lying intertwined with as much surface area of our bodies touching as possible. That night was extra special, as we both seemed to want to draw it out. Perhaps we had a premonition – like couples on the eve

39

of war – that we should treasure our time together in case the future never came.

As we kissed he'd pull apart now and again just enough to make eye contact, so I knew I was the sole object of his desire. I gave myself up fully to the moment, closing my eyes to savour being one flesh with the man I still cannot imagine loving more.

Oh, my little dove, I'd trade all those imposters that followed and the kingdoms of this world to have him back again. How cruelly, in a flash, our lives can be upended. If I'd known what would happen later that night, I'd have clung to him with all my strength and butterfly kissed and never let him go to work, nor uttered another unkind word or complaint to him.

Your father was a great lover, sublime in fact. So gentle and patient – to the extent I might have thought he lacked confidence if I hadn't seen him in his element at the plant. He'd dated other women before me, of course; but only one was serious that I knew of. She was a redhead research assistant at Arzamas. He fell hard; I think he was hoping to marry her, but she dumped him when she heard he was being transferred back to Moscow. Broke his heart. That she ran off with a country bumpkin without a university degree made it doubly hard for him to bear. So I was a mentor of sorts. He was quick learner and didn't seem to mind my leading. Not because he wasn't as proud as the next Russian man, but he was also pragmatic and genuinely wanted to please me.

Okay, I think we'd better end there for this evening, Katyusha. You're probably feeling a little uncomfortable after all the details I've shared. It must be awkward for you as our daughter when I talk of these things. But it's important to me that you should know what a fine, fine man your father was in every way, and how much we loved and delighted in each other. And to realise that you were conceived out of a deep bond of love. And that I love you, and always will, no matter what.

My darling… I've lived too long with secrets and shame. I need to let it out. Only the truth can set us free. And I owe it to you and your father to share with you where you came from and what shaped your life.

Four

Here we are again, my darling. How I stew after each session, worried that I may have offended you by saying too much.

Sorry, let me just pull up a chair by the window so I can see the view. I'm battling to stand for long now. Must be the chemotherapy.

Yes, I couldn't escape it. The blunt instrument.

Before I go on about myself, I was thinking that you probably want to hear more about your father's background.

Strangely, I learned precious little myself. He didn't like to talk about it, especially his childhood. I presume it was too painful. The orphan's burden. Like me, he barely remembered his mother. She died giving stillbirth to his younger brother. A few years later, when Yuri was about thirteen, his father succumbed to consumption, which he contracted while fighting the Nazis as a partisan in the forests about their village. The years after that when he worked as an engineer at a polluted steel plant only made it worse.

They lived in a tiny place – I forget the name – near Vitebsk in Belarus. Hmm... What else do I remember...?

Never mind, things will come to me as we go along. Let's rather continue from where we were last night, on that last Friday evening in Pripyat...

I lay with my cheek on Yuri's chest and listened to his heartbeat and steady breathing – my safe place, the absence of care – while outside it was the stillest of nights, and the moon slowly rose to fill the window, bathing the room yellow until I finally drifted off.

I woke to the realisation that the space beside me was empty. I lay still and waited. It wasn't long before I detected a movement from the corner of my eye. It was Yuri, kneeling in profile before his dresser. I could sense he was fiddling with the drawer where he kept his 'treasure' – my name for his collection of keepsakes.

The first time I'd witnessed him ferreting in the drawer was in January. He'd just returned from his shift while I was still in bed recovering from a sleepless night. I pretended to be asleep and didn't turn to look. All I heard was the rustling of papers and a drawer sliding closed, before he surreptitiously climbed into bed. Of course, not a minute after he'd left for his shift that night, I was scrabbling in his drawer… I mean, who could resist? Behind his rows of underwear I found a cherrywood cigar box. It didn't have space for much – five hundred roubles, his passport and a few letters.

Yes, I read them. This and that. A love letter from that old girlfriend. I'll get to all that later…

Now I lay still as a mannequin as Yuri returned the contents of his treasure to the drawer and slid back into our bed. Then, after a few minutes of feigned sleep, I rolled over with a groan. 'Yuri? You awake?'

'Now I am.'

'Is everything all right?'

'Why?'

'Your breathing is heavy.'

He chuckled. 'What do you expect? A lesser man would have collapsed after what you just took me through.'

'You give as good as you get, Russian bear.'

A car's headlights swept the ceiling. A whoosh outside grew louder then faded, and another, and afterwards there was just the chirping of crickets.

'Something's churning in that inscrutable mind of yours,' I chided.

He rolled onto his side, head on hand, and used his index finger to trace a path along my forehead and down my cheek, only stopping at my lips. But he didn't speak.

'You're anxious about the test going ahead, aren't you?' I said. 'Why? Wasn't it your brainchild?'

'Yes; but it's more complicated.'

'We have time.'

42

'I wish that was so.'

If only I'd listened between the lines. But I just waited.

'Even more reason to explain to me; or at least try.'

'I can't; it's top secret.'

'I'm your wife, dammit, if you don't trust me...'

He fell silent, seriously considering it. Or pretending to. 'Okay,' he said at last, 'But if a hint of this gets out it would cost me a lot more than my job.'

'I understand.'

He coughed. 'The test Yavlinsky and I argued about earlier – to see how the steam turbines' emergency system kicks in when there's a power outage, is... important – I've been promoting it since before I arrived here... but it's... not everything.'

'Say that again?' I could hear my heart beating.

'Earlier,' he continued, 'I described the *tokamak* – the fusion device at Arzamas. We designed several, progressively more advanced, up to 200 megawatts. Then we had a breakthrough, a device that could operate at a multiple of that.'

Wait a minute, I thought, he'd mentioned Sakharov and the others, but never revealed that he'd actually worked on this himself. I let him continue.

'It was larger with more complex systems, and needed more infrastructure – foundations, casings, cooling systems, emergency controls... which meant money, lots of it. Naturally, the bosses approved our proposal in a flash. Imagine how excited I was: at twenty-five, lead scientist of my workstream; my star was bright. Construction was completed in record time, and we were all set for commissioning. The race was on, you see. Our intelligence sources abroad indicated that the Americans were close. But...'

In the silence, I worried that he'd clammed up again.

'The explosion...' He inhaled. 'Terrible. Fortunately, the fallout could be contained to the area immediately surrounding the plant, which was rural, so we didn't have to evacuate civilians. As far as I know, the coverup was successful. But the bosses got cold feet. Too risky, they said, and shut down the programme.'

I gaped. It must have been devastating for him. And I'd thought I had the monopoly on disappointment. Turns out your father was every bit as ambitious as you and me; he just seldom verbalised it.

I said, 'I'm so sorry, my darling; I had no idea.' And waited for him to continue.

He turned over to stare at the ceiling. 'I thought my career was over,' he said at last. 'I drank, stayed in bed all day, missed work sometimes. I got so down... Then a telegram arrived from Ginzburg, my PhD supervisor at Moscow State. Remember him from Sparrow Hill, that dinner we hosted? Brilliant man, a luminary of science. He came right out with it: he had funding for a new phase of his research in fusion, and would I join the team?'

'Okay...' I pretended to be offhand, 'so that explains your return to Moscow, your post-doctoral research; but... what's it got to do with your work here in Chernobyl? Weren't you supposed to improve the design of the existing reactors?'

'Sort of; I...'

'Lied?'

'Lena...'

'Tss; and I thought we agreed... You're just like the rest...'

My hypocrisy. Even today, when I forget the power of grace, there are moments I still loathe myself as much as I did that night. But I was trying to keep him talking.

'What's this got to do with the turbine test – which you said wasn't everything?'

'It's just that with all the delays in the turbine test, my research on the fusion apparatus is way behind schedule. And you know what they do to a project leader in this country when that happens.'

'I'm sorry. What can I say?'

'I'm also worried that after all these delays and meddling from management, the risks in doing the turbine test have increased.'

'But...'

'They simply must be done, Lena. As soon as possible. The future of our country's nuclear industry depends on fixing these reactors before something truly terrible happens.'

I paused, absorbing his words.

'Sorry; I've said too much.'

He lapsed into silence. Then he grunted and rolled over to face me. From an apartment below us, a baby cried then hushed.

'Lenochka?'

'I'm here.'

'If… something was to happen to me…'

I sat up and stared at him. His eyes reflected the moon's glint. 'Why do you say something like that?'

And to this day, I can conjure his expression. Until then, I had thought him incapable of fear.

He took my cheeks between his hands and kissed me on the forehead. 'Now listen very carefully, and never forget…' He paused. 'Don't trust anyone. Only Sergey.'

I felt bewildered. My mind was swimming with questions but my lips wouldn't move. Eventually, I asked, 'Have you heard from him lately?'

'Nah, you don't get postcards from Kabul. Last we spoke, he was securing a pass to be here for a couple of days either side of Victory Day.'

'I wish he'd find a girlfriend.'

'It's a bit difficult if you're flying about the desert, strafing mujahideen. Give him time. There's a woman for him yet. God knows.'

'God?' I exclaimed, somewhat taken aback.

Yuri was an outspoken atheist, of course. The Revolution had killed faith in anything other than the State – demolishing or shutting any church not run by informers – but a remnant always endured, a flame that lit people's hearts and was passed on, story by story, grey hair to cradle, like the monks of the Dark Ages faithfully transcribing the holy writ by hand.

I, on the other hand, harboured an inkling that there must be a higher power – not a person but a cosmic intelligence – behind the complexities of the natural world and human consciousness. As I saw it,

45

random forces alone couldn't convert a handful of basic elements into a baby crying for its mother's unconditional love, who'd then grow up to compose poetry – or, heaven forbid, build concentration camps.

But I'd caught him off balance, which was my intent. I said, 'I was just teasing you.'

'Of course.'

He twirled a strand of my hair. 'I love you, girl.'

'Say it again.'

'I love you.'

'Why?'

'Mmm… Because you're sexy, and beautiful and clever, and…'

'Clever? Don't lie.'

'Different clever to me: you're intuitive; you know some things before I even think them.'

'Carry on.'

'I've lost my train of thought. Here…'

We kissed and afterwards lay side by side in silence. But there was a gnawing anxiety I couldn't shake. So, I said, 'Are you in trouble, Yuri?'

'Why?'

'You said just now "if something were to happen to me".'

'Any place there's a splitting or fusing of atoms, there's risk.'

I was about to ask him why he'd never mentioned that concern before, but then he abruptly sat up and reached for his packet of cigarettes, and I knew it was pointless to continue. So, I accepted a light and we smoked, and soon the smell of roasted tobacco and the nicotine and afterglow of our lovemaking beguiled me into thinking all was well in our world.

Suddenly, he stiffened, stubbed his cigarette out in the ashtray and did something that, in retrospect, still breaks my heart. He tenderly lay his hand on my stomach, closed his eyes, and concentrated like a doctor listening through a stethoscope. And then he stared at me with those piercing, normally sea blue irises that were now gilded by the moonlight – a picture still imprinted on my memory, like the one a bit later, of my only true love standing by his closet pulling on his collared shirt and trousers, doctor-white coat in hand and rubber boots. But the image is faded, not just by the haze of cigarette smoke then but more now by age. And, if I could change only one thing about that scene, he'd be smiling. How I loved his smile! But all right, an angel is still beautiful when it's sad.

Soon he'd glided across the room until his shoulders filled the door-frame. And from my position, splayed on the bed, I was thinking, my God he's handsome, never mind the bookish look with black-rimmed glasses and the trace of a stoop. He put on his head covering, the white cloth thing I called his sailor's cap.

Again he paused, as if uncertain.

I waited.

He cleared his throat. His very last words before he strode out into the night were 'Remember this: I love you more than life itself, and always will.'

Ah, my little dove... what I would give to turn back time. But not even the God of the Bible has managed that. Probably because we'd squander our second chance just like the first, when we ate the fruit of the knowledge of good and evil. Good thing the angel guarded us from the tree of life. Imagine the mess we'd make of the world if we had eternity!

Since then I've often thought about what I could and should have said to my husband that night as he left.

'I love you too, my darling' – no – 'I adore you my funny, intelligent, handsome, kindest-man-I-know husband. And don't remember me for how we met but for how we loved.' Then I'd have lured him back to bed to make love again, and afterwards held him and said, 'call in sick', whispered sweet nothings through his night shift, and let the devil care about the consequences.

But words have always failed me: either they come out wrong or not at all. Good thing I chose an art form without words.

So, what did I actually say that night?

I reminded him to take the uneaten chicken stew I had just packed him, said goodnight and watched his outline recede in the dark. Then I listened to the tramp of his boots fading down the stairwell, and the foyer door squeaking shut. Minutes later I heard the nightshift bus rumble closer, the hissing of doors and the hail of comrades. And then I was alone in the unfathomable dark, like a cavern in which my only candle had burnt out.

I could literally hear the creatures creeping from their recesses. Not unlike the feeling when my friend's mother dropped me at home after preschool and I found my grandmother at the door instead of my mother – and nothing was ever the same again.

Surprisingly though, once I'd overcome the initial grief, those three years after my mother's demise were my most carefree. Babushka doted on me. We lived cheek to jowl in her little village of Skuratovskiy, but the space was our own, and I loved it. In winter she'd make that dark Russian bread with the aroma of sourdough filling every nook. It was hardly a life of ease, though. As soon as she noticed I was doing well at ballet, she wouldn't let me miss a practice. Four times a week, minimum. Ah, Babushka, my champion… I can't think who else would have contacted the Bolshoi scouts. Certainly not my teacher, the hag. We clashed terribly. But it spelled the end of my village idyll. How vividly I remember boarding the bus for Moscow, pressing my face against the windowpane, inconsolable as Babushka's toothless smile and the red roofs of the village melted into the horizon.

But I digress…

Yuri had left for his night shift, and I never got used to him being away all night. Every time he left for work I'd get emotional. Then I'd lie there making it worse by berating myself for being pathetic. Once, in the depths of the winter, I plunged so low that I leaned over the balustrade and stared at the pavement below, feeling its magnetic attraction tipping me over. But hallelujah, I was touched by an angel: Matrushka started airbrushing my calves, meowing loudly, and wouldn't stop. I swear she knew. Eventually, I picked her up and we cuddled while I soothed her with gobbledygook and she nuzzled into my armpit.

So, that night, I got up and brought Matrushka to bed with me where I lay stroking her soft fur and smoking a cigarette till the stump burned my fingers. Soon every muscle in my body was deliciously numbed by nicotine and endorphins, and my eyelids finally closed.

My sleeplessness had started about two months earlier. Partly it was from switching from sleeping on my stomach to on my side, and maybe from hormonal changes, but most of all, from anxiety, especially in the trenches of the night! Battalions of anxious thoughts would wait at the border of my consciousness for the signal of my waking to plunder me. I'd toss and turn, then rise to close the drapes against the moonlight. Or flip my pillow to rest my head on the cooler side. Hell, I'd even try counting sheep to forty times forty. But counting rarely worked.

Lately, in despair, I'd try to conjure a picnic we'd enjoyed on the grassy riverbank downstream from the port, sailboats tacking against the stream, the ferry from Kiev steaming past while we threw daisy heads at each other like confetti. And how we'd kissed and cuddled like only those newly in love can. Then I'd imagine Yuri taking his kayak and paddling into the brown, smooth-flowing water. He'd go for kilometres up the Pripyat River, way past the cooling pond. That was my husband: no half measures. Like you, he always took things to the extreme.

But then – *suka*! Like clockwork, Sonya Yavlinsky would swan into the scene with her signature sway, sidling down to the shoreline to lift her dress and wade into the shallows, beckoning my beloved. And there he'd be, steering the kayak sharply about, smiling broadly at her…

When my fantasies morphed into nightmares like that, no amount of self-talk could prevail. My chest would contract as one negative thought led to another, especially at night when every fear and regret was amplified.

And oh, my darling, what a lifetime's worth of regrets I've accumulated!

Five

That last night in our apartment when I just couldn't get to sleep, I got up and took a sleeping pill. They were officially taboo, but as the *nomenklatura* we had ways and means – the pharmacist, in this case. I told her I was suffering terrible period pains and offered a month's private ballet lessons for her daughter. The first night I enjoyed a glorious eight hours; the next, seven; then six… by that Friday, I was sleeping perhaps four hours a night. Finally, I fell into a groggy doze.

And then it happened. A kind of thunderclap. I remember it clearly – like a distant thud, more memorable for its reverberations – windows rattling in their frames, the flutter and squawk of a stork, and afterwards a silence as if even the crickets were holding their breath.

I sat up and looked at the clock. One twenty-five. Strange, I thought. I draped a sheet about my shoulders like a toga and hurried to the balcony where I stood, bathed in moonlight, scanning the darkness. Nothing unusual, I thought, except that the sliver of reflected light above the station was perhaps more orange than yellow and a tad smudged, making it hard to see the tiny red lights that normally flashed atop the cooling towers to warn airplanes. Eventually I retired to the bathroom and then bed – and lay still as a pin, trying yet again to fall asleep.

I must have drifted in and out of a drug-induced semi-sleep because I have snippets of recollection – sirens and headlights sweeping the bedroom wall, flashes of light on the apartment ceiling, and the hiss and clack of trains running to and from Yaniv station.

The next thing I remember is a sunbeam baking my bedspread. But things were amiss: the birds weren't singing, the traffic was too heavy for a Saturday… and Yuri wasn't back. I glanced at my bedside clock. Ten o'clock! My first spike of raw fear. He was never that late. I shot out of bed, but too quickly, and the room started turning. After stabilising myself, I managed to stagger out onto the balcony.

It was so bright I had to squint, but the haze was too thick to see further than a few blocks. The air was unusually close with a burnt tinge. Feeling queasy, I leaned on the railing.

After a while, I heard a distant thudding that grew louder until it was deafening and the concrete under my feet vibrated. Next thing I was in shadow and looking up into the reptilian belly of a Mil Mi-26 – the largest Soviet transport helicopter ever produced. It seemed to hover overhead, so low I could feel the downdraft. Beneath it dangled a huge bucket spilling fine plumes of sand. Then its nose dropped and it churned off in the direction of the station.

As I stood there, puzzled, I recalled the thunderclap and glow earlier in the night. My chest tightened. The conclusion seemed inescapable: had the unimaginable happened? There'd clearly been a fire; who knows, maybe even at Reactor Number Four; which meant… Yuri could be in trouble…

I hurried indoors and grabbed the spinner, then hesitated. The receiver trembled in my hand. Yuri hated me calling him at work. My fingertip was so sweaty it slipped in the dial, but eventually I managed the numbers.

An interminable wait.

'Yes?' A female voice answered.

'It's Lena Sergeyevna Chizhikova. Yuri Petrovich's wife.' There were strange noises in the background. 'You still there? Please, I need to speak to my husband.'

'The name again.'

'Yuri Petrovich Chizhikov, Special Advisor; Deputy Chief Engineer Korolev can vouch for—'

'That won't be possible.'

'But…'

Static, followed by gushing. 'Are you not aware?'

I inhaled sharply. 'Aware of what?'

'Hold on…' More static, and a clanging of pipes.

'What's going on?' I pleaded.

'There's… been an incident… a fire… in the reactor room…'

I waited, shaking.

'Don't worry,' the voice said, 'The necessary precautions are being taken; the authorities—'

'Just tell me what happened!'

'Calm down, citizen…?'

'Chizhikova.'

'A communication will be made.'

I heard boots stamping on plastic tiles, a shout, and then static again. I said, 'Let me speak to your superior. Now.'

'He's not available.'

'Mikhail Yegorovich then.'

'Who?'

'Deputy Chief Engineer Korolev.'

She paused. 'He departed for a meeting in Kiev.'

I thought of the headlights on my bedroom wall in the night, the sound of trains. Immediately I knew. The rats were jumping ship. By the mid-80s most of us were deeply cynical. We knew the Party was corrupt, that self-interest always trumped duty. But always, a part of us hoped for better.

'Please,' I pleaded. 'Just tell me if my husband is safe.'

A pause. The line crackled. 'His name again.'

I spelled Yuri's name and patronymic twice, slowly.

'Reactor Number Four?' Pages turned. 'There's no one of that name on last night's roster.'

'Day shift then.' I rapped my fingertips on the phone handle.

'Sorry,' she coughed. 'There's no one of that name.'

'Look again! Everyone knows Yuri. One eighty-five tall, glasses, handlebar moustache, brown—' I was left with a dial tone.

I smashed the spinner down, then grabbed it and redialled, fumbling. It was engaged. I staggered through to the bathroom and had a quick wash, steadying myself on the basin. Why hadn't Yuri called to reassure me? I went to my closet to get dressed but I couldn't decide in what. Suddenly, the apartment shrank. I felt flushed, perspiring. I had to find him.

I couldn't leave in my pyjamas. The first dress to hand was knee-length in mauve and white paisley cotton with high sleeves. The fabric was faded, but clean.

After dressing, I swept through to the kitchen where my darling Matrushka greeted me, weaving between my legs lovingly, reassuring me. I stroked her and quickly filled her bowls.

A wave of nausea washed over me, either from the strange acrid taste in my throat or from hunger. I surveyed the kitchen. There was leftover chicken stew in the pan and the previous night's dishwater in the sink. The fridge offered a bowl of *kasha* and plate of blini with mincemeat and sour cream from Friday's breakfast. Instead, I opted for simple bread. I scratched in the drawer for the knife, but had to extract it from the cold, greasy dishwater. And then… for a brief blessed moment I could feel Yuri's body against me from behind, arms wrapped around me and his warm breath in my ear.

And so, on the morning of the end of my old life, I sat alone at the kitchen table with a slice of bread and cheese and black tea. Unusually for that hour, I lit a cigarette, and talked myself through my options out loud. Access to the power station was tightly controlled. Yuri had once arranged a special pass; but I needed help. Calling the *militsiya* – the local police – would be pointless. They were corrupt and useless. What else? Nothing, really. In Sovetsky Soyuz, all roads – literally and figuratively – led to and from Moscow via the local Party Office. Yet going there in person would risk seeing… I shivered. Any sensible citizen avoided the Party headquarters. But who else would know what was going on at the plant?

I vacillated. But I had to do something. The Almighty can only steer a ship that's in motion. So, I sprang up, grabbed my purse, and set off. As I was locking the front door I remembered my passport. In Sovetsky Soyuz, we needed it anytime we dealt with officialdom. Bureaucracy… the enemy of creativity.

I spiralled down the stairwell, footsteps echoing, hit the ground floor and bustled through the foyer. When I flung the door open, I was hit by a blast of oven-hot air and momentarily blinded by light. The town was abuzz with shouting and sirens wailing, especially strange as this day was *Subbotnik* – the Saturday closest to Lenin's birthday when all citizens had to 'volunteer' for manual labour like cleaning public bathrooms or picking up litter. The haze was so thick I could barely make out the grocery store at the top of Lelina Avenue. Stranger still, the road was full of puddles and water trickled along the drains.

I stepped into the street, only to find myself looking straight at my shadows – two stocky men in cheap suits diagonally across the street beside a caged beech sapling.

Yes, I was 'under observation'. Not uncommon in a police state. It could be for something as ridiculous as a snitch reporting a joke you made about a politician at the school canteen. Up to a third of the population were said to be spies in one form or another.

But I didn't recognise this pair. New blood perhaps. I straightened my dress, scowled at them, and hurried on.

Seconds later, an apparition appeared: a man in a dazzling white hazmat suit with rubber boots and a face mask. A kind of scuba-diving tank was strapped to his back and he waddled along, stiff-jointed as an astronaut, foam-blasting the sidewalk from a spray nozzle.

I felt a tightening in my chest. Yuri had recounted how whole villages had to be sanitised following previous disasters.

Gradually, I became aware of a rumble behind me. *Splosh!* I was drenched from the waist down as a tanker truck surged past, ploughing through swathes of foam-topped water. It was as if the city was a canteen kitchen being hosed down at the end of a shift. I pressed on, evading more hazmat figures. Another truck gushing water crossed in front of me, siren wailing. Soon I could see Gorkom Square, only two blocks away.

Then a troop of red-kerchiefed Young Pioneers approached, chanting their motto 'always ready'. Back then membership of the Young Pioneers was a badge of honour. If you wanted to reach the top of your profession, you joined.

Sure, I took the oath too; we were all forced to. The troop of Pioneers that morning was marching in ranks of four youngsters behind their flag bearer, swaying baskets of freshly picked mushrooms.

Incredibly, after hours of radiation! Not a word of warning from the authorities. Bastards. 'Yes, yes, yes to the sunny world!' these innocent children were singing, 'no, no, no to a nuclear explosion….'.

I watched their red kerchiefs shrink along Lelina, which continued up the gentle rise past the city limits to the bridge, beyond which the power station was obscured by thick, orange-tinged smoke. Which triggered yet another bout of alarm.

'Yurochka!' I cried aloud. 'My darling, where are you?' A passer-by stared. I didn't care. Oh, how I needed Yuri!

I pressed on toward Pripyat's city centre, a series of buildings arranged in a half-moon about the square. Among them was the Polissya Hotel, where members of Gorbachev's special commission would end up staying during the disaster. The neon sign on its façade read *Let the atom be a worker not a soldier*. The irony. In front of these buildings loomed a nine-story apartment complex for VIPs with a white façade. We anointed it the 'White House'; black humour helped keep us sane.

And then there was the Raduga grocery store where Olga packed shelves on weekends – her second 'unofficial' job to make ends meet. Raduga meant 'rainbow'. We'd joke that we were more likely to find a pot of gold there than the grocery items we needed.

I longed to go in and find Olga, but time was of the essence. So I turned right, skirted the square, hurried past the gym where Olga taught swimming and I did knee rehab – and stopped in front of the Party Headquarters, or Gorkom. Every city in Sovetsky Soyuz had one of these grotesque edifices, designed to keep the *nomenklatura* comfortable and the proletariat terrified. Still today, go to any Party Headquarters in Moscow, Kiev, anywhere. Standing before those mighty blocks of stone and the Doric columns, with the hammer and sickle emblazoned in the marble, you can sense the raw, physical power in your bones and the evil literally poisoning the air.

Moscow's was the worst. The first time I went there was to apply for a *zagranpasport* for a Bolshoi tour of Czechoslovakia, Hungary and

Poland. Domestic travel required a different passport, but these were considered foreign countries, though we controlled them like poodles. The Ministry of Internal Affairs also ran the *militsiya*. What a goose chase from one power-warped official to the next, the parasites – only to be denied permission in the end.

I was a tainted person because of Papa. Though technically it had started with the grandfather I never met, who was sentenced to five years in Kolyma for publishing an essay criticising the state housing policy. They branded him an 'enemy of the people', a standard pretext for arrest – which I heard the leader of the free world dare to call a journalist on TV yesterday. I nearly choked on my jelly!

Anyway, within six months of entering the camp, Dedushka had caught pneumonia and died. In the end he was 'rehabilitated', code for his name being cleared in the official records. That happened a lot during Khrushchev's thaw. It had to be facilitated by a bribe, of course. Babushka told me she'd sold her jewellery, but she'd done it for Mama. She needn't have bothered; the KGB's branding was made with permanent ink.

And there I stood that morning, trembling before the lesser edifice of the Pripyat Gorkom. So, as I did for stage fright, I took several deep breaths, gritted my teeth, and strode on. By the third step I was stopped by a guard, a skin-headed, pasty-faced moron with an expression so serious you'd swear the future of the Motherland depended on him.

'Permit?' he barked.

'My husband...'

He straightened, lips tightening to form '*nyet*'.

'He's—'

'Do you have an appointment?'

'No, but—'

He clicked his heels. 'Entrance is forbidden.'

I enlarged my eyes and gave him what Yuri called 'the pout', the sad, vulnerable and innocent expression with a flutter of my eyelashes. 'Please, it's an emergency. I need to speak to someone. Five minutes is all I need.'

He equivocated.

I smiled coquettishly. If you weren't lucky enough to be born in proximity to power, you had to use your wiles.

As I handed over the document, I made sure our fingers touched. But he still thumbed to my *propiska*, the residency permit that every citizen required for domestic travel in their own country.

The guard studied my mugshot, then looked up at me.

In Moscow, any hotel concierge worth his salt would recognise me. Not that I was a *prima ballerina*; but there was a rumour mill... I like to think I was more flamboyant than notorious. I added a dash of colour to their black and white world. But in truth, I hated being recognised. I was relieved when the bumpkin didn't recognise me.

He frowned, inspected it more closely.

I casually adjusted my bra strap, and he stole a glance and blushed. Then he tapped my passport and slipped it into his breast pocket. 'Counter one,' he said, 'You'll get it when you leave.'

My heart almost went into palpitations. Without that slim, red document I was screwed. It represented your essence, a permanent record of your failings and your future. Heaven help you if it got lost. To this day, I keep mine next to my bed.

But that morning, I had no choice; so I thanked the guard and stepped past into the gloom.

The foyer's only furniture was a plastic sofa and a side table with plastic flowers. There were no other people, which made it feel cavernous, though the ceiling was the standard height for an ordinary office building. There were only two fluorescent tubes overhead, no windows save for breathing portholes along the street-facing wall, and a ceiling fan. A woman, initially unfamiliar to me, was sitting at a desk reading a trashy romance novel. Her name tag read Maksimova. Her brown suit matched her hair and she had probably been attractive once upon a time.

I stared vacantly at the ceiling and waited as she continued to read. With officious little Napoleons it was best to act unhurried.

Eventually she lay her book down and looked up at me with a mixture of annoyance and boredom.

I recognised her now. The mother of Masha, a girl in my afternoon ballet class, who was sweet and willing but without talent. 'Good morning,' I ventured. But I could see her mind was elsewhere. 'I'm looking for my husband.'

'We're closed.' She turned over her book and shuffled papers.

'Please. It's important.'

'That's what everyone says.'

'With respect, the guard let me in; you're here and—'

She waved me away. Always acutely conscious of body image, I couldn't help noticing the wobble of her upper arm.

She rolled her eyes. 'The sign is clear, no?'

I noticed the sign to the right of the kiosk: a letter board found only in museums today: a black background with horizontal tracks where you slide in white letters to make sentences.

'But… it's only ten thirty,' I protested.

She set the novel aside, her lips taut. 'Are you the only person in Pripyat who doesn't know about the accident?'

'No – well, I didn't… my husband was on night shift.'

Her brows furrowed, like she was battling to put a name to my face. 'Did you call the station?'

'The lines were down.'

She appraised me. 'A precaution, I believe.' There was a flicker of recognition. 'Aren't you…?'

'Masha's ballet teacher.'

'Of course! You were with the Bolshoi, no?'

I gave a deprecating shrug.

She extended her hand. 'Angela Leonidovna… Did you file a missing person report?'

'Hah – we both know what good that will do.'

'Sorry, we're under orders to refer all enquiries to the *militsiya*.'

'Please, I…'

'Sorry.' She fished keys from her drawer and struggled to her feet. 'I'm already late.' She locked the kiosk door and waddled past me.

Alone, I immediately panicked.

'Wait!' I called, 'I remember now, at the last rehearsal, I didn't get a chance to speak to you. Sorry; I'm awfully focussed.'

She stopped in her tracks.

'I meant to tell you… Masha… she's a prodigious talent! I just think she needs some, you know...'

She turned to face me, all ears.

'Some individual attention,' I added.

She stepped back toward me and leaned forward conspiratorially. 'What were you thinking?'

I shrugged. 'A few private lessons, perhaps? I have a late Wednesday afternoon slot.'

'You sure it wouldn't be too much of a burden? A famous dancer like you must get petitioned all the time.'

'Forget about it; I love giving back.'

She hesitated.

I swallowed. Favour exchanges were routine, although transacting right there in the belly of the beast put the fear of God into me! But for Yuri, I took the risk.

Maksimova scanned the foyer. There was no sign of the guard. 'Okay,' she mumbled, 'Your husband's Party Number?'

'Sorry; he keeps his card with him at all times.'

'Full name and date of birth, then.'

She heaved herself back into her chair and reluctantly lifted a pencil.

I spelled it out, letter by letter.

'Say that again?'

I could have strangled her. I was imagining Yuri trapped under a mound of rubble, and above him a smouldering beam that could fall at any minute.

Eventually, she tore the page off, and led me through the rear door of the kiosk. Soon we were alone in a dimly lit archive filled with row after row of steel filing cabinets with hanging files. She pulled out a drawer and ran her fingers through the alphabetical card labels… drawer after agonising drawer.

'Here…' She withdrew a card.

My hopes surged.

'That's strange.' She frowned, then looked up. 'Sorry, there's nothing.'

'No!' I silently screamed. 'That's... impossible!' I managed to blurt. 'Yuri's been a member since his PhD; before that, in the Komsomol – Secretary of the Science Faculty Committee.'

Maksimova shrugged. 'There's no record...'

'Look again!' Instantly, I regretted my outburst. Never lose your cool with a bureaucrat.

'Forgive me,' I murmured, my gaze lowered. 'I'm just so worried for my husband.'

She closed the drawer. 'I'm sorry, but this is where his file would be. Now, I really must go. Our archivist is back on Monday. If she doesn't find it...'

I could have screamed. But I said, 'Thank you, Angela Leonidovna.'

'Oh, it's nothing; see it as a thank you for helping Masha. Now if you'll excuse me. Next Wednesday at, say, two pm?'

'W-wait.' I rummaged my mind for names I could leverage. We had socialised a little with a few of Yuri's colleagues but I couldn't think of anyone suitable.

Maksimova drummed her pen on the counter.

Deep down I knew there was only one person with the power to really help. I shivered.

'Come,' she touched my elbow. 'I'll walk you out.'

But he'd warned me never to initiate direct contact myself, I reminded myself. Doing so now would risk our arrangement concerning Yuri. But I had to do something.

I grabbed Maksimova's sleeve. 'One more thing. Please.'

'Yes.'

'Director Yavlinsky keeps an office here, no?

She nodded.

'Is he in this morning? I asked, though I was doubtful, considering the cars and trains I'd heard leaving through the night.

'Is he expecting you?' she asked.

'Well, no, but… we're… Yuri and comrade Yavlinsky work together and his wife and I are friends, too.'

Clearly, she was sceptical; but if she dismissed me, she risked upsetting a powerful Party official.

I acted indifferent, but inside I was trembling.

'Okay. Follow me.'

We entered a low-ceilinged corridor. Unlike in the Party offices in Moscow, this place had a cramped, prefabricated feel and the vinyl floors were soft beneath my shoes.

Maksimova shuffled along, walrus-like, pausing to catch her breath. Through a kink and into another corridor. A familiar terror gripped me.

Eventually, she stopped at a door, put her ear to it and knocked.

A grunt came from inside.

She prised the door open a crack and slipped in. After a brief exchange she was back with a puzzled expression. 'Comrade, Director Yavlinsky will see you,' she said, and ushered me into the lion's den. I…

Sorry, Katyusha I've lost my train of thought. I'm going to need to stop here for now. I'm experiencing another wave of nausea. This latest round of chemotherapy isn't agreeing with me. It's like poison. I have this bag feeding my intravenous drip, you see. My magic potion against the side effects. But it's empty. I need to call the nurse before I throw up. Ah, here's the remote. I'll just hold down the red button for three seconds. Now, let's time how long it takes a nurse to arrive. I give it sixty seconds.

Ah, footsteps coming down the corridor. See, less than a minute!

Okay, she's off to fetch me another bag to relieve my nausea. What service we get in this facility. A far cry from that public hospital up the road from us in Brooklyn where you ended up when your appendix burst. Remember that? A different story altogether. You nearly died of a secondary infection. But this place? Clean as a whistle. How can I thank you enough, my darling? Make sure you also let Bob know how much I appreciate it. By the way, I'd love to meet him before…

Sorry. I must get my thinking right, there's always hope. Modern medicine and all.

How it saddens me to think how much of your life I've missed out on these last few years apart. Your first full-time job, your marriage…

So what's he like? More importantly, does he make you happy? It seems that way. You appear to be flourishing.

Okay, I admit, I sat on a bench in that little park opposite the entrance to your office building a couple of times. Wearing a big hat pulled down low. It reminded me of how I used to come into your room when I got back from the club every night – well, early morning I should say. I'd stand in your bedroom doorway and watch you sleep. I swear you relaxed more when you sensed my presence.

My darling, I know how much you disapprove of what I did those years. But how else could I put food on the table? Mikhail? Hah! He was as reliable as a bad tooth! Sure, there was the occasional windfall from one of his nefarious schemes – that's when you'd get presents – but then things would go wrong or he'd disappear on yet another drinking binge.

Sorry, I know you hate me for speaking ill of him. But if you'd only known…

In truth it was good of him to take me in initially and arrange a waitressing job. He was literally the first person I met in Brooklyn, and I was clueless. The taxi from JFK dropped me off at the top of Flatbush, at the circle by Prospect Park. I'd heard a lot of Russian émigrés had settled in Brooklyn. Though that turned out to be nearer to Coney Island.

But within months of your birth he insisted I get back to work. Only this time as an exotic dancer. At that stage I saw no other choice. Somehow, through his underworld contacts, I suppose, he saw that I had greater commercial value as a dancer. And, giving birth notwithstanding, I'd kept my body in good shape.

I'll explain more, I promise. But that's my nurse back to tend to me. Let's call it a night, okay? *Paka paka.* Until next time.

Six

O kay, let's get right to it, my little dove, I'm feeling a bit better today. Let's pick up the story while I have the energy.

There I stood in the centre of Yavlinsky's office, like an errant child before the school principal. His desk could have seated six for dinner. But it was virtually clear, except for a notepad, the memo he was working on, a fountain pen and, naturally, the Ukrainian edition of *Pravda*, the Party mouthpiece. *Pravda* of course means truth – what gumption!

Yavlinsky's stomach pressed up against the edge of the desk and his white-collared shirt as usual had sweat stains at the armpits. His pock-marked face was proof that for a man, beauty wasn't a prerequisite for power.

His window offered a ninety-degree panorama of the park. 'The Ferris wheel,' I mumbled, 'it's rotating.'

'About time.' He signed his memo with a flourish.

Finally, he looked at me. 'I was wondering when you'd show up. Sit.' He took out a handkerchief and wiped his hand. 'So, Lena Sergeyevna, what can I do for you?'

I shook my head. 'Err… nothing.'

He fixed me with his recessed eyes. 'Forgive my cynicism, he said, 'But nine of the ten visitors I get are looking for a favour. And it must be serious, because we agreed not to meet.'

See, I'd actually called on Yavlinsky once before, after he'd threatened Yuri. Hush, hush, of course; Yuri would have killed me if he'd known. But I felt I had to do something; I'd never seen my husband as rattled. He'd said his research was in jeopardy.

Anyway, here I was again, naked before the monster. But I was not about to show weakness. I said, 'I must be desperate, no?'

'Ouch,' he replied, 'Good thing you chose ballet not diplomacy.'

'Seems we have something in common then.'

'More than one thing, I'm afraid.'

I swallowed, determined not to fall for the bait.

'So, how can I help?' he said.

'It's about my husband.'

'Again?' He chortled, his pig eyes narrowing to slits.

'It's not funny.'

'No?' He smirked. 'Go on.'

He's… missing. The a-accident…'

He stared at me with an inscrutable expression. I steeled myself. People in his profession were trained to unnerve others in this way, make you feel naked and squirm.

He said, 'I'm sorry to hear that.'

'You don't look it.'

He cocked his head; there was a click of cartilage; then he switched sides. 'What do you want me to do?'

'To care, for a start.'

He placed a cigarette lighter on the desk. It was silver and engraved with his initials. 'Do you know how many people I'm responsible for?'

'A thousand?'

'Hah! Multiples.' He aligned the lighter with the desk pad. 'And you think you're special.' He nudged the lighter. 'Makes sense, I suppose. You're married to comrade Special: special hours; special computer; special clearance.'

I tried to ignore the taunt.

He flicked the lighter to a flame. 'You're acquainted with Senior Reactor Control Engineer Toptonov?'

I nodded. 'Yuri had the team over for drinks once.'

He watched the flame dwindle, fixed me with his pig-stare. 'He died in the incident.' This was the first moment, standing there at that KGB monster's mercy, when the true horror of what had just happened sank in.

Yavlinsky shook his head. 'Tragic,' he muttered, 'Toptonov was a solid worker.'

I suddenly felt faint.

64

'Are you okay? Relax: he's the only one – confirmed dead, that is. Comrade Asimov was last seen disappearing under a rain of rubble but we're confident he'll turn up.'

I clasped my hands behind my back so he couldn't see they were shaking. 'And my husband?'

He shrugged. 'Our resident tomcat? Who knows, he was probably prowling about one of the reactors looking for trouble. Have you contacted the control room?'

'Of course; I'm not an idiot.'

He nodded. 'Many things but not that.'

'The girl who answered said she'd never heard of him, that he's not in the directory. How is that possible?'

Yavlinsky wrinkled his nose. 'I told you: your husband's an enigma.'

He'd touched a raw nerve. I leaned forward, hands on the desk. 'You're Chief of the Personnel Section for Reactor Number Four, correct?'

'The whole plant, actually.'

'Then it's your job to look after the workers' interests – every soul affected by this God-damned… incident!'

His oily, cratered face was only centimetres away. For a moment, I feared I'd gone too far.

But eventually, he relaxed. 'I'm going to make allowance for the circumstances and excuse your impudence – this time.'

I was close to tears. But hell could freeze over before I'd show weakness to that bully. Katyusha, you have no idea… coddled Western minds can't conceive how heinous those KGB people were. And forget the ignorant foot soldier simply following orders to feed his family. By the '80s, enough banned literature was in circulation, and news was filtering in from outside.

'Please. I just want to know how he is,' I said.

He stroked his double chin. 'I'd tell you if I knew, but I wasn't at the plant. The Committee met here last night, and we went on past midnight.'

'I don't believe you.'

'Why would I lie?'

'Because you do it for a living.'

65

His cheeks flushed. 'That's the second insult.'

'I'm sorry.'

He sat back in his chair and sighed. 'We both should be.'

'What's that supposed to mean?'

'Don't act dumb.' He fished a pack of Marlboros from his pocket and offered them. I felt a sudden craving for one. His fingers were stubby and carried a whiff of detergent. He lit his first. Then he reclined. Tendrils of smoke seeped from his nostrils. 'You must have heard the rumours.'

'Gossip isn't my strong suit.'

'We must be Pripyat's biggest cuckolds.'

I stared.

'Tsk, tsk. I'll spell it out then. 'Your husband and my Sonya are fucking.'

'Liar!'

Immediately, I regretted my outburst. 'Forgive me, Vladimir Semonovich,' I demurred.

Ordinarily, I'd have addressed him by his title, or comrade. But we'd met before. Worse, we'd socialised as couples – albeit only once or twice, early on, before he and Yuri fell out.

I closed my eyes, comforted by the nicotine. 'My husband would never do something like that.'

'That's what they all say.'

My shoulders tensed. 'We have our ups and downs like any married couple but…' I swallowed. 'We love each other. Anyway, what makes you think this?'

He drew on his cigarette till its end glowed. 'You saw them together in the amusement park yesterday.'

I stiffened. He must have noticed me eavesdropping from under the tree. Suddenly, the office felt like a morgue. I was desperate to escape. But if I did I'd never know Yuri's fate… I inhaled so deeply my diaphragm hurt. I said, 'Yuri's as shy as a porcupine. He wouldn't even know how to seduce a prostitute.'

Yavlinsky frowned. 'Are you implying that Sonya's the instigator?'

Like a bitch on heat, I thought. 'I only mean that Yuri isn't the type to have an affair.'

And I meant that part. His denial had persuaded me. He certainly found her attractive. But my experience of your father until then, my little dove, pointed to a man of the highest principle. He was no Puritan of course, but his personal code of honour seemed as absolute as an equation.

Yavlinsky nodded sagely. 'I'll grant you he steps to a different drumbeat.'

'Which is why you hate him so much: he doesn't worship people like you.'

'I prefer the term "respect". You need to show some too.'

Suddenly, I was weary from the verbal sparring. All I wanted was to go to bed and wake up with my husband's calming hand on my tummy.

'I need you to help me,' I said evenly.

'Why?'

'Because it's your job – or one of them.'

'Enough, gypsy woman.'

'That slur is a lie.'

'Jew then.'

I froze.

How can I describe the danger of being labelled a Jew in Sovetsky Soyuz? Here in New York City it's almost an advantage. But in Russia there'd been pogroms for centuries. Ordinary people used to slaughter Jews for sport. The Revolution was supposed to end it, and several prominent Bolsheviks were Jewish – Trotsky, Kamenev, Zinoviev. But whenever things went wrong, politicians looked for scapegoats. Like Stalin and the doctors' plot. And the mistreatment of refuseniks. I'd found out about this part of my heritage accidently from some documents in Babushka's attic when I was about thirteen, during the Bolshoi School's summer holidays. Babushka swore me to secrecy and told me the barest minimum. Her grandparents had fled the pogroms eastward from the Pale. They took refuge in Moscow and changed their names. That makes me one quarter Jewish, maybe more, through the female line. If my mother knew, she never let on. Once, when I came home crying from preschool after being teased for my dark skin, her face had a strange expression, but she shrugged and said they were jealous of my gorgeous thick hair from my Georgian *dedushka*.

Anyway, Yavlinsky was smirking at me.

'What's the matter?' he said, 'You've gone pale, if that's possible for you people. His eyes burrowed into my soul. 'Let me remind you that misrepresenting your ethnicity could result in prosecution under Article 58.' That section dealt with 'counter-revolutionary activities' or 'treason'. Conviction usually meant ten years' hard labour.

With every fibre, I wanted to run. But then I'd lose any chance of learning about Yuri. So instead, I worked myself into a rage. 'Is this the worst you can dredge?' I said. 'Fine, go ahead. I'll survive. Just know this: I have no intention of going down quietly.'

Yavlinsky looked aside. 'Thank you for confirming my hunch,' he chortled. 'I'll make a note to research the matter further on Monday.'

I felt like an idiot. Yavlinsky was sucking all the energy from me.

I rose and turned to leave.

'Sit!'

'Why?' I said, striding toward the door.

'Because you want to find your husband,' he said to my back.

I stopped. I suspected he was lying, but what other options did I have?

'Come back, silly,' he said.

I slunk back and slumped into the chair.

'Good girl,' he said. 'Now look at me.'

Reluctantly, I lifted my gaze.

'Okay, now tell me: how long did you know your husband before you married?'

'What's this got…'

'Just answer the question.'

'Five months. But you know this.'

He whistled. 'Hah, a whirlwind romance. Swept him off his feet. Don't you ever feel bad?'

'No. We ended up falling in love. I don't suppose you can relate.'

He waved smoke away, snuffed out the cigarette in the ashtray. 'Tell me: in all this time, what have you achieved for us?'

I gulped. 'I…'

Oh Katya… This is so difficult. My God, I need some courage before I can go on. Let me get my icon. That's better. Sergius of Radonezh – the healer, and the image by Nesterov.

Hmm, maybe a little nip of Stolichnaya, too.

It was Dima who smuggled it in for me. Remember the barman at the Russian Club? Oh no, of course, you refused to accompany me; you used to call it the Hard Luck Club. How right you were!

Na nashe zdorovye – I sure as hell need health right now. Every shot could be my last these days. Ah… what a smooth afterburn. Mmm, taste that birch charcoal! Those Latvians know how to make vodka, all right.

I suppose I can't procrastinate forever. The truth, Katyusha – and probably you've suspected it for some years, which would explain some of your anger – is that by the time I sat there opposite Yavlinsky that fateful morning after the accident, I'd already got myself into a deep tangle with the KGB.

But bear with me. Let me explain. I never volunteered or knew what I was getting into. No, no, the spider spins his web slowly, and with an invisible thread.

In my case, he posed as a bigwig from the Ministry of Culture, young and debonair, a ballet aficionado. Vasily Vasilyevich Ivanov. That's what he called himself, anyway. He arrived at the Bolshoi unannounced and asked to meet the cast after a performance. It was only two weeks after my fall, and I was backstage with a strapped knee, helping the girls change. Afterwards he invited us for drinks at the bar, where he sat himself next to me. I was flattered at that stage, I admit. But the next day I got a personal invitation to dinner. I was quite reluctant, but my friends thought I was crazy and egged me on, saying he was cute and powerful. We ate at the Metropol. Nothing happened afterwards, only hello and goodbye kisses. He was being a real gentleman. The next date was the same – talk, talk, talk – ballet, art, music… and then politics.

After our second glass of Soviet champagne he asked if, since I couldn't dance for the rest of the year, I would consider serving the Motherland in another way. When I asked how, he shrugged and said I simply had to get to know someone – a nuclear scientist they suspected of leaking secrets to the West – and report any strange behaviour.

Naturally, I refused. But he'd done his homework. He alluded to my tawdriest affair with a powerful man in the Bolshoi. Don't worry, he said, he'd ensure that what was in the file stayed in the file. The assignment was only for a year, he assured me. When I continued to resist, he put his hand on mine, and said don't tell anyone, but he'd put in a word with the Ministry of Health to prioritise my surgery. Then I…

No, I'd better stop there. I realise how horrible it must be to have to listen to all your mother's dark secrets.

Why am I only admitting some of these now? you may ask.

First, I wanted to protect you as a child. I'd planned to tell you everything when you came of age, after your first year in college. But by then our relationship had deteriorated to the point that we argued every time we spoke. Hardly an environment conducive to such weighty matters.

Oh, my darling, I'm so sorry I never managed to turn things around with you. I used to console myself by saying it takes two to tango. Now I realise I was supposed to be the adult in the room.

But – and this isn't an excuse – when you were a child, I was still struggling with my own issues, untreated. I wasn't well. I mean…

Never mind the details. The point is, you become extremely self-centred when you're depressed. Speaking of which, how are you, girl? How are things at work? Are you and your colleagues at the foundation making headway in saving the planet?

I understand you can't answer now. It's okay. One day…

But seriously, I'm not being cynical. I've always cared for the environment more than most among my generation.

Okay, a kind night to you, my dearest thing, until soon…

Seven

Okay... Deep breath... My darling... After what I told you about myself last night, I feared you'd shun me for eternity. Sorry, I need to sit on the edge of the bed first. I walked a little down the passage earlier but it's exhausted me. Here, first, let me straighten the sheet. That's a habit I picked up from your father. Today they might say he was obsessive compulsive. You showed a hint of that too. When you were growing up, I'd marvel at how you'd instinctively tidy away your toys. Some traits are obviously inherited. Mmm, I love the feeling after they change the linen. Gives me hope. Unlike the bedpan below my bed. My new best friend. Technically, I can still get to the bathroom unassisted, but it's becoming arduous. I'm supposed to ring for a nurse in case I fall. But you know your mother. So do the staff here by now. So they've put a chair in the shower. You won't believe the sense of accomplishment I get from getting out of this bed and cleaning and dressing myself. Oh, and applying my red lipstick, of course. A woman must keep her pride. Very important.

Okay, I think I need a tot of Stolichnaya Elit before we get going again...

Tell me, are you still a teetotaller?

Yes, I'm afraid I'm back on the bottle. I'll swallow it like a Russian. Here, one go... Delicious. Though I still scrunch my face up. Of course, I'm not wearing my bandana today which makes my face look over-drawn; the fluorescent lights don't help either. Do you know that I always scrub up before we speak? If not a shower, a splash of lipstick and rouge does wonders. Though it's becoming harder and harder to disguise the wrinkles.

Did I tell you they did CAT scans? Yes, got the results this morning.

71

They needn't have bothered though. It's this lump on the side of my neck… feels like a marble.

But don't worry; Doctor Stromer says I mustn't lose heart. He reckons that radiotherapy will do the trick. Ironic, isn't it? To use what kills us to try to save us.

Anyway, have you had time to process what I told you last night?

What can I say? I'm a broken woman. Always have been.

Anyway, a year and a half after the KGB had recruited me at the Bolshoi with the lure of corrective surgery, I found myself sitting with an unhealed knee opposite my local handler, who'd all but accused me of failing in my mission.

'So,' Yavlinsky repeated, 'what exactly have you done to return our faith in you?'

I wanted to crawl into a hole. But as Yuri would say, attack is the best form of defence.

'So,' I said, 'what happened to my surgery?'

'First answer my question,' Yavlinsky demanded.

'The problem of the chicken or the egg.'

'Okay: name just one item of useful information you've given me since arriving in Pripyat?'

'It's all in the file.'

'The empty one, you mean.'

'At least I have a happy marriage.'

'With your husband fucking another woman?'

'Prove it! And even if he did have a brief lapse in judgement, I know he loves me.

'It's not your love life I'm interested in.'

'You're wasting your time with Yuri,' I said. 'The bureaucrats who granted his top-secret clearance did their job. If there ever was an impeccable Russian patriot—'

'Just because he ticks the boxes, doesn't mean he's a team player.'

I was perspiring so badly my dress was stuck to the plastic chair seat. 'You mean, he's not willing to play on your team.'

'Meaning?'

'Don't worry, Vladimir Semonovich, your secret is safe with me.' My heart raced. 'I know all about your spare parts procurement scheme.'

He glanced about furtively and wiped his mouth.

'And how you tried to co-opt him,' I continued. 'And ever since he refused and threatened to blow the whistle you've been looking for an excuse to "harvest" him for your quota. But, apart from being an honourable man, Yuri's the one person in this town you can't touch without reason. And it's been eating you until – miracle – along comes the turbine test Yuri's been championing – to know whether the reactor shuts down in an orderly fashion when the power fails. Why's that important? Because the safety of thousands of people depends on it. And what did you do: use all your Machiavellian influence – first to disallow the test and, when that failed – to let your demons of sabotage loose.'

'Lena…' he shook his head. 'You ascribe way too much power to me.'

But I wasn't finished. 'And now you have the perfect opportunity to make this thorn in your side disappear.'

Smoke spiralled from Yavlinsky's cigarette butt. His eyes narrowed. 'You've got a vivid imagination.'

'I know how people like you work.'

'Someone has to protect our hardworking citizens from bloodsuckers.'

'Is that what you tell yourself to be able to sleep at night?'

He sighed. 'Lena, why can't you stop casting aspersions and – just for today – accept the proposition that we're a necessary evil, to protect our glorious revolution. Like everyone else does.'

'Because I'm not "everyone else".'

'Aha, we agree on something at last,' he smirked.

Ah, the curse of being different… Not a day goes by that I don't look in the mirror and wish my face would fit in, my mouth would stop asking awkward questions and my eyes would stop seeing through the platitudes. Here in New York an unusual child may be ridiculed, but they can eventually find their tribe and some peace. It was not so in Sovetsky Soyuz. Those who questioned were irritants, like sand in the engine of society.

I feigned a smile. Best to appear confident.

'Tell me,' I responded. 'With all the existential threats out there... why do you people even bother with artists?'

'Because you may be feeble-minded, but the ideas you express spread like cancer.'

'You promised I'd only have to do this for a year.'

'Situations develop.'

'Liar!' I wanted to scream. Instead, I swallowed what was left of my pride.

'Vladimir Semonovich... Please.'

He puckered his lips and pretended to consider. 'Mmm... Okay. Because you asked nicely... Remember earlier, you said you called the plant this morning, but they couldn't locate your husband in the plant's directory?'

'Yes...' Something niggled at the edge of my mind, so I paused.

'I find that strange.'

'Oh?'

'Yes. Would Angela Leonidovna not help?'

'How did you...?'

He observed with an air of bemusement; like I was an exotic bird. He said, 'I have eyes in the back of my head.'

'Sure.'

'Don't worry, I won't be harsh on her, even if she flagrantly broke protocols. Did she find his file?'

'You know very well she didn't.'

'Oh?'

'Yes, because you took it.'

'And how would you know?'

'I just do, okay.'

'Really? You just know things that us mere mortals don't.' He smirked. 'Tsk, tsk, so, the rumour is true.'

'Which is?'

'That you're a *baba yaga*.'

I'll say this about Yavlinsky: he was good at his job; he knew every chink in my armour, how to thrust the sword and when to twist. Are such monsters born that way or do the organs of state make them? In *War and Peace*, Tolstoy asked a similar question about Napoleon. After fourteen hundred pages he still had no answer.

For some reason, perhaps because I was so tired, frightened and lonely, Yavlinsky's comment finally broke me. I could no longer hold back the tears.

'Now, now, Lena.' He took my hand.

I didn't resist.

He stroked my fingers with his thumb. 'You must understand... I am under pressure to report progress and – let's be honest – you've let the side down. Nothing useful to our organisation since the wedding; first you ignored the calls from my colleague in Moscow, then mine, and you routinely give my men the slip. And all because you've "fallen in love". Then out of the blue you waltz in here demanding I help you find the subject himself – a man who's done nothing but wilfully defy me. And when I hesitate, you blackmail me with an outrageous accusation of corruption. Silly girl, do you really think anyone's going to believe some washed up ballerina cum daughter of a dissident over the Chief of Personnel Section and a KGB Major?'

I shivered.

'Lena, it's understandable you're anxious. There's been an... accident, and your husband's gone missing. Not to mention this awful business of infidelity.'

I felt nothing but hatred.

'I've been thinking...' he continued. 'Perhaps there is a way I could be persuaded to investigate this... mystery of your husband's disappearance.'

I blinked through my tears. 'You know very well where he is. You...'

'Actually, I don't.'

'Sure.'

'Believe what you will.'

An awkward silence followed. Yavlinsky leered at my chest.

I glanced down. My top button was undone. I hurried to fix it.

'You must know you're a beautiful woman,' he said.

'Creep,' I thought, recoiling and hugging myself. 'Shh… You're almost old enough to be my father.'

'Nonsense; I'm not yet forty.'

'Could have fooled me.'

'Lena… I know you want me.'

'Nonsense.'

'Really? Girls like you find power irresistible.'

The devil is the father of lies, but he also knew how to wrap his off-spring in just the right amount of truth. From my file, Yavlinsky would have known I'd come of age with an older man. The Bolshoi Company's artistic director – a sugar-coated little shit called Yevgeny something. My biggest regret was waiting until his abuse turned physical before giving him the boot. Of course, I blamed myself for succumbing to his charm. He'd had bouquets of roses delivered to my dressing room for six weeks straight. I was nineteen to his forty-five – how could I not be flattered by a powerful father figure telling me I'm beautiful and gracious and sexy? Men like him play to a woman's insecurities. And I was plagued by the same self-doubt and neuroses of all ballerinas: was I pretty enough, light enough, good enough?

I wanted to slap Yavlinsky. But as much as I despised the man, I needed him… 'What are you suggesting?'

He reached over and put his hand on my shoulder. 'That's my girl. This doesn't have to be a burden. Why should our spouses be the only ones to have fun?'

I couldn't meet his eyes.

I noticed a family portrait behind him, on the bookcase, of Sonya in a short skirt. My God, she was beautiful. And there was Little Lord Fauntleroy standing between them, to waist height, with those blonde curls and already an air of authority. The golden family. In retrospect it's tempting to feel sorry for them, to think how few of those innocent years they enjoyed before the boy toppled.

Yavlinsky slid his hand down my exposed arm, causing goosebumps of revulsion.

Then his fingers played with a fold in my skin. 'So,' he said, 'Was that a yes?'

I shivered and looked out the window, at the Ferris wheel, then obscured in the haze.

He heaved himself from his chair.

I felt churned, conflicted, desperate. Then I glanced at the photo again. Sonya's face was mocking me from the portrait! It was too much.

But what if I could get Yavlinsky to help me find Yuri? Yuri didn't need to find out. And if he did, I'd explain that I did it for love.

Hah! The problem with shoving a rock down the slope of rationalisation is that you can't control the avalanche that follows. But Yavlinsky was probably my only access to the system. I simply had to keep him onside.

He shuffled around the desk until he stood at my shoulder. Next thing his hand was on the nape of my neck – warm, sweaty and heavy, his breath reeking of garlic and cognac.

'My meeting should be over by four o'clock. Angela and the others will be long gone. Drop by then. Okay?'

I felt dirty. I wanted to run. Should have. But the image of Yuri trapped beneath a pile of rubble, writhing in pain with a ring of flames about to engulf him tormented me. My darling, I cried inwardly, forgive me, forgive me for what I'm about to do.

I inhaled. The only avenue left was to pretend.

I placed my hand lightly on Yavlinsky's, swivelled and forced myself to give him my sad, soul-searching look of longing. 'Okay,' I said with an impish twinkle, 'why should they have the monopoly on pleasure?'

'Good girl.' His warm, clammy palm slid across my bare shoulder. 'Four o'clock then. I'll brief the guard. He'll give you your passport. Angela will see you out.'

'Oh… and one last thing, if you want to see your husband again, don't under any circumstances go to the *militsiya* about this. Understood?'

Eight

It was a huge relief to get out of the Gorkom and away from Yavlinsky. But I felt sickened by my encounter with him. And I was reeling from the implied threat against Yuri and the vile insinuation that no one could place him at the scene of the accident because he'd been with Sonya. You filthy liar! I silently screamed at Yavlinsky. Damn you to hell!

But I was still no closer to finding my husband. And I certainly wasn't going to trust Yavlinsky to look for him. So where to from here? I had to find Yuri before four o'clock.

A huddle of men were loitering on the street opposite but there was no sign of my shadows. Maybe they were being inconspicuous. I walked toward the square, noticing that every approach was barricaded either by fire trucks or *militsiya*. To one side soldiers were spilling out of a troop carrier and marching to join rows of comrades.

I brushed past the *militsiya* to the edge of the square, skirting a row of soldiers. In my rage and frustration, I felt disgusted by them all – cruel, mindless organs of a corrupt state. On impulse I sauntered up to a soldier standing ramrod straight with rifle at arms and an impassive stare. I shuffled closer till our faces were a mere hand apart and smiled coyly. He remained deadpan. I wiggled my hips and pouted, taunting him. Cold fish, I thought with derision, what did they put in your *kasha* this morning? Then I stalked off.

A yell came from diagonally behind the ranks. 'Attentiooon!' Boots stamped in unison, then rifles clapped. Suddenly, all around the square, officials were shouting orders and gesticulating, and the place became a beehive of soldiering, spraying, sweeping and directing.

Then I glimpsed the Raduga's distinctive green awning. Olga! I thought. Why hadn't I sought her advice first? She was my best friend and knew a few influential people. Maybe she could help somehow. But as I approached the Raduga, I felt a jolt of disappointment. Where was the queue that normally snaked out the door? Had they closed because of the accident?

Ah, the doors were open. Inside, I could have heard a pin drop as I waited for my eyes to adjust to the gloom. Only a handful of customers became visible. As always, the shelves were mostly empty save for essentials like milk, bread, tinned meat and cheese. How little choice we had under communism!

Hurrah, I thought, recognising the athletic figure bent over the horizontal meat fridge, probably wiping a trail of blood. 'Olga!'

She spun round, momentarily flustered. Then she threw her arms wide. 'Mushka!' she cried. Don't ask why she called me a mouse. I guess I was so much smaller than her. But a rodent?

'I tried to phone you,' she gushed, 'Is everything okay?'

'Fine.' Yes, that's what we Russians always said, even as our world was falling apart. Call it Slavic stoicism. Liars, all of us.

'I've been so worried for you,' Olga said, 'The explosion: isn't it terrible? Is Yuri all right? Come here, give me a hug.'

In retrospect, I should have noted that she'd already called it an explosion. But I was preoccupied. Olga and I embraced so tightly I struggled to breathe. Suddenly, my emotional dyke cracked and I was crying real tears, sobbing into the folds of her dress.

Eventually I stopped and pulled myself together. 'The worst is not knowing where he is, Olya,' I told her. 'I keep seeing images of Yuri trapped under rubble, flames circling and all the smoke, and he's calling my name but I can't reach him…'

She stroked my hair. 'It's standard for the authorities to shut down all communications. I'm sure he's fine.'

Suddenly, I had a sense of being watched. I withdrew my head a fraction. The handful of shoppers were focussed on their selections. But then I noticed a woman behind the counter. Stout with spiky blonde hair.

'My boss, comrade Sokolov,' whispered Olga. 'Come, let's go outside for some fresh air.' The irony: the air was so thick we couldn't see the sun. Our world might be crumbling but the show had to go on, just like the summer of '41 before the Nazis came.

Olga and I huddled in the shaded alcove beneath the Raduga's awning, but after a few minutes I started to wheeze and had to spit.

'Yuck,' she said.

'Sorry. Something in my throat.'

We watched as a fire truck rumbled past.

'By the way,' she said, 'a fairy told me that about thirty emergency workers and a couple of operators were taken to the hospital this morning. I wouldn't worry – apparently, it's just a precaution, so they can be observed. Yuri was probably outside smoking when the accident happened.'

Olga had a point. Either that or pacing the grounds. Colleagues called Yuri 'The Doctor' more for doing his rounds than for his double PhD. But instead of patients, he attended to processes. Her comment was all the encouragement I needed.

'Thanks for listening,' I said, sidestepping Olga. 'I'll check at the hospital.'

'Wait,' she said, 'I'll just let comrade Sokolov know. We were about to close…'

'No. I mean… I need to see him… alone. Husband and wife business.'

She looked hurt. 'All right; I thought you'd appreciate the company.'

Instantly, I felt dreadful. I said, 'Please don't be cross with me.'

Her face softened. 'Me, angry, with you? Of course not. I'll always be here for you. Here, give me another hug.'

I accepted with alacrity. 'Olya, I don't deserve you,' I said, shutting my eyes to imbibe her comfort and warmth. How I loved her! What a friend: brusque, yes, and quick to take offence, but quicker to forgive.

'Promise you'll call me from the hospital payphone, okay? And relax; I bet Yuri's lying there safe and sound with nurses fawning over him.' She winked. 'He may not want to come home.'

'Hah, hah.'

'That's my Mushka! You're so much prettier when you smile. You two lovebirds will be having dinner together tonight, trust me. How about you and I go to the Palace for a round of *Durak* afterwards? I'm feeling lucky.' She kissed me on each cheek. 'Now go. And remember to breathe.'

I quick-marched back around the cordon of soldiers on the square, averting my gaze from the Party offices as I headed toward the river via Kurchatova Street. No coincidence that the street was named after the man who built our first atom bomb and designed the world's first nuclear power plant. And whose colleague was infamously quoted as saying the RBMK-1000 reactor was as safe as a samovar on Red Square. Indeed it would have been, if only they'd made the design modifications Yuri and his predecessors proposed.

I strode down the street as fast as my bad knee allowed, the crowds vaporising until I was alone, skirting foam-topped puddles past bleak industrial facades shrouded in thickening smog. I was fretting so much about Yuri that without the bollards I'd have walked off the pier into the water. I took a right turn with the river wide and meandering on my left. A light breeze had sprung up and cleared the smog just enough for the sun to briefly burst through and illuminate a glassy, ruffled surface and the rows of cherry trees in blossom – plumped like handfuls of popcorn with petals strewn over the ground. The water had a calming effect on me. Yuri and I loved to stroll here hand in hand, stopping for tea at a café overlooking the river. Oh Lord, where was he now?

I pressed on as the street became a canyon flanked by the drabbest of *khrushchyovky* – the prefab apartment buildings mass-produced in the '50s and '60s to solve the post-war housing shortage. Each unit was only thirty square metres made from prefabricated panels with a five-storey limit to avoid the need for elevators. They were temporary, Khrushchev had promised. When communism matured, every family would get a freestanding house bigger than the average American's. Hah! Like Gorbachev's boast of the socialist nirvana by the turn of the century. Finally, the monotony of *khrushchyovky* gave way to the school and then – my spirits soared – I spied the familiar block letters above the single-storey hospital building – 'Health of the People – Riches of Ukraine'.

Like everyone, I'd swallowed the propaganda. Don't judge. Intelligence or discernment are no match for a sustained bombardment of even the falsest of narratives. But like all successful lies, this one had a thread of compelling logic. We did have free medical care. And education. Even us ballerinas could recite poets like Pushkin, Esenin or Blok.

I burst through the hospital's saloon doors and into the foyer, where I was startled by the shambles. The floor was strewn with discarded uniforms, bandages, firemen's hats and boot print trails amid the stench of disinfectant. People were crammed onto benches around the perimeter of the room, slouched or staring ahead, part anxious, part bored, some flipping through magazines. The receptionist's chair was the only empty one in the room, though a jacket hung over its seatback.

The wall clock showed twelve fifteen. I drummed my fingers on the plastic countertop. Come on, woman, I mumbled. Then I noticed an open logbook. I angled my head to decipher the handwritten scribbles in reverse, slowly eliminating possibilities…

'Can I help?' The receptionist had arrived, dressed in a puke green uniform with her hair in a bun partially covered by a shower cap. Her face began to drift out of focus until she was a watery blur and I had to grip the edge of the counter and swallow the rising bile in my throat.

'M-my husband,' I stammered.

'Name?' she said, pencil in hand.

Painstakingly, I had to spell it out.

She laid down the pencil, paused, then shifted the register closer. Line by excruciating line, her fingernail crept down the page. I strained to read but ink smudges and splotches rendered most of the Cyrillic illegible. Only two names were familiar: a firefighter I'd once flirted with at a Palace quiz night and a junior operator at Unit Number Two. Finally, she looked up with a satisfied expression and shrugged. 'He's not here.'

'Impossible!' I cried, 'He was on duty in the control room.'

She shoved the logbook at me. 'See for yourself.'

'Isn't there a clinic at Chernobyl? Or maybe some went to Kiev…'

'No, they've been coming here first for triage.'

'B-but there must be a mistake. Maybe he was unconscious, or delirious and gave the wrong name. I'll check through the ward…'

'*Nyet!*' she said, emphasising the '*e*' and the finality of the hard '*t*'. The expression most beloved of the Russian bureaucrat after *put atkrit*: the way is closed.

Looking bored, she said, 'Listen, citizen…'

'Chizhikova.'

She gestured toward the crowded benches, 'You're not the only person in Pripyat waiting for answers. I'm sorry, but…'

'At least let me have a look.'

'Access to the ward is strictly prohibited. For your own protection.'

Ah, my little dove, beware of that expression. The communists called it 'protecting the glorious revolution'. The nanny state is a banana peel on the slippery slope to tyranny. Call me paranoid, but consider what happened after 9/11, the personal freedoms we lost 'to shield us from terror'. So nowadays you can't cough without it being recorded and stored in some NSA basement in Hawaii. And the so-called freedoms – 'free' social media apps with twenty-four-seven algorithm-curated content and 'individually targeted' ads…

The receptionist pointed to a chair that had just been vacated. 'Wait there. I'll call Director Morozov. He was at the meeting of the emergency services at City Hall. He'll know the latest.'

I sat and surveyed the room. Opposite me, a prematurely wrinkled mother cradled her child. Her husband averted his lustful gaze when I glared at him. It wasn't his fault; I was angry at everyone – the whole damn system that was stonewalling me. My heels drummed on the floor. Finally, I had an idea: the bathroom. I stood, pointed to the sign.

The receptionist nodded.

After I'd done my business, l inhaled, put my shoulders back, and strode out of the bathroom, sharp right toward the ward.

Amazing what you can get away with if you act like you belong.

The corridor was sickly green from waist height and turquoise beneath with linoleum floors. Above flickered a series of fluorescent strips connected by trunking along the spine of the ceiling and at intervals down the walls. I swallowed my rising nausea, pushed through the saloon doors, and narrowly missed an approaching nurse before slowing at an open door. I scanned the ward. My hopes surged and plunged with every reddened, browned or towel-swathed bed. But no Yuri. I moved on to the next ward, and the next, to no avail.

'Can I help?' barked a male voice with a Moscow accent.

I swirled to face a doctor so tall that my line of sight was level with the Y-junction of his stethoscope. I looked up. His cheeks were a soft, luminous white. He was handsome, in his early thirties.

'Wait… you're pregnant,' he said, looking at my waist.

Shit, I thought, was it that obvious already?

'You must leave immediately,' he said.

'I need to see my husband,' I replied, locking my feet in second position.

'Listen; there's radiation; the patients… it's not safe for your child.'

'I, I…'

He'd referred to 'my child'. It came as a shock. What was taking place inside me was still a nebulous concept to me, defined more by the effects on my body – morning sickness and discomfort – than a living person with a distinct identity I had a duty to care for. And at that moment, my thoughts were all with Yuri.

'Please, I just need to check one more room,' I said, bustling past.

He caught my wrist. 'No!'

I yanked my arm away.

He grabbed it again. 'Security!' he called.

I was stuck. Resistance seemed futile. But I knew what to do. I made my body limp, and my expression doleful.

'I… I'm sorry doctor. Please forgive my impudence. It's just… I'm so worried; my husband was on nightshift, Reactor Four. I've looked everywhere. I just need word he's alive.'

He glanced about. From the far end of the corridor, clipped footsteps approached. He lowered his voice. 'What's his name?'

As I told him, a flicker of recognition and feigned thoughtfulness swept his face. I noticed the Italian leather shoes. Imported clothing meant he was relatively high in the *nomenklatura*, perhaps head of a department.

'I'm sorry,' he said, 'Doesn't ring a bell.'

I produced a tear. 'Please; I don't know where else to turn.'

He puckered his cheeks. 'Then he bent closer. 'You didn't hear this from me,' he whispered. 'Only one person is confirmed dead… at this stage, and one missing. Neither goes by your husband's name.'

I felt desperate. I had to keep him talking. 'Will the men be all right?'

'The patients are getting the best care possible My colleagues and I flew here from Moscow first thing this morning. We're from Hospital Number Six, leaders in our field. Now, if you'll excuse me…'

'Wait. Please tell me what they're suffering from?'

'ARS: Acute radiation syndrome. It's treatable. I…' He stood tall. 'Sorry. I can't say more. You must leave.'

'No.' I squeezed his wrist. 'My husband can't simply have disappeared. Please, any information you can share that might help.' I made doe eyes.

He hesitated, glanced about furtively, then bent till his lips almost touched my ear. 'I heard a rumour,' he whispered, 'pure speculation, that the explosion was sabotage. Perhaps he's among those detained.'

I recoiled. 'Are you calling my husband a criminal?'

'*Quiet*! I'm only trying to help.'

I stared at his lounge-lizard shoes. His trouser cloth, I noted, was imported too. Then something snapped inside me. 'You're one of them, aren't you?' My nails dug into his wrist. 'You're sending me off on a wild goose chase so you can cover up the truth.'

'*Blyad*!' The doctor yanked his hand away. 'Guard! Get her out.'

An iron fist clasped my shoulder.

'No!'

But it was useless: the doctor was gone, the swing doors reverberating in his wake, and then my arm was almost dislodged from the shoulder as I was frogmarched along the corridor, cursing through the gauntlet of anguished faces in the lobby until a shove from behind sent me stumbling

85

down the steps onto the sidewalk. And by now, my darling, you're probably worrying about your exposure to radiation while you were in my tummy at that time. How it might have affected your health. All I can say is, I picked up no signs during your childhood. And trust me, I was watching for them… But so far, thank God, you've had remarkable health. So you can relax.

As for me, maybe there's a link to this cancer, maybe not. None of the white-coated wizards – professors of oncology this or that, visiting fellows from Sloane-Kettering or Mayo Clinic or their retinue of residents – have been able to give me a definitive answer. Instead, they treat me like a dumb mute, Exhibit A. One even told me what a valuable specimen I am because the pool of survivors is shrinking. How comforting to know I'm still of use to someone!

Oh, look at the time. I lose track… Dracula's due any minute, on her rounds. She's the night duty nurse. I call her that because she wakes me up before dawn to draw blood samples. All I see is her dark silhouette in profile against the window, poised with a syringe. The first time I shrieked.

Actually, she's a sweetheart. They all are. I don't know how they stay positive. If I had to pander to a lot of grumpy old codgers all day, changing bed pans, fetching, and carrying, I'd strangle someone.

Oh, speak of the devil: here she comes. And with that, my beloved daughter, I need to call it a night.

Okay. *Paka paka.*

Nine

D*obroye utro*. A morning chat for a change, how lovely. I'm about to set off for my 'walk'. Even though I'm in a wheelchair, the fresh air and change of scene are natural antidepressants – thanks to the endorphins and the sensory stimulation to the brain.

At least I can still get into the wheelchair by myself. The physiotherapist pushes me now.

At first, I had terrible cabin fever and longed for these walks. Needed a fix of the real world. She'd take me along the river up to the Mayor's Residence – which is no different from those in Soyuz. Leaders everywhere live in luxury.

But I've grown accustomed to my little world now, and I feel safer in the ward. I even start to get anxious before my outings.

Ah, here she is.

Hi Cindy!

Right, we're off. Okay, already past the first hurdle, we're out of my room. Don't laugh. These days I consider it an accomplishment just to get through the doorway. Funny how my perspective has changed, the expectations of myself. Take note. You drive yourself as hard as either me or your father. Watch for burnout.

If there was a simple solution, I'd give it. Our personality type needs a challenge. But we have our limits because we're highly strung.

I've found it helps to take a step back sometimes, and say to yourself, is this really so important in the scheme of things?

Right, this is the nursing station… and in this corridor is the geriatric stroke ward. All these old codgers staring into space. Some have been here for months. At least I'll be spared that at the current pace of my cancer.

Now into the elevator. Okay, down, down, down we go…

And through this automatic door… Ta-da… fresh air. Let's take the path around the perimeter of the grounds this time, Cindy. It's a lovely meander. Here we go through an arch. Ah, the scent of the jasmine; isn't spring lovely?

Cindy will park me here beside this little pond with the mermaid and leave us to chat in private a little, thank you Cindy. It's rather twee, but it's level ground and a quiet spot. Look, there's a gracious mommy duck guiding her newborn chicks. Too precious. Remember how I used to take you to the pond in Prospect Park on Monday mornings – after my night off from the club. We'd stand for ages throwing breadcrumbs to the ducks. But perhaps you were too young. I think that stopped a couple of years after you started school at Brooklyn Public.

Ah, I ache for those innocent days, my little dove, when we were like best friends and things were so pure and simple between us.

But enough of my wistful wallowing. Let's get back to our story.

I was on the pavement outside the hospital in Pripyat, having just been unceremoniously ejected, when I spotted my shadows, the ones who'd been outside my apartment. I hadn't thrown them off after all, it seemed.

I'd first noticed I was being watched about six weeks after our arrival in Pripyat. Presumably they reported to Yavlinsky. At the time I wondered why they went to such trouble for small fry like me. Perhaps my own chequered past, or my dissident parents? Or maybe it was standard operating procedure to keep tabs on the people they blackmailed. Strangely, they never made much effort to be inconspicuous: they wore the same white shirts and dark suits regardless of the weather.

Curiously, by now there was a virtual torrent of humanity streaming past, shuffling around me as if I didn't exist. Confused, I stopped an elderly couple to ask where they were going.

The gentleman looked at me strangely. 'To the bridge, of course. Where've you been?' His eyes sparkled. 'Come. Apparently, you can see the flames.' Disaster tourism. It's nothing new.

I hesitated, weighing the odds. I had to find out what had happened to Yuri. How dangerous would it be to follow the crowd? The authorities were doing nothing to stop them. But what about the radiation? Yuri had once explained that the human body can process relatively high levels of radiation for a limited period. I would try to be back within an hour at most.

So I joined the flow of humanity heading along Druzhby Narodiv, past its junction with Lelina to the horizon where a chimney of smoke was billowing. As I walked, I considered the doctor's speculation about sabotage. The thought was too terrible to contemplate: could Yuri have been involved? He had mentioned another purpose for the test. But sabotage? Surely not. Yet the thought niggled. It would certainly explain why Yavlinsky and the KGB were so desperate to learn about his work activities. I shuddered. But no! Not my Yuri. It wasn't possible. I put it out of my mind.

My unsmiling shadows had already melted into the stream of people heading toward the edge of town. I waited a few minutes to give some distance between us, and then fell in behind a posse of boisterous teenagers in sneakers and faded denim. Yes, plenty of imported goods were available in Sovetsky Soyuz by then, including Levis, but at a price.

Round the circle at Lelina my progress slowed as the crowd thickened in a carnival of chattering and rumour swapping: the entire reactor was toast, the fire was no accident, it was a CIA plot, a rogue saboteur… and still a blanket of silence from the authorities in the face of such an undeniable catastrophe.

The crowd concertinaed to a muttering halt. Flesh pressed in on me from all directions, along with the smell of sweat and bad breath. All I could see were the backs and necks of others below a smoky sky. Claustrophobic and desperate for fresh air, I squirmed between the bodies, muttering *izvinete* to clear my path, till I reached the perimeter of the crowd and the bridge. I grabbed the handrails and shuffled toward the highest point. From there I had a line of sight to the power station. Squinting into the sun-infused haze, I struggled to discern the rectangular hulks of the reactors. One, two, three… then only a thick, dark plume of smoke where Number Four should have been, soaring skyward and flattening into a giant mushroom cloud in shades of grey and black. I stared in growing horror.

The people about me seemed palpably excited. *Schadenfreude...* like the Parisian women knitting as heads rolled from the guillotine, the ecstatic Austrian townsfolk throwing garlands at Hitler's cavalcade, gawkers at the scene of a car crash.

A siren wailed. Bodies pressed into me. Above people's heads came a flashing red light as a yellow *militsiya* patrol vehicle passed, and another in its wake. They crossed the bridge and parked alongside each other. Two officers climbed out of the one car, one tall and the other square. The tall one set about erecting a cordon while the bald, squat officer clutched a clipboard and a loudhailer.

'*Vnimaniye*,' he said into the receiver.

The hubbub intensified.

'*Vnimaniye!*'

The crowd began to shush.

He coughed and read from his clipboard. 'There has been an unfortunate incident at Reactor Number Four. An investigation is underway. After toiling through the night, our heroic comrades in the fire department have confirmed that the blaze is under control.'

A murmur rippled through the crowd.

The officer flipped a page. 'Appropriate precautions have been taken,' he continued. 'The authorities will provide further information in due course.'

Muttering ensued.

'You are to return to the city immediately.'

No-one moved.

'Listen!' He wiped his mouth. 'At a special sitting of the city council this morning, it was decided to open the new amusement park ahead of schedule. Ice-creams are available. First come, first served.'

As one, the crowd burst into chatter again and began to surge back toward the city. *Panem et circenses*, as the Roman emperors said: distract the masses with bread and circuses.

I clung to the railing until the last straggler had passed. I was hardly going to give up on Yuri for a free ride or an ice cream. Soon I was alone on the bridge, feeling exposed and frustrated. My day had been a long series of cul de sacs: every time I thought I was getting somewhere, I hit another brick wall.

I leaned over the railing. Down below, the snow-plumped water sucked at the base of the pylon before gurgling on downstream. Just four Saturdays ago, Yuri and I had lingered here on this bridge in a cold spring fog, watching the current rush past, comfortable in our silence. I remembered him turning suddenly with an expression I'd never seen – a blend of sadness and concern – to tell me how much he loved me. This from my taciturn rationalist! To my eternal regret, I'd been lost for words. Afterwards, as we stood unspeaking with ice still crusting the reeds and the distant clattering of storks, he took me in his arms and held me close and long, as if it were our last embrace.

Now here I was, all alone, the ice long melted, while the banded demoiselles skimmed along the water's surface, and the opposite bank was covered with daisies. To say I felt empty would be an understatement; I felt like my heart had been torn open. I cried out loud, unabashed and full-throated as a nightingale.

And then, suddenly, I was overcome by what I can only describe as an otherworldly phenomenon gently assuring me that I wasn't alone. At the time, I assumed it was Yuri's spirit. But it may have been God; I'll never know. Faith is the assurance of things hoped for, the certainty of things not seen. Go ahead, laugh. But if you believe only in the measurable and explicable, how do you explain love, forgiveness and wanton cruelty?

Conscious again of a growing itch in my throat and a metallic taste, I spat, then raised my eyes. The mushroom of smoke above the reactor seemed darker, the flames below it leaping fifty metres into the air. What if I could get to the power plant? I suddenly thought. A bit reckless, perhaps, but this was now my best chance to find out where Yuri had been at the time of the explosion. Surely his colleagues at the plant couldn't pretend he didn't exist. He might even be there still! The thought gave me a quiver of hope.

A high-pitched whine from behind startled me. I swirled about. A patrol car was crawling toward me. A bare arm appeared and waved me back toward the city. I couldn't see the officer – but from the length of his arm it was presumably the officer who'd set up the cordon.

Anger and frustration washed over me. Reluctantly, I turned toward the white-blocked skyline of Pripyat. Every step I took away from the plant felt like yet another betrayal of my husband. I felt disgusted with myself. Round the circle I trudged, ushered by the *militsiya* cars.

At the fork, I was about to take Lelina Avenue, when an idea came to me. I could steal back cross country – only five kilometres as the crow flies with a river and countless trees between. Immediately, I felt a twinge of excitement at the prospect. In '79, the authorities had planted vast swathes of pines to hide the newly constructed power station from public scrutiny, much like the 'green corridor' from Moscow to Kiev: a double row of trees either side of the railway tracks, deliberately planted to obscure military manoeuvres from foreign spies.

So, instead of going straight, I veered back down Druzhby Narodiv street. Left, right, left, right, I trudged head down, along the road in the direction of the hospital. At length, I looked around. I was completely alone. Even the *militsiya* cars must have given up on me. Yet my hands still shook.

Everything outside of Pripyat, including the power station, cooling tower, artificial lake and surrounding forest, was designated 'of strategic importance' to the state. What I was planning constituted trespassing – an imprisonable offence. But if I shrank back, I'd be abandoning my husband. How could I live with myself afterwards? Besides, I stood a good chance of not being caught. I could cut through the forest unseen all the way to the access road. All I needed to do then was follow it to the power station and charm my way through security.

I looked about. Alongside the road was a wide verge overgrown with grass and then the treeline, until the electrical substation marking the city boundary. Apart from a few stragglers ahead, I appeared to be alone. I wiped the sweat off my forehead, inhaled, dropped to my hands and knees and crawled through the long grass toward the forest. My knees burned; thorns pierced my palms and hooked on my dress. But not until I reached the anonymity of the shade did I dare to stand.

The forest was silent as a morgue: no birds tweeting, no zinging of cicadas. I took a bearing from the angle of the sun through the canopy and set off. The only sound was the pad and crackle of my shoes on the carpet of needles below. Crawling had set off a niggle in my bad knee, but I put it out of my mind and kept on until I got to the river. The stream was slow and wide, the banks thick with reeds and algae. Shoes off and skirt hitched, I waded in. Soon I was almost hip deep in fast flowing water, the cold soothing my scrapes. My throat was parched, but I resisted the temptation to drink.

We had long worried about water contamination. Rumours circulated of giant fish and wolves with two heads at the cooling ponds. Daily, we were conscious of the threat of radiation. Yet we continued to live there, just as Italians still inhabit the slopes of Vesuvius.

The far bank was steep and muddy, so I scrambled up on all fours and slithered over the crest. Finally, I stood like a conquering soldier, left foot first... then suddenly the ground gave way. As my leg plunged, a stab of pain shot through my knee. I sank into the mud, clutching it until the pain subsided. A sandfly danced on my lips. I swatted it off, then wiggled my toes. At least my foot could tilt at the ankle.

So, with clenched teeth, I hauled myself forward into the forest, stepping more gingerly on my left leg. The air was hotter and drier there, and instead of resin and musty rot I could smell smoke. My knee was a little tender, but I pressed on, past one evenly spaced pair of trees after another, until finally – relief – I stumbled onto the road. But my elation quickly turned to horror. Directly ahead, above the far pines, the giant plume of smoke was spiralling, wave after furious wave, alternating between shades of white and grey, escaping from a ring of angry flames licking from below. After a while I realised something was missing. Yes... unbelievably, the turbine hall of Reactor Number Four had simply vanished! What did that mean? How much radiation was spewing out with these flames?

I checked my watch. Just after 1 pm. The thought of what awaited me at 4 pm filled me with disgust. Even if Yavlinsky knew where Yuri was, I had to find him on my own. So, I limped on, head down, in my dumb ox do-what-you-must mode developed from gruelling hours at the barre.

The bitumen underfoot burned through my soles, so I moved to the grassy verge. I was getting into a rhythm when I heard a rumble from behind and looked back. The road was straight as an arrow, blending into a mirage where it formed a T-junction with the Pripyat–Chernobyl thoroughfare. The mirage morphed into a fire truck, fast approaching. I dropped into the long grass and lay flat, shifting so I could watch its approach. Its large horizontal water tank indicated that it had come from the town of Chernobyl. Four uniformed firemen stood erect, two on each running board, brass buckles shining. Their faces were as resolute as troops riding into the glory of battle.

Oh, the naivety of brainwashed testosterone! Generation after generation, thinking war is a game. This was a battle all right, and these poor boys were nothing more than cannon fodder.

I hoisted myself on my good knee, dusted myself off, and continued down the road toward the plant. I hadn't got far when I became aware of a siren from behind, growing louder. I whirled about to see the familiar yellow of a *militsiya* patrol car with its blue stripes down the side. I froze. The car flashed its lights. Damn, he'd seen me. I needed to act like I belonged. I squared my shoulders and marched on.

Round a bend the gate came into sight. To my relief, it appeared unmanned. I broke into a limping run. But to no avail: the patrol car drew up alongside me. I slowed and glanced sideways. The officer at the wheel had his window open. He was speaking into his radio but staring at me as if I was a rabid dog. It was the officer who had made the announcement earlier. I hoped he wouldn't recognise me and tried to ignore him.

'You,' he called, 'this is a restricted area.'

'I'm late for a meeting,' I called without slowing or turning.

'You work there?'

'Yes,' I shouted.

'Wait!'

I hurried. I couldn't afford to tangle with the *militsiya*, especially after Yavlinsky's warning. Soon the huge rectangular administration block of

Reactor Four loomed no more than fifty metres away. To my relief, the guardhouse looked unoccupied. Firefighters and workers in overalls were bustling about the yard. Thirty, twenty-five… I counted my steps, nearly inside. Perhaps the *militsiya* had believed me. But now I heard the car scrunching on loose stones behind me. Then it passed me by a few metres, came to a halt and the passenger door swung open. As the officer stepped onto the tarmac I veered away across the road.

'Stop!' he barked.

'I have a message for the senior duty engineer,' I said, striding on.

'Really?'

'Yes, its urgent.'

He smirked. 'You can tell me. I'll be sure to relay it.'

'It's confidential.'

'You can trust us.'

'I have strict instructions.'

He frowned. 'From whom?'

Now what? If I named Yavlinsky, they might radio him to confirm.

'Deputy Director Brukanov,' I said.

'Sooo, you've got a secret message from the big cheese.' He looked at my muddied dress. 'Where've you been?'

'I slipped beside the road.'

'Liar. We've been patrolling it for the past hour.'

'I took a shortcut. Now, if you'll excuse me…' I walked past him.

'Hey!'

On impulse I made a run for the gate. I could hear shoes pounding and a hand grabbed my upper arm, fingers biting into my flesh.

'Let me go!'

He yanked my arm. 'Nice try,' he sneered, shoving me toward the car. 'In.'

Inside, it was gloomy and smelled of hair oil. The plastic seat covers were torn. I tugged the door handle. Locked. I clawed at the grate separating me from the officers. Damn, I thought, what use will you be to Yuri in jail? Idiot!

The car lurched forward, tyres screeching, and I was thrust back into the seat. Once we were cruising, the tall officer twisted about to take a proper look at me. 'Let's see who we have here,' he said, grinning. His ruddy, pockmarked skin and stubble looked incongruous with his neatly pressed uniform. 'Well, if it isn't the pretty ballerina!'

'Huh,' the shorter officer said. 'She appears out of nowhere on a deserted road. Must have fallen off her broomstick.'

They guffawed.

'My husband is special consultant to Unit Four,' I said in my haughtiest voice. 'A nuclear physicist with top secret clearance, and he's gone missing in the explosion.'

'In the what?' said the driver. He slowed and lurched to the left, then he twisted to face me. 'Did I hear you say explosion?'

'I meant accident. The rumours...'

'Be careful what you say, girl.'

'Yes, sir.'

We drove in silence until the bridge.

'Officer...'

'What?'

'Please let me out here. I promise I won't try to come back. I... I suffer from claustrophobia. Please, I'll do anything...'

'Really?' the driver chortled.

The car sped up and, the forest became a blur. Every milestone toward town felt like another nail in Yuri's coffin. And mine.

We slowed at the bridge where a fresh cluster of gawkers had gathered. The driver leaned on his horn. Slowly, they parted, and we crawled through. Free, we accelerated through the circle, and peeled off into Lelina. The traffic was mostly departing the city, and in places it was stop-start. I began to wilt. My eyelids drooped...

A screeching of tyres woke me as my head whipped forward and, as the car shuddered to a halt, the smell of burning brake pads seeped into the car.

'*Blyad*!' the driver hissed.

The tall officer stuck his head out the window. 'Why aren't you lot at work?' he yelled.

'We're going to the train station.'

'Like hell.'

'It's true, officer.' I could hear the raw fear in his voice. 'We've been given the weekend off. Sent home.'

'Where's that?'

'Moscow for me, sir. The others Uzbekistan.'

'Huh. Present passports.'

The workman held up a crumpled letter, his hand visibly shaking.

The officer waved dismissively. 'I said passports.'

The men delved into their pockets and bags.

He scrutinised each with painstaking thoroughness. To inspect papers is what every law enforcement official in Sovetsky Soyuz lived for.

'Go ahead.' He shook his head. 'Jump ship if you must. Rats.' And he tossed their passports on the ground.

We continued up Lelina. As we approached our *khrushchyovka*, I ducked and twisted my head to glimpse our balcony. My darling, my darling, my heart cried. Not twenty-four hours ago we'd been up there together sipping vodka…

Then I froze. Something seemed to sweep across behind the sliding doors, a human shape. Yuri? But how…? Had I imagined it? What if he'd been elsewhere at the time of the explosion, detained in the ensuing milieu, and had now returned? I didn't know what to believe.

'Stop the car!' I cried, fumbling for the door handle. '*Blyad.*' I was trapped. The car seemed to have shrunk. My palms were sweaty and my breathing fast. I yanked at the door handle. No give. I tried to look back up at the apartment, but I couldn't see it properly any more.

We were approaching the city centre. The number of buses had mushroomed and now lined both sides of Lelina for several hundred metres. The square was abuzz. A troop carrier had pulled up alongside, and out poured soldiers in fatigues, trotting off with rifles aloft to join the green-grey ranks. Just then a glint beyond the Palace building caught my eye. The top quarter of the Ferris wheel, still turning. 'Yuri, look!' I wanted to shout.

The car stalled. I craned to see the problem. Traffic. We were right opposite the Rainbow store. It was still open, with a queue snaking to its entrance along the sidewalk on my side. Which sparked an idea. Olga worked at the other branch, but Pripyat's retail community was close knit, and the managers all knew each other. So, as surreptitiously as possible, I tested the window handle. Hallelujah, it moved. Frantically I wound it down and thrust my head out, where a fine mist licked my face.

'Excuse me,' I called to the line of shoppers. Most ignored me but a military man in air force grey, junior by look of his epaulets, said 'Can I help?'

Momentarily, my voice failed.

'Hey,' said my tall captor. 'What's going on there?'

I stretched for the officer's cuff and tugged.

'Please, sir,' I said, 'I need a favour.'

'Yes?'

The engine revved.

'Ask the store manager to pass a message to comrade Sokolov at the Raduga for Olga. She works there. Tell her Lena is with the...'

The car lurched forward, and the window frame smacked my temple. I continued pleading, but my words were lost to the wind.

The driver took one hand off the wheel and turned to glare at me. '*Suka!*' he spat.

Again, the same: Bitch, witch, whore. The insults always stung.

Why such universal revulsion for me in Pripyat? What had I done to deserve such loathing? My lifestyle was no different from the average artist. We were Moscow's avant-garde, taking liberties other citizens wouldn't have dared to. The authorities gladly turned a blind eye to the lifestyle of ballet dancers to portray a liberal impression of Soviet life to Western diplomats attending the Bolshoi.

But how would word of my past find its way to this rural backwater of Pripyat? It made no sense. Suddenly, a new thought struck me, and it seemed to make sense. Yavlinsky. I was almost certain he'd deliberately planted these rumours for the express purpose of isolating me.

I know what you're probably thinking now, Katyusha. That I've justified your view that I was thoroughly immoral. I know how the gossip about my exotic dancing followed you right from Brooklyn Public through Fordham and even to Columbia. Never mind that by the time you were in middle school, I'd been promoted to managing the bar. My average take-home pay dropped – I earned less in tips – but the reliability of a steady salary allowed me to enrol you in after-school tutoring, chess lessons and so on.

Oh, my darling, I don't blame you for judging me harshly... It must have been terribly embarrassing as a teenager to have a mother like me. But I dared not explain myself back then. It would have opened a can of worms and forced me to reveal my complicity and – ultimately – my previous identity. I must at least give Mikhail credit for keeping his side of the bargain; he never went public about my past in Russia. It could have put both our lives in danger. Yes, yours too. The KGB's tentacles reached far and wide. And probably still do. If you don't believe me, talk to Trotsky's widow, Sedova. They managed to assassinate him in Mexico City of all places. Chilling.

But enough. These matters are draining, albeit necessary. So I'll say good night now... to be continued!

Ten

Hi, my darling, you're back! Ready for another episode of this sorry saga?

Overnight I was reflecting on those firemen who passed me on the road to the plant, unwittingly riding to their deaths. Funny how it's easier to see things clearly from the distance of thirty years. Not to mention the additional facts that have come to light since. Yes, the truth shall always out!

Isn't it astounding how the authorities kept the ordinary citizens of Sovetsky Soyuz ignorant of the danger. With typical Soviet bravado, the helicopter crews dumping sand and boron onto the burning reactor chose not to wear their lead suits. Red Army conscripts were handed shovels and dropped onto the roof of Reactor Number Three to heave still-burning graphite fragments off the edge after the mechanical robots failed from overexposure to radiation. They could choose between two minutes of this in Chernobyl or two years fighting in Afghanistan. And knowing no better, most chose Chernobyl.

But here's the irony – would the outcome have been any better if the disaster had happened in the US? Would there have been volunteers for these suicide missions? Including the later one, when a far larger secondary explosion seemed imminent, which would turn much of Western Europe into a wasteland. To prevent this, miners from the Donbass dug a tunnel beneath Reactor Four – shirtless and proud with picks and shovels. Could an even greater catastrophe have been averted because the accident happened in a one-party state? Crazy thought, isn't it? But all conjecture.

But there I was, my darling, with you inside me, being bundled out of the car by the *militsiya* on a street in Pripyat. I was escorted into a building, where I stood smarting in a dimly lit corridor.

'*Prakhodi*,' a gravelly voice beckoned from behind a door.

The officer flung the door open, shoved me in and left.

A man rose to his feet behind a large desk. He struck me as surprisingly urbane and pleasing to the eye: tanned face, dimples, high cheekbones and a full head of hair with a hint of silver at the temples. I noticed his imported navy suit jacket and an open-necked shirt. He removed his reading glasses.

'Please.' He gestured at the seat opposite. 'Excuse me while I finish this memo.'

His desk was clear save for a notepad, a jug of water with two glasses, and a cigarette fuming from the lip of an ashtray. Beyond was a bookshelf filled with lever arch files and a triptych of family photographs atop. On the wall behind him was the obligatory portrait of Lenin with his ominous frown and a framed print of *The Tank* by Deineka. You'd recognise it: a sangfroid soldier trying to out-march a tank. The zenith of Soviet Realism.

The man signed his memo with a flourish. He had the soft hands of the pampered elite. He took a drag on his cigarette till its end glowed. 'Sorry for earlier,' he said. 'My men can be rather… direct.' He leaned back, appraising me.

Something was odd about his face, I thought. Perhaps the eyes. They were a little too close. According to Babushka, that meant he was hiding something.

Smoke escaped from his lips and his eyes narrowed. 'And?' he said.

I kept silent. This was clearly an interrogation. I needed to say as little as possible for as long as possible.

He reached for a file from the bookshelf. 'I see they've trained you well.' He put on his spectacles and read, 'Lena Sergeyevna Chizhikova…'

Strange, I thought, the Tsar's Russian from a local *militsiya* officer of the Ivankiv region in Northern Kiev Oblast. Barely a trace of a Ukrainian accent. He'd probably grown up in the republic before going to Moscow or another major centre. Most senior government or industrial posts in Pripyat – or any other important city in the republics – were occupied by ethnic Russians. See, we also committed colonialism, like every empire.

Perhaps he was part big city boy and part *ukrop* – the derogatory term for a Ukrainian.

He cleared his throat. 'The name I just read,' he asked, peering at me over his glasses. 'That's you?'

I gave my dumb insolent look.

He looked down again. His brow scrunched. 'This handwriting is terrible. Idiot spilled coffee. Let's see… Suspect apprehended while attempting to enter front gate of Reactor Four. Claims she was looking for her husband.' He eyed me from above his glasses, 'Care to explain?'

At some point in an interrogation, it becomes counterproductive to keep stalling. It's a fine art to know when to throw them a bone.

'I went for a walk. Is that a crime?'

He seemed to be debating something in his mind. Then he straightened and said jauntily, 'Tea or coffee?'

'I'm fine, thank you,' I lied. I was running on adrenalin.

'Water?'

I didn't respond.

He poured anyway.

I eyed the droplets forming on the glass. My throat was parched. I hesitated.

If you accept the smallest kindness from your interrogator, you enter his web. But water is life, and how could I know when I'd get another opportunity. I accepted it, and my God, was it good!

He smiled. I knew it was an act; but it was hard not to fall for his debonair show of concern.

He extended his hand. 'Captain Dermichev; Alexander Ivanovich; Senior Detective, Ivankiv Distrićt.'

Captain? Unlikely that a man this suave and mid-thirties would hold such a middling rank. 'I haven't seen you about town,' I said.

'I've only been here a month, from Moscow.' His palms were soft and moist, but his handshake was firm and the contact lingered a fraction longer than necessary.

'With respect, Captain, while we exchange pleasantries, my husband

remains missing, his workplace is in flames, and every official I've managed to speak to claims ignorance. I need to know what's going on.'

He nodded sagely and flipped to a clean sheet on his notepad. 'I was
going to ask you the same thing.'

'Am I under arrest, Captain?'

'Not yet.'

'Then what?'

He leaned forward, elbows on the desk. 'Let's start with a bit of
context…'

I waited.

'Okay… This morning… You woke up…'

Careful, I was telling myself. This one is clever; he's keeping things
open-ended. So, I gave him my best blank-ignorant stare.

'You need to work with me, if I'm to help you, comrade Chizhikova.'

The age-old conundrum: tell the whole truth and give him rope to
hang you or lie outright and find yourself tied in knots later. The trick
was to strike the right balance between silence, obfuscation and par-
tial truths.

Dermichev inhaled. 'And then?'

'I was worried.'

'Why?'

'My husband hadn't returned.'

'What time was that?'

'Approximately ten am.'

'What time would he normally get home?'

'It varies. Lately, around nine.'

He frowned. 'Night shift ends at eight, no? And the bus runs like
clockwork. Why the delay?'

Our eyes connected. I knew he knew. Such people are trained to read
a person's suspicions and fears. So…

I shrugged and said, 'His job is his life.'

'Tss; with such a wife…'

It was shameless flattery, but damn, it felt good!

'Presumably, you couldn't get hold of the station with the lines down,' he continued.

I nodded.

'So, what did you do then?'

'I went to the Party Office.'

'Not the *militsiya*?'

'The Party's closer.'

'You don't strike me as being lazy, comrade Chizhikova.'

'With respect, Captain: your institution is not known for its customer service.'

He chuckled. 'Who assisted you at the Party Office?'

'Angela somebody.'

'What did she say?'

'That my husband doesn't exist.'

His eyebrows rose. 'Meaning?'

'His file was missing.'

As he nodded, he pulled a slip of paper from his top drawer and read, 'Yuri Petrovich Chizhikov...'

Just to hear my husband's name in that moment brought a lump to my throat. Where are you Yurochka, I silently prayed. Tell me where you are…

When my mind returned to the present, I found Dermichev staring at me with a puzzled expression.

'Comrade Chizhikova?' he said.

'I-I'm sorry?'

'The name I just read: is it your husband's?'

'This is ridiculous.'

His smile vanished. 'Just answer the question.'

I nodded.

'What do you think happened to his file? Assuming he is a Party member of good standing, as you imply.'

'Not just 'imply', Captain.'

Surprising for a scientist so young, no?'

I bristled. 'My husband was National Young Pioneer Leader, Komsomol Committee Member, Chair…' I stopped, but too late.

It was rookie mistake: volunteering more than asked for.

Trying to avoid eye contact, I looked at the photographs in the triptych behind him. I could make out a couple and two teenaged children. Strange: the man's face… it wasn't Dermichev! So, this wasn't his office. Whose then? Perhaps I was right, he was too sophisticated to be regular *militsiya*. Who then? KGB? Surely then he'd have liaised with Yavlinsky and wouldn't be asking such questions.

But the organs of state would come at you from several angles to catch you out. Either way, I figured I had more to lose by not cooperating.

He coughed, then said, 'You're proud of your husband. That's natural; but why were you so desperate to find him today, enough to cross rivers and forests and risk arrest?'

'Yuri's a special consultant to the management of Reactor Four, on night shift. He spends at least half his time in the control room; that makes it a one in two chance he was there when the explosion happened.'

Dermichev's eyebrows rose. 'What makes you think it was an explosion?'

'Accident then. What does it matter?'

'Words are important.'

'Ah. We agree on something, at least.'

'You must learn to control your cynicism, comrade Chizhikova. It would be a pity if I felt compelled to add that tendency to my notes.'

Suddenly, the room felt icy.

Under Sovetsky Soyuz law, cynicism was considered a character weakness, and if directed at the state, a mental illness, which meant you were institutionalised, like my father. Of whom Dermichev knew all right. With the KGB there was no such thing as coincidence. It didn't necessarily mean I was of special interest – meaning under observation. The organs were obsessed with gathering personal information on citizens. The first thing they extracted under pain of torture in the Lubyanka was a list of friends and associates. Imagine if there'd been social media back then. There'd have been no need for torture.

'Comrade Chizhikova?' Dermichev said. 'You all right?'

I squeezed out a tear and let it run down my cheek. 'Fine,' I said, adjusting my bra strap. 'I just want my life back.'

Being so powerless in a corrupt police state meant that feminine wiles was one of the few resources I could draw on to try to get some small leverage. It came with risks, but it was always a last resort worth trying.

Dermichev gave me an understanding smile. 'I know how distressing this must be. Trust me: I want to find him just as badly.'

I searched his soul with my eyes.

'I want to help you. Just promise me you'll answer my questions truthfully: lives depend on it. Okay?'

I nodded.

'Good. Now: this Angela at the Party Office – what did she look like?'

'An overweight mouse.'

'Be serious.'

'Mousey hair, mousey nose, a grey suit and more than a few kilograms too many.'

'And you say she found nothing on your husband?'

'I saw the empty file hanger.'

'What then?'

'I left.'

'You didn't meet with anyone else?'

'The place was deserted.'

'You sure?' His eyes bored into mine. 'Think before you answer.'

I swallowed.

It was like walking a tightrope. If he'd been acquainted with Yavlinsky he could have picked up the phone and instantly corroborated my story. But I figured he would have done that already. He was more likely asking these things because he and Yavlinsky were rivals. The KGB – like the Politburo and the rest of government – was riddled with vying factions. Typical in a one-party state. And division in the enemy's ranks equals opportunity. So…

'Yes,' I said, deadpan.

He frowned. 'You're aware that lying to an officer of the law is a crime?' He twirled his pen and watched it spin. 'Comrade Yavlinsky and I have a call scheduled this evening.'

I drew a sharp breath. I was doomed. But I'd have to stick to my story and hope. 'Fine,' I said.

He puckered his lips, then smirked. 'I saw you looking at the photographs behind me.'

'Forgive me. I didn't think that was illegal.'

'Cute wife, I must say. Pity she's not mine.'

I shrugged. 'If you're tight with Yavlinsky, why bother questioning me?'

He leaned back. 'You're good.'

I waited.

He shifted. 'I've been assigned to investigate improprieties committed on the part of local officials. And there have been rumours that Major – sorry, Director – Yavlinsky has been running his own fiefdom in Pripyat; with a few – shall we say – side interests.'

'And what has this got to do with me?'

'We'll get to that. First, after the Party Offices, where did you go?'

I was caught in another dilemma: if I told him I went to the Raduga, I'd have to mention Olga and ensnare her in my web. But if I didn't, he could catch me in a lie. Olga was my best friend and would certainly be in my file. So, he'd know where she worked on a Saturday morning, put two and two together, and call her boss. Another trick in the art of withstanding interrogation – after silence and denial – is to keep things as vague as possible. Avoid names of people or places at all costs. But there are three reasons to make an exception, each to be used with great caution: to buy time, build credibility, or entrap an enemy.

I said, 'the hospital.'

'No detours? Why?'

'Someone told me the injured firefighters were taken there overnight for observation.'

'Who?'

'A… *starik*, on the square.'

Clearly, he was sceptical, but he nodded. 'Tell me about the hospital.'

'Lots of anxious relatives in the foyer. And what a mess – discarded uniforms strewn about the floor.'

'You found the firefighters and operators then?'

'Correct.'

'But not your husband. Were you able to look?'

I hesitated just long enough to think whether to be honest; or not.

'They wouldn't let me into the ward. Said the radiation levels were dangerously high.'

'So, you just nodded politely and left?'

'The guards frogmarched me down the passage and shoved me out the door.'

He chuckled. 'So, you pick yourself up, dust off your dress, and decide you'll walk to the reactor and poke around a bit yourself?'

'It wasn't like that.'

'How then?'

Could the suited thugs across the road from the hospital have been Dermichev's, not Yavlinsky's? That would explain why I didn't recognise them. No doubt they followed me down to the bridge. But back? Then they'd have seen me take the shortcut into the forest and told Dermichev. That would explain the *militsiya* car patrolling the deserted road. But…

'Let me help you remember…' Dermichev scrutinised his notes. 'Apparently you were seen lingering at the bridge for at least ten minutes after the general proclamation to return.'

So… I thought, either he doesn't know what I did next, or he's testing me.

'I got emotional seeing the flames up close. I eventually obeyed.'

He removed his glasses. 'You mean you pretended to. Last seen heading back to town then found on a deserted road going in the opposite direction half an hour later.' He produced a silk handkerchief, breathed on his lenses, and wiped. 'In a restricted area?' He replaced them and read. 'The suspect ignored our instructions, circumvented a roadblock…' He peered at me again.

'How was I to know it was off limits?'

108

He smiled knowingly. 'This says the access roads were blocked, that you must have cut through the forest and over the river or… maybe the rumours are true.'

'Which rumours?'

'That you're a witch. The part about the broomstick.'

I remained silent.

'Apparently, they call you Baba Yaga. Tss: small town people can be terribly narrowminded.'

I dropped my gaze to the floor. 'So, I trekked across the countryside. Is that what you wanted to hear?'

The air felt stifling. I brushed a fly from my cheek.

Dermichev rose, walked around his desk, and stopped behind my shoulder. I was too terrified to turn. I felt his breath on the back of my neck and shivered, thinking he was as diabolical as those forest spirits that terrorise villages in Babushka's Belarussian folk tales.

He placed his hand on my shoulder. 'Why are you shaking?' he whispered.

'It's cold in here.'

He squeezed my shoulder lightly, almost as if with compassion. 'If you were innocent, you'd have nothing to fear, would you? He ran his hand across my shoulder. 'But relax; believe it or not, I'm on your side.'

My neck muscles tensed. Experience had taught me that those words mean the opposite. Like starting with 'to be honest', or 'this is going to hurt me more than you'.

'Now, now,' he said, soothingly. 'If I were intent on harming you, I'd have thrown you in a cell and left to join my wife and children at the *dacha*.'

He had a point. He'd been civil throughout. Perhaps he really was here to investigate local corruption, including Yavlinsky's procurement scheme, and wasn't aware of our arrangement. As I said, they had factions. Who knows why one lot might want to keep knowledge of an operation from the others?

I forced my shoulders to sag.

'That's my girl.' He released his grip and returned to his seat. 'Now,

109

we're almost done; just a bit more background and I'll arrange bail for you. Then we can both go and enjoy the holiday weekend, okay? Good. Now, your husband, the soon-to-be-famous scientist...' He flipped through the file with fingers as delicate as that of a concert pianist. 'Admitted to the Department of Physics and Technology of the Moscow Engineering Physics Institute. After graduation he volunteers for military service. Afghanistan for a year. Then he enrols at Moscow State University and – in record time – gets his doctorate in theoretical physics under the supervision of Vitaly Ginzburg.' Dermichev peered over his glasses. 'A Jew.'

'Like many a loyal Bolshevik,' I retorted.

He returned to the sheet. 'Rumours are, Doctor Chizhikova was almost a candidate for the 1986 Lomonosov Gold Medal for outstanding achievement in the natural sciences. Research into civilian applications of nuclear technology.' He turned the page. 'He's then assigned to the closed city of Arzamas – sorry, I'm not supposed to name it.' He scrutinised me.

'Is that a question, Captain?'

He sighed. 'We all know why a 'closed city' is called that.'

'Your point?'

'You didn't find it strange?'

'What?

'Your husband does his post-doctoral research in Arzamas. Then back to Moscow and, after a short stint, he's transferred to Pripyat but still reports to the same people in the Ministry of Medium Machine-Building Industry.'

'Both civilian and military nuclear power now fall under the MMMB, Captain.'

'Yes, but what's he doing in a civilian nuclear power plant.'

'The RMBK-1000 is based on the military prototype,' I hit back.

'The 1000 what?'

Damn, I thought, I've blown it! I just revealed that I know confidential details of Yuri's work!

'It's a channel-type reactor,' I said. 'Don't ask me what that means.

The term's common knowledge here; the engineers bandy it about in their bar talk. I believe they are cheaper to run and easier to maintain than other designs.'

My hunger, exhaustion and worry were starting to catch up with me, and Dermichev's face started to blur. 'May I go now, Captain?' I said.

'When you've answered my questions.'

'I have.'

'With the truth.'

'Since when do you people give a damn about the truth?'

'You people?'

'The government.'

He shook his head and muttered.

I smiled inwardly. I'd managed to frustrate my interrogator. Maybe I could get him to make some mistakes.

He inhaled, rolled his eyes toward the ceiling, and said, 'So...'

I waited.

'How did you meet your husband again?'

Blin. He was skilful. The moment I started feeling smug, he changed tack. I'd overestimated my ability. How could I hope to outsmart someone who'd trained for years at the Moscow Academy and perfected his craft over years in the field. They lull you into complacency with seemingly arbitrary banter and then drive a stake through your heart.

'What's wrong?' he said. A smile played at his lips. 'You're pale.'

'I'm tired and hungry.'

'Sure. So... a beautiful, vivacious, almost-famous Bolshoi ballerina just happens to cross paths with a reclusive genius still raw from being jilted by his childhood sweetheart and – miracle – five months later they're married. And as if that weren't fanciful enough, our wannabe prima throws her career down the toilet to follow him to Pripyat, of all places.'

My palms felt sweaty. From what he'd said so far, I could deduce he had access to my regular KGB file. But it was just possible that my case was run outside of the official channels..

I said, 'No comment.'

111

He closed his eyes and inhaled. 'This is so frustrating. She spurns her only lifeline.' Then he stared at me. 'Is that your position then?'

I didn't respond but inwardly I was panicking.

He shook his head. 'Why Lena? Why give it all up, the glitter of the Bolshoi, to come to this godforsaken little town in the sticks?'

I studied his face for a sign of sarcasm but there was none. And then it dawned on me that he really didn't know anything about my reporting on my husband, Ivanov's promise to arrange surgery for my knee, or me and Yavlinsky. I shivered. Either he was a pretender, not part of the KGB, or there was a part of my file that was extraordinarily secret. But why?

I said, 'I've been offered a position in the corps in Kiev.'

'A come-down, I'd say.'

'Beggars can't be choosers.'

'And your husband will follow?'

I had to make a critical decision – and fast. Trust Dermichev or Yavlinsky? But I didn't trust either of them further than I could spit.

I chose Dermichev.

I met his scrutinising stare, paused, then said, 'My career was as good as over.'

'Yes… I read the news reports. Sorry: it must have been humiliating – all those important people watching; not to mention the pain.' He paused and twirled his pen. 'But a knee injury is common in ballet, no? It doesn't mean the end of a career.'

'It could if it's the anterior cruciate ligament; especially if it's a repeat. We're talking a minimum of six months' rehabilitation, more often a year.'

He counted on his fingers. 'That means you could be back on stage by now.'

'It's taking longer than expected.'

'Why?'

'The body isn't a machine.'

'And surgery?'

'It wasn't offered.'

His eyebrows arched.

'Someone altered the radiology report, said it wasn't warranted.'

'You going to return to the Bolshoi?'

'Eventually, if they'll have me.'

'Otherwise?'

'I told you.'

'But Kiev? Your husband's job is here.'

'Why not, Captain? I came here for him. Article 22 of our Constitution created equality between the sexes. Or one of us could commute weekly.'

He smiled. 'That would be a sacrifice on his part, no?'

'It's called love.'

'Hah! The fairy tale marriage… Do you believe in magic?'

'It's easier than believing the crap you read in *Pravda*.'

His lips tighten. 'Need I remind you of Article 190-1 of the RSFSP Criminal Code, that slander of the Soviet State carries a three-year term?'

'These days the General Secretary encourages robust debate.'

'Touché.' He offered a wry grin. There was a long pause.

'To return to my earlier question – how did you and your husband cross paths in the first place; you have precious little in common, no?'

Inside, I was squirming. If I had to choose, I would confide in him over Yavlinsky. But I was still reluctant – partly from my ingrained distrust of the system. Essentially, I wasn't ready to be open. So, I was caught in yet another dilemma of the interrogated: if I refused to answer, he'd assume I was hiding something; if I answered, I'd be giving him rope to hang me. Lying of course, is always an option. But you must be good at it. Deception is safer.

'Sheer serendipity,' I replied. 'Yuri was in Moscow on a weekend pass. We got chatting; somewhere along the river; I can't recall exactly; we were in the same line for an ice-cream.'

This, of course, he had no way to disprove. But if I'd said a drinks party, for example, he'd have asked whose, who else was there, and so on; and then he could check out my story.

Dermichev nodded, but his pupils were dilated and his shoulders tense. Which meant he wasn't convinced. Then he smiled, leaned back in his chair, and hauled out a pack of Marlboros. He offered me one.

I shivered. My God, was I tempted. I hadn't smoked since breakfast. Dermichev lit my smoke.

I inhaled and our eyes locked. Hell, it felt good: the intimacy with another human. For a moment I forgot that it was an interrogation. As the aroma of tobacco filled my senses, it felt like I was floating.

He lit his own and watched the tip until it glowed. Then he blew a smoke ring, appraised me through narrow eyes and the haze, and said, 'You're obviously not the fragile Russian doll from the photographs: though I must say, you're every bit as beautiful.'

I hugged myself and, with my free hand, rubbed the goosebumps off my forearm.

Men made passes at me all the time: from flowers with a note attached that they'd throw on stage, to knocking on my changing room door after a performance for autographs. And those were the pleasant interactions. Russian men felt it was their birth right to make lewd comments or grab your backside. Normally I'd fob them off and think nothing of it. But there was something sinister when it came from someone with authority over you. Like the time the Director of Choreography cornered me in his office after a late practice and said if I slept with him, he'd elevate me from a nameless swan to a stand-in Odile/Odette.

Dermichev positioned his cigarette on the lip of the ashtray. A strand of smoke unfurled in the air between us. 'Relax,' he said. 'I'm not going to hurt you. Unless you leave me no choice.'

'What is it you really want, Captain?'

'The truth.'

'Which is that I am in love and happily married.'

A smile teased his lips. 'We both know there is more to your relationship with the eminent scientist.'

'No need for sarcasm, Captain.'

'Nothing of the sort. You don't get proposed for admission to the Academy of Scientists of Sovetsky Soyuz under thirty if you aren't a prodigy.'

114

'Yuri's smart, but he's no Sakharov.'

'Sakharov…' His lips curled a fraction. Then he picked up his lighter, a silver one with a Soviet star engraving. He flicked it open, shut, and open again, but there was no flame. 'He got off lightly because of his profile in the West. Your husband on the other hand…'

I met his gaze. I reminded myself to stay strong, show no fear. 'I don't care. Just tell me where Yuri is, and I'll tell you anything. Literally.'

'Ah, that's better; at last. So… what did he say before leaving for work last night?'

I maintained my veneer of calm but inside my heart hammered. 'It's a bit – how should I say? – awkward; what a husband says to a wife just after they've been… intimate.'

He chuckled. 'I'm not squeamish.'

I closed my eyes. But I was only pretending to think. I was reminding myself not to tell a soul about Yuri's admonition to me not trust anyone but Sergey. So, I said, 'Mmm. Yes… I remember now: he said goodnight. And my darling, of course.'

A cloud passed across Dermichev's face. He stubbed out his cigarette and leaned forward. 'You're aware of what happens to people who fail to cooperate in a state investigation? Especially someone with such a… questionable history.'

I felt faint.

'Yes.' He tapped the file. 'I have your antics within the Bolshoi community here in graphic detail.'

I was falling apart inside but had to act unperturbed. 'Hah,' I said, offhandedly waving my cigarette. Ash fell on the desk. I wiped it off. 'So, I'm not an angel; so, what? Do you have any artist friends, Captain? Thought not. It's in our DNA not to conform. But that doesn't make us all dissidents.'

'Who called you that?'

'You people. Declared me *neviyezdnoy.*'

Which literally means, denied permission to travel abroad. The doing of the OVIR – the Office of Visas and Registration in the Ministry of Internal Affairs. *Neviyezdnoy* was a terrible stain on your reputation.

115

The Jews suffered the worst. In the aftermath of the Six Day War in '67, many tried to emigrate to Israel – which meant quitting their jobs – but were denied permission; mostly on the grounds of having been exposed to information vital to national security. Social parasites, people called them. Such was the stigma that they were virtually unemployable. The system's cruelty knew no bounds.

Dermichev responded, 'You were allowed to tour Prague, no?'

'Huh; you call that abroad? What about the tour of Paris and London? The day before I was meant to leave the OVIR declined my visa. I'd packed my bags already, the bastards.'

'Tss; your language, my dear.' He paged through my file. 'It says here you were a second stand-in and they needed to save on costs.' He looked up. 'Have you considered the possibility that you just weren't good enough?'

I finally snapped. 'Damn you!'

He closed the file. 'Enough! You're wasting my time. I'm going to keep you here for the weekend and on Monday we'll decide whether you need to be shipped to Moscow or not.'

Stay calm, I told myself, Yuri's life – if not yours – depends on it. Keeping my hand as steady as possible, I extinguished my cigarette. 'I'm sorry. Please understand. I get upset talking about these matters. My career was my life.'

'Was? Don't despair, comrade Chizhikova, where there's a will, there's a way. If you cooperate, I'll most certainly put in a good word for you at the Ministry of Arts and Culture. Please, just give me something to work with. I know this is hard to believe, but we want the same thing.'

'Which is?'

'To find your husband.'

'So, you can arrest him?'

'Not true.'

'Why should I trust you?'

He shifted over to stand beside me. I got a whiff of cologne, the real thing.

Dermichev's fingertip touched my temple.

I was paralysed, entranced by the scent; I didn't want to move.

His finger twirled on a lock of my hair. 'Do you have a choice? He softly stroked my neck.

This is wrong, I was thinking. Trouble with a capital T.

He continued to fondle my hair. 'Tell me to stop.'

Still, I didn't budge.

'Thought so,' he crowed, 'You're a sensuous woman; ruled by the flesh. They were right.'

You fool, I scolded myself for not protesting.

He ran his fingers across my shoulders.

I clenched my eyes. Steady, I said to myself, but inside I was crumbling. He was a professional if nothing else.

'Now,' he said, straightening. 'Has your husband's behaviour been strange in any way: yesterday, the evening, the weeks before?'

Get up; run; die rather than talk, I screamed to myself.

But if I refused to cooperate I'd be locked up for weeks and no help to Yuri; so, I may as well talk just a bit, and at least partly cooperate.

'W-what did you ask?' I stammered. I couldn't look him in the eye.

'Your husband: did he exhibit any strange behaviour recently.'

'Not that I noticed; though I've been rather self-absorbed lately.'

'How so?'

I shrugged. 'I can be selfish sometimes.'

'Okay, let's try another angle... Do you have a spinner at home?'

'For Yuri; in case the control room needs to reach him urgently. I was opposed; it's like an invitation to the world to steal your peace. Most people would kill for the privilege. What can I say? I'm not normal.'

He laughed. 'Did he receive any calls over the past two weeks?'

'If it rang five times since they installed it, it would be a lot.'

'Just answer the question.'

'No.'

'No, what?'

'No, the phone didn't ring in the last two weeks.'

'For three weeks?'

I paused. 'Not that I know of.'

117

'You're happy for that be put on record?'

I felt a stab of panic and glanced about the room. 'You didn't tell me we were being recorded.'

He smiled. 'Relax. It's only a formality.' Then he fished in his cigarette packet for another Marlboro. This time, he didn't offer me one.

Whoosh went the lighter, a pause, and that intoxicating aroma flooded the room again. My limbs relaxed, my head swam, and I craved another smoke. But I was determined not to ask.

Avoid getting into debt with your interrogator. I'd already broken the rule twice; but these matters call for judgement; there's always a trade-off.

'The day before yesterday...' he said, eying me through the haze. 'At the funfair...'

I remained deadpan.

'Your husband had an argument...' he continued.

I felt the perspiration in my armpits; no doubt it showed through my dress. If he knew about the argument, he must be hand-in-glove with Yavlinsky. I'd been a fool. I desperately needed a pause.

'Could I please use the bathroom,' I said.

When flustered during a negotiation, it helps to get out and take a physical break to gather your thoughts. And an interrogation of course, is a type of negotiation: your opponent wants information and you want freedom – there's a give and take.

Dermichev looked dubious.

I clenched my teeth.

His hand moved toward his phone. 'Okay. My secretary will escort you to the ladies' room.

There, my escort waited by the row of sinks while I locked myself in a stall. I took the opportunity to relieve myself, but then remained for a minute, wracking my brain. But the conclusion seemed inescapable: Dermichev and Yavlinsky were surely in league. I must tread carefully.

Back, I sat across the desk from him. He crossed his legs. I crossed mine. I let my eyes drift to the bookshelf, to the ceiling. 'And?' he said at last. 'Are you going to tell me about the argument?'

I fixed him with a blank stare. 'My name is Lena Sergeyevna Chizhi-kova,' I said, slowly and deliberately, 'I work as a dance instructor at School Number Four, Pripyat. I have nothing further to say.'

He scowled. 'So, you're throwing the book at me.'

'You chose to record us. That makes this an official deposition.'

'Deposition? Hah! You've been watching too many American TV series.'

'I can't, they're illegal.'

Technically, I was correct, although the authorities showed little concern with non-political *tamizdat* from Hollywood during *glasnost*. But Dermichev was furious. 'Don't get smart with me,' he said, 'I could have you beaten for this attitude.'

I studied his face. It was almost impossible to read. I shivered. My handler in Moscow had roughed me up once. It happened during my third report-back session after our 'agreement', not long after Yuri and I tied the knot. I'd told him I had nothing more to report, that my husband was true to his file – a thoroughly patriotic citizen. It was a lie, but I'd fallen headlong in love. His backhander struck so hard that his wedding ring split my cheek, and left blood trickling down to my chin. The bastard would no doubt kiss his wife and hug his child when he got home.

'All right,' Dermichev shrugged. 'If you insist on making this difficult.' He pulled out a photograph from the file. 'Here's one of you crouching under the *kashtan*, not thirty metres away.'

I swallowed.

'Just tell me what the conversation was about,' he said, 'and you're free to go tonight. You have my word.'

It was tempting; oh, so tempting, but I said, 'My name is Lena Serge-yevna Chizhikova, and I…'

'Damn you!' He slammed his fist onto the desk. 'I know they were arguing.'

I met his eyes. 'Why don't you ask your fellow officer what he's got against Yuri?'

'So, you admit they've clashed.'

'Who wouldn't, with that pig.'

'Ouch. Shouldn't you rather be angry with his wife?'

I jumped up. I wanted to slap him.

But inside I wanted to cry. Was I the last person in Pripyat to accept the rumour?

Instead, I said, 'It was public knowledge that they clashed. But I'm not a lip reader. I was taking a break in the shade, minding my own business.'

'Voices carry hundreds of metres when it's windless.'

'Maybe, maybe not. I have better things to do than eavesdrop on other people's conversations.'

'It was about the test, wasn't it?'

I shrugged.

Feigning nonchalance is the next best delaying tactic after silence.

'*Blyad*!' He pulled out a sheet of paper and waved it at me. 'Your charge sheet…' He straightened it and read, 'Threat to the Security of the Motherland…' He stopped. 'Should I go on?'

I didn't respond.

'Think carefully, comrade Chizhikova. If you don't play ball now, I'll ensure that the only dancing you'll ever do in future is with a fellow *zek* in a cold shower.'

I crossed my legs to stop them shaking.

A conviction for that charge was a 'twenty', being twenty years of hard labour. I must have been five the night they came banging at the door and led Papa down the garden path to the police van. If he didn't survive the halfway measure of an asylum, what chance did I have in a camp?

I closed my eyes and inhaled, drawing courage from deep within.

This tactic of clamming up at that point was risky; but it was worth a shot; sometimes bravado pays.

'My name is Lena Sergeyevna Chizhikova,' I repeated. 'I work as dance instructor at School Number Four, Pripyat, and I have nothing further to say.'

He ran his hand through his hair. It was thinning at the crown. Suddenly, he was no longer the slick, handsome man I'd seen on entering the room, just another lowlife functionary, with hair protruding from his nostrils and a yellowed shirt collar.

'Okay,' he said, 'fine.' He signed the charge sheet. 'Lucky for you, you'll have the weekend in this little hotel of ours to acclimatise to confinement before the next transport to Moscow.' He lifted the phone's receiver off its stand and dialled.

'You can't do this,' I protested.

'Yes, I can.'

'I know my rights.'

'Hah, hah.'

In theory the Soviet Legal Code was the most extensive on the planet, but in practice it wasn't worth the paper it was written on. Nor was the free 'legal representation' the state was obliged to provide. Anyway, they could detain you for weeks without charge.

Dermichev paused before dialling the last digit. 'Tell me, why are you trying to protect him.'

'Because he's my husband,' I replied evenly.

'Tss, tss; I know how it goes. First, you learn they've cheated on you. Okay, you rationalise, he strayed on an impulse, it happens – I'm where his heart is. Then he's working late more often, and you say he's ambitious. You hear the rumours but ignore them. And if that's not bad enough, he does a disappearing act on you…'

'Whoa; what are you implying?'

'Have you stopped to consider that he may have run off with her last night, that this fire or whatever it is, was an elaborate smokescreen – excuse the pun?'

'That's preposterous.'

'Really? Who do you think removed his details from the plant directory and his file from the Party Office?'

'You people.'

'Okay; have you seen Sonya since yesterday at the funfair?'

'No.'

'I thought not.'

'But…'

'Yes?' He smirked. 'You were saying?'

'Nothing.'

I shifted and crossed my legs the other way, determined to keep my indignant façade. But inside I was crushed. The thought that Yuri might have cheated on me, and so soon after our marriage, was painful enough. But perhaps he got carried away in the moment after drinking. Who knows? It was his disappearing act that was finally getting to me. Not that I consciously believed my Yuri was capable of an act as heinous as causing a nuclear accident to run off with a KGB official's wife and abandon his wife to a lifetime of not knowing. But the evidence was troubling: Yuri's erratic hours, the flirtation with Sonya, that mumbo-jumbo before he left for work about not trusting anyone – and, of course, his missing records.

Eleven

There was a sudden scuffing of shoes on linoleum from the passage outside, and then a knock at the door.

'Yes?' Dermichev said.

'It's Vera, sir.'

'I'm busy.'

'Please. It's urgent.'

'Okay,' Dermichev muttered. 'Come in.'

His secretary tottered in, shoulder-length blonde hair bobbing. 'Sorry, sir. There's someone here to see you.'

'Tell him to wait.'

'He insists he needs to see the suspect.' She looked at me.

'Well, he can't.'

'He-he's military.'

'Name?'

'Yakovnev. Lieutenant-Commander.'

The name sounded vaguely familiar.

'What!' Dermichev said. 'A junior officer?'

'He says he's an aide to Major-General Grachev.'

'Of the 103rd Airborne Division?' Dermichev's eyebrows lifted.

As did mine. Major-General Grachev – later known as 'Pasha Mercedes' for being on the take – commanded our special forces in Afghanistan. According to Yuri he had a reputation for being tough as nails and dangerous.

Dermichev shoved my file aside. 'Fine, let him in.'

I heard the door creak open but dared not turn.

The hairs on my forearms stiffened.

Clip, clip, and the bootsteps entered.

'At ease. What's your business, comrade Yakovnev?'

'Yakovnekov. Sir.'

I recognised the name and the voice but was too astonished to be able to put a name to them.

Dermichev got up. 'Huh – Vera said Yakovnev. Come, let's speak in the briefing room.'

'No, sir. My orders are the suspect must be present.'

Sergey? But surely not. Yet it was; his Belarusian way of accentuating the first syllable. I felt an inexplicable lightness in my spirit.

Dermichev frowned. 'Okay; I'll get another chair.'

'Thank you, sir; but I prefer to stand.'

I slowly started to turn.

'A man of action.' Dermichev's eyes scrunched. 'What do you have there? Order of the Red Star, Kutuzov 2nd Class… Impressive. Where from?'

'Afghanistan.'

'So, it was Sergey!' I wanted to leap up and shout it from the hilltops.

'Ah,' Dermichev quipped, 'A futile struggle. Chasing Dushmen from hilltop to hilltop.'

Dushmen being a derogatory term for the Mujahedeen guerrillas.

'It's more fun than pushing a pen around a desk.'

'So, how can I help you, comrade?'

'I have orders to transport the suspect to Vulytsia Volodymyrska, immediately.'

I was confounded; I felt a chill: 33 Vulytsia Volodymyrska was the KGB headquarters in Kiev, in the old city centre, directly opposite the monastery complex of St Sophia. The irony… Today the Ukrainian government still occupies the building as is.

Unable to contain my curiosity any longer, I tentatively turned. What I noticed first were his boots – so shiny you could see your face in them – and then the sharp trouser creases. My heart thumped.

To this day, I don't know how I managed to suppress a gasp. Yuri's oldest and dearest friend standing there like a knight in shining armour. What a sight! He was good looking on a bad day, and here he was in full officer dress of the elite counterinsurgency landing troop division of the air force. Like the Green Berets, except their berets were blue. In Sergey's case it was folded so straight it could have been ironed in place. Dead centre of the forehead was a red star, in line with an almost identical one on his buckle.

Sergey didn't display a trace of recognition. 'Lena Sergeyevna Chizhikova?' he asked.

I nodded but was confused.

Sergey took a piece of folded paper out of his top pocket and placed it on the desk. 'It's all in there, sir,' he said offhandedly.

Dermichev read, brow creased, then tossed the paper aside. 'Thank you, Lieutenant-Commander, you can wait outside. When I'm done interviewing the suspect, I'll—'

'With respect, sir: the orders say immediately.'

Dermichev glared. 'Leave; now, or I'll have you arrested for interfering with a state investigation.'

'I'm simply following orders, sir.'

Silence.

'Please, sir: just countersign the letter and let us go. I was detained at a roadblock on the way here and must be back at eighteen hundred sharp.'

'I can read. But tell me: how do I know this letter isn't fake? Anyone can forge a signature.' He groped for the telephone. 'I didn't survive this long in my line of work without being careful.'

'Understood,' Sergey said, nonchalantly. 'The general's number is in the footer. Or you could try First Secretary Shcherbitsky.' First secretary referring to the head of the Communist Party of Ukraine.

Dermichev started to dial, clockwise...

Sergey glanced at his watch. 'Fourteen fifteen... I'm not sure either of them will take too kindly to their after-lunch snooze being interrupted.'

Dermichev continued to dial, but with each number, he slowed.

'Engaged. I suppose every man and his dog is calling a relative in Kiev.'

Sergey stepped forward, towering over the desk. The cotton twill of his olive shirt was heavily starched, and open at the neck revealing the horizontal white-and-blue-striped undershirt.

'My transport's waiting outside, sir. I'd better be…'

'I heard you the first time, Lieutenant.'

'Lieutenant Commander.'

'The impertinence,' Dermichev shook his head. 'I was getting so close.' He scribbled his signature on the orders. 'When you make your report to the General, don't forget to add how you fucked up my debriefing.' He fished a pair of handcuffs from his drawer and shoved them across the desk. 'Now go. And if I hear she's within twenty kilometres of this city by sunset, by God I'll make sure you both never see the outside of a barbed wire fence.'

Sergey slipped the paper into his chest pocket. 'Thank you, sir.' Then he clasped my arm and slapped the irons over my wrist. His face was impassive. 'Come with me.' Through the door we marched, along the dimly lit corridor, past Vera's empty desk, the foyer, so fast I had to skip to keep up. He shoved me through the revolving front door. I was disorientated by the glare and had to squint so hard I could barely see. But how glorious the softened sun felt on my face after all the fluorescent lights and blank walls. The air was warm and snowing *kashtan* seeds with a scent of freshly cut lawn. Then came that tickle in my throat again, and the smoke. Sergey was drawing me toward the street, and from behind a starter motor coughed. Seconds later, a UAZ vehicle pulled up beside us. The full name was Ulyanovsky Avtomobilny Zavod, the vehicle factory founded in '41 when Stalin moved vehicle production to Ulyanovsky to escape the Nazis. Another dismal wasteland I once performed in and couldn't wait to leave. Its only aesthetic feature was the Volga. By the way, Ulyanov was Lenin's real surname. But Vladimir Ilyich Ulyanov doesn't have the same ring, does it? 'Lenin' is from the river Lena in Siberia, where the Tsar violently suppressed a mine workers' strike.

Sergey bundled me into the rear of the UAZ and hopped into the passenger seat. We took off with a screeching of tyres, braking just in time to avoid rear-ending a bus. Another surge, left, right, straight until *wham* – a pothole – and I was bounced right off the seat, my head touching the ceiling. On we sped. Suddenly, I was flung forward as we

126

slammed on brakes for a hunched babushka with a shopping bag limping across the road.

I swivelled about. No car seemed to be following. Our engine revved high, then at an idle. The air was filled with a mixture of diesel, khaki and sweat, as the UAZ shuddered and vibrated. I felt an urge to vomit. And pressure was building in my bladder. I knew myself: I'd be desperate for the bathroom long before we got to Kiev.

'How are you doing back there?' Sergey called.

I hesitated.

'It's all right, Lena, you can speak your mind. I trust Lieutenant Svechin with my life. We've served together for two years.

'The driver nodded but remained focused on the road.

'So, Sergey, aren't you supposed to be in Afghanistan until next week? Yuri said…'

'It's a long story.'

'Did you fly here direct?'

'Via Moscow. Spent a few days there.'

'How's your mother?'

He looked out of the window.

'What's wrong?'

'Her cancer's back.'

'No…'

'They give her six months.'

'Oh, Sergey; I'm sorry.'

'It's okay; she's had a good life. It's her suffering I can't bear. As if she hasn't had enough already.'

I was deep in thought, struggling to make sense of what had just happened. I said, 'How did you know I was being detained? Olga?'

'Hell no.'

'How then? That soldier?'

'Which one?'

'Outside the Raduga. I asked him to contact comrade Sokolov.'

Sergey stared ahead, then gave a slight nod. 'You could say.' And whoosh… the UAZ ploughed through a puddle.

'You aren't really General Grachev's aide, are you?' I said, 'and that business about Shcherbitsky…'

Sergey turned to face me. Suddenly, he was deadly serious. I searched his eyes but only saw a soldier's resolve.

'You're not really taking me to First Secretary Shcherbitsky, are you?' I said.

His dimples appeared; then a chuckle, which turned to a deep-bellied laugh.

I felt a surge of joy. This was the Sergey I knew – the gentle giant, life and soul of a party.

Ah, the relief and lightness of spirit I felt as we hurtled along the street parallel to Kurchatova toward the square. Glimpses of the neon sign of the Polissya flashed by between buildings. Seconds later, a sign for Lelina Prospekt appeared. We're going to our apartment, I thought, buoyed with hope. Perhaps I hadn't imagined the shape passing over the window earlier…

Suddenly, I was thrown against the door as we cornered hard right with tyres squealing, then sped up again. Now an intersection loomed and I was thrust forward as we braked behind a crawling fire truck. The smell of burnt brake pads filled the vehicle, so I wound down my window and stuck my head out. Usually, you could see the cooling towers in the distance from there; but the air was thick as pea soup, and orange from shielding the sun.

A voice crackled over the radio up front, but Svechin killed it. A black Volvo pulled up behind us. I was anxious by then. What if we were being followed?

A fireman hopped out of the truck ahead and unreeled a hose. He fiddled with the nozzle until foam began to spew. Soon a jet was blasting like an ocean wave over the sidewalk.

'Is all this cleaning because they're worried about radiation?' I asked.

'Waste of time,' Sergey grunted.

'Why then? They must know this.'

'Officials have to look like they're doing something.'

'What would you do?'

He pointed skyward.

'Oh! So is your squadron here to douse the flames?'

'Not exactly. It's complicated. Antoshkin's crew was assigned. They're expecting the go ahead any minute.'

'Then what was the helicopter I saw earlier?' I said, remembering the rhythmical thudding as its shadow passed over our balcony.

'Probably one of the locals.'

'But... I'm confused.'

'How so?'

'I don't understand what you're doing here in Pripyat, so soon,' I glanced at my watch. 'How long does the flight take from Kabul?'

'I told you: I came from Moscow.'

'But still.'

Sergey hesitated, as if thinking. 'Let's just say, last night I was asleep in our barracks in Moscow, dreaming of skiing off-piste at Sochi. We weren't even given a chance to pack a bag. You'd swear Sovetsky Soyuz had been invaded.'

'Is the situation here that bad?'

'Worst case. I saw as we flew in. We did a few passes; every so often the smoke clears.'

I felt the knot in my stomach again.

'The reactor roof is totally destroyed.'

'But... what about all the redundancies in the design? Yuri called it a double shell.'

'All I can say is we measured eight hundred roentgen equivalents at two hundred metres.'

'Say that in plain Russian?'

'The safe limit's eighty.'

It took a few seconds for me to process what Sergey had just said. Then I said, 'Then why were you flying there earlier?'

The steely look he gave me said it all. Sergey was a soldier. Living in the West In this age of ease and cynicism, it's hard to comprehend the concept of unconditional patriotism. Who are our heroes today? The Kardashians, Justin Bieber? Sometimes I shake my head in disbelief.

129

Our driver revved the UAZ till the engine sang. Then he tooted his horn. But the fire truck didn't budge. The pressure in my bladder was becoming unbearable. Fortunately, we were now close to our apartment, I thought, an image of Yuri flashing through my mind.. I rolled down my window again and leaned out, wincing at the reek of detergent and the foam-topped pools littering the road. Step by painful step, the fireman worked his way across the intersection, spraying every nook and cranny at least twice. Finally, the fire truck was gone and the UAZ clanked into gear. But instead of continuing down Lelina Prospekt, we turned left.

'Where are we going?' I said, 'Our apartment's the other way.'

No response. We accelerated.

'Please,' I said, 'Yuri might have returned by now. We must go…'

'That's the first place they'll look.'

'But he'll be worrying about me.'

'He won't.'

'How do you know?'

'Trust me.'

I swallowed.

'This isn't the way to Kiev,' I said.

'Third right!' Sergey commanded, ignoring me.

The UAZ cornered so hard we rose on two wheels, surged forward and then zigzagged through increasingly deserted side streets. Sergey tapped Svechin on the shoulder and pointed ahead and then we skidded to a stop beside a heap of white sand. Sergey and I got out. The engine hissed but otherwise the street was silent except for muffled traffic sounds and the far-off shouts of kids playing. Rubble all about us, stacked bricks, the smell of fresh paint and concrete and graffiti on the walls. Part building site, part ghetto. I was still taking it all in when the UAZ coughed back to life and roared off.

'I need to wee,' I groaned, pointing to the bricks.

'Wait,' Sergey produced a set of keys. 'Let's go.'

Suddenly I heard the *thuk-thuk* of a helicopter, faint at first, then ricocheting about the buildings. It was hard to tell where it was coming from. Louder, the monstrous chopping grew until it cast a shadow on the tarmac ahead of us. The downdraft kicked up a puff of cement powder. Instinctively, I ducked. Dust flew about and my eyes stung as the chopper circled overhead.

'Dermichev's checked out your story!' I whispered. 'God help us!'

I'm too tired to continue any further tonight, my little dove. All I can think of is how heavy my eyelids are becoming. Forgive me, but could we call it a night?

Twelve

Good morning my darling. You'll have to forgive me again today, I'm feeling a bit flat. The results just came back from my latest tests.

It's bad, I'm afraid. My 'markers have deteriorated', whatever that means. Essentially the cancer has spread further. There are new signs in my liver and kidneys.

Yes, there's always hope. But it's a slender thread. Doctor Stromer tried hard to talk me into experimental treatment. He's just returned all fired up from an oncology conference in Kuala Lumpur. Apparently, there's a clinical trial with a targeted approach – something to do with genes. But the expected success rate is twenty per cent! I asked about the other eighty per cent. Guess what he said: they're terminal patients anyway. Hah! Like we're rats in a laboratory. And even if it's successful, I would only get remission for a year at best. I told him not to bother.

Oh Katyusha, I don't mean to burden you; there's nothing more anyone can do. And I thank you every day for what you're doing for me already. Quality of life is the greatest treasure, especially when you know the days are few. And this place has it all: privacy, pain relief, comfort and distractions. Though those are becoming fewer as I'm confined more and more to bed. Television only goes so far. I've taken to sitting up in bed writing. A crude journal. Burn it when I'm gone. But it helps clarify my thoughts for when we speak like this...

My darling, I so appreciate being able to talk to you so freely at last. It's like a weight falling from my shoulders. An unexpected benefit of this terminal illness.

I can't tell you how rare it is to find a person in this country who is genuinely interested in my past. My friends at the Russian Club say the same. It seems that the lot of the émigré is to have no history. At first it was my salvation, because I needed to keep it quiet. But what a lonely way to live. The first twenty-six years of my life were simply obliterated overnight. It was like I'd just been born.

And of course when I arrived here I couldn't even speak the language, so people treated me like a four-year old. I'm serious. They'd raise their voices as if I was deaf. Or they'd just speak past me like I didn't exist. I've always been the outsider who doesn't belong. Even at the Russian Club I'm an outsider among outsiders.

You were my sole purpose in life when you were growing up, Katyusha – to shelter and provide for you, to be the mother and father to you, which I myself never had.

Ah, my little dove, there was a time you were so affectionate with me. How could I forget how you'd come and tug at my skirt and ask for a hug? You must remember. You were still doing it until your tenth birthday. We'd bear-hug till one of us couldn't take the pressure! That warm feeling is starting to return now that we're speaking again. How I've missed you!

But yesterday I was telling you about the helicopter that was circling above us. For a moment it stopped and hovered directly above us, but then to my relief, it continued overhead and disappeared. I followed Sergey as he strode toward the raw concrete façade of a newly constructed *khrushchyovka*, its reinforced steel protruding and plastic still visible between the concrete slabs.

Sergey removed a piece of cardboard that jammed the door in place and next thing we were in a stark, unfurnished foyer that reeked of fresh paint. The pressure in my bladder had returned with vengeance. I watched, desperate, as Sergey slotted the key into the keyhole and fiddled.

Hurry, please, I silently urged. When the door finally swung open, I bolted ahead, past a surprisingly well-equipped kitchenette – with a *radio-tochki* which appeared to be on – and into the living room. But my eyes were scanning for the bathroom as I broke into a run, not caring to shut the door, lifting my dress in the nick of time…

I emerged a different person and returned through the living room from which a sliding door led to a courtyard. Sergey was at the sink filling two glasses. He handed one to me, which I drained in one go and scanned the room. The only furniture was a sofa. 'An antique Moldavian,' I said. 'I take it this place doesn't belong to a woman.'

'Hah, hah. It was allocated to an infantry colonel I know from Kabul. A sort of pre-retirement posting. He asked me to do a snag list and buy him some furniture.'

I sat down on it, and said, 'Weren't you supposed to take me to Vulytsia Volodymyrska?'

'Of course; stupid me.' He grinned.

'That was a fabrication?'

'We are going to Kiev, though.'

'Are we?'

'I'll explain.'

Silence ensued.

Then Sergey said, 'They've declared an exclusion zone around the plant, manned by check points. Supposedly to protect citizens from possible exposure to higher than optimal levels of radiation.'

'Are you worried Dermichev has figured out you tricked him?'

'If not yet, then soon. The duty officer at Vulytsia Volodymyrska is one of us; he'd have corroborated my story if Dermichev had called earlier. But there's a shift change soon.'

'So, why not run the gauntlet of the *militsiya* now?'

'The army has taken control. We'll go tomorrow. There will anyway be an alert out for you.'

'Me? I don't understand. Because I trespassed?'

'No.'

'What for then?'

'It's complicated.'

'Well, we have until tomorrow, no?'

'Unfortunately, I have to go soon. Some business at the barracks. I'll fetch you tomorrow.'

'I'm confused.'

'I'm sorry. You're just going to have to trust me.'

I shivered.

Those were Yuri's last words to me the night before. Trust only Sergey.

I sank onto the sofa, trying to think. Eventually, I said, 'So, how will waiting for tomorrow help?'

'We're arranging papers for you,' he said.

'Papers?' But I have my passport right here.'

'No; a new one.'

I was dumbfounded.

In Sovetsky Soyuz it was next to impossible to get a forged passport. Thoroughness – though not efficiency – was the hallmark of the Russian bureaucracy.

'But… why all this trouble? All I did was trespass on state property. Surely a good lawyer could limit it to a fine or short prison sentence at worst? Especially now with *glasnost.*'

He leaned against the wall, his expression pensive. 'How can I explain…? This thing is bigger than you – way bigger.'

'*What* is? Talk straight with me, Sergey.'

'Sorry,' he said, 'This is a lot to take in: the explosion, Yuri missing, your run in with the law, now this cat and mouse game…'

'No, please Sergey! Please be straight with me.'

'I'm sorry, I can't…'

'Dammit, that's what they all say.'

We sat in silence. At length, he said, 'Lena: how much do you know about Dermichev?'

'That he's not regular *militsiya*?' I said warily.

'Go on.'

'KGB?'

'Sort of.'

'Meaning?'

'The agency is more divided now than ever – mainly between the pro-reform faction aligned with Mecheny and the conservatives.' Mecheny being another nickname for Gorbachev. 'It's pretty much a mirror of the Politburo.'

'And which faction is Dermichev?'

'I was hoping you could tell me.'

We lapsed into silence again.

'Anyway,' I said eventually, 'What does any of this have to do with me? If it's not about my trespassing.'

He inhaled slowly, then exhaled. 'Have you considered the KGB might have been planning to take you in anyway – and you just happened to give them a perfect smokescreen?'

'What could interest them about a not-quite-famous ballerina.'

'Ex-ballerina, you mean.'

Those cruel words again. My spirit plunged. Despite the constant insecurity and self-doubt, to be a successful artist I had to fervently believe in myself, that I had something valuable to share with the world. Ballerinas are probably the worst. Our egos inflate like hot air balloons, but one pinprick and we crash.

Sergey, for all his macho bravado, had the sensitivity to notice.

'Oh Lena,' he immediately said, 'I'm so, so sorry; that was a terrible thing to say.' He sat down beside me with his arm around me. 'Forgive me.'

'It's fine,' I sniffed. 'It's the truth.'

'Nonsense. Some of the greatest ballerinas get injured and return to the stage.'

'Like?'

'Maya for one.'

'I'm no Maya.'

'Alla then.'

'They're special.'

'So are you.' His fingers pressed into my shoulder. 'Don't ever forget it.'

'But it's been a year and a half and I still can't dance on it.'

'Just keep up the rehab, do the drills and trust the process.'

Tears welled. I couldn't look him in the eye. 'If it was only a physical problem,' I mumbled.

He shifted closer. 'Every professional makes mistakes. That's how we learn. God knows, I've made enough…'

'Yes, but you'd be dead by now if it was a serious one.'

'Hah, if only you knew. You see this?' Sergey lifted a medal off his chest. 'For courage in the line of fire. Only it wasn't courage. The only reason I kept my hands at the instruments was trained instinct. The luck involved... Do you know how many rounds are fired in a thirty-second strafing? If I could, I'd turn in this worthless piece of tin. It's just a talisman to stop survivors from drowning in guilt.' He stood. 'Okay, enough heavy talk.' He smiled. 'Listen to me Lenochka: you're going to perform Odette one day, and I'm going to be in the loges; I promise – if I have to trade the paintings that I inherited for the ticket and fly back from Vladivostok by helicopter for the night!'

'Ah – you're so sweet.'

'Hardly.... But tell me: why drive yourself so hard? You've already had a good career, achieved what every girl in Soyuz dreams of, performing in the Bolshoi – why not call it a day, settle down and focus on say... teaching?'

In an instant, I was seething. 'Listen...' I puffed my chest. 'The day I graduated from the Academy, I promised myself I'd retire on my own terms.'

'Things are different now.'

'How so?'

'You're married, for one thing. And expecting...'

'You think Yuri and I didn't discuss it?' I snapped. 'The very day we were engaged.'

Oh, that autumn morning...! He'd taken me for the weekend to Tolstoy's estate, about two hundred kilometres south of Moscow. He knew I had a whole shelf of Tolstoy, with *War and Peace* beside my bed. We were strolling up the birch-lined avenue in a cold December mist, from the gate to the manor house, my hand in his. We'd only known each other three months but it felt so comfortable and right to be joined at the hip like that. We paused as a fox trotted past and the next thing Yuri was in front of me, hands on my shoulders and an uncharacteristically awkward expression. Then he popped the question – confidently, without preliminaries or explanation. Of course, it came as no surprise; I'd been planting the seeds from the day we met – on the KGB's orders. Except by now, I was falling in love. There I stood beneath dripping boughs, wrapped in furs against the cold, but with a warm heart. With every fibre in my body, I wanted to shout yes and hug him and twirl about yelling hallelujahs. But I loved him too much not to first tell him my view on falling pregnant. That I hadn't practiced ten hours a day since childhood, contorted myself beyond the limits of the human body and made pain my daily companion just to throw it all away by having a child before I retired.

Sergey nodded sagely. 'Yuri said so. I told him he was crazy.'

'Thanks a lot.'

Sergey winked. 'He didn't listen, of course.'

'Of course.'

For a while we sat without speaking.

'So...' I said at length, 'you propose I retire? Are you implying I'm old?'

He laughed. 'Of course not. I just assumed ballet was like soldiering – best done young.'

'Maya Plisetskaya danced the dying swan in her fifties, not a pretender in sight; only retired at sixty-five.'

'And Osipenko at sixty,' he quipped.

'Hah, I'm impressed. How did you know?'

'I have a friend who's an aficionado.'

'Tell me more...'

'It's platonic, I assure you.'

'Really? Look, you're blushing...'

'Yuri tells me you were offered a soloist position with the Kiev troupe?'

'A lucky break; Alexander's uncle is the director there.'

'You stay in touch?'

I shrugged. 'Ballet's a small world; it's a bad idea to keep enemies.'

'Agreed: I shoot mine.'

'Ha, ha.'

'Sorry,' he smiled sheepishly. 'Tell me: Kiev's two and a half hours away; how is that going to work with Yuri here?'

'I could board at the theatre school.'

'Aren't they doing renovations?'

'Only to the theatre building. The troupe will still train.'

'And you'd live apart during that time? What kind of marriage is that?'

'We'd see each other on the weekends and between seasons.'

He smiled and shook his head. 'You're not normal.'

'And proud of it.'

'Careful: they say if you go against the grain of the universe, you get splinters. Especially in a one-party state.'

'Fortunately, a certain amount of rebellion is expected from artists; even Stalin indulged it. These days, the Mineral Water Secretary actively encourages different views.' That being a derisive nickname for Gorbachev for restricting the sale of alcohol.

'For now.'

'You know something the rest of us don't?' I studied his face.

'No, why?' he said, but he didn't look me in the eye.

'Just asking.'

After a silence, he said. 'I need to ask you more about Dermichev.'

'Okay.'

'What sort of questions did he ask you earlier at the *militsiya* station?'

'A lot about Yuri, actually.'

'What exactly?'

I shivered. 'Do I have to replay the whole scene? It gives me the creeps.'

'Sorry. It's important. Did he ask about Yuri's research?'

I nodded.

'And?'

'I had nothing to tell him.'

'Did he mention the tests?'

I hesitated. I was still a bit sceptical. 'I can't recall.'

He searched my eyes. Then he stood up and wandered to the kitchen, filled the kettle and fired up the stove. 'Tea?'

'Thanks.'

'So, what do you think?' He ferreted through the cupboards.

'That you got there just in time.'

'Oh? Tell me: did he specifically ask about the week or two leading up to the accident?'

'No, but Yavlinsky…'

I stopped, but it was too late. Oh, you blabbermouth Lena, I cursed myself. You've blown it!

Sergey pounced immediately. 'You mean Yuri's boss?' he said.

'Not quite.'

'Chief of Personnel Section then?'

I looked at him quizzically. 'Yuri's told you?'

'Just that he's an ogre.' He took the steaming kettle off the stove. 'So, why were you talking to him?'

'I was desperate. They didn't have a clue at the plant. Sounded like chaos. Anyway, Yavlinsky was already in Kiev.' I felt bad about this lie. But what choice did I have? 'Fortunately, his secretary answered,' I continued. 'Poor thing will get it in neck for giving me his number.'

Sergey's expression was guarded. He put the tea and a plate of cookies on the coffee table in front of me and sat down. Clearly retired army personnel had access to better provisions that anything we could find at Raduga. I helped myself – I was starving.

He leaned forward and looked at me intently. 'What did he ask you – about the lead up to last night?'

'I don't recall. Sounded like he was just fishing. His type like to gather information that they can use later against a person.'

'What do you think he has against Yuri?'

'I'm not sure. Probably professional jealousy. He hates it that Yuri has free reign in designing the tests. He did whatever he could to thwart them.'

Sergey stroked his chin. 'And now they'll no doubt blame Yuri for the explosion.'

Suddenly, the apartment felt as cold as a tomb. The words of the doctor at the hospital came back to me. 'That's ridiculous,' I said, 'Yuri's been warning them for months that the reactor design is flawed and urgently needs modification.'

'I know.'

'Yuri tells you these things?' I said, dumbfounded. 'His work is supposed to be classified.'

'Relax. Yuri and I are like blood brothers. We've known each other since we could speak.'

'Still…' My mind was roving far and wide. 'What else did he tell you?'

'It's complicated.'

'Meaning?'

'I'm sorry,' Sergey said, standing. 'I've already told you too much.'

'No!' I got up and stepped toward him. 'Don't speak to me in riddles,' I said, tears pricking my eyes.

'I'm afraid I have no choice. For your sake. And Yuri's.'

'So, he's alive?'

'I didn't say that.'

I closed my eyes in anguish.

'Lena… There is every reason to believe there's just been a big misunderstanding, and that Yuri has already been admitted to hospital – either here, or in Kiev or Moscow – and he's getting the best possible medical care.'

But his words were cold comfort. I was already sobbing.

Sergey handed me his handkerchief,

'Thanks.' I wiped my face. 'Sorry.'

'No need. After what you've been through… I've seen hardened soldiers cry for their mamas for less.'

'If it's any comfort,' he continued, 'I've heard the talk in the officers' mess… only two men have so far been reported dead. On the other hand…' He winced. 'I must be honest: if, in a disaster like this, a person missing from the site isn't found within forty-eight hours, it tends to mean the worst.'

Terrified, I gazed into his face.

'Come here,' he said.

He drew me to him and wrapped me in a hug. The pretence of bravado I'd worn all day crumbled as he pressed my face against his shirt collar. Luckily, there were no neighbours in that unfinished complex to overhear my wailing. I was like Juliet discovering that Romeo had killed himself in vain.

Gradually I felt Sergey's strength and security flow into my body. When I'd cleared enough snot and tears to see, Sergey was still there, ramrod straight and impassive. I closed my eyes again, rested my head on his shoulder, and for a brief but glorious interlude, I was convinced all would be well.

Sergey eventually released me from his embrace. He glanced at his watch. 'Four thirty; I need to go.'

I felt a jolt of anxiety. In all the drama, I'd actually forgotten about my four o'clock meeting with Yavlinsky. But it was too late to do anything about it. 'Where?' I said.

'The base.'

'And me?'

'You'll be safe here tonight. I should have your papers ready first thing. Then you leave for Kiev.'

I bit my lip and averted my eyes. I wanted to cry again.

'What's the matter?' he said.

'I'm not leaving,' I said. 'Not while there's a chance Yuri's still in Pripyat.'

'Come now, Lena – think. Every firefighter and policeman within a hundred-kilometre radius has been rushed to the scene. What are you going to do that hasn't been tried already?'

'I don't care; I'm staying.'

His face hardened. 'I can't allow that.'

I plopped myself down on the sofa, arms crossed. 'Carry me then.'

'Lenochka, be logical. If Dermichev catches you in town from tomorrow, there's nothing even I can do for you. Besides, Pripyat's no longer safe with the radiation. It's time.'

'For what?'

'Evacuation.'

'For whom?'

'Everyone.'

I found it hard to believe but said nothing. In retrospect though, all the signs were there: the heavy traffic out of town, the itinerant workers sent home, and the growing number of buses I'd witnessed about the square. The *nomenklatura* were of course the first to jump ship, while the rest were kept in the dark, and then peddled the myth of Soviet stoicism. Eventually they too would have to be evacuated. Like the summer of '41, when the authorities waited until Hitler's panzers were halfway there before ordering the evacuation of Moscow – 'important' people first, followed by scientists and skilled workers from the arms industry along with whole factories dismantled and shipped lock-stock-and-barrel across the Caucasus, then groups of 'strategic national interest', like the Bolshoi.

But evacuation or not, I was adamant about not leaving Pripyat without Yuri. I stared defiantly at Sergey.

'Please.' He put his hand on my wrist.

I pulled mine away. 'No!'

He said, 'I'm not at liberty to explain now but, as Yuri's oldest and closest friend and a person who loves and cares for both of you, I'm pleading: believe me when I say it's what he'd want.'

'Sorry. You're only trying to help. And I'm grateful for you coming to my rescue today, truly I am. But…'

'At least think it over. I understand you've been bombarded with a great deal in the past twenty-four hours.'

'Maybe, but I'm not going to change my mind.'

We sat in awkward silence. At length, he said, 'Shouldn't you be considering…?'

I waited.

He pointed at my belly. 'You know…'

'How do you even know that I'm pregnant?'

'Yuri told me.'

'I should have guessed. Your intimacy could make me jealous.'

He chuckled. 'We shared a locker, not a bunk.'

We fell silent. Eventually, he said. 'Isn't that reason enough to get out of here – to avoid the radiation?'

'No. I'm not going through with the pregnancy.'

Sergey looked momentarily shocked, but quickly recovered.

'Does Yuri know?'

'It's not his decision.

His eyebrow lifted.

'I told you we'd discussed it in advance.'

143

'Probably, with the evacuation, the procedure will be postponed. Maybe use the time to reconsider.'

I leapt to my feet, shoulders back. 'Are you suggesting that – after a year of intensive rehabilitation, just as I finally – and hopefully soon – overcome my injury – I put my body through the trauma of childbirth and take on the responsibility of being a mother?'

Yes, my darling, I was still thinking like that. But not for much longer.

'Surely it's not that bad?'

'Easy for you men to say; you're not the ones sacrificing.'

'Okay, but think what you'll gain.'

'I don't think you understand, Sergey. I was born to dance; since the age of five, I've never wanted to do anything else. Imagine if I said, "from tomorrow you can't be a soldier"?'

He grimaced. 'After what I've done today, that's a distinct possibility.'

'I'm sorry.' I looked into his eyes through a blur of tears. 'But why are you doing this for me?'

'What?'

'Risking your career.'

'It's complicated.'

'I have time…'

The roar of the UAZ outside startled me.

Sergey checked his watch, unfazed. 'Unfortunately, I don't.' He stood, beret in hand. 'Sorry, I really must be going. Lieutenant Svechin is here.'

'But…?'

He strode toward the door. 'Make yourself at home,' he said over his shoulder. 'There are some provisions in the cupboard. I'll be back first thing tomorrow.'

'No, please don't leave me here.'

He paused at the door. 'It's not paradise, but it'll do. Don't – I repeat – *don't*, under any circumstances, leave the apartment until I return. Don't touch the telephone or the door. And keep quiet. It's for your safety and for others. Understand?'

After Sergey left and the UAZ engine died down the street, I wandered the apartment in a daze. My thoughts were spinning but I could no longer think coherently. I felt drained and exhausted by all that had happened. Eventually, I went into the bedroom and flopped onto the bed. Nothing made sense. Talking to Sergey had raised more questions than answers.

My mind drifted to the night before, in my own bedroom, where it was dark except for the starlight from the window. I was delirious from the afterglow of our lovemaking, watching my true love getting dressed.

Ah, if only that could have been my last memory. How many times over the past three decades haven't I wished I'd never woken up? Not that I had the courage to take my own life. I outright failed that test in those final weeks on the balcony in Pripyat.

But I'm glad I lived on. Because then I got to know my other great love, my darling. And that was you. The joy of your first smile and the way you cooed. Sonorous as a dove. That's how you got your nickname.

Speaking of names, do you know the meaning of the name Chernobyl? It's the local name for the herb wormwood. And a remarkably prescient name it turned out to be. Wormwood is specifically mentioned in the Bible in the Book of Revelations. If that even rings a bell for you. As I recall, you never really took a liking to the Good Book. Which isn't surprising. In your early years I was still an atheist. My spiritual awakening was slow.

But let me read the passage to you. I'll just get my Bible. Here, I have the page bookmarked. Revelations chapter eight, verses ten and eleven.

'And the third angel sounded, and there fell a great star from heaven, burning as it were a lamp, and it fell upon the third part of the rivers, and upon the fountains of waters. And the name of the star is called Wormwood: and the third part of the waters became wormwood; and many men died of the waters, because they were made bitter.'

Now, tell me if that isn't prophecy, girl! And yet when it was fulfilled in Chernobyl, did the world heed the message? Of course not. Hard hearts. Let's take a break here. The telling has taken it out of me today.

Thirteen

Right, here we go again, my little dove. I'm going to get right into the story. My energy is becoming more and more finite.

After Sergey left me in that apartment I must have drifted off to sleep on the sofa, because I awoke numb in every fibre and completely disorientated, unsure of where I was and whether it was evening or morning.

Then reality flooded back and my anxiety returned. So much had happened since I'd woken that morning that I could hardly comprehend what was real and what wasn't. All I knew was that something great and awful had befallen me – and quite possibly my husband – I was now a fugitive from the law, and my only hope had just been driven off in a UAZ.

I began to pace the apartment, trying to assure myself that by next week Yuri and I would be together again. Sergey would fix everything, and I must just be patient. Mercifully, I didn't know the extent of what still lay ahead as I wandered about inside the living room, which was now bathed in dusk. But the walls seemed to close in on me. I felt cooped up. Inaction was against my nature. *Lose yourself in action lest you wither in despair*, said Lord Tennyson. In Babushka's words, pray and row for the shore.

I tried the sliding door. At first it wouldn't budge, so I wedged my feet against the wall and heaved. When it finally gave way, I stumbled out, almost toppling over a loose paving stone. 'Slipshod workmanship,' I could hear Yuri saying.

The spaces between the tiles were chock full of weeds, tall and thick stemmed with yellow flowers and leaves broad enough to make shade. Across the road was a giant mural of three sturdy peasant women in multi-coloured pastels hoeing a ripened wheatfield. Workers of the world unite.

146

But I soon felt that now-familiar acrid taste in my throat. I went back inside, pacing again.

Then I heard a spinner ring. I located the telephone and stood, rigid, until the ringing stopped. But afterwards, I couldn't take my eyes off the phone. Somewhere beyond that crab shaped contraption and a copper wire was another human being. How I craved connection. I thought of Olga. I was just a few simple hand movements away from her reassuring voice. Talk about temptation. Sergey had warned me... But he'd also left me all alone at this moment while my world was falling apart.

Finally, I lifted the receiver. My index finger quivered at the dial. One, two, three, four, five dials. *Click, click...* static...

'Yes?' said the operator.

I was trembling. 'Er... Lena Sergeyevna Chizhikova.'

'Number?'

I rattled the off the five digits. I'd long since memorised her number.

It rang for an eternity. I was about to give up when there was a click.

'Yes?' I was so relieved to hear Olga's voice.

'It's me!' I blurted.

'Mushka! I've been worried sick. Where've you been?'

Hearing her voice, someone who cared and knew me well, was like balm.

'I'm fine. No: actually, it's terrible.'

'Did you go to the hospital?'

'Yes, but he wasn't there; not that I could see; and no sign of his name in their records. I tried to peek into the wards, but they were so rude; they literally marched me out.'

'Oh, you poor girl. What happened then?'

'The doctor had the nerve to suggest he might be among those detained.'

'Oh...?'

'Something about sabotage. I'm worried sick, Olga. And then I went and got myself arrested...' I was hyperventilating. I took a deep breath. 'It's a long story. After the hospital I joined a throng heading out of town to the circle. There was a crowd at the bridge. Crazy. Everyone gawking at the damaged reactor. Smoke billowing, fire…'

I got a strange feeling, like a caution.

'Are you still there?' Olga asked.

I sniffed. 'I'm just upset; it's all too much.'

'Shh. I'm here for you. I heard about your run-in with the *militsiya* – some garbled message via the grapevine; I was worried sick; called the station right away; but all the duty officers would tell me is that some air force commander came to transport you to Kiev. Is that where you're calling from?'

I hesitated.

'Mushka?'

There was a scratching on the line.

'Where are you?' she asked.

'I'm not supposed to tell anyone.'

Silence.

'Lena Sergeyevna… we're best friends.'

Oh dear, I've hurt her feelings, I thought. I vacillated, loath to defy Sergey's warning. After all, he'd risked his career for me. But the thought of losing my only friend in the world at that moment was terrifying. 'I'm not sure,' I eventually said, 'At a friend of Sergey's.'

'Sergey? Is that the air force officer that came to transport you to Kiev?' The Sergey I met at the Energetik last year? Don't tell me the air force hunk is in town and you haven't told me?'

I laughed. Already, I felt better. 'Stop,' I said. 'Leave him, he's way too sweet and innocent for you.'

'But okay for you? Hah!'

'He's Yuri's best friend, silly.'

'Don't laugh, it happens. A girl like you…'

'I'm a home girl now.'

'That's easy in Pripyat; there's nowhere to go.'

I chuckled. 'Fair point.'

'See, I've cheered you up already. Isn't it good to laugh? I've missed you, friend; the last few weeks you've been so preoccupied. Let me come and see you, for my sake if nothing else. Not every girl is lucky enough to find love young like you. We need to rely on our friends. You've forgotten what it's like returning to a cold, empty bed night after night.'

'I'm sorry, Olga, don't take it personally, I…'

'Listen, my dear, I'm coming over. Where did you say you are?'

What she'd said was true: hell, I relied heavily on her friendship; I could never survive in Pripyat without her, even with a husband. But still, I hesitated.

'Don't you go quiet on me again.'

'It's just… Sergey will kill me if he finds out,' I said.

'Is he there now?'

'He's back at the base. Said he'd come by in the morning.'

'Perfect! I'll come over right away; we can have dinner, and then I'll be gone. He'll be none the wiser. Come my dear: you've been through hell. Two is always better than one.'

'That's not what you said last month after that fellow dumped you…'

'…for that wench! Her boobs were so big she could hardly stand upright.'

We both laughed. It felt good. I said, 'I love you, friend.'

'Then let me come and comfort you.'

I was out of excuses. The truth was, I was yearning for her company, any company. 'Okay.'

'There's my girl.'

I started to describe the zig-zag route but I hadn't taken note of the street name or number. 'It's two rows behind Lelina,' I said, 'I'll hang a sheet from the window. Don't laugh.'

After we hung up I went to fetch a sheet.

Soon Olga arrived at the door clutching a bunch of yellow roses so big it hid her face, and a paper shopping bag overflowing with provisions. She was dressed in a tightfitting dress that accentuated her slim, muscular legs. 'To cheer you up,' she said, handing over the flowers.

'Ah, that's so sweet, they're gorgeous.'

I plunged my face into the bunch and drank in the scent as the petals tickled my cheek. I was choking with emotion, but I had to be strong. I laid the flowers on the hall table. 'You're too good to me,' I said, taking the bag. 'And this?' I peeked in. 'Salami, bread, veggies and cream, mmm… no, you shouldn't have – *salo*, my favourite, and tea and wine!' I put the bag down and threw my arms around her. Eyes closed, I clung to her for life. Then she lifted me high in her strong arms before plonking me down again.

'Aren't you going to invite me in?' she said.

'Of course; sorry.' I waved her through to the living room.

She placed the bag on the kitchen counter and took in the apartment. I noticed she'd applied lipstick and a touch of rouge.

She narrowed her eyes. 'What are you doing in this dump?'

'It's a long story,' I said.

'Really?'

'I'll explain later.'

She looked put out. 'If you insist.' She ran her fingers over a section of exposed brickwork near the door handle. 'Your so-called friend expects you to stay here?'

'There's everything I need.'

She put her other hand on her waist. 'Tell me: how well do you know this Sergey guy?'

'I told you. He's Yuri's oldest friend.'

'That may be,' Olga said. 'I thought he was nice enough in the beginning at the Energetik, but after we spent some time together, I realised there was something odd about him.'

'What do you mean?'

'The way he looks at a woman, for one thing.'

'That's no surprise, considering the dress you wore.'

'And what was wrong with it?'

'Only that the neckline dropped almost down to your belly button.'

'You can turn heads yourself, kitten.'

'Not with these bee stings.'

She laughed. 'You have other assets.'

'Anyway, it doesn't matter; I have my man now.'

150

Immediately, I regretted my words. 'Sorry,' I said, 'I didn't mean it that way. You being single.'

She shrugged. 'It's okay, I don't need a man to complete me.'

'Listen, Olga, you mustn't be so hard on Sergey. He'd been in Afghanistan, probably hadn't seen a woman not covered by a hijab for six months.'

'It wasn't just the way he looked at me.'

'Aah, I thought so, naughty girl.'

She grinned. 'We drank too much, though that didn't stop him. Your boy is anything but the gentleman he looks in that uniform.'

'Then you two were made for each other.'

'That's rich coming from you.'

We chuckled.

'Come,' I said. 'Let's brew some of this delicious tea you brought.'

I headed to the kitchen, put on the kettle, and got out clean cups.

'I don't suppose this place has a television,' Olga said, scanning the room.

'Only a *radio-tochki*.'

'We should listen for the announcement.'

'About what?'

'You haven't heard the rumours?'

'You mean the evacuation? Sergey mentioned something. I thought he was just trying to scare me. I mean, a whole city of what, forty-five thousand people? Ridiculous.'

'Tell that to the villagers of Chelyabinsk.'

I recoiled. Yuri had once told me about the accident at Chelyabinsk, the very first closed city, but it was supposedly a state secret.

'How do you know about that?' I asked Olga.

She appeared to blush, though perhaps it was the rouge. 'You don't have a monopoly on state secrets.'

I stared at her.

'Relax, you're suspicious of everyone. Do you think I accepted this teaching post in Pripyat, a stone's throw from the biggest nuclear plant in the world, without doing my homework?'

151

'You make it sound like you found this out at the local library.'

'You scratch hard enough, and you find, Mushka.'

I was irritated.

'What else have you found in your scratching? Some dirt on me?'

She rolled her eyes. 'If you're going to be nasty, I'm going.' She was about to pick up the flowers but stopped. 'Keep them.'

I felt panicked. Don't leave me alone, I silently screamed. There was a tremor in my hands, sweaty palms. 'I'm sorry,' I said. 'Can you forgive me? It's just, so much has happened, I...'

Her face softened. 'Of course, my darling. But I'm not letting you sleep here alone.'

'But what if Sergey returns early? He made me promise.'

'And then he abandoned you in this dump? Wake up, Lena. They don't fly helicopters after dark. He's in the officers' mess drinking with the boys – or girls. And you trust this man more than me? Do you think it's just a coincidence he shows up in Pripyat in your hour of need like a knight in shining armour? You know better than to believe in serendipity.'

'Stop,' I said. 'He's a good man.'

'I beg to differ. Listen: come spend the night at my place. We can return at first light. I insist.'

'No. Dermichev's men may be watching your apartment. It's no secret that you and I are best friends.'

She recoiled. 'Who's Dermichev?'

'The officer who questioned me. He's smart. Not your ordinary *militsiya*. You should have seen his face when Sergey and I walked out. Thunder.'

'And it was all, as you put it, a ruse? I told you he's fishy. I'm staying here. Maybe talk some sense into you.'

My eyes darted to the phone.

'How long can you remain a fugitive Mushka? It's crazy. The punishment for evading the *militsiya* will make a trespassing conviction like a slap on the wrist. Go now, give yourself in; a girl I coach on the swim team has a lawyer for a father who owes me. You're a first offender. And any magistrate with half a heart will take your distress into account.'

Olga had a point. 'But I can't betray Sergey, not after what he's risked for me.'

She shook her head. 'Hell, you can be a mule.'

'I'm sorry.'

'At least let me stay over tonight.'

'But that would make you an accomplice.'

'Don't worry about me; I have connections.'

'But a crime is a crime.'

'Hah; you're not that naïve... This is Sovetsky Soyuz.'

I wavered. 'Aren't you playing *durak* tonight?'

'They won't miss me.' She bent to remove her walking shoes. 'In fact, they've been looking for a reason to dump me in favour of that gossip Svetlana. 'Right, that's settled.'

She strode to the kitchenette. 'You must be starving. How about a stew?' She delved into the brown paper packet. 'Let's see: onions, carrots, potatoes, butter, fresh garlic, a side of beef and... ta-da, red wine.'

'A saperavi!' I exclaimed. 'You naughty girl. That's a month's salary.'

She winked. 'Only if you pay.' She fished out a bottle opener, cut the foil and opened it. 'We'll let it air, shall we?'

As we prepared the ingredients and made girl talk, I became filled with conviviality, thinking how lucky I was to have a friend who'd stick by me through my trials, even at the risk of her freedom.

Fourteen

I watched as Olga filled two glasses with saperavi, dark as blood with a rich bouquet. Not thinking to question how she'd procured such expensive wine.

It was easy on the throat with enough tannin for an afterburn and then the kick from the alcohol. One glass, two, and I was floating. Waves of emotion swept over me – gratitude at first, for friendship and the finer things in life, and then a deep longing for my husband. Oh, how terribly I missed him, how worried I was. The dam wall broke and the tears flowed.

'Darling, darling.' Olga placed her hand on mine. 'You've been so brave. What you've been through...' She took my glass and put both on the floor.

I said, 'It scares me to think how dependent I've become on a man. After that Gosbank director I swore I'd never give my heart away again.'

'Sounds like you fall in love at the drop of a hat.'

I smiled weakly. 'I'm a ballerina – we give our hearts away every night. You know Olya, deep down I still fear Yuri might turn out like the others. It's as though I'm waiting for the flat of his hand or another woman to rock up. And how could I blame him for looking elsewhere – after how miserable and neurotic I've become?'

'Nonsense.' She stroked my hand.

After a brief silence, I said, 'I've been suspecting him of having an affair.'

She waited for me to continue.

'With the Yavlinsky woman – can you believe it?'

'Hah, no. Yuri, the squarest of engineers, who only had one serious girlfriend before you?'

'Yes, it sounds ridiculous. I confronted him yesterday. Of course he denied it. Oh, Olya – have I driven him away?'

'How so?'

'I had this terrible thought earlier: imagine if he's used this accident as an excuse to disappear.'

Seemingly nonplussed, she passed me a tissue. 'Go on, cry – it's good to feel deeply.'

'It's also frightening,' I sobbed, 'my mood is like a rollercoaster.

'Men…' She shuffled closer. Our thighs touched. 'I've never found one I can trust. Why do you think he's having it off with Sonya Ustinova?'

'You know her?'

'Of her. Everyone does. Vamp. But what makes you think Yuri…?'

'They work together at Unit Four.'

'So do thousands of others. There must be other reasons you're suspicious.'

'Oh, little things… He's been coming home later sometimes, his clothes dishevelled, too much deodorant…'

'How long has this been going on?'

Olga had a curious expression when she listened intently. Head cocked and stripes on her brow; it made you feel like you were the most important person to her in the world. *Da* – a skill as rare as hens' teeth in this self-obsessed and distracted world.

I blew my nose. I was feeling better already, just for having talked. I shrugged. 'About six weeks, I guess. At first, I ascribed his working late to his obsession with those tests he's been planning since we arrived.'

'Tell me about the tests.'

'I would if I could…; you know how secretive he is about his work.'

She looked sceptical. 'Come now – a woman always knows.'

'No, really, he's disciplined that way.'

'What about papers lying about, the things you overhear on the phone. Amazing what you discover, especially after sex. I've had lovers talk in their sleep.'

I crossed my arms. 'What does it matter? I just want him back.'

'Don't be touchy; I'm only trying to help.'

155

'Sorry; I know.'

'Maybe there's a connection,' she continued. 'The tests and the accident and...'

'Don't you also start now!'

'What?'

'Implying that this was somehow all Yuri's fault – his obsession with seeing what happens when the reactor's power fails.'

'Oh?' She tensed with that querying expression again. Suddenly I knew I'd gone too far. I'd have to extract myself slowly. But before that, I'd need to give out more line.

'His area of research – from before, at Arzamas – had reached its natural end; it required scaling up. That's why he was transferred to Pripyat.'

She nodded.

'Don't ask me to explain. I just know that it's got to do with the core of the reactor; and that the outcome of the test was important for the course of Sovetsky Soyuz's entire nuclear programme.'

'Interesting.' She leaned closer. 'Any out-of-the-ordinary phone calls the past few weeks? Visitors?'

Instinctively, I shifted away. 'Stop: you're starting to sound like Dermichev.'

She bristled. 'Who?'

'I told you. The *militsiya* captain earlier. I think he's KGB.'

She sighed. 'You see the KGB behind every bush.'

'Well, aren't they?'

'Listen: I can see you're getting defensive. Why don't we lighten up a bit?'

'Good idea. I'll go and check on dinner.'

The stew was bubbling away furiously, almost fully reduced. I turned the flame down, added a dash of water, sprinkled in salt and pepper, and stirred. Done, I dished it out and topped up our glasses.

'Sorry,' I said, 'Ordinary, even by my standards. But I'm starving...'

'Thanks.' Olga crossed her arms and frowned. 'I'll bring more interesting ingredients next time.'

Clumsy fool, I berated myself. She'd trekked across town with flowers and expensive treats, offered to stay the night despite the risk to herself, and how was I thanking her? By criticising the food and suspecting the worst.

Ah, some people are experts at making you feel that way. It's always your fault.

'So, is it true,' she said, after swallowing the dregs of her wine, 'what they accused you of – trespassing?'

I drained my glass. 'How do you know that was the charge?'

She blinked. 'I called the station, remember.'

I should have asked her why the police would divulge that sort of detail to a member of the public. Probably, I'd had too much wine. Regardless, I was afraid of aggravating things between us.

Olga leaned forward, elbows on the table, accentuating the bulk of her shoulders. There was a strong sensuality about her, despite her rather heavy muscles.

Olga looked at her glass, running her finger around its tip. 'It was a foolish thing to do, Matrushka – walk straight into the mouth of the beast with all that radiation spewing, but I admire your courage.'

My hand slid instinctively to my stomach. I felt a stab of guilt.

I hadn't told her I was pregnant. Perhaps subconsciously I had my doubts about how well she could keep a secret.

I shifted my plate aside, and leaned forward, chin on my palms. 'I'm sorry if I seem cagey, Olya. It's just that Yuri and I have such an intense relationship.' Her knee touched mine and remained there, but I didn't move away. 'I'm only his second lover – imagine. It's like the classic fairy tale in reverse, where the innocent man is rescued by the woman of the world. Of course, he has his faults, but in a strange way I feel purified by simply spending time with him. And God knows, I'm in need of that!'

'You're too hard on yourself. I think you're an angel.'

'Fallen angel, don't you mean?'

She chuckled. 'Don't let your failures define you; learn and grow stronger; that's how our species got out of the primordial sludge.'

There it was again, our 'gospel of determinism' – evolution. We had it force-fed from our first Young Pioneers camp.

Olga splayed her legs; her thigh brushed mine.

I felt a jolt, a strange mixture of delight and unease. I needed to get away. I stood up, queasy from the wine and the fatty stew.

'I wonder if they'll report the accident on *Vremya*?' she said.

'National News?' I laughed. 'A meteor is more likely to land on the Kremlin.'

Bad news was a rarity in Sovetsky Soyuz. Crimes like muggings, thefts or murders weren't possible in a utopia which, according to Mecheny, would be a fait accompli by '96.

'There's no TV here, anyway,' I said and excused myself to go outside to think.

With the moon yet to rise, and smoke-muffled starlight, it was darker in the courtyard than a Crimean fog. And almost as quiet; the only sound was a distant screech of a train braking. My spirit felt troubled, but I couldn't pinpoint why. Olga's questions perhaps? Or the way our legs touched. But my eyes were soon stinging and that metallic residue was collecting at the back of my throat again, so thick I had to spit. Then a hand grabbed my wrist and I swivelled about.

'*Blin*, Olya, you frightened me.'

'You all right?' she said.

'Just thinking.'

'Come.' She pulled me toward the door. 'You shouldn't be outside.'

After all the exertion of the day, I desperately needed a shower and bed. Olga said she'd freshened up, so I showered and rinsed out my clothes. There were no towels, so I scrounged a tablecloth from the kitchen. I offered Olga exclusive use of the bed, but she wouldn't hear of it after all I'd been through. So, we agreed to share the bed and sleep in our birthday suits.

'Won't you help?' she asked, fumbling at the back of her dress.

'Sure,' I said, but by the second button my hands were trembling. When her dress slipped to the floor, I stepped back. She had broad, muscled shoulders in perfect da Vinci proportions, a surprisingly nar-row waist and slender but athletic legs. Then she turned and took my breath away – her breasts were two sizes larger than mine, yet pert above a taut stomach. I'd seen countless naked bodies backstage during costume changes, where privacy was a foreign concept, but dancers were invariably skinny and small-breasted.

My eye was drawn to the dark figurine tattooed between the swell of her left breast and collarbone, with a diameter smaller than a rouble coin, which made me gasp. In Sovetsky Soyuz, body art was taboo – not from religious mores, but because the Party saw it as an act of subversion.

'You like it? Come here, feel how smooth it is.'

I hesitated. We were barely a foot apart. I could feel her body heat. Tentatively, I ran my finger over the image. It was exquisite, the wings indigo, orange and translucent like a stained-glass window. 'Where did you get that done?'

'I'll tell you in bed. Let's chat before we go to sleep.'

We slipped under the covers, head to toe, both in soldier position. At first, we were silent. From where I lay, I could see out the window to where the moon had risen – a cheesy yellow one, past half, with a faint halo. My thoughts turned to Yuri. My darling, my darling, I called silently, are you out there somewhere, gilded by the same moon? But soon my thoughts turned to worry. Why did nobody at the plant, the Party Office, the *militsiya* station, or the hospital have any record of him? Surely, it was too much coincidence to simply be bungled paperwork. Immediately, I feared the worst. Had he been deliberately 'erased'? No! I silently cried, I'm too young to be a widow! And what if my injury doesn't heal? How will I dance and make a living?'

Olga cleared her throat. 'You still want to hear about the tattoo?'

'If it helps me understand you better.'

She took my hand. 'That's so sweet.'

'First, tell me,' I said, 'Why so high on your chest? Aren't you worried someone will see it?'

She laughed. 'That's the last thing we worried about in Barashevo.'

I was stunned.

Barashevo was an infamous prison in Moldova, part of a network of camps called the *Dubravlag*. My mama was in one called Yavas. I was never supposed to find out. But once, back in the village for summer break, I'd come upon a letter from Mama under Babushka's bed. The colourful postage stamp drew my attention. Babushka promised to show me the next letter, but it never came. Mama was long dead. Most inmates at Yavas were 'politicals' – academics, intellectuals, poets and teachers branded dangerous to the state simply for being free thinkers who dared to express their conscience.

But Olga had never struck me as a dissident. So, when she uttered the word Barashevo, I stared in shock.

'You – in prison? Why?'

'This stays between us, okay?'

'You have my word.'

She paused. 'I killed a man.'

'What?' I was flabbergasted.

'The bastard. He'd been beating me for months. My only regret is he didn't suffer more in the process. That night he came back blind drunk, slapped me around, vomited on the bed, then ordered me to clean it up so we could have sex. If I didn't, he'd shove my head in a bucket of water. By then I'd taken precautions. A knife…'

She exhaled. So, there you have it: my deepest, darkest secret. The real reason I retired early from swimming.'

'Not the LA boycott! Olya, you poor thing; I'm amazed you're so together after that ordeal. I'd rather die than go to prison.' By then *tam-izdat* had done the rounds, and most citizens had learned the terrible truth from survivors like Solzhenitsyn.

'*Zeks* who said things like that didn't last long,' Olga countered. 'Better to accept your new reality – even if you were blameless.'

I didn't press her further. All she volunteered was that the KGB hammered at her door at two in the morning. A neighbour had heard the argument and seen Olga throw the knife in the trash. After a week in the Lubyanka basement, she spent three days in a cattle car with a few dozen other women to reach a snow-covered siding in the middle of nowhere.

Then we slipped into light-hearted girly talk. I told her about my time at the Bolshoi, which cheered me no end – the good times, the camaraderie, the adoring audiences. How wonderful it felt after all the

160

anxiety and uncertainty of the day to completely relax and be myself with a friend. Soon, waves of sleep were lapping over me until I struggled to keep my eyes open.

When I awoke, the moon was no longer visible from the window. I felt uncomfortably warm and peeled the blanket off. Surprisingly, Olga no longer lay top-to-toe, and her leg lay across mine. Where our skin touched it felt wet from perspiration, but I was reluctant to wake her. So, I lay, listening to her gentle, rhythmical breathing. Usually, on a windless night, I'd hear the creatures of the forest – a nightjar twittering, a whoo-hoo or the howl of a wolf. But they'd all fled.

How did they know, these so-called wild animals? With no standing army, no government, no bureaucracy, they had the sense to leave – and then return to our 'wasteland' at just the right time. Less than a generation on, foxes, elk and mushrooms all flourish in a thicker, brighter green forest.

Olga's breathing grew shallow and irregular. We both knew the other was awake but neither wanted to be the first to talk. The minutes ticked by until I started nodding off. Then I felt Olga's hand slide across my stomach. Dreaming, I thought, and rolled into a foetal position. She shifted closer until her knee touched my back. I kept feigning sleep. She snuggled closer until her body matched mine, contour for contour. By then, every muscle in my body had tensed.

Not from scruples. I'd seen a lot. Moscow in the '80s had a thriving bohemian scene – dancers, poets, painters, musicians, almost like before the Revolution. But the punishment for 'homosex' was five years' hard labour in a camp. Strangely though, it only applied to men. The authorities generally turned a blind eye with women.

Olga wiggled closer until our bodies were like peas in a pod. I could feel her nipples pressing against my back.

'Olga?'

'Yes.'

'What are you doing?'

'Just cuddling.'

'Okay.'

We lay still, but I couldn't relax, let alone sleep. Then I felt her hand slide up the side of my thigh.

Yet again, I kept quiet when I should have spoken.

'Just say and I'll stop,' she whispered in my ear. Her fingers moved over to my stomach.

'Stop,' I said without conviction.

I sensed her stiffen. She withdrew her body a fraction.

'Sorry I bothered; you're in another world.'

'Wouldn't you be?'

'Yuri?'

'Of course.'

'My darling… Don't be such a worry wart. I bet he's safe and sound in some clinic, being discharged as we speak.'

'But what if…? I can't bear to think he might be suffering and I'm not there for support.'

'I know, but there's nothing either of us can do to help him right now, is there? What's wrong with enjoying some comfort from each other?'

'I'm married, for one thing.'

'Hah; so now you're Miss Faithful; you, of all people.'

I should have heeded the signs. I'd never told her anything of my dating in Moscow; she'd only known me as a faithfully married wife. Instead, I muttered something about not wanting to hurt Yuri.

'Fine,' She retracted her hand and rolled onto her back, arms folded. 'Be like that. I was only trying to be a good friend. Goodnight then.'

I was beginning to feel desperate. I couldn't bear her being angry with me. I was so lost and lonely and worried, but also angry and jealous of Yuri's attraction to Sonya, and physically and emotionally exhausted. I longed for comfort, to be held by another human being and feel warm and safe in the fantasy that someone cared for me.

After another silence, Olga said, 'Are you going to trust me to help you or not?'

I turned on my side to face her and nodded.

'You promise?'

'Of course, you're my best friend. Why do you ask?'

'Remember that time on the ferry from Kiev – when we promised each other there'd be no secrets?'

'I do.'

'Then why are you hiding things from me?'

'Who says I am?'

'I'm not stupid, Mushka.'

'What do you think I'm not telling you?'

'Things.'

'Like?'

'Let's start with Yuri...'

'Yes?'

'When you got to Pripyat, you two had stars in your eyes. These last few weeks, you're in parallel worlds.'

'He's been obsessed with his job, the stress of those tests.'

She inhaled, paused slightly and said, 'Any strange behaviour recently?'

'I've told you about my suspicions.'

'That woman? Forget about her. If anything, it'll be over in no time; she's no match for you. It must be something going on at work.'

'I don't know.'

Silence. Then she rolled over with her back to me. 'Okay, if that's the way you'd like to play this.'

I panicked. I said, 'There was a phone call...'

'Go on.'

'About a month ago... during lunch hour. I came to the apartment to get my purse. Yuri didn't hear me. You know how I move like a cat.'

'And the caller?'

'Yuri addressed him formally; I assumed it was his superior in Moscow. He assured him that preparations for the test were complete, for the twenty-sixth. Then there was a disagreement.'

'Oh'?

'Something about whether the documents were ready.'

'A contract?'

'I'm not sure. From the context I thought it might be a *propiska*. I

163

remember feeling hopeful that, finally, he'd realised how truly miserable I'd become, and was arranging a transfer back to Moscow.'

'And then?'

'I felt a sneeze coming on. I suppressed it, backtracked and left.'

'And that was it?'

'Yes.'

'Mmm…'

'Why are you asking?'

'There's something fishy about Yuri's disappearance.'

'Oh?'

'If our government excels in anything, it's accurate records. Dead and missing reports are seldom wrong. And surely, if there'd been a mix-up, Yuri would have tried to contact you by now.'

'Maybe he's already tried,' I said. 'Think: if he's released, he'll either try to call or physically return to our apartment. He could be there as we speak.'

'He could also call Sergey.'

'No. Yuri wouldn't have known Sergey was in Pripyat; his visit was unplanned; he flew in this morning on the containment mission.'

She chuckled, 'He should have called me.'

'Very funny. I thought you only swapped body fluids.'

We both laughed. I was feeling cheerier already.

She took my hand. 'I tell you what: let's go over in the morning and have a look.'

'No. I promised Sergey. Besides, Dermichev must have posted surveillance. It would be suicide.

But Sergey could arrange something; I have no doubt.'

'Well then…' She gently squeezed my hand. 'There's nothing else to be done till morning.'

And so, we lay holding hands in silence. But neither of us could sleep; we were too aware of each other's breathing. At length, I felt her pulling my hand toward her, palm down, on her thigh, then up toward her waist…

She shifted closer. I stiffened.

'Do I repel you, Lena?'

I shook my head.

'Are you scared?'

I shook my head. All my senses were heightened.

'What's the problem, then?

'We're best friends, for one thing.' I ran my finger across her collar-bone and down to her tattoo. 'Did you learn to... in the camps?'

She remained silent.

'You should have told me about your ordeal earlier. The thought of just one day of strict regime labour terrifies me. I don't know how you survived for... how long?'

'Three years, nearly. A person can get used to anything.'

In retrospect, I should have asked her why not the usual five.

'Would you still have been my friend, knowing that I killed a person?'

I kept still as a statue.

'It's all right, you don't have to answer.'

I inhaled sharply, but still I was rigid.

Ah, my little dove, I suppose there are some things even a mother and daughter shouldn't talk about. I didn't love her; I wasn't even particularly attracted. I just desperately needed a friend right then. It was a moment of tenderness and mutual kindness – or so I believed at the time. Regardless, I've never touched another woman that way again.

Fifteen

That night I lay awake gazing through the window with Olga asleep beside me. What had I done, I kept thinking? I had finally succumbed to her desires, but now I felt dreadful.

In retrospect, I'd been flirting with depression for years. Perhaps the trigger was being orphaned, or wrenched from my village, or being the outsider. And maybe a genetic chemical imbalance. Who knows?

Of course, it was never diagnosed. That was a fate worse than death in Sovetsky Soyuz. Unlike today when it's almost fashionable to talk about your feelings. No matter how dreadful I felt – even to the point of suicide – I didn't dare breathe a word for fear of *psikhushka* – a psychiatric ward. Papa's fate.

So what can I tell you about your grandfather, my darling? I wish I'd known him better; perhaps I was too young. Besides, he was either away or working. He was an educationalist. Apparently, he started out teaching Russian literature at the local school, became principal, and then went on to Narkompros, the Commissariat for Education.

But according to Babushka, he was too ambitious and outspoken. So, eventually one morning they came. They 'diagnosed' him with a cocktail of sluggish schizophrenia, anti-social personality disorder and anti-Soviet thinking.

Only three of his letters ever got through the censors. Then they simply stopped, as though he'd gone for a stroll and never returned. The official cause of death was tuberculosis. More likely *psikhushka* broke him.

And so, during my time in the old country, I made sure to avoid being diagnosed with depression.

Not that things are much better here in America. You're virtually uninsurable if you admit to a mental illness. That's one of the reasons I only sought help in my late thirties, when you were going into middle school. And I didn't have much choice.

It was terrible. Remember I told you I was promoted to manager of the bar area, but worried about losing my outsized tips as a dancer? It was irrational fear. But any sudden or major life change can trigger depression. Anyway, I didn't sleep for three months. I wouldn't wish that endless trudge through the dark valley on my worst enemy. It's no coincidence that the organs used sleep deprivation for torture.

When finally – hallelujah – I got diagnosed and put on anti-depressants, it was a revelation, like a mist had cleared and I could see things in perspective. I also realised I'd been living for most of my life at a level of happiness several notches below normal. Within weeks I was calm and slept like a log. I can't tell you what a relief that was.

But pills only help for so long. You need the head doctor to properly straighten the twists in your psyche. Which is a long and expensive process. By the time I could afford it – only at the end of last year – I didn't know it but I already had one foot in the grave.

Fortunately, it's always seemed to me that you inherited your father's cheerfulness. I'm very glad of that. But don't take it for granted; you never know when the black dog might bite. Above all, my darling, guard your sleep. When darkness falls and you're alone, and the day's distractions fade, the worst of possibilities can take root in a vulnerable mind. One bad night can become two and then three… and soon you're always second-guessing yourself.

Like that last night in Pripyat. I lay awake feeling horrified at how much I'd told Olga. In contrast, Olga slept like a baby, her face as peaceful as an angel. But who was she? I'd known her less than a year… What if…?

Then I pulled myself together. I had to focus on the here and now – what to do next. Returning to the plant would be suicide, and the hospital had been a fruitless exercise. I could go to Yavlinsky; evil was always an option. But the mere thought of seeing him again nauseated me, and I'd have to try to explain why I'd missed our afternoon 'meeting'.

Then I thought about the shadow I'd seen in our apartment from the *militsiya* car.

My heart leapt.

If only I knew the number of our spinner, I'd call to see if he was there. But it was Yuri's secret connection to Moscow. No point asking Sergey to take me there tomorrow. He'd already refused, because Dermichev's men would be watching it. But what if Dermichev hadn't yet discovered Sergey's duplicity? There was still a slender window of opportunity, but I'd have to go now, under cover of darkness. Yes, Sergey would be appalled after all he'd risked for me. Yet there comes a time when you must choose what matters most. I had to find Yuri.

I shifted to the edge of the bed. Olga muttered. I froze. Then she moaned and rolled over. I waited.

My watch said three forty-five. I must have drifted off! I slipped out of the bed and onto the floor. I got up, did a *bourrée* across the floor to retrieve my still damp clothes and purse, and was outside without a stir from Olga.

The moon was mostly eclipsed, the night was dark and my footsteps loud. I heard a scuffle ahead on the pavement and peered into the gloom. Nothing. A movement… As my eyes adjusted, the outline of a rat materialised. It ogled me with glinting red eyes and scurried off. On I walked, hearing the sounds of an occasional vehicle as I neared the intersection with Lelina Avenue. There, I waited in the shadow of a building to observe. Smoke swirled about the streetlamps, casting a ghostly yellow halo. Nothing in sight. After a few minutes, a bus passed without passengers, then another. When I was confident the coast was clear, I set off down Lelina, hugging the shadows of the juvenile beech trees lining the sidewalk. There was no sign of the sprayers or fire trucks. Perhaps they'd moved on to other parts of the city.

Fortunately, no vehicles passed in the couple of minutes until I arrived at the entranceway of our *khrushchyovka*. There I tensed, thinking that just last night Yuri had trod this same path to the bus, his colleagues hailing him, while I basked in the afterglow of our love. How quickly my life had changed! Like a runaway train.

I glanced about furtively. Only one car – a dark olive, hard to see exactly – was parked across the street without lights, otherwise our street was deserted. It was now or never... I inhaled, darted through the foyer and... phew, I was in! My hopes grew as I spiralled up the stairwell, and by the time I'd glided the length of the corridor, I could picture Yuri on the sofa reading a magazine.

I eased the key into the door. It swung open. I called his name, but only an echo greeted me. I tiptoed in. The door closed behind me. It was pitch black, but instinctively I sensed the emptiness.

Suddenly desolation overwhelmed me, and a primordial howl burst from deep inside. I sank to the floor in the darkness, heaving with sobs. At that moment I didn't care if I woke every damned soul in the building.

The something soft stroked my ankle.

'Matrushka!' I cried, delighted and ashamed at the same time. She rubbed up, purring, and I scooped her frail body into my arms and cuddled her. 'Oh, my darling. How could I have forgotten you? I'm so sorry. Forgive me.'

Finally, I rose. A flashing red light flickered across the interior wall. Perhaps a fire truck? It helped direct me to the window to close the drapes. Then I switched on the light.

Chaos! Everywhere I looked, chairs were overturned and cupboard doors open, their contents strewn on the parquet floor. The kitchen floor was sprinkled with spilled flour, broken eggs and shards of crockery.

For a split second I took the shambles to mean Yuri had been back to make food and fetch his belongings for some reason. But he was obsessively neat. I navigated through the mess to the bedroom. Not as bad as the living room, but a few items tossed around, and Yuri's lampshade broken.

I stood trying to process it. My first thought was the KGB. But what didn't Yavlinsky already know? His men had scoured the apartment before we moved in. In the following weeks, they'd also done the occasional clandestine search. I'd noticed little things like a rug out of place. But it had stopped when Yavlinsky became more concerned with his nefarious self-enrichment scheme. Which made the wanton destruction in the living room this time seem strange. There was no indication of a thorough search. Had it been done in a hurry? Or to make a point? Dermichev had stated clearly that he was looking for Yuri. Could that be the reason? Having not found their man, might his henchmen have made the mess out of pure spite?

Then another, more sinister idea occurred to me: if Yuri had returned to the apartment earlier this evening, could the shambles be because he'd resisted arrest? Was he locked up somewhere?

My speculation was interrupted by a rap at the door. I froze, my heart thumping. The KGB! That car across the road…

I heard a jingle in the corridor. This time I'd surely get a criminal record, and I could kiss goodbye any hope of dancing again.

Another knock. I thought of hiding. But no, they'd already seen me. Best to be confident. Anyway, since when was it a crime to be in your own home? I padded toward the door, rose onto my toes, and peered through the peephole.

Pyotr Pavlovich! *Phew…* Never had those hooded eyes of our busy-body neighbour been so welcome. Dressed in his pyjamas he looked comical. I considered ignoring him. But he'd obviously heard my howling. And he would surely call the *militsiya*. I straightened my dress, plumped my hair and opened the door.

'Lena Sergeyevna?'

'Yes, I live here,' I replied sarcastically. 'What are you doing up? It's past four in the morning.'

He eyed my clothes. 'What's going on?'

'I wish I knew.'

Then, looking past me, his jaw dropped. '*Blin!*' he said, 'who did that?'

'I'm hoping you can tell me,' I replied.

He shrugged. Then his eyes narrowed. 'Where've you been?'

'Uh… with a friend.'

'And Yuri?'

'I don't know; that's the problem; he didn't return from his shift.'

'Which reactor is he at again?'

'Number Four.'

His eyes dropped to the floor. 'I heard. Is he all right?'

'I don't know; he's missing.'

'I'm sorry. I'm sure he'll show up soon. How are you?'

As if you care, I wanted to say. We eyed each other for a few awkward moments.

'Well then,' he said, stepping back. 'I'd better be going. Let me know if I can help.'

'No wait, before you go, did you hear anything over the past few hours?'

He pretended to think, then shook his head.

'Please. If you remember anything… I'm worried sick for Yuri; and I have a feeling all this…' I pointed toward the floor, 'might somehow be connected with his disappearance.'

He ran his fingers through his hair. Then he checked the corridor. 'Okay,' he whispered, 'But you didn't hear this from me…' He leaned closer. 'Must have been shortly past twelve.' He crossed his arms. 'First I thought it was KGB. But wouldn't they bash the door down? The knocking was soft. Then a scratch and a click. I assumed it was your husband returning early. But then there was scraping, like furniture being moved and breaking glass. I…'

'Pyotr!' came a shriek from down the corridor. Martina's voice was so shrill we use to joke that it could penetrate a bunker. I'd only met her once, on our second night, when she came to complain about being woken when Yuri left for work.

'Pyotr!' she yelled again.

'I'm coming, dear.' He looked at me, dolefully. 'Sorry, I must go.'

'No, wait,' I cried, grabbing his wrist. 'You were saying?'

He fended me off. 'I've told you everything I know; I was probably hearing things; I'm sorry.' He slipped deftly past me and disappeared along the passage, back to the comfort of his wife. I was left alone in a sterile corridor. Dejected, I turned. As the door clicked shut behind me I burst into tears.

Fortunately, Matrushka brushed up against my ankles again. At least they hadn't harmed her. I lifted her to my chest, and then took her to the kitchen to get her some food. Instantly, I felt better. Then I noticed the sky bluing. I had to get back before Olga woke! So, I hurried across the living room toward the bedroom, scrunching over shards of glass. I took in the carnage with fresh eyes. Our love nest, our sanctuary, had been deliberately violated, and the pictures had been ripped off the walls. What if Dermichev had phoned Vulytsia Volodymyrska after the shift change and spoken to someone Sergey hadn't briefed? Had he learned that I never arrived in Kiev? He'd surely order his men to search our apartment. But the ransacking seemed so wanton. I replayed the interrogation in my mind. Like Yavlinsky, Dermichev had been fixated on Yuri, asking the same stupid details – work habits, phone calls, papers, the days leading up to the accident. Did they both seriously suspect my husband of sabotage? Preposterous!

Nevertheless, my heart was thumping. And my spirit was beginning to crumble.

Would I ever escape the clutches of the KGB? They'd already taken my grandfather, my father and my mother, then threatened Babushka to force my collaboration. Now both Yuri and I, it seemed, were next on the list.

I felt a wave of gratitude that at least I'd been able to protect Babushka in her final months and she'd never discovered that her own granddaughter had become a snitch.

Ah, that's another cat out of the bag now... Ivanov's lure of knee surgery when he recruited me in Moscow was only half the story. He'd threatened to institutionalise Babushka. Somehow – probably through her doctor – he'd discovered that she'd been diagnosed with dementia. But it was in the early stages, and she could have enjoyed several happy years of independent living in the village. So, after much agonising, I agreed to spy on Yuri, on the assurance it would only be for a season. I wasn't to know that she would die of a stroke just a month before Yuri and I married. My last remaining relative. The only sliver of light from that tragedy was that the KGB lost some leverage, emboldening me to defy them later.

By now, barely eighteen months since the KGB had drawn me into its web, it already felt like a lifetime: I was drained by the constant surveillance, the threat of being summoned and the need to lie repeatedly. But what choice did I have? It wasn't the kind of organisation you could simply resign from.

My thoughts were interrupted by the sound of a car coming to a stop outside. I peeked out the bedroom window. A sedan had just parked across the street, out of the lamplight. The passenger door opened, then the driver's door. Two stocky men alighted, both looking in my direction. I nipped behind the drapes again. They sauntered across the street toward our building. Every instinct in me screamed to get away. But I waited until I was sure they'd passed from the line of sight beneath the balcony before moving. I guessed I had a minute, maybe two... and headed straight for the bedroom.

Sixty seconds to take stock of my life and distil my priorities into a single small kit bag.

I grabbed my dance bag off the floor, which was empty but for my pointe shoes. I snatched up some clean clothes and underwear and threw them in. Then, I reached under the bed for *Chetki*, my beloved book of Akhmatova's poetry.

I felt under the beside drawer for the envelope with my emergency stash of roubles. Mercifully it was still there. Thank God they'd left without searching our bedroom.

I went to the bathroom for toiletries and lipstick. A glance in the mirror made me recoil from the bags under my eyes.

Finally, I remembered Yuri's treasure. I pulled open his dresser drawer, crouched and shoved in my hand. The cherrywood box was still there. Whoever had been in wasn't looking for our possessions, that was clear. Or they'd been interrupted. In trepidation, I slid the top off, lifted the pouch, and shook the contents onto the bed: his passport, roubles, papers, a photo of our wedding – and surprisingly, an orthodox cross, perhaps a family heirloom. Downstairs I heard muffled voices. I returned his passport to the drawer, stuffed the rest into the kit bag, grabbed a photo of Yuri from a broken frame and bolted from the bedroom. But before I reached the front door, I picked up dear old Matrushka. Her eyes were dilated and she appeared listless. Feeling terrible, I cuddled her, letting her face nuzzle in the crook of my arm and her whiskers tickle my skin. Then I hurried to the kitchen for a tin of pickled fish and spooned it into her bowl together with the remains of our *salo*. How desperately I wanted to take her!

Finally, I snatched up my purse from beside the door and marched out into the corridor. Still deserted, luckily. But from the stairwell came the echo of bootsteps. I shuffled toward the fire escape. Down I spiralled, feet barely touching until I hit the ground floor. Soon I found myself in a musty, windowless enclosure, so dark I couldn't see my hand in front of me. Predictably, I stumbled into the door. From upstairs came a muted rapping; probably the two thugs at our apartment. I fumbled at a handle. It was horizontal and solid, so I pulled. Nothing happened. I pressed. Still nothing budged. Finally, I leaned my full weight and bounced up and down until it finally swung open to a rush of fresh air.

I stood staring down an alleyway, toward Lelina Avenue. A car light flashed past. I turned. The alley was deserted. From above came the whimper of a baby. A frog croaked nearby. I slipped onto the back street and broke into a limping jog, keeping to the shadows until I'd zig-zagged two blocks. Then I stopped to catch my breath. The sky above held a hint of dawn. On I strode as normally as I could with the discomfort in my knee, expecting at any moment to be apprehended.

Somehow, I successfully retraced my steps to Sergey's apartment. I put my ear to the door. Silence. The door squeaked open. I tiptoed across the lounge and peeked into the bedroom. Still sleeping. I retreated to the living room and slumped onto the sofa, trying to calm myself with slow, deep breaths, watching through the window as the sky gradually lightened.

The daylight helped to vanquish my ghosts. Pink and blood orange it glowed, warmer and brighter until I thought the sky would burst into flames, though in the end it simply smouldered to a dull yellow. I must have fallen asleep eventually, because when my eyes struggled open, a curtain of sun cut across the living room, causing the wall beside me to glow. Disoriented, I reached over for Yuri. Oh, the ache in my heart when I felt the strange sofa and realised he wasn't there…!

Then I heard a rumbling outside, like a bus idling. Still in a daze, I swung my legs to the floor. wrenched the sliding doors open and staggered into the courtyard. As my foot struck sand and brick I came to my senses. Sobered, I mounted the sandpile and peered into the street, just in time to see the UAZ. Sergey was back! I gasped, could it be that late? I rushed inside and, using the window as a mirror, straightened my hair and dress. At least my dress had dried. My face was pale as death against my jet-black hair, so I dabbed on some lipstick. Back in the living room, I shoved my kit bag behind the sofa.

Outside, a car door closed. I scanned the apartment. The bedroom door… Oh no! Olga had promised to be gone before he arrived. I pressed my ear to the wood. Thankfully, silence. But then came a groan.

A confident tread approached along the path. Sergey, no doubt. What to do? It was too late to get rid of Olga.

'Lenochka,' he called. 'You there?'

My mind was all over the place.

He rapped again. 'Lena!'

'It's open.'

Click, woosh, and there he stood in the doorway in full dress uniform – the greys and charcoals ironed to perfection with the DVD insignia on his peak: an eagle clasping a sword, like the Romanov coat of arms.

I was breathless.

'You look terrible,' he said, removing his peak.

'Thanks.'

'Sorry. I'm a soldier, I shoot straight. You tired?'

'I didn't sleep well.'

'The bed's not comfortable?'

'No, no, unfamiliar surroundings, that's all.'

'You'd tell me if something was wrong, wouldn't you?'

'Of course.'

'You going to invite me in?'

'Ah…' I feigned embarrassment. From behind, I heard a doorhandle turn. But Sergey had already taken a step forward. I waved him in. 'Sorry for the mess.'

Sergey was looking past me.

I turned. 'No, Olga,' I mumbled, 'that's not fair.'

She had emerged from the bedroom in her crumpled dress with one shoulder bare and her hair a dishevelled mass of curls.

'Um…' I ventured. 'Sergey, you remember Olga?'

'Sure, from the disco last year.'

She blushed. There was an awkward silence.

'Olga was such a dear to come over,' I said, 'I don't know if I could have managed alone.'

Sergey glared at me. 'I told you…'

'Olga's like a sister.'

'Wicked stepsister, maybe.'

'Huh?!' Olga spat. 'Take that back.'

Sergey remained deadpan.

'All right, then,' she said. 'If this is the thanks I get…' She flounced into the bedroom and slammed the door.

Sergey and I stared at her wake, and then at each other.

He was frowning. He shook his head in disgust. 'That was a big mistake,' he said, taking a seat at the table.

'Sorry,' I said. 'Really. It's just… a person has to trust someone in this life. How else does one function?

'Still, you promised.'

I shrugged apologetically. 'Would you like some tea?'

The tension in the room was palpable.

I was aware he was watching me throughout. I found tea in the cupboard and tossed some leaves into the samovar. Then I lit the stove.

Suddenly, the bedroom door flew open. There was Olga in the same skin-tight outfit with her hair in a ponytail so taut it narrowed her eyes. She stomped past us toward the door.

'Where are you going?' I called.

'A girl knows when she's not welcome,' she said, shutting the door without a good-bye.

'Oh, well…' I got out two mugs and placed the samovar on the table, sat down opposite Sergey and poured.

He warmed his hands on his mug. 'I have good news,' he said.

'Ah… at last… please.'

He paused. 'You're no longer under investigation.'

'What?'

'You're clear.'

'You mean the trespassing charges…'

'Dismissed. Extenuating circumstances. You simply did what any faithful wife would do. The *militsiya* apologised – verbally, that is.'

'But…' I gaped. I was about to ask about the trashing of my apartment last night, but instead said, 'I'm stunned. You mean, I'm free to go – just like that? How did you do it?'

He paused. 'Well, yes and no. Officially, you're clear. But I'd be lying if I said there's no risk.'

'What do you mean?'

'Sometimes individuals within the security apparatus pursue their own vendettas.'

'Oh?'

'Dermichev, for example. I could see he took what happened yesterday very personally.'

'I suppose.'

'So you need to be careful. That's why I'm urging you to get out of Pripyat as soon as possible. He's been given a fair degree of latitude down here to conduct his "special investigations". There's no saying what he might do.'

I considered this a moment. It was sobering. 'I see. Anyway, how did you do it? Arrange to expunge my case?'

He winked. 'A friend at the Ministry of the Interior, Kiev Oblast. He's a Lieutenant-Colonel, formerly of our helicopter unit.'

'But here in Pripyat…'

'Yes, but he's got clout.'

My mind raced. 'But you just said Dermichev was a law unto himself?'

It was true that his questions the previous day hadn't focused on my trespassing, but rather on Yuri.

Sergey stared into his mug. 'Down here, yes. And he'll be smarting; but for now he's under pressure to accept it.'

'Really? He struck me as well-connected – Moscow through and through.'

'He's a lightweight.'

'Compared to whom?'

Sergey gave a wry smile. 'How's Deputy Bureau Chief?'

'Whatever that means.'

'A dog barks in Siberia and he knows about it.'

I shivered. 'I didn't know you associated with those monsters.'

'Knowing them doesn't make me one.' Sergey sipped his tea. 'But what matters is, you're free.'

'And my file – will there be a record?'

'Well, I'm not a magician. But you weren't convicted. It will say something like insufficient evidence.'

'So… you mean…?' I stared. Then I flung my arms about him, crying. 'How can I ever thank you enough?' I embraced him with all my might. I nestled my face in the crook of his shoulder, thinking, my benevolent warrior, my Soviet Achilles, don't ever let me go.

Eventually, my crying faded to a whimper. But still, I shook like a leaf. He held me tight, stroking my hair and whispering comfort in my ear. Only when I finally relaxed, did he pull away.

'Sorry,' I said, wiping my face with my sleeve. 'More tea?'

'No thanks. I must deliver a briefing at eleven.'

'Oh?'

'Our squadron flies to Kabul today. Bloody Mujahedeen decide to attack our base again. It could mean months in that godforsaken country.' He flicked a speck from his chest.

'What about going to Kiev?'

Sergey replaced his peak. 'I've arranged a place for you on the noon ferry. Lieutenant Svechin will fetch you just now and take you to the terminal. Be ready from eleven am. That's in an hour.'

I shook my head. 'I told you, I'm not leaving Pripyat before I know Yuri's fate.'

He stepped toward me. 'Come on, Lena, don't…'

'No! I'm not fleeing while he could still be out there, trapped in that wretched inferno.'

He took my wrist. 'Listen: there's nothing you can do; put one foot on the road to the plant and you're finished; not even I could help you. Besides…' He glanced at my stomach. 'Yuri would want you out of harm's way.'

'Don't you dare start with that again!' I shrieked.

He looked agonised. Then he seemed to mull something. 'What if I told you my sources say someone matching Yuri's description was admitted to Hospital Number Eighteen in Kiev yesterday afternoon?'

It's impossible to describe the surge of hope I felt.

'Where did you hear that?' I blurted.

He muttered something unintelligible, then said, 'Don't get your hopes up. It's second-hand information. Anyway, I must warn you: this person's burn wounds were so bad that a positive ID was impossible.'

'Exactly,' I replied, 'What if it's not him? And he's still stuck under that mangled concrete and steel, exposed to the radiation and the smoke? How could I live with myself if ran away before I'd done everything in my power to help him? Sorry: I can't, and I won't!'

He sighed. 'I don't understand you, Lena.'

'Don't try.'

He looked down, fiddled with his buckle. 'It's just…'

'What?'

'Well… Yuri made me swear that if anything happened to him, I'd watch out for you.'

'That's sweet, but I'm not a helpless baby.'

Sergey looked as if he was about to manhandle me to the car; instead, he rose on his heels. 'You're a stubborn woman. Just promise me you won't resist the evacuation orders.'

I nodded, just to please him.

Good, I'll get your name on the right evacuation list. He fished a small piece of paper from his pocket. 'As soon as you arrive in Kiev, which is where they're taking residents from this section of Pripyat, find a pay phone and call this number. They'll arrange your papers. My contact here couldn't get them done in time. Do exactly as they tell you; and don't breathe a word of this to a soul.'

I stared at him.

'Don't worry, you should be all right getting to Kiev. If you don't delay.'

'But... I thought you said I've been exonerated?'

'Yes and no. I can't explain now. Just do what I say.'

'Will I see you there? You said you had business...'

'As I said, I'll be en route to Kabul. And anyway, we can't be seen together. The only people you can trust are on the other end of this line. He tapped the paper. I know none of this makes sense to you now. You just have to trust me. Okay?'

Yuri's words again. Though confused and afraid, I felt a certain comfort. But as I tucked the paper into my bra, it was impossible not to tremble.

Somehow, I knew I'd never see Sergey again. Don't ask me how.

He touched my arm. 'Lena, I'm so sorry you have to go through this.'

I dabbed a tear and sniffed. 'Until now I've been so hopeful that Yuri will turn out fine. That he's propped up in a hospital bed being pampered by some pretty nurse, that he's simply been mistaken for a fire-fighter, and all will be well. But every hour that goes by it seems less likely. I can't bear the thought of being alone in this world.'

He held my hand in his palm. 'We're never truly alone.'

I stared at him. 'Since when were you religious?'

'That's not what I meant. There's always someone; a lover, a friend...'

'You're right. At least I have you and Olga.'

He tensed. 'How long have you known her?'

'We're best friends.'

'Really? You met in Pripyat – what – twelve months ago?'

'Yes, but...'

'How much do you know about her, Lenochka?'

'Everything. We're confidantes.'

'She's what, twenty-six?'

'Seven.'

'And a swimmer, if I recall, with two podium finishes at the All-Union Games.'

'And if not for the Americans, she'd have been at the Olympics.'

'Exactly. So, she's successful, athletic, intelligent…'

'And sexy, judging from how quickly you two disappeared together after the disco.'

He laughed. 'A slip-up. What can I say? But why would a winner like her be posted hundreds of kilometres from civilisation to teach indulged teenage brats to stay afloat?'

'The fairy tale doesn't work out for everyone, Sergey. She fell from grace. There could be many reasons: a bad decision, insubordination to the coach…' In that moment I felt a cocktail of emotions and averted my eyes. 'Just look at my career.'

'I'm sorry,' he said, 'Your situation is different. You chose to leave for a season; soon you'll be dancing solos again, I have no doubt.'

Suddenly, there was a rap at the door. I looked at Sergey. He nodded, so, I opened it. Before us stood his adjutant, Lieutenant Svechin, fresh-faced and clean-shaven, his uniform starched and spotless. He did a double take, perhaps because I was braless under my rumpled dress with dishevelled hair. But then he saw Sergey, snapped his heels, and saluted. 'They're expecting you in ten minutes, sir.'

'Thank you, Lieutenant; I'll meet you in the car.'

Expressionless, he clicked his heels again and was gone.

I turned to Sergey. 'I guess it's goodbye then.'

There was an awkward moment as we both seemed uncertain whether to embrace. Then he said, 'Our intelligence is that the general evacuation will be mid-afternoon. So, it's over, Lena. I'll tell Lieutenant Svechin to come back here within the hour and drive you to the waterfront. The last ferry leaves at thirteen hundred hours. No doubt it will be packed like sardines; but the captain's a friend of mine; he'll take you, even if he has to put you in the engine room.'

'Thank you. I appreciate it. But no. I'm staying till the end.'

He shook his head. 'Okay, it's your choice. But I've committed to getting you safely out of Pripyat. I'll instruct Lieutenant Svechin to make sure you get on the right bus.'

That felt like a curtailment of my freedom, but he pre-empted my protest. 'Right,' he said. I'd better be off.' He bent and kissed me. 'Goodbye, Lena.'

He paused, and with his forefinger he twirled a strand of my hair. 'Yuri's a lucky man,' he said, with a faint blush.

'No, I'm the lucky one – to have a friend like you.' At the same instant, we flung our arms around each other and embraced as if our lives depended on it. I wanted to stay there, enjoying the feeling of another human being close to me, one who cared and had no expectations.

But he disengaged, stepped back, tipped his peak and departed without another word. I was left staring at the door as the jeep's starter motor whined, the engine roared to life and, with a crunch of tyres, they were gone.

After Sergey left, I sank, bereft, onto the sofa. For several minutes, I stared vacuously through the window. A weak sun had broken through the haze and lit the apartment building opposite. As I focussed on the wall, a pastel-hued mural was lit up. It showed a giant stork, stick-legged with a long, slender, orange bill and black and white plumage. Ukrainians believed the stork was sacred. If one nested near your home, your family would have a settled and prosperous future. Not once, I realised, had I caught sight of a stork during my year in Pripyat.

Soon the walls of that paint-fumed apartment closed in on me. I got up and paced some more, unable to order my thoughts. Eventually, I lit the flame under the samovar and made myself some tea. Soon I started to feel better. Then I remembered my kit bag behind the sofa. Yuri's treasure! I emptied the bag onto the kitchen table.

First, I counted the roubles. Five hundred and fifty-five altogether. About four months' worth of Yuri's salary.

I put the photo aside and held the letters. With a trembling fingernail, I worked loose the staple that held them together. The writing on the first page was precise and heavily slanted. I cringed; it was from me to him. Next was a congratulatory epistle from his grandfather on his graduation. Sweet. I'd read these before when I first discovered his treasure. But the next letter… even just seeing it a second time stung. It was from the redhead in Arzamas who'd jilted him. I lifted it to my nose. I swear I got a whiff of perfume. Again, I pictured Yuri buying it for her from GUM, the massive department store off Red Square.

I skipped to the valediction. *Ya lyublyu tebya.* I love you. It made me want to puke just thinking about it. But at least he'd told me about her.

I scrunched the letter and tossed it aside. Three individual sheets of paper remained. I hadn't seen these before. Strange, I thought, perhaps they'd been stuck to the others. Or had Yuri added them later? The first was in untidy cursive, as if written in a hurry; with no valediction or signature, just a watermark with the initials D.M.I. They didn't ring a bell. But the address in the footer did: Bolshaya Ordynka St; the Ministry of Medium Machine Building. Yuri's employer. It was dated 1 April – less than a month before, and the subject line was blank. *Dear Yuri,* it read, *your telegram yesterday refers.* My throat felt dry.

Only matters of vital importance warranted a telegram.

Continue as planned with… The memo continued with mostly technical jargon and a barrage of acronyms – alphas, betas and gammas – which were literally Greek to me. I skipped to the closing paragraph, but before I could read it, I was interrupted by a peremptory rap at the door.

And that, my darling, is as good a place as any to break for today.

Until tomorrow. *Paka paka.*

Sixteen

Before we continue today, I've pulled out those precious photos to show you; the only ones I have of me and your father from before you were born. I've kept them hidden all these years. Remember, I was supposed to destroy all vestiges of my previous life before I left Soyuz. If they'd been discovered by the wrong people, my identity could have been compromised. And both of us would have been in danger, remember.

You must be dying to see what he looked like. Sadly, only two photographs of him survived the evacuation. Here… I keep them as bookmarks in my bible now.

This one is of Yuri as a child. He told me he was ten at the time, perhaps his stepmother took the photo. Sweet, he was camera shy. Just like you, my little dove. See how he averts his eyes. And the curls… Now you know where you got the wavy hair from.

The other is the two of us on our wedding day. Look how happy we were; innocent as babes; who would have thought, with all those secrets we both held? If you take a closer look: his face is grainy, but you see the resemblance, where you got your height and your fair complexion.

The affair was modest enough: only two *svideteli* to stand witness, Sergey and a colleague of mine from the corps. Yuri's stepfather – his uncle – was there too, but his consumption was sadly so advanced he could hardly breathe without coughing. By then he was a grumpy old man. He and Yuri had a fractious relationship from the outset. Mainly, they argued over politics. Yuri, like his father, was a conservative; his uncle was for reform. Regardless of the crusty veneer, the man had a kind heart. Yuri would never have admitted it, but I surmise it was this uncle who had seen his potential and nudged him to spread his wings and aspire to greatness. And it was he who gave us our pair of crystal glasses to smash at the ceremony: the number of resulting fragments was supposed to represent the years we'd remain married. Ours only broke in two, though we laughed it off at the time. What a happy, carefree day. We had the civil ceremony at the local Department of Public Services, followed by a visit to the *Shtyki*, the monument to the defenders of Moscow on the outskirts of the city. You may have seen photos of it: a giant concrete plinth with bayonets on a grassy slope where newlyweds liked to pose – marking the site where the Red Army gave Hitler his first bloody nose.

I'll leave them for you among my things. How I wished over the years I could have kept more! But I had to content myself with what was in my mind. Like almost everything these days, being virtually confined to this bed now.

But I'd better put them away for now. I'm starting to cry. Let's rather keep going with the story.

I was barely finished reading the last sentence of the telegram from Yuri's employers when there was pounding at the door.

I panicked, imagining a *militsiya* officer with handcuffs ready.

Another knock.

I started stuffing the money and clothes back into the kit bag.

'It's me,' called a woman's voice.

'Olga!' I cried, instantly forgetting her flouncing and the awkwardness of the night before. Before gathering the letters, I flicked to the final salutation, *Matushka Rossiya*. I was aghast. The phrase the Whites used during the Civil War. To utter them – even in jest – in Bolshevik Russia, was tantamount to treason.

There was a scratching at the keyhole. Strange: I didn't recall giving her a key. Hurriedly I tried to gather the papers but they splayed out on the table. Then I saw the last one. It was in Yuri's precise handwriting. My heart leapt.

My darling Lenochka, it started.

The door jerked. I folded the paper together with the others. Probably, it was one of the letters he'd written to me while travelling, but never sent. He'd sometimes show them to me afterwards. Late night sentimentality.

Suddenly, the door burst open. I stuffed the last of the contents into my kit bag with my ballet shoes on top.

Seconds later Olga breezed in. Clearly, she'd been back to her apartment because she'd changed into a checked floral blouse and a black skirt. She'd also applied mascara and lipstick. 'What's that?' she said, eyeing the bag.

'My ballet kit,' I said, withdrawing one of my shoes and stroking its toe.

She sat down alongside me and folded one leg over the other. 'Dreaming of a return, are we?'

I nodded.

'Dreams are good; just be careful, they can be shattered.'

'You seem to have survived.'

'I go through the motions.'

'You should be kinder to yourself, Olya. Your trials weren't your fault.'

'You're right. You of all people understand. Before I met you, I felt like the only girl in this sanitised, make-believe town who's known real hardship. Listen, Mushka, I'm sorry about earlier.'

'It's okay.'

Silence.

'I was grumpy,' she said. 'I didn't sleep well last night. And you?'

My heart skipped a beat. Had she noticed me leaving?

'Terribly,' I said, 'I didn't want to disturb you, so I slept on the sofa.'

'Ah… that explains it; I thought I heard the door opening.'

'I even tried pacing the courtyard – but nothing worked. Eventually, I went out for a stroll.'

'I see.' She shifted closer, and her leg brushed mine. She took my pointe shoe from me and inspected it. 'Beautiful.'

'I wore them the night it happened.'

She placed her hand on my thigh. 'Tell me about it.'

So, I did. I described it all. How it had been my dream come true – to dance a solo in Giselle. And in the Bolshoi Theatre itself, packed to the loges. How flawlessly I'd danced the fouettés in the pas de deux of Act One. Then Act Two, feeling so alive from all the attention, so completely possessed by the music and totally absorbed in my character. And then, that one glance at the Tsar's box, that moment I dared to gaze up at Gorbachev's face and he looked straight into my eyes!

Perhaps it was hubris, but in that moment my sole purpose was to make him proud. Instantly I felt an extra spring in my step, and my bourrées took on a reach-for-the-stars quality. I was living my fantasy... the temptress in sweeping white veils... starlet, goddess, queen-of-the-night...

When everything came crashing down.

Olga shook my leg. 'What is it, Mushka?'

'Nothing. It's too painful.'

Outside, there was the roar of an engine. Instinctively, I sprang from the sofa and ducked behind the drapes. I could hear tyres scrape on gravel and brakes squeak. I scampered through to the bathroom, splashed my face, and checked my hair in the mirror.

'Who's that?' Olga said.

'I'm guessing it's Sergey's aide.'

'I thought Sergey had abandoned you.'

I glanced at my watch. 'Oh, no, time for the final transport.'

Outside, a car door opened and closed.

'Come on.' I prodded her in the side.

'What?'

I poked her in the ribs.

'What? Why can't a friend stay over?'

'Just get into the room!' I wanted to scream at her. I grabbed my kit bag and cast about for a place to hide it. Boots approached in the foyer.

'Go; quick!'

There was a knock at the door. 'I'm coming,' I cried. Meantime, Olga finally staggered off the sofa. I steered her into the bedroom and shut the door on her.

'Lena Sergeyevna?' a man's voice boomed.

Strange, I thought, it was an older, gravelly voice, vaguely familiar, but I couldn't place it. And then the hairs on my forearm rose. No, it can't be... 'One minute,' I called, 'I'm just getting changed.' I dropped the kit bag behind the sofa and hurried to the door. There, I hesitated to look at my reflection on the wall. I daubed a smudge of lipstick away, smoothed my hair, and prised the door handle open.

It was Yavlinsky, in black trousers and a white, short-sleeved shirt with sweat stains at his armpits, tucked in, which accentuated the bulge of his paunch. His face was red and glistening from exertion.

'How did you know?' I blurted.

For a split-second he glanced past me. 'I have my sources. The more pertinent question is: why are you here?'

I shrugged.

He frowned. 'We agreed to meet at my office at four yesterday, no?'

'Sorry; I was detained.'

'Don't say I didn't warn you, Lena Sergeyevna. Just what I said you shouldn't do. You cross a protected site; blunder down the road in full view, subtle as an elephant. You should stick to ballet, silly girl.'

'The case was dismissed.'

'I heard. But just because your boyfriend has a powerful *krisha* in Moscow doesn't make you innocent.'

'He's not my boyfriend.'

'Sure.' He breezed past me into the apartment.

'Err… I'm expecting a friend any minute.'

'I see.' He surveyed the scene.

I gestured to a chair. 'Please, sit. Water?' I poured two glasses.

We sat facing each other. His eyes bored into me. I tried to look calm but was terrified Olga would sneeze or worse. I desperately needed to divert his attention. So, I said, 'How's your son's head?'

'Fine.'

'You sure? It was a nasty fall.'

'He's a cry baby,' Yavlinsky sneered. 'The X-ray isn't conclusive. Sonya's paranoid: she wants to consult a specialist in Kiev. But I think it's simply time that child started acting like a man. All he seems to do now is mope around the house, staring and mumbling.'

'He's only five.'

I waited.

'Sonya blames you and your husband,' he said.

I felt a chill.

'She believes you could have stopped it.'

'And what do you believe?'

'There are always two sides to a story.'

'She doesn't blame herself or you? You were both there.'

'I was too far to intervene.' He sipped his water.

'If you're here to learn more about Yuri,' I said, 'You're wasting your time.'

'Who says I'm here for him?'

He was observing me like I was a painting. I shifted in the chair.

'For me…?'

He nodded.

I felt a chill. 'Haven't you people got bigger fish to fry than a middling ballerina eager to find her missing husband?'

'Middling?' He sucked in his cheeks. 'Drop the modesty.'

'Most of my career was in the corps.'

There was a shuffling sound from the bedroom. I winced.

Yavlinsky raised an eyebrow. It looked as if he was about to say something, but then changed his mind. We stared in silence.

Eventually, I said, 'What do you want? If you think I'm—'

'Relax,' he chided, 'I'm here to offer you a deal.'

I was concerned Olga was listening. But what could I do? If I'd ushered Yavlinsky to the foyer, he'd have suspected something. 'I'm listening,' I said.

He cleared his throat. 'You keep quiet about my procurement enterprise and our… relations, and I'll leave you alone.'

My mind reeled. 'What about your bosses?'

'Leave that to me.'

'It sounds too good to be true. Why now?'

He swallowed. 'You met Major Dermichev…'

'Major?'

'Don't act. You could hear he wasn't a local.'

'Go on.'

189

'He's here to investigate me. Someone made a complaint.'

'And you think it was me?'

'Not really.'

'He asked a lot about you, by the way.'

'Exactly,' Yavlinsky said.

'How do you know I didn't rat you out?'

'I know things.'

I waited.

'Dermichev has managed to persuade the powers that be to redeploy me.'

'So why do you need a deal with me?'

'Because a post as head of staffing at Kaliningrad shipyard is preferable to prison.'

'Kaliningrad, you say. Not too far, at least.'

'You're supposed to say sorry, you'll miss me.'

'That would be a lie.'

'Tss, if you think I'm bad, wait until Dermichev shows his colours.'

'He seemed pleasant enough.'

'He's a charmer.'

'That's rich coming from you.'

'I didn't come here to argue.'

'What then?'

'I told you: to offer you a deal.'

'I'll have to think about it.'

That golden rule of negotiation again: to pause before agreeing to anything.

Yavlinsky filled in the silence. 'It's now or never. Besides, I might change my mind.'

'How do I know your replacement will honour what we agree?'

'You don't. But I can make your file disappear.'

I paused. I was tempted. I couldn't think of a downside. But I said, 'And Dermichev? What about his file on me?'

'He let you go, didn't he?

'Yes, but…'

He waved dismissively.

A stifled cough emanated from the bedroom. Surprisingly, Yavlinsky didn't seem to notice. He sipped his water and wiped his lips with his sleeve. 'It's your husband Dermichev is after. He couldn't care less about you.'

'So, the mess at the apartment… wasn't you?'

'What mess?'

Yavlinsky seemed genuinely surprised. I told him what I'd seen, just the basics.

He nodded sagely. 'There's nothing new to find, is there – since our last visit?'

'Of course not; I would have told you.'

He looked sceptical.

I said, 'What do you think Dermichev will do now – about me?'

'That's a good question. Your soldier friend caught him off guard yesterday. He's been humiliated; he'll be looking to get even.'

'How will your deal help me then?'

'I can at least give you a head start.'

'To do what?'

'That's up to you. Leave Pripyat. Lie low for a while or – even better – disappear. If the damage at the reactor is as bad as my sources indicate, the authorities are going to be distracted, up to all-union level. They may even be forced to allow international inspectors in, or experts to assist. Maybe you'll get lucky, and they'll forget.'

Believe it or not, I was inclined to believe him. In that moment, after months of being under Yavlinsky's yoke, the prospect of even a few weeks' freedom was tantalising. The naivety.

'All right,' I said. 'But on condition you answer two questions.'

'Let's hear what they are first.'

'Where is Yuri?'

'To be honest…'

'Please do.'

'I wish I knew where your husband is. My men are looking everywhere.'

'I see.'

Something instinctively told me that what he'd just said was the truth.

'And your other question?'

'Will you still put in a good word for me at the Ministry of Culture? Your cousin...'

'Sorry; she's been reassigned to someplace trans-Ural; apparently she didn't kowtow enough to Gorbachev's faction.'

'You're lying.'

He frowned. 'Anything else I can help you with?'

'Just get the hell out of here.'

'Fair enough,' he said, resignedly. 'My helicopter's waiting. You should also leave before the rush. I can help if...'

'Thanks; I'll take my chances.'

'Well then, I suppose it's good-bye.'

I said nothing.

'Right.' He got up, was about to turn, then added, 'These... dealings between us... I know they've been hard for you; truly, I didn't want to... but I had a job to do.'

I gazed imperiously at him.

'No hard feelings then, okay?'

Reluctantly, I nodded.

Part on good terms, they say – if you can. Even if it's insincere.

'Good,' he said, 'When this temporary evacuation is over, you should come to the office after work for a drink and *zakuski*; for old time's sake. Before I move to Kaliningrad.'

I wanted to slap him, but I forced myself to say, 'Perhaps.'

He smiled. 'Good. Because... I don't know how long this evacuation will last and what will transpire, but I want you to know that I've grown to... like you, Lena. A lot.'

As the door swung closed on Yavlinsky that morning I felt dirty, like I'd done a deal with the devil. I should have been overjoyed that I'd secured an exit clause. He'd told me I was free, except I didn't trust the snake further than I could spit. I instantly regretted not pressing him harder for information on Yuri. The KGB never loses a person's file. But

I was desperate to get rid of him before Olga appeared. And now my last hope of a lead had left town. It was another damned if I did, damned if I didn't situation. Oh, how I agonised and castigated myself.

Within seconds I felt a hand on my shoulder and swirled about.

'O-Olga?' I stammered.

'Is everything all right?' she said. Her cheeks were a tad flushed, and there was a hint of concern in her eyebrows.

'Fine,' I said, 'I suppose you heard everything?'

'Heard what?'

'Very funny.'

'Okay, but only the gist.'

'Do you despise me now?'

'How could I?'

'I don't understand.'

She glanced away.

'What is it, Olga?'

'There's something I need to tell you.'

'What?'

She cleared her throat. 'I... I told...'

From the kitchen, the *radio-tochki* crackled and hissed with static. 'Dear comrades,' came the announcer's voice, 'we ask that you remain calm, be organised and maintain order during this temporary evacuation.' And then something about adverse radiation conditions developing. Pack an overnight bag, they advised, with a change of clothing, toiletry bag and personal effects like your passport and some cash.

The cheek! As if we were going away for a few days on a summer camp. Truth is, many people knew better. By the mid-eighties, the average citizen in Sovetsky Soyuz was a card-carrying cynic. Unlike the stereotypes the Western media peddled. I've seen the footage: faceless ranks of brainwashed soldiers slow marching zombie-like across Red Square. Do you think they had a choice? If you'd asked any thinking Russians in private whether they believed a word they read or saw in the state media they'd have laughed.

So, in the end they gave us two hours warning. Imagine, my little dove, packing up your whole life into a kit bag in two hours!

For someone like me who thrives in artistic chaos, it was one thing. But imagine how someone as meticulous as your father would have struggled? Or you for that matter. So, now you know where you got your proclivity for things like studying instruction manuals.

In fact, Yuri was far more pedantic than you. That's the way his logical, ordered mind worked. Which made him a formidable chess player. I only dared take him on once. I think I lasted six moves. He played on the national stage, you know, while still in high school. In Moscow. That's where he got the vision beyond his village and Vitebsk, to go and study in the capital. Similar to your story, interestingly. Except he didn't need scholarships like you did for Fordham and Columbia. In Soyuz education was free, and entrance was entirely merit based. In theory, at least.

Okay, let's break there.

Seventeen

Right, where were we last night?

Oh yes… Olga left without a proper farewell, presuming we'd be evacuated to the same location. In the end we never saw each other again. She's probably still teaching swimming in some provincial Russian city. An aging *nasedka*. Or stool pigeon. Every prison in Sovetsky Soyuz had them. They'd come alongside a bewildered newcomer and offer companionship in exchange for information.

I was left alone, pacing the apartment, wrestling with what, if anything, I could still do to find Yuri before being forced to leave. In truth, though, despite my bravado with Sergey, I had already tried every possibility I could think of to find Yuri in Pripyat. The only slim hope that remained was the one Sergey had dangled – Hospital Number Eighteen in Kiev. But if that person was indeed Yuri, what were his chances of survival? Finally, I was no longer able to hide from the awful possibility that I might have to face a future without my beloved Yuri by my side.

A ghastly hollowness opened inside me, as if I had been disembowelled. I sank onto the sofa and began to wail in despair. How could I possibly live the rest of my life as a widow, without Yuri?

I longed to clutch my darling Matrushka to my bosom for comfort, but the thought that I had abandoned her all alone in our apartment made me feel even worse. My wails erupted into wracking sobs that shook the walls.

Finally, when all my energy was spent, I lay limp on the sofa, too numb and dejected to move.

And then I felt the strangest sensation. A kind of butterfly flutter in my belly. Then another. I gently placed my hands on my tummy. Nothing.

Then it came again.

Yes, my little dove, that was you! It was as if you deliberately chose that quiet moment to announce your presence, to call out to me, telling me you were a real person. It almost felt like you were reminding me that I wasn't alone. That you were here too, right there inside me. My child. Yuri's child. The product of our love...

Another flutter! Such a wave of tenderness washed over me in that moment. If felt an instant connection to this tiny new being who was trying so hard to communicate with me. For the first time it became real to me that perhaps I wasn't only a ballerina and a wife. I was also a mother-to-be. I had another role, another purpose. And I wasn't alone. I had you. And through you, Yuri's love was with me too.

And I can promise you, Katyusha, with my whole heart, from the moment you came into this world and my life, you've been my greatest joy.

I was still lying there on the sofa stroking my belly in wonder when I heard a loudhailer outside. I leaped up and ran to the door.

'The evacuation is underway!' a male voice boomed. 'All residents are to assemble outside their building with their hand luggage and wait for the bus.'

'Ensure the lights and gas are turned off and taps tightened,' the announcement continued. 'But don't lock the doors.'

I hurried through to the bathroom to wee, then stole a peek in the mirror. My hair was dry and knotted, my skin pale and creased. I could be forty, I silently lamented, I had to do something.

So, I tied my hair in a bun, put on my sunglasses and positioned my beret – part of my bohemian look.

Then I grabbed all my toiletries and some snacks, stuffed them into my kit bag and swung it over my shoulder. I paused with my hand on the doorknob, inhaled and thought, 'God, this is hard.'

The soldier nearest my doorstep was in full battle fatigues, rifle over his shoulder and a clipboard in hand.

'*Zdrávstvujte.*' He was formal and impassive. 'Passport.'

Oh, how they loved to ask for our passports! He inspected it, page by painstaking page. The way they were trained to, to make us nervous and tempt us to fill the silence.

I swallowed the heartbeat in my throat and smiled sweetly.

He ran his finger down the list on his clipboard.

My heart beat harder, convinced he wouldn't find my name. Only Sergey's assurance kept me hopeful.

He looked up with a blank stare. 'It says here you live at 101B Lelina.'

'I stayed the night with a friend.'

'And where is she?'

'He. In the air force.'

'Mmm.' He scrutinised his list again. 'It says here you are married to a Yuri…'

Phew, I'd cleared the first hurdle. This soldier was just a junior official, not under Dermichev's command. Still, my story had to be good. 'Officer,' I said, 'If it's marital unfaithfulness you're concerned about…' I pouted and offered my wrists. 'Then go ahead and arrest me.'

For a moment it looked like he was considering just that. But then he swallowed a smile and, returning my passport, said, 'the bus departs in fifteen minutes.'

He was true to his word. Soon I heard the rumble of an engine approaching followed by the creak and hiss of brakes. I stood on the tips of my toes and peeked out the window. Sure enough, it was the bus. And there was already a snaking queue of residents at the stop. Also, I noticed, standing a few metres apart, Lieutenant Svechin was looking in the direction of our building. So Sergey wasn't bluffing when he said he'd ensure I left with the evacuation.

Finally, I thought, it was time to decide. Though it hardly felt like a choice. At best I could delay. So, chin up and eyes straight ahead, I strolled out into the foyer.

By the time I got there, the queue had shrunk, and after a nod and wan smile to Lieutenant Svechin, I ended up being the last to board. It was one of those tinny buses with ceilings so low, even a waif like me felt cramped. The driver was doing a crossword puzzle and barely acknowledged me. Alone in the first row sat another official in a mud brown uniform. He accepted my passport and began to page. While waiting, I glanced around. The bus was packed: every centimetre of the overhead racks was filled and there were no empty seats. Many people had either

197

a bag on their laps or a child. Most were quiet and staring out of the window with anxiety on their faces. To my surprise, the official waved me past.

I scanned the interior, considering where to sit. No-one budged.

I felt the familiar stab of rejection. The outsider again.

Finally, there was a shuffling in the second last row and a vacant window-seat appeared. I shuffled down from the centre aisle with my eyes lowered, cautiously optimistic but still expecting a tap on the shoulder. The authorities could be letting me think I was getting away, so I would become complacent, while they followed and watched, giving me enough rope to hang myself. It was a well-known ploy.

I squeezed past the pairs of legs toward my seat, avoiding eye contact. What a relief to finally get there. I looked at my watch. Three fifteen pm. Surreptitiously, I scoped out my surrounds. Behind me was a family of four. The pigeon pair – aged maybe ten and twelve – were animated, as if embarking on a Pioneers' camp. And across the aisle from them was an older lady, presumably their *babushka*. That was an unusual sight in a city as young as Pripyat. Perhaps she'd come to visit for the weekend.

The air in the bus had become stale and close. I slid the window open a crack. But the air was rancid. Eventually, the doors swished shut and we were off. As the bus stopped and started through the backstreets, my emotions veered from relief at escaping the radiation to despair at the thought that I might be deserting Yuri.

At the intersection with Lelina, the bus slowed to an idle. Two lanes were converging where the bus station lay ahead. Bus after bus rumbled by until finally, a driver took pity and waved us ahead. As far as I could see down the boulevard, it was bumper to bumper, and we took forever to progress the two city blocks to our *khrushchyovka*.

I gazed up at our balcony, feeling a stab of wistful pain. Just forty-something hours ago, which already felt like a lifetime, I had sat beside my beloved husband with Matrushka at my ankles, clinking glasses, drinking to life, and talking, talking, talking. Poor Matrushka was still inside. I sent up a prayer for her, feeling terrible that I was being saved while leaving her to a dreadful fate.

The bus edged forward. The railing was directly above us when something within it caught my eye. My heart leapt. It seemed to be the figure of a man. Yuri? Call me mentally disturbed, call me a witch. I don't care. But I simply had to go back and check!

'Wait!' I shouted, 'Stop the bus!' As I struggled past legs to the aisle and made my way forward, I was aware of people staring. The official at the front rose from his seat and gesticulated for me to sit. I tried desperately to explain, but my pleas were drowned by the engine. Soon the other passengers were irritated. One remonstrated with me to return to my seat.

Dejected, I finally conceded. I was angry with myself, but too cowardly to kick up more of a stink. I battled to suppress my tears of frustration.

Meanwhile, our bus trundled on, one small segment of an endless giant caterpillar creeping metre by painstaking metre out of town, over the bridge, past the huge, block-lettered sign 'Welcome to Pripyat 1970' in the direction of Chernobyl town. I pressed my face against the pane, gawking at the nightmare unfolding outside. The ghostly column of smoke was still spewing tirelessly heavenward from its launchpad of flames, occasionally clearing enough to reveal the mangled ruins of what until then had been the pride of Soviet ingenuity, where my husband had spent his nights for the past year. It was like a front row seat in a disaster movie. Yet, it never occurred to me at the time that I was witnessing history.

Soon our bus had left the fiery wreckage of the reactor behind, and we were in the countryside. The inversion in the atmosphere that day meant that the smoke hung thick for kilometres about the plant. For a moment I lost my bearings until a breath of wind briefly cleared enough smoke to expose the tops of the half-completed cooling towers of Reactors Five and Six. Topless monuments of futility, I thought. The Kremlin had just lost its bragging rights to the world's largest civilian nuclear power station.

After the towers came the cooling pond – a shallow, twelve-kilometre strip hugging the Pripyat River, where catfish thrived in the warm water. Onward the convoy rumbled, with the cooling pond on one side and the forest on the other. Tree after tree, evenly spaced in perfectly straight rows.

Then the clapboard buildings of Chernobyl town finally materialised from the foliage. First came the fire station – a nondescript single-story structure recessed twenty metres from the road.

The town appeared deserted, the only signs of life being uniforms and uncurled hoses strewn about the yards. Further along the main thoroughfare, doors and windows were already boarded up. Here and there we passed a citizen or a soldier. But there were cats and dogs aplenty, moping about on porches and on windowsills. They all seemed to know they had been abandoned.

Our bus stopped at the hotel for a bathroom break. We formed a line each for men and women under the watchful eyes of officials. There was a buzz in the air, as if we were off on a weekend vacation. Done, we reboarded and set off. A ninety-degree right turn at the square and in a blink we were through the town centre and swallowed again by trees.

Featureless kilometres followed as our bus rolled on. The oncoming lane was mostly empty, but for the occasional convoy of UAZs and troop carriers rumbling past. All were brimming with fresh-faced soldiers clutching rifles and about to face an invisible enemy, as completely unprepared as their compatriots in 1812 and 1941. Even the fortunate few who were issued with face masks and gloves were too macho to use them. Those who didn't die within days wished they had. Small comfort, they were made Heroes of Sovetsky Soyuz, their bodies wrapped like mummies in layers of plastic and their relatives kept at a distance.

My fellow passengers were growing restless. Chattering waves swept up and down the bus – with speculation about where, why and for how long we were being taken. I overheard the couple behind me saying most buses were being diverted east to Chernihiv where the authorities were erecting makeshift tents. The man to my right – a mechanic and bachelor as I learned – was sure some small village nearer by would host us. Yet another, a young man in construction overalls, said Kiev. I prayed he was right.

I turned from the gossip and stared out the window. I felt low – not just from exhaustion. My anxiety was as unremitting as the forest on either side of the road. The only thing on my mind was Yuri's fate, and my own if it came to widowhood. Every now and then I stroked my belly, drawing comfort from the tiny presence inside.

When I finally wearied of my relentless worry, I turned my attention to the other passengers. Most were young families or groups of friends. For a moment I felt some peace, the solidarity that comes from being in the same boat as others, shielded by four walls and the care of the state. Despite socialism's faults, it can also be a balm – an uncomfortable comfort zone, if you like – where you trade the cruelty of the natural world for the tyranny of the collective.

But soon a sense of loneliness seeped in as I listened to the companionable chatter among the people. And a hint of nausea from motion sickness, as much as the pregnancy. I slipped my hand into my kit bag and felt for my copy of Akhmantova's *Chetki*. Immediately, the line came to me, *'I've learned to live simply, wisely, to look at the sky and pray to God'*, and I gazed out over the countryside again.

Forest, forest, forest and fields stretched unbroken to the horizon. Overcome with exhaustion, I stuffed my little shawl behind my head and lay back against the seat. Soon the vibration of the engine and the warm, oxygen-starved air lulled me to sleep.

A sudden hiss of brakes snapped my head back upright. A roadblock with a guardhouse loomed ahead. We slowed to a crawl and stopped. A soldier in fatigues hopped on board. He stood up front, blocking the aisle, rifle across his chest and cap pulled low over his deadpan face. I tensed as he scanned the sea of faces, terrified he was after me.

'Exit the bus and line up there,' he ordered, pointing to the shoulder of the road where three more soldiers stood abreast – one with a rifle, the other a clipboard, and the third a pole. I craned for a better look. At one end of the pole was what looked like a mirror, and at the other something resembling a camera bag, which, being married to a nuclear engineer, I knew was a dosimeter.

The guard sauntered up to the bus and stopped outside my window, before ducking out of view. Meanwhile, the first row of passengers had stood to disembark. In single file they traipsed outside, where the soldier with the clipboard checked off names – a rather awkward process due to his facemask and gloves. The process continued in solemn, orderly silence but I was so scared I wanted to puke. I slid out of my row and shuffled forward, thankful for the anonymity my overweight seatmate provided me. Before the exit, I paused and stretched, enjoying the warm forest-fresh air on my cheeks. When my turn came to step down, I was reluctant. I stood in a daze. Only when the solider with the clipboard beckoned, did I will myself down.

'Present passport.'

I clenched my passport to steady the tremor in my hands, but inside I was a wreck. I handed it over. The guard opened it slowly. Then he glanced at me, and down to my shoes.

'Is Pripyat your permanent residence?'

I nodded.

'Occupation?'

'Teacher.'

He frowned. 'It says ballerina.'

'Retired ballerina,' I said. Which was close enough to the truth, and sufficiently brief.

The guard's eyes narrowed.

Had he recognised me from an alert or an old newspaper? Just my luck to run into a warrior who loves the arts.

I saw a hint of a smile. 'So young?'

Immediately, I relaxed. I shrugged coquettishly.

He smiled. 'So, what made you move to Pripyat?'

Silently, I winced. It was a question I'd asked myself a hundred times by then. Why hadn't I resisted the KGB for longer? Surely, I could have found another way to get the surgery I needed. And once I'd fallen in love with Yuri, why hadn't I delayed the move?

'I followed my husband,' I said.

'And? Where is he?'

I feigned a blush and gave my best schoolgirl smile.

'You're not together anymore?'

I dropped my gaze and looked sad. 'He didn't deserve me.'

The man behind me in the line cleared his throat loudly. The guard scowled. 'Be patient,' he hissed at him, before resuming his leering at me.

I fluttered my eyelids. 'What did you ask again, officer?'

'Err...' The guard's eyes strayed to my chest. 'Nothing.'

From the guardhouse, came the crackle of a two-way radio. The soldier ignored it, but the voice was insistent. I strained to hear.

'Calling first perimeter control,' the voice repeated.

I was too nervous to breathe. My mind leaped to that windowless room with fluorescent lights. Oh, my darling Yurochka, I mouthed, please help me to find you!

Suddenly, a shot rang out from the trees close by. Instinctively, I startled from the shock and ducked. The sound ricocheted and geese rose cawing from a nearby thicket, followed by silence.

The guard chuckled. 'That's my commanding officer hunting. Couldn't even hit a bear from twenty metres with a shotgun.'

I breathed out.

The radio crackled to life again, but before I had time to tense, there was a bleating from the thicket that turned to a whine then a whimper. The guard laughed. 'I was wrong. Sounds like he got a boar. They've told us to shoot anything that moves.'

The passengers in the line behind me were muttering impatiently. I leaned closer to the soldier, who blushed. Then the radio hissed, shriller than before.

Another bus sighed to a stop. Then ours started up again, revved, and let its engine purr.

The soldier appeared agitated. I was terrified he'd answer the radio.

'Here,' he said, waving my passport. 'Good luck.'

With trembling hand, I accepted it. 'Thank you.'

I returned to my seat with my head lowered while the guards processed the remaining passengers. No hitches, fortunately, and soon our bus was moving out into the road. Please, I silently pleaded as the soldiers melted past the window, wait before you answer.'

Our bus rumbled on – twenty metres, thirty. We were gaining speed. Forty, fifty, sixty, until – finally – I plucked up the courage to turn…

Blin! The guard stood on the centre line waving with both hands. Had our driver seen him? We rounded the bend.

The seconds ticked into minutes.

In the end, the relief came to me slowly, as I reflected on my narrow escapes. First, Sergey had freed me from custody, then Yavlinsky had tracked me down to tell me he was leaving. Now I had presumably slipped through Dermichev's cordon, if that's what it was, and with every kilometre we were moving away from the radiation. I was leaving Pripyat's soulless conglomeration of *khrushchyovky* and narrow-minded inhabitants. And for now, the journey offered a temporary respite in my search for Yuri. There was nothing I could do.

In a way, Katyusha, I have a similar feeling now. Here I am, immobilised in one of the world's best hospitals with every life-monitoring device and medication known to science, fawned on by more overqualified specialists than nurses. The world out there can rage and I may be dying, but for once I can relax. What will be, will be. It's liberating.

Be sure to allow yourself some moments like this too. Like me, you're a fighter, you like to be in control. That's already got you a long way in life. Look at you, smart girl, a leader in your field in your twenties with a fine husband and a beautiful home. Just beware the darker side of perfectionism.

Okay. Why don't we stop here. It's late. There's the moon, almost full. Not often I see it through the lights of the city. Gotham at its best.

Ah… I hear boot treads. That's the new night nurse. Dracula got promoted to the day shift.

Okay, I'm turning in.

Paka paka. Till tomorrow then.

I love you girl!

Eighteen

Before we continue with my story, I want to say something about survivor's guilt, in case you ever experience something similar.

I've had a few close brushes with fate over the years, and though I've suffered along the way, I've always managed, so far, to stay alive. And each time I survive, I have this initial sense of relief, which can last from ten minutes to several weeks or more. But the moment I finally process my ordeal enough to enjoy a moment of happiness, guilt rears up and kicks sand in my face. Then the endless sham trial starts, with me as both prosecutor and judge. My crime is that I got to live instead of worthier people, like Yuri. What did I do to deserve my escape? There's no winning my case. On the flip side, I castigate myself for not being happier. You're one of the lucky ones, my accuser whispers, you're in the West; you have hard currency, fifteen breakfast cereals to choose from and the freedom to say what you like – as long it's politically correct of course.

Sadly, I've never overcome the condition. Like an alcoholic, there's no cure, I'm always recovering. But a burden shared is a burden halved, and discovering that I'm not alone has helped. My bridge group at the Russian Club are all fellow refugees.

Better by far, though, is being able to share it with you. Do you have any idea what a blessing you are to me, my beautiful, intelligent daughter, and how much I love you? Even more so after these years apart.

Last night I described my narrow escape from the checkpoint in that endless convoy of buses on the road to Kiev. As we rolled on, a horse-drawn cart approached in the oncoming lane: hunched figures up front, a farmer and his wife, their faces prematurely gnarled. Just another day for them, just another load. Soon they'd passed us, and their village appeared – ramshackle cottages, broken walls, rampant ivy, a yield sign – then in a blink it was behind us.

From there the forest grew denser, the road narrowed, and from either side, natural-growth elms and beech trees arched toward one another until we were enclosed in a tunnel with walls in a thousand shades of green – fresh as lettuce at their bases rising to dark ancient tops and browns in between. Round a bend we went, and the shadows became dappled with shards of light from the sinking sun. Ahead loomed a barn, its roof collapsed, and beside it a rusted tractor and peasant huts with thatched roofs and mossy walls.

Suddenly, a boy on a scooter appeared from a side lane, skidding to a halt just in time before we rumbled past. Then one cottage, two, a schoolhouse. Another cottage with a street-facing porch with a *dedushka* in a rocking chair, pipe in hand, watching. I wondered what the old man made of us. Russian peasants were always the last to be told but the first to know. How many invading armies – reds, whites, Germans – had he seen come and go? How many more might he live to see?

Soon the village receded behind us. Vegetable patches, dilapidated barns, the spiral of smoke from a chimney, followed by pink-blossomed plum trees and the white of the apple trees in full glory, almost luminescent in the gathering dusk. But my emotions had plunged, the aching beauty only served to accentuate my sadness. Every kilometre travelled snapped another strand connecting me with my beloved. My heart was collapsing as the hope inside me bled away. I had to try to believe that Yuri was somewhere in Kiev.

The forest came and went, finally melting into an ocean of blazing yellow canola fields, unbroken to the horizon, with scattered islands of beeches and the smudge of a village. Above was an endless blue sky, ranging from unnaturally dark to postcard clear, streaked with wisps of high cirrus. And then the fields turned fallow brown, and a tractor the size of a truck tore steadily across the wide, flat horizon, a train of the finest dust billowing in its wake.

Eventually we entered forest again. The bus pulled over in a clearing. A bathroom break, they said. I sprang out of my seat, my desperation reflected in the faces of my fellow passengers. The disembarking passengers fanned out into the woods, each searching for a modicum of privacy.

Fortunately, the trees were plentiful and thick and soon I was alone. Or so I hoped. Next thing a dog barked nearby followed by the squeals of children at play. One couldn't get far from civilisation in the bread-basket of Soyuz.

I returned to the bus aware of a growing hunger and thirst and chided myself for not packing more snacks for the journey. But I arrived to find the authorities handing out food parcels to each boarding passenger. How thoughtful. Back in my seat I wolfed down the cheese and lettuce sandwich and the chicken wing but left the apple, which looked unripe. Then I reclined and watched the remaining passengers board.

Finally, the doors sighed closed, the vibration rose in pitch, the bus jolted, and we rolled onward out of the forest. The sun was lower now, more orange than gold. The fields too, were aglow and the air began to cool, tinged with the smoke of stoves. From horizon to horizon the darkening land was flat or gently rolling, marked here and there by a windbreak or a village made small and insignificant against the sheer vastness of the steppe.

Onward we rode as telephone poles slid by, up a gentle rise, down and up again, now into a forest before the vista opened up again onto fields fringed with trees. But then I observed that we seemed to be heading away from the fading light and south, which meant…

I tapped the fellow in overalls in front of me on the shoulder. He turned.

'Seems you were right,' I said. 'We're heading for Kiev.'

He smiled and shrugged. 'My boss at the factory is connected.'

'Clearly. I'll listen to you next time.'

'What's your name?' he said.

I hesitated.

'Irina,' I said. 'Would you like my apple?'

He gratefully took it, and we chatted a little. But soon I felt the need to be alone again and excused myself to stare out the window. The driver must have taken the long route, because there was no sign of Kiev's *khrushchyovky* or its golden domes. Just more land.

Ah, Russia, Russia, as Gogol would say, from my beautiful home in a strange land, I can still see you...

Almost imperceptibly, the vegetation was changing. Soon we were passing through planted pines and undergrowth. Then I glimpsed the waters of the Kiev Sea, calm and foreboding in the fading light, and knew we were approaching the outskirts of the city. There before us lay the gracious Dnieper, wide and slow, splitting the flat land with a mighty bend.

As we crossed the gargantuan steel bridge I stood to get a glimpse of the water. Though it was almost dark, I could see a strong current swirl around the pylons before surging downriver with its familiar trail of soil-blackened foam before fanning out to meander through a patchwork of low, flat islands. The roadway on the far side hugged the far bank of the river, past the Plodil District. Then we headed inland and got bogged down in traffic. We stop-started until the turnoff, where we eased onto Prospect Peremohy with its double lanes and ample shoulders, straight and undulating to the horizon. Soon our indicator lights flickered and we slowed. Sensing that we were arriving, my fellow passengers broke into excited chatter. We made a turn, crossed a boulevard, turned awkwardly down a side street and came to a stop at last. The doors opened.

The area they offloaded us in seemed more like a remote building site than a residential neighbourhood, except there were streetlights. Mighty *kashtans* bowered the streets, their canopies plumped with drooping-heart leaves. They were adorned with snow blossoms glowing in the dusk, so bountiful you could hardly see the lattice of telephone cables and power cables for trams. Wooden observation towers loomed every fifty metres as if we were in a prison, though they appeared to be unmanned.

There I stood on a broad, weed-dotted sidewalk with my kit bag at my feet, surrounded by huddles of people chattering. I looked around. The mood was expectant. From the washing strung on balconies and windows that had drapes, only one in five apartments seemed occupied. From some, faces peered.

What, if anything, the authorities had told them I had no idea. But they looked terrified. Yes, of us. Never mind that we weren't foreigners, that we shared the same language, culture, history and values – in a stroke, we had become aliens, indelibly marked. We might as well have been lepers.

I patted my chest, thinking about the slip of paper, and Sergey's instruction to call the number. But I couldn't see a pay phone. As unobtrusively as possible, I drifted away from the crowd, and was almost struck by a tram trundling past up the street only to stop diagonally opposite me. Two men in dark suit pants and short-sleeved shirts stepped out, smoking and chatting, approached with a swagger. I froze. Could they be Dermichev's men?

Twenty metres, fifteen... ten... then they veered off up the path.

Shaken and trembling, I looked around. I was out of earshot of the crowd now, beside a black wrought iron fence. It was high enough to house a tennis court, but instead it enclosed a playground with a slide, jungle gym and swings, and beyond that, a bench. The gate was open, so I headed for the bench, where I sat to settle my nerves.

I heard the voices of children approaching, and some young boys from the bus came tumbling through the gate, followed by their mothers. Thankfully my side of the bench was in a shadow. I hoped they wouldn't notice me. Right behind them a *starik* entered. I guessed he was about seventy years old, dressed in a dark turquoise jacket, creased black pants, and a flat cap. Tapping a cane, he limped toward me. I shifted to the far edge of the bench. He acknowledged me with the barest flick of his cane and sat. We stared ahead in silence. Eventually, curiosity got the better of me and I peeked. His clothing was shabby and loose, emitting whiffs of naphthalene, and his chin had a three-day stubble, but his chest was covered in medals. I don't remember them exactly: lots of hammers and sickles and stars. They were dished out like chips in those days.

The crackle of a loudspeaker behind gave me a jolt. The regime hung them in many public places, from telephone poles to trees. We were never far from Big Brother's spokesmen.

'A roll call will commence shortly,' the speaker announced, followed by a cough and a bus number. It must have been ours, because the mothers gathered their children and filed out of the gate. I tried to stand

209

but the veteran pressed his cane down on my thigh. 'No rush,' he said, they're reading names alphabetically.'

Again, I tried to rise; but the cane was surprisingly firm. 'Excuse me,' I insisted, 'They'll be calling me soon.'

'I know,' he said, 'You're a "C".'

A tingle spread up my spine... Dermichev?

He removed his cane and turned to me. 'Pleased to meet you, comrade.'

I stared.

'Smoke?' he said, padding his jacket. 'No? I don't bite, lady.'

'Thank you. But my mother taught me better than to talk to strange men in the big city.'

'I see. Odd: I don't detect a country accent.' He lit and then drew on his cigarette.

'I'm originally from Moscow.'

'So, what do you think of your new neighbourhood?'

'Who cares – it's temporary.'

The *starik* watched his cigarette tip glow. 'Temporary can end up being a lifetime.'

He was giving me the creeps. I grabbed my bags and stood.

'By all means go on, but you may find yourself at your *khrushchyovka* behind us just as those two are searching it.'

My chest tightened.

'The idiots marched straight past you,' the *starik* continued, 'Must have assumed you were on the previous bus.'

From over the loudspeaker, came the yell, 'Andreyevsky, Antomov.' Then some warning about wandering off without permission before falling silent.

I watched the *starik's* eyes. His pupils seemed open. I said, 'How do I know you're not one of them?'

'You'd be in a police van by now.'

I was determined not to show fear. 'They could be regular family men returning from work. Anyway, thank you for your concern, sir, but please excuse me...'

He rose with surprising ease. 'Wait...'

I stopped. He ruffled in his jacket, scribbled something, tore off a small page and held it out. 'Does this number look familiar?'

I froze.

'Go ahead,' he urged, 'Compare them.'

I hesitated, then fished in my bra. The paper was soaked in perspiration. I carefully smoothed it in my palm. The ink was smudged but just legible in the fading light. The number matched.

The loudspeaker crackled again. 'Belinski, Boroin...'

I felt dizzy.

'Come.' He took my wrist.

I resisted. 'Where to?'

He sighed. 'Lena Sergeyevna...'

At the sound of my given names, I felt an immediate comfort.

He leaned closer and lowered his voice. 'Listen; this is important: from now on you won't know where you're going ahead of time, nor who you'll meet.'

I hesitated all of a few seconds. I could obsess about the most trifling decisions like what to cook for dinner, but when it came to matters of life and death, I was as decisive as a general.

'Fine, comrade...?'

'Vladimir Alexandrovich Zhukov. Follow me.' He shrugged his jacket into shape, hunched over his cane and tap-tapped out of the playground and along the sidewalk in the direction our bus had arrived from. I was several paces back, feigning sangfroid, but expecting a tap on the shoulder at any moment. The voice on the loudspeaker started to fade. Come on old man, I was thinking. But Zhukova was in no mood to be rushed. He turned and glared at me before continuing. We were nearly at the corner when the announcer called another name. Ahead, a car horn tooted. 'Don't worry,' the announcer said, 'The government will look after you; every family unit will be allocated a room and a hundred roubles to tide you over.'

The original nanny state, you could call it. The idea is appealing, no question; the mass of humanity welcomes it with open arms. And why

211

not? It's like being offered heroin before you're addicted. For a time, you feel warm and safe, until you can no longer function without it.

Zhukov's stride had lengthened and his limp was gone as we turned into the broad boulevard, Prospect Peremohy. We hugged the footpath which was recessed from the traffic as it passed through intermittent parkland, on and on until, finally, I saw the sign for the metro.

Down the stairs we eased, and onto the landing. Zhukov directed me to the wall map of the metro and told me to study it while he went to the ticket office. Soon I had refreshed my memory of the main lines of the subway network. Minutes passed… I moved onto the hotchpotch of notices tacked onto the adjacent board. More minutes… he seemed to be taking his time. I was growing anxious.

Then a prod in my ribs sent me whirling about in a panic. 'Relax,' he breathed, taking my arm. 'You'll draw attention.' He guided me to the opposite corner. After scanning the crowd, he surreptitiously pressed a small wad of papers into my hand. 'There's five hundred roubles, a one-way ticket and an address,' he said. 'Don't speak to a soul until you get there. Understood?'

I nodded.

'And don't – under any circumstance – mention your name, ever, not even when you get to that address; understood?'

'But…'

He glanced about. 'Promise me!'

'Okay.'

'Good. Now get going.'

'And you?'

'Here's where I leave you. We operate independently.'

Questions were swirling, but words deserted me. I felt bereft and alone again.

'Don't worry, my dear.' The crags on his face softened. 'They'll take care of you.' He touched my cheek with the back of his hand, like a father; and glanced at my stomach. 'Both of you.' Then he melted into the crowd and – yet again – I was alone, fighting back tears.

Nineteen

T he train wove and clattered through the bowels of Kiev. I was sitting beside the exit, staring at the subway map opposite. Though alone in my carriage, I was convinced I was being followed. Around corners we went, screeching, straightening, screeching again, then a drawn-out hiss of brakes as we slowed, and the doors swooshed open. A handful of commuters stepped out onto the platform. Only a girl of about my age boarded. We made the briefest eye contact before she found a seat alongside me.

I fumbled in my purse, feeling through the wad of notes Zhukov had given me and found one that was a supermarket receipt. On the reverse was a scribbled address – *Saksaganskogo 58B*, and below it Universytet, the metro station near the university. I knew it – on a downslope from the Golden Gate, near the Old Botanical Gardens. I looked back at the metro map on the wall opposite and counted the stops.

More commuters boarded each time the doors opened until there was standing room only. Gradually, I grew aware of a balding, briefcase-wielding businessman sitting opposite. I tensed. Were they already following me? He pretended to read a newspaper, but I sensed him ogling my legs. I crossed my arms and turned away. When that didn't work, I glared at him. He seemed to blush but continued to read. I breathed a little easier. Perhaps he was just another lecher.

The girl next to me pulled a book from her satchel. I strained to make out its cover. Ah, a spy thriller I'd read, with the CIA as the villain. I lost interest. Two more stops. I grew increasingly nervous. The lecher was staring again. Go to hell, I wanted to shout, but Zhukov's caution rang in my ears. As we approached the Universytet stop I stood and shuffled toward the doorway as we slowed. The lecher stood and grabbed the adjacent strap. As the carriage swayed, our bodies moved in sync but fortunately didn't touch. Was he an informer?

The platform was thick with commuters. I waited for the torrent of fellow passengers to spill out onto the platform.

'Stand away from the doors,' screeched a tinny recorded voice.

I hopped off a split-second before the doors sucked closed behind me, and the train creaked away into the tunnel. Soon the escalators had drained the platform and I was alone. Or was I? I glanced about, feeling paranoid. I'd become a fugitive in an all-seeing, all-knowing, all-powerful state.

I took the escalator, rising past poster after poster of socialist realism, Gorbachev and occasionally Lenin. One landing followed another. Up and up we went, until finally I was disgorged through a turnstile into a concourse. I ambled over to the street map on the far wall. Saksaganskogo Boulevard was there – long and curved – but without any apartment block numbers. A middle-aged couple materialised. The husband poked his finger and said they should take a shortcut through the Old Botanical Gardens. When they'd left, I took a closer look: if I took the same route, I'd arrive midway along Saksaganskogo. I fell in with a herd of commuters shuffling toward the concourse exit but soon felt claustrophobic and an urge to lash out at the people bumping into me. I became aware of a heightened protectiveness toward my belly. But soon the air grew fresher, and suddenly I was outside. But by now it was darkening outside. Down a flight of stairs I pattered, into a garden. I passed flowers and more flowers, all about, luminous whites and pinks, until I entered a forest. The thinly spaced streetlamps offered little light here, so I trod carefully as the path wound downhill. The shrubbery was thick and cast ominous shadows as I hurried on past the debris of a knocked-over bin, around a curve, and onto asphalt. Here was the brightly lit intersection with Saksaganskogo Boulevard. And a choice. The nearby buildings weren't numbered. I chose the uphill path first, to the right. No sign of a number 58, never mind B. It was exasperating, especially when I arrived at the intersection at the end of the road. *Blin*, I muttered under my breath, why did I ever trust that old man?

214

My inner critic rose to the occasion. You fool, Lena, you could be enjoying a warm meal with fellow refugees instead of wandering about lost with nothing but a kit bag, a few roubles and a fake address.

I backtracked, stopping at every doorway, asking at some. I felt parched, my knee was niggling and my vision was blurring. Eventually, I stumbled upon a plaque with the number 58 and looked up to see the crumbling façade of one of those old town pre-war blocks that had only survived the Nazi retreat because some of the explosives they'd planted didn't detonate.

To enter these pre-war walk-ups required passing through an archway and across a courtyard, exposing me to prying eyes. By the time I reached the door my hands were shaking. It was pitch dark, I was completely drained, and now I stood on a strange doorstep staring at the intercom button, with no idea who, if anyone, might answer.

I pressed. Nothing. Again. Nothing. I looked up. There were four or five stories, tiny balconies, some open windows, pot plants and bric-a-brac. It was all dark; except… was it? Yes, the hint of a light from the top. I rang again. Still nothing.

Finally, there was a crackle.

'Yes?' A woman's voice croaked. 'Who is it?'

I stooped to the microphone. 'L…'.

But I mustn't give my name! What now?

'Hello?' the voice said.

I froze. Finally, I plucked up the courage and said, 'I…'

'Please speak up.'

'I… was given your address.'

Silence. What now? Either Zhukov was a conman, or he'd given the wrong address. I took out the page. It was too dark to be sure. *Blin…* Was the old bag calling the *militsiya*? I turned to flee. But as I passed through the arch, I heard a crackle. I ran back and put my ear to the intercom.

A faint cough came over the line, static, then, 'What colour was his jacket?'

'Err… turquoise.'

There was silence. Then, 'There's a key under the mat. Turn twice and shove.'

True enough, the key was there, but the steel door required all my body weight to creak open. The entrance hall was lit by a single electric bulb dangling from the ceiling, which cast shadows on the black and white floor tiles. I passed a row of empty post boxes. The stairs were of stone worn smooth from use. At the second turn was an enclave with a bedraggled pot plant, then a landing. But no light from beneath any of the doors. So, I continued up, eventually to the fourth and final floor, apartment 58B. A faint trace of light about the door gave me hope. My fist poised. I put my ear to the door. From inside came a shuffling sound. I knocked. A jingle emanated, and then the door swung open.

The woman at the door was my height but triple my age, her silver hair in a bun, wearing a plaid skirt and cream shirt. Her skin was surprisingly smooth and seemed younger than her voice. Which was unusual, because unlike performing artists like me, most women didn't have access to all the lotions and potions of our counterparts in the West.

Her face lit in a smile. 'Ah, I was wondering what took you so long. Come in; let me lock the door behind you; there. Now, give me your shoes; I'll put them here, like this, straight; that's better. This place is so tight, it's like living in a submarine; one must keep order. Right, let's go talk in the kitchen. Please, after you.'

Within a few strides, I'd passed two closed doors, wheeled right, and reached the kitchen. Just before that was a doorway to a toilet-cum-bathroom-cum-laundry. One of its four walls was shelved floor to ceiling packed full, and one had a shower curtain, presumably hiding a bath. The kitchen wasn't much bigger. The table filled most of the floorspace even with its four straight-backed chairs tucked in. I squeezed into one and sat hugging my bag. Directly ahead was a window framed by lace curtains and below them an oil heater draped with crocheted towelettes. On the windowsill stood a glass jar filled with shells.

'From the Crimea,' she said. 'We vacationed there.'

'What's it like?'

216

'Beautiful. Towering cliffs, dark, cool water with numberless inlets we'd explore by boat. My husband was in the navy…'

'Which explains your reference to submarines.'

She laughed. 'Igor used to say, discipline is the only way to avoid going mad or getting food poisoning. A place for everything and everything in its place. I mocked him, but it must have rubbed off on me. He was a strong character.'

'I'm sorry,' I said, looking down at the linoleum.

'It's all right; he's been gone ten years now.'

There was an awkward silence, in which her face turned grave. 'Did anyone follow you?'

'No.'

'You sure?'

I shrugged. 'It was dark.'

'Mmm… Do you know why you're here?'

'No.' I reached for my bag. 'I was just given an address on a scrap of paper from a tramp with the name…'

'Shh. We don't talk about those before or after us in the chain; only a distinguishing detail or two.'

'Who's we?'

'Excuse my manners,' she said, and offered me her hand. 'Anna Ivanovna Angelov.'

'Which, I assume isn't your real name.'

Her nod was barely perceptible. I accepted her hand anyway. Her fingers were cold and surprisingly smooth. I said, 'Lena…'

'Shh!' She patted my hand reprovingly. Her hazel eyes were intense. 'You're not to use that name again. Not ever.'

'But…'

'Not even in your thoughts. Clear?'

'What do you mean I can't use my own name? That's impossible.'

'Just don't, all right. Ever again.'

I pondered her words. The implications were too ghastly to contemplate. I had just lost my home, my cat, possibly my husband, and now my identity, too? 'You don't understand,' I said, 'The authorities have dropped all charges against me. I'm a free woman.'

She didn't move, just eyed me. 'Then why are you here?'

'Because...' I reached into my bra. 'This phone number... a friend in Pripyat gave it to me, said I should call it when I got to Kiev... it matched the one... I mean, the *starik* with the turquoise jacket gave me.'

She smiled. 'I see you're a quick study.'

I took my seat and said, 'Sorry, I'm exhausted.' I fiddled with my fingernails.

'I hope to have your new passport within a day or two,' she said. 'We're talking about a new one; of a different person.'

My jaw dropped. 'What do you mean?'

'What I say.'

'But why?'

'It's not safe for you; too many people are looking for you; people with power.'

'That doesn't scare me; I've spent half my life mingling with influential people; I'm married to...' I shook my head in silent frustration. The enormity of the task – to never again mention the name of my husband – was dawning on me.

From near the stove, a clock ticked the half hour. On the surface I was confused; but on a deeper, subconscious level, I understood. So, I just swallowed, fixed her with my eyes, and said, 'But... changing my whole person? Surely, it's not that simple.'

'You're right. It's going to be the longest, hardest act you've ever danced.'

I stared. 'You know I'm a ballerina?'

She nodded.

'And my new... "character"?'

'They don't tell us until the last minute.'

I sighed. 'How long do I have to keep it?'

'Forever.'

'Meaning?'

'Forever. For as long as you live.'

I frowned, confused.

She inhaled. 'As of tonight, you must expunge all memory of your life...'

'What?'

'Name, village, family members, friends, profession. Not a word to a soul.'

'Basically, you're asking me to die.'

'No, I'm telling you to.'

I was reeling. It was too much to take in. How had I got to this point? A scruffy *starik* handed me a scribbled address... madness! All because of a throwaway line from Yuri –while high on hormones and tobacco – about trusting Sergey. And who was this woman, I thought as her words echoed in my ears. *Expunge all memory of your life.* I stared at her.

'But that's impossible,' I said, 'in a police state like ours.' As I said it, I realised it wasn't strictly true: the new recruits at the KGB spy school did just that. But that was sponsored by the state.

'Shh.'

'But it's never been done... successfully.'

'How would you know?'

'Touché.'

She smiled weakly. 'I'm not denying that it's daunting. That's why you must get out of here – and soon.'

'But where to? I'll be more conspicuous in the countryside.'

She shook her head. 'Out of the country.'

'Where – Bulgaria, Germany? I don't speak more than a handful of words other than Russian.'

She just looked back at me.

Then it dawned on me. 'Y-you mean... abroad?' I was flabbergasted. 'Like in permanent exile?'

She nodded.

'Impossible!'

'Why so?'

'I would never abandon my husband.'

'Unless…' she looked down, rapped her fingertips on the table, 'it's what he wants.'

'You – you mean he's…?'

'I didn't say that.'

'What then?'

'Sorry, my dear.' She stood. 'I've already said too much.'

'No!' I slammed my hand on the table. Glasses rattled. 'You can't casually mention my husband as if he's alive, and then go silent.'

She skirted the table and stood in front and above me. Her eyes were cold as ice. 'Listen. If you don't want to trust me or the people I work with, you're welcome to leave, right now.'

My spirits plunged. The thought of being alone on the street again, lost in the dark, was terrifying. 'Forgive me,' I said. 'But please – if you say he's dead, I'll accept it – I almost have already; at least I would know for sure; but if by some mercy he's survived, at least have the humanity to tell me.'

She placed her hand tenderly on my shoulder. 'Tomorrow evening, I'll tell you what I know – which, I must warn you, isn't likely to be much. I promise, okay? Good girl. Now I'll heat up some *borscht* from lunch. I've already eaten.'

'Thanks, but I'm nauseous.'

'Not surprising, in your state.' She took a bowl from the fridge, scraped its contents into a pot. After lighting the stove, she turned to me with an impish grin. 'I also used to hold my belly all the time.'

I looked down. Involuntarily, I raised my hands to the tabletop.

She dipped her finger in the soup. 'Another minute or two.' She stirred. Silence. Then she said, 'Congratulations on the baby.'

The comment unnerved me. She must have seen that because her expression changed, the creases in her skin seeming to have softened. And I was thinking, she must have been beautiful in her youth; she still was. But then I looked at the table, suddenly choking up.

She turned down the gas. 'What's wrong?'

I felt a tear forming.

She came over and gently placed her hand on my shoulder. 'My dear girl… I've learned the hard way not to dispense advice unless someone asks for it. But I'm going to make an exception because I can see you're in turmoil.'

The moment I looked at her, I burst into tears. Something in her manner triggered a memory of my mother.

'I know you're planning to abort,' she said matter-of-factly.

How did she know? I wondered.

'Was planning,' I said.

'Oh? And when did that change?'

'I'm not exactly sure. But I'm having feelings I've never had before. I'm becoming attached. It's so confusing.'

'I'd never tell you what to do in this situation. But – and I say this from bitter experience – if, at this point, you have any inclination to keep the child, do; because there'll come a day – which may take years, decades even – when you'll regret it.'

'But… couldn't you say the same about having the child?'

She paused in contemplation. Then she said, 'I've got two children. When they were young, I'd go into their room after finishing the dinner dishes and just gaze at them sleeping… the faces of angels.' She returned to the stove and began to ladle *borscht* into a bowl and placed it before me together with a half loaf of *borodinsky*. 'Go on,' she said. 'You'll feel better on a full stomach.'

The aroma stimulated my hunger and soon I'd wolfed down a hunk of bread and cleaned the bowl.

'How was that?'

'Delicious. Thank you.'

'What's bothering you?' she said.

I looked into her eyes. I sensed she cared. 'The radiation… it can damage a foetus, no?'

'It depends how much and for how long.'

'I know. I…' I paused. How much should I confide?

'I know about your arrest,' she said.

'How's that possible?'

She smiled sympathetically. 'Never mind. So, what happened?'

I hesitated. 'How much detail do I share?'

'Less is always better, my girl – almost always.'

I said, 'We'd been on the bridge, on the outskirts of town, watching the reactor fire… On the way back, I was anxious that my husband might be lying trapped beneath smouldering debris. I had to try something. So, instead of returning to our apartment, I took a shortcut through the forest. The territory was off limits. For all I knew, there could have been barbed wire or landmines. But I would have walked through fire. I…'

'And?' she urged me.

'The *militsiya* picked me up before I got to the gate.'

'So, you never entered the grounds?'

'No.'

'How close did you get?'

'I'd say five hundred metres from the reactor. All in all, it couldn't have been more than twenty minutes' exposure within a kilometre of the source.'

'Oh… my dear, I wouldn't worry.'

'But… what if the child's… abnormal? How could I live with myself?'

She shrugged. 'You're the only one who can decide.'

I wiped my eyes. But by then my thoughts had returned to Yuri. Again.

'Now what's wrong?' she said.

I paused to make sure of my words. 'My husband… Even if he does wish me to leave the country without him – how is it possible? A person doesn't just hop on a plane.'

She paused. 'Let's just say… we've been planning for this eventuality.'

'We? None of this makes sense.'

'I'm afraid, my dear, it may never.'

My hostess wouldn't be drawn further. She said she'd explain more when she returned from work the next day, and then repeated her warning not to leave the apartment. Just for a day, she assured me, make yourself at home with my bookshelf and record collection. I protested until she threatened to withhold my second helping of *borscht*.

After dinner she handed me pyjamas and sent me off to shower. 'Leave your clothes behind to soak,' she said, 'You're glowing like a lantern.'

And what a shower! There's nothing like a massage of piping hot water to soothe anxiety. Standing in the bath with barely a centimetre between the crown of my head and the nozzle, I scrubbed and scrubbed. I lingered until I imagined tentacles of steam reaching beneath the door along the passage. Then I basked in the afterglow until the last drop fell from me and trickled down the drain.

In retrospect, my hostess probably wasn't exaggerating about me glowing. Though the little she knew about radiation was dangerous. For example, she'd never heard of taking iodine to prevent the thyroid gland absorbing the unstable isotope 131. I advised her to buy some tablets before stocks ran out. Which happened a week later, when the authorities finally deigned to inform the residents of Kiev about the cloud of radioactivity overhead and the need to shower regularly and wash their fruit and vegetables.

Interestingly, a similar thing happened here in New York State, at Indian Point nuclear plant, only thirty-six miles away as the crow flies. Different reactor design, different cause, but same outcome… Now you know why I always kept iodine tablets in the toiletry cupboard.

Angelov then showed me to my sleeping quarters – a single bed, a dwarf's desk and a bookshelf. Despite a whiff of must and a fine layer of dust, the place was neat as a pin. A teddy bear seated against a pillow suggested that it had been a child's room. But judging by the heaviness of her spirit as she wished me goodnight, I dared not ask.

'Remember,' she said before leaving, 'You go nowhere tomorrow. No answering the door, no noise, no opening the drapes. But enjoy sleeping late. I'll leave fresh *kasha* on the stove.'

I scanned the bookshelf. Nothing but children's classics. I switched off the light.

Seldom had a soft mattress felt so welcome to my soul. I snuggled under the covers and lay on my back – the only comfortable position now – imagining kinder times. Evenings at my late aunt's home in the village when Mama and Papa visited for dinner, and I'd be bundled up in a blanket and left to doze off amid the warm, comforting drone of adult chatter.

Just as I felt tired enough, the pressure built in my bladder, forcing me to the bathroom. Wide awake again, I felt the onset of dread as my fears multiplied in the dark: Yuri trapped under a tangle of radioactive steel and concrete or, according to the authorities, a ghost who'd never existed. But then I chided myself. Much of what we worry about rarely materialises. My fears were all still speculation, and without proof of death there was always hope. But the only real lead I had was the man spotted at Hospital Number Eighteen in Kiev. If memory served me, it wasn't far from Universytet Metro Station. I resolved to look for a street map on Angelov's bookshelf in the morning.

With a jolt I remembered that I'd promised to stay home. How could I betray her, after all her kindness? But how could I betray Yuri by not trying to find him? I drifted off to sleep mired in guilt and anguish.

When I finally blinked awake from my troubled night a shaft of sunlit dust was hovering above my chest. I wanted to sneeze but suppressed it. Then, as I recalled my surroundings and my thoughts cleared, I sprang up and got dressed. The clothes Angelov had lent me were a fuddy-duddy plaid skirt and white blouse, but they would have to do.

There was no sign of her in the kitchen, so I peeked into the lounge. Good taste in furnishings, I thought, a Yugoslavian sofa. Yuri would approve. The thought brought a stab of pain. Yurochka, I silently sobbed, I know you're alive! You're a survivor.

And in a way I believed it. No matter how deluded I was, I needed to believe it to endure the marathon ahead. And make-believe, after all, is the foundation of a ballerina's art.

Beyond the sofa was an upright piano, a fireplace filled with dried flowers, and a mantelpiece cluttered with photos. My eye caught a black and white snap of a family of four on a crowded beach – Odesa presumably – with Angelov on the kinder side of middle age. A beauty indeed, she had her arm draped about a teenage boy, blonde as a Swede, presumably from her submariner husband beside her with a short buzz cut. But the sight of this happy couple triggered my dread and I moved to the bookshelf. What an impressive collection! My eyes settled on The

Master and Margarita by Bulgakov, which got me wondering. I vaguely recalled reading that he once lived in Kiev.

I spent the morning lounging around making countless cups of tea and slipping in and out of books like television channels. But I couldn't resist studying the street layout of the city – specifically, around the hospital. It was so close! Oh, how my resolve was tested in that claustrophobic apartment. But I stayed indoors. I owed Angelov that. Besides, if Yuri was in Hospital Number Eighteen, I persuaded myself, he'd be in the best hands; one day wouldn't be critical.

It was five fifty-five by the time I heard a key in the door.

'*Zdraztvye!*' Her tone was friendly but the salutation formal. 'See what I brought,' she said, holding up a brown paper bag. 'Salmon and sour cream.' She led me to the lounge where she unlocked the cabinet under the television. Then, presenting a bottle of Georgian red and two glasses, she pointed to the sofa. '*Sidet.*'

Her manner seemed slightly strange.

'*Na vashe zdarovye,*' she said, raising her glass.

We clinked glasses and sipped and then sank into an awkward silence. She too seemed familiar with interrogation techniques, as if she was holding back to see what I might offer.

I sat quietly.

She made some innocuous comment about the warm spring weather, and how her husband came from a line of naval officers going back to Tsar Nicholas the First. The only vaguely useful thing I learned about her was that she worked in a government department.

Suddenly, I'd had enough. I drained my glass and plonked it on the coffee table.

'Okay... so, where is he?'

Her face darkened.

I feared the worst.

'No, not that,' she said.

'What then?'

'All I can tell you is that he's alive.'

I let out a cry.

Words can't describe the elation I felt hearing that after days of agonising uncertainty. My husband lived! In that moment, I didn't consider the question of whether or how he might be suffering. He breathed. He was on this shore of the ocean between life and eternal stillness.

'I must caution you,' she continued, 'he's gravely ill.'

I searched her eyes and her posture but saw no traces of deception. 'Where? In a hospital?'

'I'm not allowed to tell you.'

But I pressed on. 'Number Eighteen?'

She remained deadpan.

'I'm right, aren't I? Sergey…'

Her glare stopped me cold.

'Sorry,' I said. 'I'm tired. It's just so hard to keep up the pretence.'

'I'm afraid you have to get used to it.'

'I will. I can act. But please. If Yuri's just around the corner…'

She shook her head. 'It's too dangerous; they'll never let you in without a security clearance.'

'But…'

She stood. 'Perhaps we can arrange something when your papers are ready. Hopefully tomorrow.'

'But you promised by today!'

'I promised no such thing. I said a day or two, and that I would tell you what I could today, which I have.'

I sat back, chastised. Suddenly, I felt bad. 'I'm so sorry,' I said. 'I'm behaving like a brat. Obsessing over my own problems. I just so badly need to know Yuri's all right. And if there's anything I can do to help him.'

Her expression softened. 'I understand. And we're doing our best to get your papers ready as soon as humanly possible. But these official processes take on a life of their own.'

I nodded meekly. 'Trust me, I know.'

There was a peaceful silence.

'Right,' she said, standing. She opened a cupboard, produced an instamatic camera, and laid it on the table. 'I need to take a few photos for your passport. But first we need to give you a chop.'

And that was the end of my China doll image. I sat on the kitchen chair as the scissors hacked away, watching in horror as lock after precious lock fell to the floor.

'There,' she said, and stood back triumphantly.

I stood gingerly, shook the strands off my shoulders and ruffled what was left of my hair. I went to look in the bathroom mirror. I was aghast. She'd given me spikes, like a punk. I felt naked. I knew it was me in the mirror, but it wasn't the person I recognised. Yet another layer of my identity had been snatched away.

And funnily enough, Katya, it's happening to me again right now. Seriously. Beneath my bandana, I'm becoming as bald as a vulture. Every morning great tufts come out and clog the shower drain. It's devastating. Hair is so much part of a woman's identity.

Oh, my darling, there's no point beating around the bush: my cancer can't be stopped now. My blood markers took a turn for the worse overnight. They even sent in the hospital padre to visit me this morning. A Catholic was apparently the closest they could get to an Orthodox. Or – who knows? – perhaps you arranged it; I remember while you were at Fordham you got into a Catholic crowd for a while; perhaps they influenced you. Anyway, he even asked if my affairs were in order. Huh!

Who knows how long I have. Not a doctor in this country will dare give a definitive timeframe; they're too scared of being sued. But they don't need to – I can read the tea leaves.

Sorry, I'm crying. I hope you don't also get too upset now. But this time I'm not going to apologise. In the end, it's better to be honest and face facts. And in truth, there's nothing like a good howl to revive one's spirits.

Okay, my little dove, I'm exhausted. Let's call it a night.

You might be just as tired. I imagine you both work like Trojans. Especially Bob. I looked him up. Impressive. But I'm sure that fancy law firm gets its pound of flesh. Watch, he'll make partner soon. Maybe even district attorney. I recognise ambition...

Sorry. I'm getting emotional again. Must be the medicine. I just can't help thinking about your father. Yuri was ambitious too, though he never admitted it. I found that attractive in a man. Always striving toward a higher goal.

Do this for me, my little dove: next time Bob gets home from work, take him in your arms and hug him as tightly as you can and tell him how much he means to you. You'll never regret it, I promise. But one day you might regret not doing it.

And again: make sure you thank him, from me, especially for his part in arranging this lovely room of my own. Funnily enough, the more I'm bedridden, the more I appreciate it. Probably because I'm living almost exclusively in my thoughts, which can so easily be disturbed by the mere presence of others.

But don't be alarmed, there's still some time; this old mother of yours is a fighter; I'm not going anywhere until I'm done with this tale.

Twenty

Ah, here we are again, my girl, ready to start. I feel better in the mornings than the evenings now. A nice cup of coffee after a delicious scrambled egg for breakfast and I'll dive right back into the next episode! We're on the home stretch now.

I was telling you how Angelov hacked my hair off for my passport photo.

And I didn't have to look at my notes… See, my mind, at least, is still in working order.

Well, she'd barely swept my locks off the kitchen floor when she summarily excused herself, apparently exhausted. But not before telling me to help myself to the meal in the fridge, and that I wasn't under any circumstances to leave the apartment tomorrow, save for a fire. If a nosy neighbour was insistent at the door, I should say I was her cousin Masha from Moscow. And with that she went into her bedroom and closed the door.

I felt destitute. Angelov had teased me with the news that my husband was alive but in critical condition perhaps not a kilometre away as the crow flies. But I wasn't to try to see him: I must leave him to suffer and possibly die without ever setting eyes on each other again, and then disappear forever to become someone else in a strange country God knows where. And now she'd closed her door in my face.

Fortunately, I had no inkling of how hard the rest of the journey would be. I thank God every day that in his wisdom he shows us no more than the immediate hurdles in front of our noses.

Unsurprisingly, I struggled to sleep that night, such was my tortured self-talk. But my self-pity soon morphed into trying to figure out how to gain access to the hospital. Using my existing identity would be suicide.

Dermichev must have become wise to Sergey's ruse by now and alerted the hospitals. But what if Yuri died while I continued to prevaricate?

And now there was the additional worry that more time out on the streets could expose my baby to radiation. Yes, my little dove, I'd started seeing you as my baby – and caring about your needs. You see, becoming a mother is a process. But once the flame of a mother's love is ignited, it can never be extinguished. There's a Lebanese saying that when you have a child you never breathe alone again. I loved you already then. And I love you still. I want you to remember that long after you throw the last handful of dirt on my casket. And don't let that make you feel sad. Dying's the most natural thing in the world.

And so, on my second day in Kiev I woke again to an empty apartment. I felt frustrated and anxious, but after a cup of tea and some *kasha*, I calmed down. Perhaps I had been too harsh on Angelov: getting me a false identity couldn't be easy. And Yuri was getting good medical care. Besides, I had no choice but to trust. Or at least try to...

But soon after breakfast I found myself pacing every square centimetre of the apartment like a cooped-up hen. I wondered how on earth people in prison survived solitary confinement.

I paused at the bathroom mirror to examine myself again. Somehow, removing most of my hair had changed the entire shape of my face. I was barely recognisable. Immediately, it struck me that this would make it easier now to move around Kiev incognito.

With this thought, my mind wouldn't stop spinning. I returned to the kitchen and drew up a chair so I could look into the courtyard. I scanned the far walls. They were criss-crossed with external plumbing but only a handful of apartments had open windows. Presumably, most people were at work. I leaned forward to get a view of the paving below. It was deserted. I watched and waited. One minute, two... Then I saw the shadow of a man in the archway. But no: either he'd ducked away, or I'd imagined it. Minutes ticked by and there was no movement of any kind. Who would be the wiser, then, if I slipped out for a few hours, as long I got back before the residents started returning from work. Angelov wouldn't know. Kiev was a big city, so it would be easier to stay anonymous. I had to take the risk for Yuri. How could I live with myself if I didn't try while I had the opportunity?

Within minutes, I was out on the bustling sidewalk of Saksaganskogo Street, a stone's throw from the apartment, wearing a head scarf and my hostess's sunglasses. On the downslope I could see the rooftops of Vokzalna Train Station – that great southern hub from which important people took *electrichkas* to their weekend *dachas* or long-distance trains to the far reaches of the empire. But, from the map, I knew to head uphill, along Lva Tolstogo Street toward the greenery of the gardens. So, there I was, like a twelfth century travelling minstrel arriving in Kiev, staring up a rubble-strewn slope to the remains of the Golden Gates where Yaroslav the Wise failed to fend off the Mongols, who ended up ruling Russia for two hundred and forty years.

A yellow tram rattled past and squeaked to a stop just beyond me. Passengers alighted and boarded. How at peace they seemed, how set in their ways. A couple of men in grey suits, briefcases in hand, approached with the ease of the middling *nomenklatura*. Before, I'd have despised their narrow lives and routines; now I felt a pang of envy. They had purpose, jobs, homes, and, most of all, each other. My aloneness felt more than I could bear. Yuri, I silently cried, if by any miracle you're still alive – breathe on; I'm coming to ease your pain, to nurse you, and to tell you how much I love you!

I suddenly became aware that I was disorientated, unsure of my directions. Approaching was a boy in his late teens with frayed jeans. A safe bet he wasn't a ballet aficionada who might recognise me. 'Excuse me,' I said, 'where's Hospital Number Eighteen?'

'Keep going,' he said without hesitation. 'Past the gardens, Lva Tolstogo veers right; afterwards, on the left before the university, there's a shortcut. My aunt's a nurse there.'

I suppressed my curiosity.

'A radiography technician,' he added, as if reading my mind.

'Interesting.'

'Are you visiting someone there?' he said.

'I'm in Kiev on business. I want to drop in to see a friend from high school.'

His eyes lit up. 'Is she from Pripyat?'

He knows, I thought. Just my luck. 'Yes... I mean no. She has burns... her apartment had a gas leak.'

He looked sceptical. 'You don't have to be ashamed, miss.'

'What do you mean?'

'My aunt works in the emergency ward – she told me about the accident, that there'd be many more patients in the days ahead.'

I felt a knot in my stomach. 'I don't know what you're talking about. Thanks for the directions.' I marched off.

'But miss!' he called out.

I paused, deciding it was better to hear him out to avoid suspicion. I turned.

'The army's taken over the hospital,' he said. 'You need papers to get in. They even turned me away.'

'Thank you again,' I said, and strode off. But I was spooked. A military guard meant body searches, questions and cameras. My scarf and dark glasses would be scant disguise indoors. Yet I'd got that far, I should at least reconnoitre the hospital. I'd just have to avoid my ballet duckwalk and stand tall. But I sensed the boy looking after me, so I took a detour through the gardens to calm myself.

The air was sub-tropically warm and humid, and the shrubs were all in flower. The scent of almond blossom was so potent that I was soon wandering along the path in a trance, over slate pathways covered in confetti of fallen petals. Rounding a bend, I saw a *starik* sitting on a bench beneath a cherry tree, tossing breadcrumbs to a pigeon. I felt a rush. Could it be my guide Zhukov? As I drew closer, he turned. Just another tramp.

I tensed. He could also be a snitch. One of the government's myriad eyes and ears. It was rumoured that bums were paid in vodka to inform on suspicious activities.

'Hey!' he shouted.

Damn, I thought.

'Go!'

I froze.

He stood, waving. But not at me, I began to realise. A crow was picking its way over the litter that had spewed from an overturned trash bin. The crow stopped, plumped self-importantly, and poised for flight. I eyed it. Crows could be as terrifying as Yak fighter jets, heading straight for you with swift, aggressive flaps, only flinching at the last second if you didn't.

As I walked on, the *starik* watched me with hooded eyes. I sped up, eyes fixed ahead until I'd passed him. Round the bend, I broke into a limping jog up the arc of the pathway, where I was glad of the sunlight. But I only breathed a sigh of relief when I saw the sign for the Universytet Metro. Past the entrance to the platforms I hurried, before entering the gloom of the underpass tunnel with its reek of urine.

I popped out again into the dazzling sun on the bustling Tarasa Shevchenko Boulevard. Diagonally opposite was St Volodymyr's Cathedral. I crossed over and joined the pedestrian current down the gentle incline, growing increasingly claustrophobic. Then I stopped dead. Barely fifty metres ahead, an ambulance was double-parked outside a stately three-story building with fenced grounds. I started to tremble. On a gate, partly obscured by the branch of a *kashtan*, was a sign with the number eighteen!

Oh Yurochka, I inwardly cried.

Inexorably, I was drawn forward until I was directly opposite the hospital. Every fibre in my body was twitching, ready to bound across. Instead, I waited. Nothing. Pedestrians muttered behind me, and I moved aside as a bus rumbled by. Eventually, the taillights of the ambulance flickered, then its indicator, the iron gate swung open, and it turned.

A guard in military fatigues appeared from nowhere.

My heart sank.

He raised his hand to stop the ambulance. The driver unwound the window and handed over papers. The guard scrutinised them.

What was taking so long?

He spoke into his two-way radio.

This is going to be difficult, I thought.

Finally, he waved the ambulance through. It entered an archway and disappeared.

The kid was right, the hospital was guarded like the Lubyanka.

I stood, debating whether to risk entering, when the guard swirled around and stared in my direction. Was he looking at me? Yes. My heart sank. I'd have to come back later. I looked at my watch. Ten o'clock. If I returned in say two hours, he might have gone off shift, or be on a lunch break. Or be less likely to remember me.

What should I do in the two hours? It would be stupid to return to the apartment. And just as foolish to waste the window of freedom in Kiev. But an idea was forming. I could go to the Party's regional headquarters...

I shivered. I'd been there a few months back with Yuri for some official business and he'd introduced me to a couple of important people. One in particular seemed to be well disposed toward Yuri, as if he owed him something. A comrade Morozov, if I recalled correctly. There was surely a better than even chance he hadn't heard of me being taken into custody in Pripyat or leaving with Sergey. Perhaps if I spun a strong enough story, he'd tell me if he knew Yuri's whereabouts. Or, on second thoughts, perhaps I could...

Never mind, let's get to that later.

But wouldn't visiting the Party Offices expose my hostess? Not necessarily. There was no need to mention to the authorities where I was staying. I paced up and down the sidewalk, wrestling with a conflicted conscience. But I could find no resolution. Except that I had to keep moving. So, I decided to take a roundabout route to the headquarters to avoid anyone following me and give myself time to decide along the way.

Reluctantly, I turned up the nearest street, Volodymyrska, which led to the hill toward the heart of the old city. As I passed the Opera House where I'd once performed on tour, I wistfully recalled those heady days, when I'd just been made stand-in for the role of Carmen and my star was rising. Sadly, in the end, I never got to dance the lead role, my shot at glory, because Miss Perfect never faltered. She was even a nice person,

234

making it hard to wish her ill. How often career opportunities depend on the bad luck of others!

I glanced across to the road abutting the theatre school and smiled. There was the restaurant where we were tacitly allowed to dine with VIPs after our performances, despite official orders to retire early for beauty sleep. I paused to admire the theatre's grandiose Baroque façade. Ah, the memories... After the Bolshoi, Kiev was the largest stage I'd danced on, and one of my favourites – despite being the site where Stolypin, the last Tsar's prime minister, was assassinated.

I'd been imagining this would soon be my new company. But what now? It didn't bear thinking about. The door was boarded up. 'Closed for renovations,' the sign read. It seemed to sum up my life.

I marched on up the cobbled street canyon of pre-war apartments and office buildings, up the gentle rise to where it curved right to reveal the onion domes and green copper spires of St Sophia's Cathedral and the monastery. One glimpse and my spirits rose, remembering Babushka's bedtime stories. The church had been named for the Holy Wisdom – Hagia Sophia – by Vladimir, the first Christian king, and survived allegedly because of the protection of its saint, unlike St Michael's further on, which Stalin had blown up.

I crossed the street and cautiously approached the crumbling stone wall of the monastery. There, I pressed my face to one of its many gaping holes and peered through. Ah, what blessed relief from the heat in the shade of a tree and between the cool stones.

The main edifice was a modest Byzantium structure surrounded by several single-storey satellites set among a garden in full spring blaze. Sitting quietly on a bench in the shade of a blossoming cherry tree, I spied a so-called priest. Most clerics the authorities tolerated were likely to be informers.

Then another priest appeared, strolling ramrod straight with his cassock scraping the pathway. Stiff as formal religion, I thought, until the corners of his eyes crinkled into a broad smile as he sat down beside his colleague to converse. How my heart ached with loneliness as I witnessed their connection. It dawned on me that if I disappeared, no one would even notice.

Soon, they rose and wandered off. I tore myself from the cool of the aperture and faced the city. Directly opposite stood the KGB headquarters, the very building Sergey had assured Dermichev he would transport me to. At street level, the walls were clad in roughly hewn stone broken occasionally by tiny, barred windows. All designed to project the power of the state, instil fear, and cower the populace. Precisely what the state had accused the church of doing by building steeples that were visible for kilometres, reminding the peasants that they could never hide from the Almighty's reach.

A gaggle of men in dark suits were descending the steps with a self-important air. They began to congregate on the sidewalk, where a thick-set individual held court. Suddenly, he raised his hand to hail a taxi, and something about his manner seemed familiar. Then he looked my way...

Yavlinsky!? Surely not. I felt flustered. He was being transferred to Kaliningrad. But maybe not right away. It could be he was spending some time in Kiev first. So this was where the helicopter had taken him from Pripyat. But if Yavlinsky had fallen foul of the system as he'd said, why would he now be fraternising with KGB dignitaries so publicly and with such authority?

A police van drew up, shielding him from view. Seconds later it joined the traffic, leaving an empty sidewalk; and I was left doubting and uneasy.

But I dared not linger. I needed to keep moving, take detours. So, I continued toward Sofiyivska Square. My leather shoes sounded on the cobbles as I marched. The square was deserted save for a huddle of *stariki* at a lamp post, and a *babushka* walking with a basket. What was I doing here? I asked myself in anguish.

Feeling the stares of the *stariki*, and worried that somehow they might recognise me as a ballerina, I hurried across the square and melted into a side street and toward the river park.

Finally, I was alone again. I could return to the conundrum of whether to visit the Party Headquarters. I checked my watch. Ten forty-five. Time wasn't an issue. But was it worth the risk?

On I wandered beneath a canopy festooned with candelabras of blossoms on paths sprinkled white. The trees were mostly *kashtans* and maples, their bark freshly striped with whitewash to stop beetles boring during the winter. The vegetation was thick about me, but now and again I glimpsed the river snaking peacefully far below. I reached instinctively to point it out to Yuri and his absence struck me like a physical blow. A great void opened in my heart that no natural beauty or pleasure could ever fill, so big it felt like an effort to breathe.

The further into the forest I went, the more my loneliness turned to anxiety, until every shadow became the KGB. Suddenly, I was desperate to escape. But how? The path seemed to stretch on forever. Fortunately, I'd studied the map. The park hugged the river, which meant it was long and thin. So, I veered off on a cross-path, over a tarred road and up, out of the forest gloom to the grassy slope and sunlight. Up the hill I strode, a modest incline, barely fifty vertical metres, until I reached a ridge with a view. There were trees everywhere, between buildings, lining the streets and courtyards all the way to October Revolution Square below and beyond...

The Kiev offices of the Committee of the Communist Party of Ukraine. I felt goosebumps on my arms. Could I really be contemplating another visit to the belly of the beast? It felt like I'd been playing a game of Chutes and Ladders, and I'd just slid down the longest ladder yet and had to start from the very beginning again. For minutes I was paralysed with fear, unable to decide whether to continue.

Anyway, the dull ache in my knee forced me to move. So, I set off down the slope toward the square in search of a bench. There was a tidy crowd down there for a weekday, mostly old folks seated in pairs or groups, many staring into the distance through a haze of cigarette smoke.

I slumped onto the first free bench and surveyed the scene. At the table nearest me a pair of men were engrossed in a game of chess, chuckling and smoking. They had the familiarity only long friendship

237

or military service can engender. And, not for the first or last time that week, I cried. My sunglasses misted up until I had to remove them.

I was wiping them on my skirt when I was startled by a soccer ball against my shin. I looked up to see a little boy approaching. I noticed his Nike sneakers first, then his face… it was Alexander Yavlinsky, Sonya's son!

I picked up the ball. 'Is this yours?' I said brightly.

He remained rooted to the spot, his face impassive. A rivulet of snot ran from his nose.

'Come, take it,' I said, offering it to him.

He slowly shook his head.

'You sure?'

He remained mute, the same blank stare as if I was a perfect stranger. Then he turned tail and scurried off.

I started to panic. I had to get away fast to avoid an encounter with his mother, never mind father. But it was too late.

'Well,' said her familiar voice. 'The porcelain doll.'

'Hi Sonya,' I said awkwardly, and passed her the ball.

'Hi. What are you doing in Kiev?'

'It's a long story,' I said, flippantly.

'Vladimir told me some of it.' She handed the ball to her son and patted him. 'Go play by the fountain, darling. I'll be right there.' She watched him amble off in slow motion, then turned to me. 'He said you were looking for Yuri.'

I didn't respond.

'Is he all right?'

'Do you care?'

'I won't respond to that,' she said. 'So, did you find him?'

I shook my head.

'I'm sorry,' she said.

'I'm sure.'

'What's that supposed to mean?'

'You know exactly.'

Her face darkened. It was hard to tell if it was from embarrassment or anger. But when she spoke again, it was clear.

'How could you, Lena?'

'Could I what?'

She gestured toward the fountain. 'What do you see?' she said.

The boy stood by the water's edge, unnaturally still, staring straight ahead.

As I watched, my uneasiness grew. Another lad of similar age ran up and grabbed the soccer ball from him, then turned and ran. But Sasha continued staring blankly ahead. Finally, he turned, saw his mother and started tottering toward us. 'Mama,' he gurgled, whimpering into her skirt.

'It's all right my darling,' she said, stroking his hair. Then she turned to me, seething. 'You see now?' she spat. 'From the fall. Just yesterday we saw a specialist here in Kiev. The initial diagnosis is brain damage.'

'I'm sorry.'

'Well, that won't bring me my son back.'

'You're not blaming me, are you?'

She didn't answer.

'You can't be serious,' I said. 'I've done nothing.'

'Exactly. You stood and watched.'

'Think what you like,' I said. 'Just leave my husband alone.' I stalked off, diagonally across the square toward the metro sign on Khreshchatyk Street, feeling terrible, but not looking back.

I tottered down some steps into the metro ticket hall, where I paused to get my bearings. Hurried commuters scurried around me while the clatter and clang of trains rose from the deep tunnel below.

There was a protracted screech of a train arriving and a warm wind followed. I skirted the turnstiles and the kiosks and followed the signs for the far exit. The tunnel was long and winding, and by the time I popped up above ground, dazzled by the sunlight, I was halfway up Instytutska Street, on the slope opposite the square, above a VIP hotel.

I waited at the exit for a gap in the current of suited *nomenklatura* surging past. Their conversations sounded as earnest as the architecture around us. It felt like I'd moved from the heart of the city to its cerebral cortex. Up, up I strode, and then veered onto Bankova Street, hugging the contour of the hill until ahead loomed the Gorkom. Monstrous Corinthian columns, too high to describe, and as hard and cold as the hearts of the brutes oozing power as they strutted or gathered in clumps to smoke, swap favours and plot.

I still get the shivers thirty years on. Few empires in history could boast an authoritarianism as effective as Russia's. And always from a powerful centre – be it Novgorod, Kiev, St Petersburg or Moscow. The Kremlin was like the hub of a giant spider's web, with a thousand spokes and sub-spokes – where every union, republic, district, city and village or collective farm – hell, every man, woman and child and their thoughts – were ultimately controlled by one man.

Who knows, maybe it's a necessary evil in a country so vast. Even in its shrunken form today, the Russian Federation has the largest territory of any country on earth, spread over no less than eleven time zones. It's also the oldest, dating from AD862, depending how you determine it. Who said a kingdom couldn't endure for a thousand years?

Everything in history is debatable. Even the real reason I went to that evil edifice in those precious couple of hours of freedom I had stolen in Kiev that day, against the insistence of my hostess.

Sorry. I'm still finding it a struggle to tell this part. I'm doing my best, but I'm a house divided, just as I was then. I've carried these secrets for a generation. Shame is a poison that thrives in the dark, and it's still gnawing inside me after all these years.

There was a reason I first walked that long, circular route through the city and its parks, thinking through my options. I was wrestling with my conscience.

Sorry, I need a drink of water. Let me call for the nurse. I'm not trying to avoid the topic. Well, okay, maybe I'm procrastinating. But don't worry, I'm going to tell you the raw truth. I've got nothing to lose now.

In truth, I wasn't only going to the headquarters of the Ukrainian Communist Party to ask a certain comrade Mozorov for help. How on earth could I expect some random individual, even if he was fairly senior

in the organisation, to know where my husband was? No, my real intention was to go straight to Yavlinsky's boss who, like Yavlinsky in Pripyat,
kept an office at the Gorkom.

I was planning to confess to my failure as an informer and for feeding
them nonsense in the name of love. And then, after pleading for clem-
ency, I was going to tell them everything I knew about Yuri's work. All
of it, in exchange for their help to find him.

Yes, I know, just two days earlier, Yavlinsky had come to assure me
that I'd been exonerated. But having seen him here at the Gorkom in
Kiev, it was obvious that I'd been naïve to believe him. I'd allowed
myself to be duped yet again. I was certain now that the organs – whether
Yavlinsky or Dermichev or some other arm – were going to catch me
sooner or later.

You'll be wondering why I would throw myself into the hands of the
KGB even though I knew Sergey, Angelov and the others were arranging
me a new passport, a whole new identity, and an escape route to the free
world. The truth is, I saw no possibility that their scheme could work. It
might be hard for you to see it as I did then, but in the 1980s, the idea
that an anti-government conspiracy could succeed in Sovetsky Soyuz was
unimaginable. The KGB was simply too powerful; its tentacles were inescapable. In fact, I had a suspicion that Sergey, Zhukov and Angelov were
also connected by some roundabout route to a faction within the KGB.

I had only agreed to inform the KGB for love of Babushka, and only
reneged out of love for Yuri.

But leaving the KGB was a cat-and-mouse game I was bound to lose.
And now I no longer had the leverage of Yavlinsky's corrupt moon-
lighting scheme that I'd discovered in Pripyat, because he was being
moved elsewhere. Although he'd made it sound like he was being side-
lined, what I'd seen earlier outside the KGB offices told a different story.
And according to Zhukov, the KGB was still looking for me.

So from the look of things, it was only a matter of time before they
tracked me down. I couldn't escape them forever by hiding. Besides, all
they wanted from me was information. And all I wanted now was to
find Yuri before he died, if indeed that was to be his fate. Confessing

might be the only way to achieve that. What other hope was there but to face the KGB head-on and try to negotiate a deal while I still had a trump card?

Sorry, let me get some water.

That's better.

I've found it excruciatingly difficult to tell you this part, my little dove. I'm not proud of any of it. But do we ever really escape ourselves or our failings? I don't think so, it's more what we do despite them. Yet my very act of telling this is already a triumph.

My darling, I hope in time you'll see it the same way when this tale is done. And that you'll find it in your heart to forgive me. Such matters of the heart can take years to heal, I know, but hopefully, with more understanding of my struggles you won't stay bitter for life.

Okay, enough for tonight. This is taking its toll on my stamina, though. Even the act of talking tires me now. Your mother isn't feeling well today. I'll tell you more next time.

Twenty-one

I hope you haven't given up on me, Kayusha. I can only imagine how shocked you were after what I revealed last time. I couldn't sleep either. I tossed and turned until after midnight. Though it didn't help that it was hot and humid.

Still, the view from this window was lovely. The city lights seem extra bright when there's no moon. And the reflection on the wall... The bridge looked like a string of pearls.

Of course the sky is pretty much all I can see these days from this angle. But don't worry; if I get bored, I count helicopters. It's astonishing how many criss-cross the sky on Friday and Saturday nights. It's a wonder they don't collide.

After the last session, I also came to realise how circular my story must sound. If I were a novelist my protagonist would have completed her character arc by now. After the inciting incident she'd have courageously overcome one challenge after another until she finally changed for the better and – drum roll – won a glorious victory and lived happily ever after. But my story plays out more like a stuck record. The protagonist just goes down at every hurdle.

And as the author of my own story I take full responsibility. Like millions of others, I stood by while that evil system flourished and spread. Not a day has gone by that I haven't thought 'if only'. But self-flagellation is pointless, and hindsight is a hypocrite. The truth is, I'd probably do the same again. How could an orphan not accept any bargain to protect the only living relative who'd stood by her and raised her? And what orphan wouldn't be tempted to join a noble group of citizens purportedly supporting the Motherland? Oh God, how I wanted to feel I belonged to something bigger than myself. Which ballet provided, in a way, especially in the corps. It filled the void for a while, until I realised that most

243

of my so-called friends were connivers who'd sell their grandmothers for a kopek to get a better part.

But here's the biggest irony of all. Imagine for a moment that I hadn't agreed to inform for the KGB. Would I have met Yuri or given birth to you, the two great loves of my life?

Anyway, that day outside the Party Headquarters in Kiev, after all that agonising, I didn't do it. I didn't go in and confess. In fact, maybe that moment was the turning point in my journey to redemption, second only to my decision to stop giving them useful information on Yuri. I just didn't recognise it at the time. Instead of feeling virtuous, I felt only self-loathing for coming so close to betraying everyone who had trusted and helped me, including Yuri.

Instinctively, at that moment I felt an urgent need to immerse myself in nature as a form of spiritual cleansing. Fortunately, I wasn't far from Kiev's new Gryshko Botanical Gardens, so I asked a passer-by for directions to the nearest bus stop and the line number. The trip, though a short distance, took a good half hour with all the stops.

The entrance to the gardens had a carnival atmosphere. The ticket office was flanked by an ice-cream kiosk and a news stand, each with a modest queue of customers. I paid my pittance and entered.

The grounds were palatial: trimmed hedges, wide pedestrian boulevards and freshly turned black earth in the beds. Craving seclusion, I headed away from the crowds toward the river. I sat for a while on one of the benches half-hidden in the shade of a fern bank. Then I passed a variety of exotic shrubs, pausing to read the plaques. Afterwards I meandered down the gentle curves of a leaf-dappled path. Below I could see the swollen river where a barge was plying its way against the languid flow. Beyond lay the sawtooth of the city's outer suburbs. With every step, the full-fronted sun seemed to coax the surrounding vegetation to further bloom until I was in a tunnel of lilac. I felt compelled to press my face deep into the blossoms to revel in the scent.

When I finally retracted my head, I noticed a gap in the hedge and, down in the vale among trees, the neglected roof and dome of Vidubitsky Monastery. Another place Babushka had spoken of.

Feeling somewhat restored, I continued down past the neglected monastery, and back along the road until I linked up with the river park. At a relaxed pace, I returned past the Lavra to the metro station.

I glanced at my watch. Almost two hours had passed. It was time to return to the hospital. But maddeningly, the same guard was on duty outside the hospital as I approached. And before I had time to hide, he'd spotted me. Just then a delivery vehicle pulled up and blocked me from his view. Thwarted, I got away as quickly as I could before the delivery van moved.

I was comfortably back in the apartment before my hostess. There I was, innocent as a lamb, to receive my hostess's perfunctory greeting and exchange pleasantries. Dinner was more bread and *borscht*, this time with chunks of beef. But mostly, we ate in silence.

She seemed to be avoiding conversation, which was fine with me. I was thankful not to have to make up lies about my day. Finally, after washing and drying the dishes in silence, we retired to the lounge to watch the news.

'Measures were being taken to eliminate the consequences of the accident', the *Pravda* newsreader waffled. Aid was being given to those affected, and a government commission had been set up. This, believe it or not, was the first official broadcast of the tragedy – several days after it had happened.

That night I barely slept a wink because you were fluttering and wriggling inside my tummy! It was like you were teasing me: you'd wait until I began to drift off and then you'd start again. Ah, the sense of wonder and awe at this new little spirit moving inside me, like a little bird. Slowly, it began to sink in that I was no longer alone. I lay and stroked my tummy where you'd moved, cooing softly to you, promising that I'd love and care for you no matter what. It was the happiest night I'd had in months.

Until I started fretting again. About Yuri, or rather his absence, my guilt for another wasted day, and the emptiness of my bed... Even when he was on night shift I'd pine, even though I knew he'd return a few hours later. But at least then, when the loneliness got too much, I could phone him. How he hated that! The engineers on duty would tease him mercilessly; they called him a kept man. But I couldn't help myself; I'd get into such a state.

I also agonised again over whether to try to find Yuri in the hospital again, once more betraying my hostess and, by extension, Sergey. Guilt, grief, fear and indecision – a perfect cocktail of psychological torture. By then I felt exhausted and desperately needed sleep. I shifted the pillow, turned it this way and that, but my mind simply wouldn't be stilled. So, by the time the light of day replaced the gloom, I felt like I'd spent the night in an endless loop of *fouettés*.

Angelov was at the stove, nursing a pot of tea. She smiled, but her eyes were hard. Clearly, there was tension in the air. 'Morning,' she said, 'rough night?'

'Nah, I just have trouble sleeping when it's warm and humid.'

She filled two mugs and handed one to me. 'Here. You'll feel better.'

The liquid seared my throat. Slowly, from the vapour, my sinuses cleared. We sat in silence until, finally, she eyed me and said, 'Any plans for today?'

'Err... Not sure.' I picked up the newspaper. There was nothing in the headlines about the explosion. I said, 'I suppose I'll pace this prison anti-clockwise today and wait for the identity papers you promised.'

Her expression darkened.

'What's wrong?'

She shook her head. 'You couldn't last more than a day before betraying my trust.'

'What?'

'Don't insult my intelligence, young lady. Did you think I wouldn't find out? I told them it was a mistake taking you in. Personally, I don't see what a man of Yuri's integrity saw in you.'

I stared, lost for words.

'What did you tell them? Should I expect a thumping on the door tonight? Answer me!'

I looked down at the red and white checked tablecloth. 'It's not what

246

you think,' I said, feeling angry and ashamed. She'd probably had me followed from the moment I left the apartment.

She leaned forward. 'Tell me, dammit. The truth this time. If you know what that is.'

I stroked my hair, considering my options. But, in short, I had none. She knew everything, anyway. 'Okay,' I mumbled. 'I admit, I went. I planned to throw myself at the Party's mercy. When you came home without my identity papers, I began to doubt everything. I thought you and Zhukov might be having me on, that anyway it's a lost cause trying to change my identity, because if the authorities want me badly enough, they'll find me sooner or later.

'Rubbish. They're not gods.'

I paused, flicked a grain of sugar off the table. 'I couldn't do it though.'

'I know.'

'So, you had me followed.'

'Did you think I'd trust a snitch?'

I was gobsmacked. How could she possibly know?

'How does a person like you live with yourself?' she continued.

She'd struck a raw nerve. I was feeling awful. But I returned her stare. 'If you despise me so much, why did you take me in late at night?'

She looked away. 'It was Yuri's sole precondition.'

'Yuri's precondition?' I was shocked. 'For what?'

'I'm afraid I can't give you the details.'

'A summary then.'

'I can't.'

I stood. 'Well then,' I said, 'I'll have to find out on my own.'

'Enough!' she snapped

We glared at each other.

Eventually, she exhaled. 'The less you know the better, for everyone's safety, yours included.'

'I don't care if I die, so you may as well tell me everything.'

'It's the torture you have to worry about.'

'Tell me anyway. Please.'

She puckered her cheeks. 'Okay. Sit.' She sighed. 'Sergey's arrival at just the right time to rescue you from the *militsiya*... wasn't serendipity.'

I nodded. It was too good to be true. I'd started having my own doubts. Of all the helicopter pilots in Sovetsky Soyuz, why had Sergey been re-called from active duty abroad? And so early.

'Unlike Sergey and others, your husband didn't really care for the politics – who was reformist or conservative, this faction in the Kremlin or that. He's a scientist's scientist. All he wanted was to continue his research. He was convinced they were close to a breakthrough that would revolutionise the nuclear industry – both civilian and military. And, as a necessary temporary measure, he wanted to correct the weaknesses in the existing reactors to make them safe.'

I stared at her. Of course, I knew some of this already. But I needed to keep her talking to find out if she knew where Yuri was.

'I don't know enough of the technicalities,' she continued. 'But I un-derstand the kind of reactors used in Chernobyl are prone to accidents. Something to do with the water in the cooling system boiling too quickly. Your husband's boss in the military has been sounding the alarm for years and agitating to make the necessary design changes. Apparently, he'd originally developed those reactor types and his team, including Yuri, were best qualified to implement the improvements. The author-ities, unsurprisingly, ignored them, not wanting to disrupt the power supply.' Then she paused.

I shifted in my seat. 'Yes,' I said. 'Yuri seldom talked about his work, but I know the intransigence of the authorities distressed him greatly. Tell me, please, do you know where he is now?'

She looked severely at me, then rose. 'Excuse me. I need to get to work.'

'No, please.' I jumped up, grabbed her shirtsleeve. 'Don't leave me hanging.'

'I need to go,' she said.

I released her sleeve. 'Sorry. It's just... If he's alive... why can't I see him?'

She cleared her throat. 'Trust me: you don't want to.'

A hollow was forming in the pit of my stomach. 'Please,' I begged. I was close to tears. 'If only to say goodbye.'

Her expression turned grave. 'I'm sorry. Yesterday, I still thought it might be possible; that we could take you to the hospital; but… it's worse than we thought. He's deteriorated. And our sources say no one is being allowed near those who were exposed to extreme levels of radiation; not even close relatives.'

'I don't care!' I blurted. 'I need to see my husband. I…'

She frowned. 'Do you realise that this is not only about you? And do you have any idea of the risks people are taking on your behalf? Good people.'

I felt tears welling, and slumped.

Angelov touched my wrist. 'It's okay. All will be well… in the end.'

'But…'

'My dear, dear girl… I can't promise you a fairy tale ending. Everyone dies in the end – and we all suffer. But one thing I can tell you is: there is life for the living beyond tragedy – meaningful life, even joy.' Her voice cracked and she looked down.

I waited, feeling terrible.

'I lost my husband… when his submarine went down – so deep, it was never found.

Her lips were quivering.

'I'm so sorry for my petulance.' Tears spilled down my cheeks.

She looked up at me and opened her arms wide. 'My dear…'

As we embraced, I felt a comfort beyond words.

Then she said, 'Can I give you some advice I would probably have ignored myself?'

I nodded.

'Even if – by some miracle – they permitted you to visit him in hospital,' she continued, 'I'd urge you against it. Go to the library, read what a body looks like when it's been exposed to those radiation levels. No, rather keep your memories of the proud, vigorous man you married, a great scientist. And then consider the future – the future he wanted for you and your child, his child – and use the fresh start his sacrifice has gifted you to do some good in the world to honour his legacy.'

'Which is?'

'A safer world. And a strong and secure Russia.'

'With respect, that sort of slogan has been used to justify all sorts of madness.'

She grimaced. 'This has nothing to do with politics. Your husband strove to make this country a leader in scientific research and its application for the betterment of all. And to uphold the qualities that have sustained our people for a thousand years before the red tide swept over us, and will do for aeons hence – family, faith, valour, hard work, poetry, belly laughs and the boundless black soil of the steppe...'

Abruptly, she stood, purse in hand. 'I've said too much. I must go to work.' With that, she turned and strode into the passage.

'Oh...' She popped her head back into the doorway. 'If you try going to the hospital today, I'll tell my colleagues to abandon all plans for your exile. I think you know what that means.'

I nodded.

'But relax, I've been assured your papers will be ready before the parade.'

I stared blankly at her until I remembered the next day was May Day, a public holiday. 'Okay...' I said, nodding.

'And I tell you what,' she added, 'Assuming we get your papers in time, we'll give you a chance to walk the streets a bit, test out your new identity. The crowds will be good cover. See you this evening.' Then she left and the door clicked shut and all fell deathly quiet.

For a long time I stared at the wall, wrestling with my thoughts. To cut a long story short, I decided to stay put for the day. Surely Yuri would last another few days at least, being in such good care. And the safest option was to wait until I was allowed to go out, and then slip my tail.

But within minutes I was thinking, what if the papers weren't ready the next day or Angelov was purposely stringing me along? I needed a backup plan. So, I approached the window and, clasping the drape, peered out over the courtyard. I waited and waited, until, sure enough, what I expected appeared. Clever: he was dressed like the concierge of a typical apartment building of the *nomenklatura*, those thugs whose chief reason for existence was to report on residents. And skilful: unobtrusive yet covering a lot of ground as he strolled about, stopping here and there to smoke or check a crack, varying his routes. By lunch I was confident I'd deduced his patterns enough to give him the slip.

Then I went into the lounge to relax and kill time. I paged through a coffee table book on the Crimea for distraction. But as much as I tried to immerse myself in its world of tall, dark, rugged cliffs and pebble beaches, I couldn't. My thoughts kept turning to Yuri and my heart would race in panic.

When Angelov returned unexpectedly at three o'clock, I was still there reading. In she breezed, with barely a greeting, and tossed a newspaper – *Pravda*, Ukraine Edition – onto the seat beside me.

'Read,' she said.

The headlines were the usual propaganda and obligatory mug shot of the General Secretary with his wry smirk and benign uncle expression. I paged through the entire paper and then again back to front before looking at her quizzically.

'Nothing strange?' she said.

'No more than usual.'

'Anything on the evacuation?'

'No.'

'And there hasn't been since the explosion,' she added. 'Doesn't that strike you as odd?'

'I suppose so,' I said, thinking as I spoke. 'From what I saw there really was major damage to the reactor. The consequences for the environment, surely, will be dire.'

She nodded. 'Dire enough to cause them to evacuate a city like Pripyat of forty thousand residents, not to mention the other nearby villages. Yet there's nothing in the news.'

I had this sinking feeling as it slowly dawned on me that as far as the government was concerned, all the evacuees and probably a great many others had become ghosts. Officially, we didn't exist.

'Anything else catch your eye?' she asked.

I picked up the paper again and read, my eyes scrunched in concentration. Finally, alongside a scandal involving a local Party chief, I noticed an article about the May Day parade. The text was a tiny photograph of the prior year's celebrations – ranks of drum majorettes in short skirts marching down Khreshchatyk Boulevard behind their baton-twirling leader, smiling faces plastered with make-up and crowds lining the street.

'The parade's going ahead!' I exclaimed.

'Exactly. While my contacts tell me there's a cloud of radioactivity moving south toward Kiev as we speak.'

I exhaled. It was hard to take it all in.

'I'm told some are arguing against the parade. Zgursky, for example, Chairman of the Kiev City Executive Committee, and First Secretary Shcherbitsky. But Moscow is insisting. And guess who's going to win that battle.'

Moscow, of course, as history attests. And thousands of innocent people were needlessly exposed to radiation.

Yes, my little dove, it's enough to make a person cry just thinking about it. And this while the headlines of every newspaper beyond our Western border were screaming that a cloud of radiation the size of an average country had moved north of Pripyat while another stream moved south over the skies of Kiev. As far away as France, people were too afraid to harvest mushrooms from the forest.

Somehow evil men seem to flourish in this life. But always, even during a calamity, there's reason to hope. The winter of evil may last long, but take heart: always, spring will come to call forth the dormant seeds and flourish. See how the church in Ukraine flourishes today, despite decades of persecution. Look at Pripyat itself: contaminated so badly they had to bury trucks and cut down forests. Disease and death reigned, and doomsayers said it would take a thousand times a thousand years to recover. Yet a mere thirty years later, the trees are so high and lush they hide the ruins and give sanctuary to wildlife. Also, humans. A handful of old folks were the first to return; saying they'd rather die than live in exile. And now the area is a tourist attraction. Yes, people pay to enter the exclusion zone, as I did, traipsing through ghost towns like stepping into a computer game or a horror movie to gawk at the pain of others. You must have seen the photos in the news. They publish them every year on the anniversary. I've got some in the *National Geographic* among the magazines beneath my bed.

Take a look. There's an image of the school I taught at, with the text-books still open on the desks. Here's one from the kindergarten, with a teddy bear on the bed; and there, a pair of shoes. But perhaps it's all staged. Nothing is sacred these days, not even our memories.

All these years later, and still the tears come when I look back and think of Yuri. I've never stopped loving your father, Katya, and wishing you could have known him and he you. But better to have loved and lost, my little dove, than never to have loved at all.

Twenty-two

So, as I was saying last night, my hostess surprised me by suggesting she'd let me leave the apartment to stretch my legs, as she put it, and grow accustomed to my 'new self' in public amid the anonymity of the May Day crowds. Looking back, I suspect she knew I'd run off and look for Yuri anyway. But at the time, I was incredulous.

'Really?'

'Yes, but only short walks, a few blocks and back. Possibly as far as Revolution Square. There will be lots of people all along the way.'

'But I don't have my identity papers yet.'

'Tss, you of little faith.' She fished in her bag. '*Voila!*' she said and handed me a passport.

I barely recognised the pigeon head in the photo. Strangely, I felt exhilarated. Like the start of a new adventure. They'd done a thorough job I realised as I paged through, even a stamp and a few splotches. My first name had been changed to Yelena. From Helen of Troy, I thought, clever of them: close enough to the name Lena to create ambiguity, yet opposite in meaning.

Still, I was sceptical. 'Are you saying I'm a free woman, that you trust me?'

'Hell no!' she laughed. 'Not as far as I can spit. Our men will follow you.'

'Still…'

'You need to get accustomed to your role sooner rather than later; there isn't much time.'

'You still want to send me abroad?'

'Yes. I know it's hard to believe anyone would go to such trouble for someone of your ilk, but it seems you have friends in high places.'

'Sergey?'

'Higher.'

I was puzzled, but I held my peace.

'I still can't bring myself to approve or agree,' she said. 'As far as I'm concerned, you're nothing but trouble.'

I've spent three decades since trying to persuade my inner critic otherwise.

Despite her misgivings, Angelov remained the consummate professional. She insisted we run through every possible question and angle to my new character before turning in for the night. She got me to repeat my new name, place of birth, hometown, siblings, traffic violations and so on, until I felt my head would split. Then she handed me a sheaf of notes which she told me to study until the facts were second nature. She warned me that I'd need to pass my first brief test run in the morning, and then said goodnight. My mind was in overdrive after that, and I battled to fall sleep.

First, I struggled to come to terms with my new identity as a dance instructor at a reputable, albeit middling school; a non-religious Jewess who was single, after her fiancé – a physics teacher – died in a car crash on the outskirts of Moscow.

The other, bigger reason for my sleeplessness was that I was rehearsing how to breach the defences of Hospital Number Eighteen. I had a simple plan: to follow a delivery vehicle up the drive, and when the guard was distracted, slip around it, through the arch and around to the rear parking lot.

Finally, there was my conscience: it would mean betraying my hostess's confidence yet again. But in the end it wasn't much of a struggle. I had to do it. My husband was suffering, probably terminally ill. I couldn't live with myself if there was a chance of seeing him and I didn't try, especially with so many unanswered questions swirling in my mind.

How I slipped my tail the next day is a long story. But I'd had enough practice in Pripyat.

By the time I woke, Angelov had left for work. After fortifying myself with a bowl of *kasha* with apple sauce and a cup of strong, black tea, I slipped out of that tomb-like apartment onto the sidewalk of Saksaganskogo Boulevard – pretending not to notice my tail – and allowed myself to be swept along by the crowds. By ten o'clock the crowds were already heaving and swaying to the sounds of martial music. Westward we surged in the direction of Khreshchatyk Street, onward to Revolution Square. There was a carnival mood: families carrying picnic provisions, kids with ice creams, lovers together. It was a perfect spring day, the chill lingering from the night but with the promise of warmth enough for short sleeves and dresses. The crowd continued along confetti-blossomed sidewalks under baby green *kashtan* canopies, where squirrels scurried overhead and far, far above, the sky was so blue it might have been painted.

How normal that May Day seemed in contrast to the calamity unfolding just a hundred and eighty kilometres to the north. Time and again my mind returned to the scenes of hell fire and billowing smoke my dumbstruck fellow evacuees and I had witnessed from the ruins of the reactor. Block after block the swelling crowd flowed, past crumbling apartment blocks and tattered storefronts, one tributary of humanity joining another, surging toward Revolution Square like lambs to the slaughter.

I had the dubious privilege of attending, to listen while dignitary after dignitary spewed their drivel. But I didn't endure to the end. Instead, I used the hiatus to give my tail the slip.

I returned via a circuitous route to Lva Tolstogo Square, back where those elegant but crumbling pre-war apartments overlook the botanical gardens and trams rumbled by, offloading their cargoes of purposeful men. I was suddenly plagued by the likely futility of my mission, and the prospect of a fugitive's life in exile. But this was no time to feel sorry for myself. I powered back up the incline so fast that I missed the shortcut and had to double back. Soon I was among trees, the gardens to one side and the university grounds on the other. For a moment, lost in my thoughts and fears, I forgot I was in the centre of a bustling city. Until I glimpsed the four-storey hospital building behind the foliage. I waded through the undergrowth to the fence. The wire was covered in ivy and blackberry thorns, but I managed to press my head through to the mesh to look.

Along the side of the building were rows of parked cars – presumably belonging to senior administrators and doctors. But a delivery van got my attention. It was in a loading bay across the lot, with two workmen ferrying boxes from its rear into the hospital's goods entrance. My ticket in, I thought, as I withdrew from the foliage. I just needed to get past the guard. I hurried along the lane and stepped out into the hurly-burly of Shevchenko Boulevard, this time approaching the hospital entrance with caution, using a clump of chatting pedestrians as camouflage. When I got close enough, I paused to observe the comings and goings through the front gate of the hospital.

As the seconds became minutes, my anxiety grew. I had at most half an hour before my tail alerted Angelov. Worse, the pedestrians in front of me had dispersed, exposing me. For a moment, I was convinced my life was over.

But at that very moment – don't tell me by coincidence – another delivery van rolled up and turned into the driveway. The guard stepped out with his hand raised.

With feigned confidence, I sauntered out from the huddle, and crouched behind the far side of the van.

'Present passport,' The guard demanded.

The driver obliged.

The van rolled forward.

I followed, keeping low and out of the guard's line of sight, until we were through the archway. Then I wandered across the paving and slouched against the far fence. Shoots of blackberry vine tumbled through the mesh about me. I lit a cigarette and scanned the rear of the building, noting two entrances, one marked *Oncology*. The delivery van was parked between them with its sliding door open. I dropped my cigarette butt into the bramble below. This was as good a time as any...

But my legs wouldn't obey, try as I might. I remained slouched, flushed and sweating. Too risky, a voice in my head shouted. Go back, throw yourself at Angelov's mercy, and give up. But somehow my bloody-mindedness kept me there.

Just then, the saloon doors swung open and two orderlies burst through, wheeling a trolley. One, two, three and they'd loaded the trolley's boxes. And then the van was off, the orderlies back inside, and my legs had found inspiration.

It was so dark inside the building that I had to pause for my eyes to adjust. I found myself in a passage that ended at the base of a spiral staircase, beside which was an elevator entrance. To my right was an open doorway. I peered in. It appeared unoccupied, so I stepped cautiously inside. There were two interleading rooms. The first had tables and chairs, dog-eared magazines, coffee mugs and a sink and kettle in one corner. The other was lined with lockers, most of which were locked except.... I pried one open and – bingo – a doctor's coat on a hanger.

Suddenly, there was a scuffle from the passage. Footsteps. I froze, coat in hand, sure I was done for. But then they faded. I heard the saloon doors swing open and closed, and it grew still again. I tried the coat on. It was a few centimetres too long, but not far from my knees. I noticed an authorisation card pinned to the breast. The photograph was faded but – my spirits soared – it was a woman! I strained to read: Doctor Raisa Alexandrovna Yudin. And short hair like me – what were the odds? All I needed to do was to act the doctor. The key was to identify one hundred per cent with my character by looking from the outside in to develop an artistic schizophrenia. My speciality.

Out of the staff room I bustled, into the stairwell, where I spiralled upwards, surprised at the griminess: cracked concrete, peeling paint and a cigarette stub in an empty preserve jar. Up I hurried, level one, two, three… deciding to start from the top floor, where surely they'd keep the Chernobylites, out of the way, both to maintain secrecy and isolate the radiation.

Soon, I was on the top floor, gasping in front of a closed door with a small, glazed window. I pressed my face against it.

The foyer was an ants' nest, orderlies and nurses bustling about in pale blue uniforms and the occasional doctor passing. When my breathing had slowed sufficiently, I pushed through the swing doors. For a few seconds, the fluorescent lighting left me disorientated and light-headed. Be strong, I urged myself, slipping into the wake of a pair of orderlies.

We passed the nursing station and entered a corridor. The walls were freshly painted in baby blue and turquoise – and the floor was a patchwork of slate. The passage kinked left and the orderlies disappeared ahead. Another kink, and the corridor straightened again. I found myself in front of a towering steel gate. I grabbed the prison-thick bars and rattled. Locked. I patted my coat. Damn, no keys.

Then I stopped. Footsteps were approaching from behind. My heart raced. I was trapped.

A nurse brushed past me, muttering gibberish like the cat in Alice in Wonderland. Then she reached into her pocket, and after a jingle of keys, the gate swung open. 'Doctor...' she said, waving me ahead.

'Thank you,' I mumbled, avoiding eye contact as I strode past.

The foyer was spacious and cheery, with sun streaming in through a window, bisecting a row of pot plants on the sill. The far wall was lined with a row of empty plastic chairs.

Just then, an elderly woman in white with a cane, sidled up. She was looking at me expectantly.

It was a fifty-fifty call: either I was supposed to know her or not.

Neither was a problem, but I needed to know where I stood. In situations like this, a pause dramatically improves the odds of success. So, I hesitated.

'Can I help you doctor?' she eventually said.

'I... Where's the radiation ward?'

She looked confused. 'You don't...?'

'Sorry. I should know my way by now,' I muttered. 'This place is a rabbit warren.'

I scanned her chest but there was no identity card. So, I said, 'What did you say your name was again?' And waited.

'Nina,' she said, 'You saw me yesterday.'

I stared.

'I'm the patient in room 3, remember...'

'Yes, yes, of course. Nina. How are you?'

'Well, thank you,' she said with a smile, 'The new medications are helping.'

'Good, good,' I said.

Nina coughed. 'Are you looking for someone doctor?'

'Err... Actually... I need to check on another patient; the husband of a friend.'

Her eyes flashed from my face to my identity pass and back. 'His name?'

'Yuri.'

Her brow furrowed. 'Maybe he's new.'

'Yes, came in recently.'

'Sorry. Seems like I don't know everyone after all.' She chuckled, and – to my relief – walked around me.

I continued past.

But then she stopped. 'Doctor...'

I was frozen to the spot.

Her expression was quizzical. 'The radiation treatment ward is behind us. You'll...'

'Of course,' I said with a self-deprecating smile, 'I'm going mad. That's what working a double shift does.'

There was an awkward silence. I wheeled about...

'Aren't you going to suit up, doctor?'

'Of course,' I said. 'Silly me.'

'Don't worry if you've forgotten,' she said, 'I've seen the other visiting doctor get gowns and masks from the nursing station. This lot that came in over the weekend are getting the royal treatment.' The hint of a knowing smile formed on her lips. She pointed behind me. 'That way, remember...' And with that, she *tap-tapped* away and down another corridor.

Busybody, I thought, I'd better hurry; Dr Yudin might already be looking for her coat.

Above the entrance to the far corridor was the universal symbol for radiation in a black and yellow triangle. Instinctively, I clutched my stomach with both hands.

I glided across the polished slate floor into the corridor, slowing before the first ward doors, which were half ajar. My heart leapt. Could I have found Yuri? Carefully, I poked my head in.

Six beds were crammed into a space smaller than a normal private room. The poor men lay cheek by jowl, the taller ones with their feet hanging over the ends of their beds. The floor was littered with crumpled sheets, tissues, and dirty plates and the place had the smell of death. Absurdly, I felt no dread or fear that my husband would be one of these disfigured, about-to-die ogres breathing like thirsty radiators. I was still in that blessed state of naïveté of those who think such calamities only happen to others.

'Please,' the nearest patient groaned when he saw me. 'More medicine.'

As I turned to him, I had to suppress a gasp. His neck and face had brown and pink splotches and both arms were bandaged. His eyes were pleading. I moved from patient to patient, inspecting faces. 'Not Yuri, not Yuri,' I muttered, until the last, who was wrapped to the chin like a mummy and again from the forehead. What was visible of the face too disfigured for his features to be distinguishable, but there was something familiar.

'Yurochka?' I mumbled, as my hand extended. 'Is it you, my darling?'

'Don't touch!'

I froze.

'Turn around, now, or I'll call security.'

Slowly, I turned. The voice belonged to a woman of about forty, dressed in green trousers and a white blouse. Her face looked familiar, but I couldn't place it.

She pointed at my chest. 'Where did you get that?'

'I… err… I can explain.'

'You'd better.'

I figured the game was up, so I told her I was an evacuee from Pripyat, looking for my husband feared lost in the accident; and that the authorities had left me no choice but to steal into the hospital.

'What's his name?' she asked.

I hesitated.

If I gave Yuri's name, I could potentially expose myself, and by extension Sergey, Angelov and their network. But if I didn't, how could she confirm his presence? So I told her.

She closed and opened her eyes, her face pained. Then she shut the door behind her, approached me. 'My dear lady,' she said, 'I'm afraid...'

I followed her gaze to the furthest bed. Oh, no... Empty.

A sense of horror engulfed me. As if the bottom was falling out of my world.

'I didn't treat him,' she said, still gazing at the bed.

'Who then?'

'Doctor Abrikosov. Unfortunately, he's no longer here. He was transferred back to Hospital Number Six. Departed last night. An emergency, apparently.'

I slumped.

But she delved into her top pocket. 'He gave me a copy of this – in case you came.'

I unfolded the note. *Certificate of Death* was all I could read before my eyes misted.

'I'm sorry,' Dr Yudin said, 'I'm told he passed peacefully in the early hours.'

I felt dizzy. My spirit was spiralling, down, down, down... The past few days of uncertainty had done nothing to prepare me. News of his death had a finality for which I was wholly unprepared.

Dr Yudin placed her hand on my shoulder. 'It's for the better; he was in a bad way.'

I stared at the bed. It was empty, even of sheets, with only a folded blanket at the end. I was reeling, or maybe it was the room, because the strip lights above me began to rotate like the blades of a fan. I felt a terrible sense of abandonment, knowing I was now utterly alone.

'Where did they take him?' I stammered.

She shrugged. 'I don't know; some secure site. Not even relatives are allowed. They've declared the bodies state assets.'

I winced. 'But... I want to see him!'

'I'm afraid I can't help you,' she said. 'But it's better you don't see his body. People have nightmares. Here, look.' She stepped toward the mummified patient and peeled the bandage a couple of centimetres from the chest. The skin didn't look burnt but soft and formless like old cheese. My first reaction was horror.

'Your husband had this over much of his body. But take heart, his suffering was limited. Anaesthetics are sophisticated these days; he was barely conscious in the end.' She replaced the bandage. 'Now, you'd better get going before security arrives.'

There was so much I wanted to ask her. What exactly had happened to Yuri, what was he like in the last days, did he call my name in his sleep…?

But all I could muster was, 'Are you sure you don't know where they took him?'

She shook her head. 'But I could enquire about the location of the burial. I'm sure there will be a plaque.'

The life of my Yuri reduced to a name engraved on a strip of metal? I wanted to cry – I still do. In the end, Yuri never even got that much.

Doctor Yudin assured me she'd make further enquiries about Yuri's body. 'Here's my number,' she said, scribbling on the back of an old prescription sheet. 'Call me at around three. Oh, and be sure to use the public phone in the park up the road. You can't miss it, beside a shady park where *stariki* sit at tables playing chess and smoking.'

Before I could object, she gently retrieved her white coat from me, took me by the elbow and steered me down the passage to the elevator and all the way past the guard house to the street. I was left marvelling at her kindness. And this toward a stranger who'd dared to steal her coat and impersonate her. Grace defined.

I left the hospital and wandered about the nearby streets in a stupor, feeling like the last pillar supporting my life had been yanked out from under me and I was falling, falling. I stared forlornly at the shop windows and crowded cafés. The sight of friends chatting and couples together compounded my pain.

Eventually, I stole a glance at my watch. It was two fifteen. I had time to kill. Then I recalled Dr Yudin's instruction to call from the park.

263

I wondered why she'd been so specific about the time and place. But did it matter?

On I drifted up the street, careful not to linger in one place or stray from the anonymity of the crowd. Sooner or later, I'd have to return to the apartment and face Angelov. But first I needed to exhaust all other avenues of finding Yuri. Part of me still didn't fully trust her... or anybody.

I found the park, though it was more of an enclave. Sure enough, there were two tables of *stariki* in a cloud of tobacco smoke with a phone booth behind them. I passed by and continued to wander the streets until ten to three.

As I returned my doubts grew. For one thing, most public phones in Sovetsky Soyuz didn't even work. So, it was with heightened anxiety that I entered the phone booth and lifted the receiver. My free hand shook so much that my index finger kept missing the digits. Once I got it right, the ringing seemed endless and I started to wonder if she'd given me the right number. Then, all of a sudden, I was through.

'Yes?'

'Doctor Yudin, please,' I blurted.

Silence. 'I'm afraid there's no-one by that name.'

I varied the spelling.

'Sorry. I'd know her. We're a small team.'

'Impossible! Someone must know her. A middle-aged doctor.' But it was to no avail.

I staggered away from the phone booth, defeated. In a daze I slumped onto the nearest bench, hugging myself for comfort, fighting back angry tears. I had left it too late; I should have tried harder to find Yuri earlier. Why, why did I obey Angelov and stay home? Now it was too late: the worst had happened. Yuri had died alone without me ever finding him. I had wasted my chance. How could I possibly live with myself?

As I gazed blankly in front of me, numb all over, I gradually became aware of something moving closer. A turquoise jacket.

I raised my eyes, confused. One of the chess players was standing facing me now, leaning on his stick. 'Comrade Zhukov?'

264

He pointed at the empty bench. 'Mind if I join you?'

I shifted to make space and stared vacantly at my feet as he sat alongside. We sat in silence, just as when we first met in the suburbs. It felt like a lifetime ago.

'And?' he said at last.

I stared at the ground. A pigeon hopped toward my feet.

'Any luck?' he ventured again.

I had nothing left to say.

'Silly girl! You must have known we'd follow you. You still think you know better? That you can beat the system alone? Why did you do it? You could have ruined everything.'

'To find my husband,' I choked.

'And did you?'

I swallowed. 'He's dead.'

'You saw his body?'

I shook my head. 'The doctor—'

'Probably said you couldn't see his body, that the authorities have it.'

I looked up, confused.

'I told her what to say.'

I stared.

'She's one of us.'

'Oh.'

Finally, it was dawning on me why Dr Yudin had insisted on me using this specific phone.

Zhukov struggled up. 'Come with me.'

I made no move.

'Come.' He pointed at the metro with a trace of a wry smile. 'It's time I took you underground.'

'But...'

Something in his manner rekindled a glimmer of hope inside me. 'It will become clearer. Follow me.'

My heart seemed to flutter. Or maybe it was you, Katyusha. I stood up and followed.

We passed through the turnstile, down an escalator. He was ahead of me, walking along the platform at a surprising clip. Then he suddenly doubled back, and we were going up again, then down to another platform, where a train was grinding to stop alongside. We boarded, walked through to the next compartment, and slipped off again to wait behind a pillar for the next train. We rode it for a couple of stops to Universytet Station where we switched lines and rode until Arsenalna. There we alighted and headed down endless escalators. Arsenalna, situated directly beneath a bank of the Dnieper, was exceptionally deep.

Along the way, I pressed Zhukov for an explanation, but he fobbed me off. Eventually, we surfaced on a stately boulevard parallel to the river. First it ran straight; then it kinked and passed a long, shady park.

Residents were out enjoying May Day on the lawns or picnicking beneath the trees. In a sunlit spot, two lovers lay side by side on their backs chewing clover. I felt a pang of pain.

Then I noticed a boy polishing a red apple on his shirt and lifting it up to bite. I couldn't help but think of the cloud of radiation.

'No!' I shouted.

'*Shh!*' Zhukov hissed. 'Don't draw attention.'

On he strode. God knows how such an old man could be so sprightly. Eventually, the park gave way to a whitewashed wall of thick stones twice my height. Now and then through a crack I glimpsed the onion domes of an ancient monastery. 'Kiyevo-Pecherskaya Lavra?' I gasped, thinking of another of Babushka's favourites – the Orthodox holy of holies, where St Anthony had supposedly dug his home into the banks of the Dnieper.

Finally, we arrived at a wooden door with a brass handle, above which was a stone arch. Zhukov glanced about furtively, rapped on the door and then put his ear to it. A murmur came from within. He coughed twice and waited. There was a rattle; a sliver of light appeared around the edge of the door and very slowly it creaked open.

He stepped inside, and I followed. Before us towered a cassocked, hooded figure covered head to toe in a black robe pleated below the waist like a dress.

The door creaked closed under its own weight. After stooping to lock it, the priest led us into a courtyard, where we crunched across the gravel. We strode past a sanctuary, rounded a corner, passed what looked like a dormitory, then a library, various stores and a workshop. It was as if we'd entered a medieval village.

As we followed the priest through the grounds I noticed a series of faded-gold domes to the left and far below, another church with a green buckled roof below that, beyond which a vast canopy of trees stretched down to the snake of the Dnieper, old mother river. Its water was the same blue as the sky and streaked with islands, with a wide beach on the far bank.

We paused at a bronze statue of two men. Cyril and Methodius, the priest told us. 'The Greek missionaries who brought us the light. And our alphabet, of course.'

Along a cobbled path we continued, down, down, past trellised vines and pink-blossomed orchards. Finally, we reached a level platform set against the bank, after which the ground fell away to yield a panorama of the river and the other half of the city beyond. The priest turned ninety degrees and walked straight toward a near-vertical bank. I thought he would bump his head but at the last moment he brushed aside a drape, stooped and disappeared, followed by Zhukov. I was left gaping. Until I remembered – perhaps from Babushka, or from school – about the network of underground tunnels and caves on the bank of the Dnieper.

Again, I vacillated. I couldn't face yet another disappointment. But what choice did I have? Inside was a cave with just room enough for a narrow table and chair, where a younger priest sat writing on a scroll by candlelight. The same man, I could swear, accepted my entrance fee twenty-five years later and handed me a beeswax candle, while I muttered, 'My house shall be called a house of prayer, but you have made it a den of thieves.'

The priest looked up, acknowledged us with a nod and handed us each a candle, before resuming his writing. Our priest-guide thanked him, brushed aside a sack of hessian, and stepped into the dark beyond, with Zhukov and me in his wake. The tunnel was barely wide enough for single file, and the rock floor was heavily footworn. We descended, one twist after another. With every step the air grew warmer and closer, and I grew more disorientated. I must have fallen into a trance because at a point I became aware that I was alone, save for the distant scraping of feet. I sped up, faster until…

Bam! I bashed into Zhukov and my candle toppled. All I could see now was the outline of his back hunched over something. As my eyes adjusted, I could make out a waist-high cabinet with a smooth flat surface. Ignoring me, he genuflected, then stooped.

I fished around for my candle and struggled to relight it on his, which he'd placed on the floor.

'*Blin*!' I muttered.

'Shh…'

What were we doing here? If there was any glimmer of hope that Yuri was still alive, time was of the essence. I couldn't endure any more delays. I leaned around for a better look.

Impossible! I thought. I was staring through a glass cover at the unmistakable shape of a corpse – a short, shrivelled figure, lying on his back.

'Quiet,' Zhukov cautioned. Then he bent, kissed the glass and straightened. 'St Gregory,' he said. 'Revered for keeping a vow of silence.'

It was too much. I shoved my way past him, turned around, and glared. 'You're just leading me on, aren't you?'

He genuflected yet again, as if I didn't exist.

'This is a trap, isn't it!' I continued. 'You and Angelov are just another arm of the organs, I know it!'

He kissed the glass face again.

I was furious. 'So, I'm right!'

He slowly straightened. 'My dear…'

'Don't patronise me,' I spat, 'I know your modus operandi.' Something had snapped inside me. 'First, I have a fall. Then a charming man shows up dangling knee surgery and threatening my *babushka*. Next I'm forced to accompany my husband to a dump in the forest to almost die of isolation. So you send me a 'best friend' who's also one of you lot!'

'Zhukov placed his hand on my wrist. 'You've got it all wrong.'

'Hah! You're all the same. Then that thug Yavlinsky couldn't get enough information from me, so they sent Dermichev, and now you, just to lure me here and have me arrested. And all to get at Yuri.'

He placed his candle on the casing and looked at me. 'Are you finished?'

I nodded.

'Good. Now, if we were going to arrest you, it would have been a lot easier when you trespassed on hospital grounds, or skipped roll call on arrival in Kiev. And why would Sergey risk his career, if not his life, to spring you from Dermichev?'

He had a point. But I wasn't about to believe him that easily.

'Look, you need to trust me. There's no benefit to us in helping you. It would spare us a great deal of risk and trouble if we didn't have to arrange your emigration.'

I hesitated.

'You're free to leave,' he said. 'You can turn around and walk back the way we came; it's impossible to get lost, we haven't passed any side tunnels yet. And don't worry; I'll tell Sergey of your decision; though I doubt you'll see him again, anyway. Thanks to your carelessness he's now in danger of being court-martialled at a minimum.'

I stared. His face was in shadow, but I could tell he was serious. Yuri's words came to me, to trust only Sergey. Could I believe this man? My bravado crumbled and I was fighting panic.

'My dear girl…' his tone was softer now. He put a hand on my shoulder. 'I don't blame you for distrusting everyone and everything; it's not a bad starting point. I can't imagine the conflicted emotions you must be experiencing right now.' He picked up his candle. 'Come, it will be clearer soon. Have faith.' And he started shuffling down the passage.

And of course I went! Wouldn't you, my little dove? We go where there's hope. Also called faith, Zhukov's final word. Perhaps it was a relic from my childhood that decided me, hanging onto the coat-tails of Babushka's faith. Aided by a setting seeped in millennia of belief: shelters like the Lavra had kept the candle of the gospel flickering through many a tyranny. Communism was by no means the first, nor will it be the last. Think of the centuries under Mongol rule. My darling, when you eventually travel to Kiev, please do the pilgrimage, if not in faith, then for me.

Now I must call it a night. I'm exhausted again. I'm afraid it's a near permanent state now; I'm getting tired of saying I'm tired! But don't worry, we're into the final stretch.

Twenty-three

Dobro vecher, maya daragaya, Katyusha.

Sorry; toward the end it seems I'm reverting to familiar things – like my mother tongue. It's like becoming a child again. Life becomes smaller. It's hard not to notice the shrinking in a place like this. I don't mind, though. We're all just pilgrims in this weary land. How much does a person need to be happy, anyway? Apart from good relationships.

The trick is not to shrink your mind or spirit. That's why these conversations are so good for me: I'm forced to revisit the expanses I once strode. And vast they were – the two greatest empires the world has ever known and the biggest stage.

You'll notice my breathing is laboured now. They've upped my morphine. But it's still not enough!

Anyway, let me continue while I still can.

I was hurrying to keep up with the two older men down that warm, dark tunnel toward a smudge of non-darkness. After what felt like an eternity of bends, I saw a light ahead. The air seemed fresher, and a cave opened before me.

From the altar and icons the space probably served as a sanctuary. Then from the far end of the cave below a kerosene lamp came a soft grunt. I strained but I couldn't see anything obvious.

'Come over here, my dear.' It was the priest's voice from the same direction.

Tentatively, I shuffled forward. The priest was kneeling beside a low bed, his shoulder illuminated by a lamp hung on the wall. A copper wash basin lay on the floor below the light, and, beside it, a towel.

'Closer,' the priest urged.

I was confused, but I obeyed.

'He sleeps a lot lately.'

I felt my heart throbbing against my ribcage.

'Who is it?' I ventured, careful not to hope.

'Come, Vanya,' Zhukov piped up. 'Let's give them some privacy. Time is short.'

The priest stood, lifting his cassock. 'We'll give you a few minutes alone.' He shuffled past me, his hem dragging on the floor.

I turned. The two men stooped into a side tunnel.

'No,' I cried. 'Don't leave me alone like this!'

But they ignored me and disappeared.

Confused and frightened, I edged toward the bed. In the shadows I could make out a body. It was covered to the shoulders by a blanket and the head was propped by a pillow with a wet towel draped over the brow. Above me the lamp swung gently, casting a flicker across the face. I battled to discern features, except that the person's skin was dark and splotched and... had heavy stubble. A man, I thought, my spirits daring to rise. And a sheen on his brow. I froze. The silence in the cave was absolute. Finally, I summoned enough courage to bend... I gasped. The large head and square jaw were his... I bent further. The face was too heavily scarred to be sure, so I turned my ear and listened. The breathing was rhythmical but laboured.

'Yuri?'

He didn't respond. The stillness felt oppressive. A half-light flickered.

Then I thought I caught his scent. Every man has one. But there was no sign of movement. I was shaking, convinced I was too late, that I'd been abandoned, finally, and for all time, tricked by the organs or their lackies. A setup. And the worst was, I felt I deserved it. Wretch that I am.

I took the kerosene lamp off its hook and – with a trembling hand – held it over the face.

'Yuri?' I cried.

But there was no movement or sound. I wasn't even sure he was breathing now. And immediately, I was doubting again, thinking he was dead. What a cruel trick. I set the lamp back on its hook, bent and kissed his cheek and...

I felt the tickle of air on my nose. A breath? I placed my hand on his cheek. It was warm! Or was it the air in the cave? 'My darling,' I murmured. 'Don't go, not now; and if you must, just know that I came.'

His lips were moving! Or was it a play of light?

There was a murmur, which turned to a muttering. Even though it sounded like gibberish, I wanted to shout with joy.

His head shifted. The breathing grew hoarse.

'Shh...' I said, patting the pillow beside his head.

He relaxed, his head sinking back. I took the damp cloth and stroked his forehead. 'Yuriok... tell me it's you.'

He appeared to be trying to lift his head, but the effort was too weak. 'Lenochka...'

'So, it is you,' I murmured, 'my darling.'

His chin tilted in a nod.

At which point I knew for sure that it was my Yuri and he was alive.

'What happened? Why?' I said. My shock had already morphed from disbelief to anger. God knows, I wish I'd reacted otherwise. If I'd realised how little time was left, I'd have dropped down, there and then, and kissed every exposed square millimetre of his face – sores or none – and his neck and beyond, and then I'd have lain down beside him and held his hand like we used to do when trying to fall asleep. But instead, I just repeated that single word question. 'Why,' I said, ' Why did you do this to me? Why, why, why?'

And I'm still asking!

Then I softened a little, running my thumb down his cheek. 'The doctor told me you'd died.'

He tried to rise, but only managed to lift his head a fraction before it slumped back onto the pillow. His lips were moving but all I heard was a gurgle.

'My darling, I've tried so hard to find you,' I cried, 'please believe me. From the moment I woke and realised you weren't in bed beside me. I searched everywhere. I even tried to get to the plant. I'd never have left Pripyat if I'd known...'

'I know,' he croaked.

'But... how?'

'It doesn't matter.'

'But I need to know!' I was almost shouting.

He coughed. So wet and hoarse that it frightened me. 'You should conserve your breath.'

'It's okay,' he said, 'I'll rally. I've felt better today, believe it or not. I was just sleeping when you came. They say a remission is normal before the end.'

I waited.

He continued, his voice clearer. 'I was taking measurements beside the reactor when… the control rods didn't work. The opposite. They caused a power surge. No one could have predicted… I got trapped in the rubble. Fortunately, one of our people extracted me.' He paused to cough.

'My angel… I've missed you so much.' I was trying to sound reassuring, but something about his look terrified me – his neck and face above the stubble were covered in splotches, and his expression was gaunt. The look of death, though I hadn't learned to recognise it yet.

My practical nature kicked in.

'My darling,' I said, rising. 'Let's get you to a doctor.'

'No…' he groaned. His hand lifted and slumped.

'Why not? Look at you. You must be in agony.'

'I just came from the hospital – last night.'

'But…' And then it dawned on me. I said, 'Dr Yudin?'

He nodded.

'How did you get out of the hospital? It's a fortress.'

'In a hearse.'

I stared.

He smiled. 'You could say, I'm already dead.'

'No! Darling, don't joke like that.'

'They've done all that's possible.'

'I won't accept it!' I cried. 'As you always say, there's nothing science can't resolve.'

'I was wrong.'

What? My proud husband admitting to an error?

'No,' I said, 'There's got to be something.'

274

'They think I took up to a thousand milliroentgen per hour.'

'Okay,' I said, daubing his forehead with the cloth. 'But don't say words like that over yourself.'

'I'm dying, Lenochka.'

'No!'

'Come closer,' he wheezed, 'So, I can see you properly. I want to take the memory of your face with me into eternity.'

Strange, I thought, my most ardent rationalist defaulting to the mystic.

I bent down until our faces were within centimetres, but then hesitated.

'Don't worry,' he said, reading my mind. 'Radiation at these levels is only harmful if it's sustained. Let's treasure these few minutes we have alone.'

I bent further but stopped just short of his face.

He struggled to raise his arm, and with a quivering fingertip, stroked my face. 'My little bird...' he breathed, 'how I love every millimetre of you. My God, you're an angel; I'd forgotten how beautiful... Did I tell you I adore you, that no woman ever came close?'

In the moment, instead of bathing in the delight of those words that every lover wants to hear, my spirit was in anguished confusion.

'What's wrong?' he said.

Everything, I wanted to shout. Never mind that I'd just been reunited with the love of my life, all I could think of was that petty, unproven indiscretion.

'Out with it,' he said. Dying or not, he could still read me like a book.

'You were having an affair with Sonya, weren't you?' I blurted.

No response.

'Don't try to deny it this time, Yuriol.'

He grimaced, as if from pain. Then his body slackened; it was as though the fight had gone out of him.

Immediately, I felt dreadful, like a coward who spears a stricken warrior.

And then, from the shadows, he spoke up, in that measured, emotionless way of the rationalist.

'I can promise there was no affair.'

'Yuri don't...'

'Shh... Yes, she's attractive and she turns men's heads. And yes, she flirted with me. Day in and day out. Especially at work. You know we were on shift together.'

I winced.

'I showed no interest, but she wouldn't let up.'

I waited, holding my breath.

'She seemed so determined. Finally, she cornered me on the balcony at that office party. Unfortunately, there was no one else around, and she started kissing and touching me.'

'*Suka!*' I swore.

'But I didn't want any other woman, Lenochka. I had you. I managed to extract myself.'

'You promise?'

'I promise, Lenochka.'

'How often did you end up kissing her?' I blurted, still burning with jealousy. I had to know.

'Just that once. I made sure she could never corner me again.'

He exhaled. 'I'd long suspected that Yavlinsky was using her as bait to get me fired. He was desperate to get rid of me. I think they were in cahoots. I even doubt it was a coincidence she was sunbathing at the amusement park on Friday. They knew where we walked at that time of day.'

I was stunned. The possibility of Yavlinsky's complicity hadn't crossed my mind.

We sat in silence. The candle sizzled. When he spoke again, it was with difficultly.

'I love you, Lena. Only you. Why don't you trust me?'

'Of course I do!' I cried. And I meant it then, with all my heart.

I took his hand and gently squeezed it. And he smiled!

Ah, that impish grin... As only your father was capable of. A person couldn't help but smile with him. I realise that I've hardly spoken these past weeks of the happy times. We had so many! Picnicking beside the river, fossicking in the forest, paddling in his double canoe, dance lessons on Saturday evenings at the Palace of Culture…

And then he winked. The light wasn't the best, but I saw it – no doubt. 'Will you kiss me?' he asked.

I recoiled. 'But I thought…?'

'If we're quick, the exposure will be minimal. Come, just once, for me to take to the next life.'

I was shaking, almost convulsing with fear, until I got within a whisker of his lips and then I stopped. And drew back.

Coward. Why didn't I believe him? He was a nuclear physicist. I could bury myself with regret.

My darling, if you learn nothing else from this sorry tale… Don't let fear be your ruler. It was the thorn in my side, but it doesn't have to be yours. You're your own person. Yes, you inherited many of my genes, but an equal measure from your father, and he didn't even know how to spell fear. This was the only time I saw the slightest chink in his armour, when he must have sensed the final abyss approaching. But who wouldn't be afraid of facing eternity?

Just then, Yuri coughed, violently this time, and struggled to sit up a few centimetres higher on his pillow. Then he glanced at my stomach. 'How is he coming along?'

'How do you know it's not a girl?'

'I don't. I'd love nothing more than a daughter. I'm sure she'll be every bit as beautiful as her mother. A beauty queen!'

We laughed.

'Except that would be a waste,' he said.

He hated pretence, and valued intelligence above all. Like you, my darling, daddy's girl. Ah, there's so much I still want to tell you about your father. But I'm exhausted. Every word seems like an effort. As it must have been for Yuri that day. Fortunately, he wasn't one to waste words.

An awkward silence had descended between Yuri and me. The lamp hissed and flickered.

'Are you still determined to...?'

I shook my head and saw the glow in his eyes.

'What made you change your mind?'

I paused to think. There were so many reasons, I realised. 'I can feel her moving inside me,' I told him. 'I've fallen in love with her.'

He reached a trembling hand to my belly. 'Promise me,' he said, 'when our daughter is old enough to understand, that you'll tell her not to believe the lies they'll spread about me, my associates, and our cause.'

I nodded, though I didn't really understand.

I still don't, fully.

He reached his shaking hand to the floor, lifted a glass of water and took a sip, spilling it slightly. 'And tell her that her daddy stroked her forehead once, and told her how much he loved her and always would.'

The floodgates of my emotions finally broke and the tears flowed. 'Don't talk like that,' I begged between sobs. 'You're going to overcome this; you're the strongest man I know.'

He gave a wan smile and passed his glass to me to put on the floor. The lamp flickered.

'Yuri?'

'Yes.'

'There's something I have to tell you.'

It was my turn to confess. I still tremble at the thought. My transgressions made his admission as trivial as frowning at a school picnic. So heinous they were that for three long decades, I've kept them buried.

'What is it?' Yuri said.

'I... there's something... I couldn't live with myself if I didn't tell you before...' I wiped my nose with my sleeve and try to compose myself.

'There's no need,' he said evenly.

'But... no... I must, I...'

'I already know.'

I stared at him. 'You mean...'

'Everything. And why.'

From far off, down a tunnel, I heard a faint chanting. I shivered.

'Sergey urged me to divorce you,' he croaked. 'Three months into our marriage. Their people in the organs had investigated you.'

I was stunned.

'By then I was hopelessly in love with you,' he continued. 'So, I refused. First, I wouldn't listen. Then, when the evidence was irrefutable, I convinced them it was better the devil I knew than the one I didn't.'

'The devil part was right,' I said, averting my eyes.

'Don't be so hard on yourself. I know why you did it.'

'It's no excuse. I—'

'You were protecting your grandmother, Lenochka.'

I had to choke back the tears. It was dawning on me how much he loved me. Not only had he not exposed me; he'd indulged me, protected me even, let me see or hear things about his job that he deemed inconsequential, just so I had things to report to my handlers, first Ivanov, then Yavlinsky. My only consolation was that my betrayal played no significant part in the failed test and the explosion. Or Sergey's fate.

Then – typical of Yuri – just as he had me scrambling to catch up, his train of argument took an unexpected turn. 'Did you read my letter?' he asked.

I kept my expression deadpan. 'What letter?'

'Don't pretend. From my valuables in my drawer. I know you used to scratch there. So, I left you a message. The last letter in the bunch.'

'But we were evacuated.'

He frowned. 'Stop lying to me, Lena.'

'But...?'

'Our people were at the apartment, after you left via the fire escape.'

I fell silent. Another piece of the puzzle had just fallen into place. Though the ransacking of our apartment must have been Dermichev's or Yavlinsky's men, the men who surprised me there were from Sergey's hardliners. 'I'm sorry,' I said. 'I had no business...'

'This isn't the time. Just tell me you read it.'

'The others yes... But I was interrupted after the love letter – from that bitch who broke your heart.'

'Funny…' He coughed. 'I suppose a bit of jealousy shows you care.' His eyelids flickered, then closed for a few seconds, then reopened. I gently shook him awake.

'Sorry. The medication… it causes me to drift off.'

I was startled by a cough from behind. I swivelled about. Zhukov and the priest stood in the entrance.

'He'll fall asleep any moment,' the priest said. 'He's rallied for you, but I'm afraid he's weak. Dr Yurin said she'd be surprised if he makes it till tomorrow. We're so sorry.'

I felt a hand on my wrist. It was Yuri's. He tugged me closer. 'Come here my darling.'

I leaned closer and stroked his forehead. He struggled his head up a centimetre or two. 'So, you never read my letter – to you,' he whispered. 'But you have it?'

'Yes.'

He struggled for breath. 'In a safe place?'

'With Angelov.'

'Good. After this, you must return. Don't worry; she knows you're here. Then read the letter. Promise me you will. It will explain the rest. Enough of it, anyway. Some of it not even Zhukov can know.'

'Okay,' I said to please him.

To be honest, Katyusha, even after reading his letter that night in Angelov's apartment, I was confused. I suppose he had to keep his written words to a minimum in case the letter fell into the wrong hands. How I wished I'd read it before, that night I found it in our Pripyat apartment! I could have asked him to elaborate now. What I did learn from the letter though, was that Yuri was part of a team tasked with developing a space-based missile defence system to match the threat of America's Star Wars programme. They'd done the conceptual design and tested it with a prototype at Arzamas, so the KGB was aware of the project. Which meant it must have been sanctioned by the Kremlin, if not the General Secretary himself.

Yes, the same man lauded by the West for championing disarmament! In fairness, he might have approved it in principle, but the project was run by a distinct grouping within the military industrial complex, headed by a member of the Politburo Yuri didn't name. He said that Yavlinsky's faction of the KGB wasn't privy to the research but desperate to learn more.

Interestingly, Dermichev had been sent to Pripyat by the General Secretary or his loyalists in the Politburo to find out what was going on with the project they now regarded as having gone rogue – under the cover of investigating Yavlinsky's procurement racket.

Then Yuri's letter got a bit technical for me. Something about key components of their missile defence system being designed based on nuclear fusion-based technology, which promised to give it a massive advantage over Star Wars. The reason he needed to be in Chernobyl was that some processes couldn't be validated in a laboratory; they needed the infrastructure of a full-scale conventional reactor. But along the way, the hardliners – represented chiefly by Yuri's boss and Sergey, though they weren't named in the letter – had tried to recruit Yuri to their cause. What convinced him was the ability to continue his research and testing on the missile defence system and the opportunity to test and fix the design flaws of the RBMK-1000 reactor. This was clearly his greatest concern – the safety of the country's nuclear industry. His bosses at Arzamas had been warning Moscow of the dangers for years.

In his letter, Yuri even quoted the chief designer of the reactor who said, when admitting to problems, that 'we ourselves lie and teach our subordinates to lie, and no good will come of this.'

'The long and the short of it is,' Yuri said, 'Reactor Number Four's turbine test was a terrible failure. Instead of saving our nuclear industry, it's going to give Gorbachev's men a perfect excuse to scale it back.'

He sighed. 'We knew there was a risk. But it was calculated. We had to try. Something like this or far worse would have happened anyway. Almost certainly. You only have to look at the track record.'

'My darling...' I lightly stroked his arm. 'You did what you knew was right. No one can take that away from you.'

'Regardless,' he said. 'There'll be reprisals. Against those involved and their families. Chiefly me. But we planned for this eventuality. Which is why you must leave the country.'

'And Sergey?' I said. 'Will he be court-martialled?'

'Perhaps. He's reconciled to the worst. I'd say there is an even chance he'll be all right. He has friends in high places – in both factions. And there's no tangible evidence to link him other than our friendship.'

'But what about Dermichev – he's a KGB colonel; they don't forget; trust me.'

'Lena, Lena… Do you think we could have sprung you from custody and arranged for your emigration without support from the Politburo? Or expunged my file? Funny to think I'll be interned down here, like a saint. Alongside an urn with the ashes of every formula, notebook and design sheet of ours that we've incinerated.'

'Stop,' I urged. He was breathing heavily. 'Don't talk like that.'

Of course, at that point, I didn't know what he was talking about, but I listened anyway.

'Like our hardware…' Yuri continued. 'Which by now would be buried under superheated reactor fuel and tonnes of boron and sand by now.' Then he sank back onto the bed. The rest seemed to invigorate him because his eyes lit up and he said, 'Mark my words, Lena, there will be enquiry after enquiry. Scientists in the West discovered the radiation long before our people had a clue. It will be Gorbachev's undoing. They won't take his glasnost seriously unless he allows their inspectors. Serves him right, the charlatan; it's just a pity the Russian people all have to suffer for….' He coughed, picked up the glass of water and drank. His head was visible in the light now, and I could see he was almost bald.

'But as I said, there'll be scapegoats,' he continued. 'The operators, engineers… And, even if my colleagues manage to bury all the evidence associating me with the tests, there'll be rumours. My memory will be tarnished, and with it yours. That's why you must go; make a new life.' He fell silent, then he drew breath and continued. 'Promise me you'll explain all this to our child. Tell her that all her father ever wanted was a safer world, where one superpower can never gain unlimited power

282

over another. And that technology itself is never inherently bad, only the people that abuse it.'

'I promise,' I said. Then I knelt by the bed and lay my cheek on his chest. With my eyes closed I took in the scent of him, and the sound of his laboured breathing.

I didn't care about the sores on his neck, or the folds of mouldy skin, I just wanted to lie alongside the man I'd always loved one last time. And I've never regretted it.

'Don't be sad,' Yuri whispered hoarsely, 'You can make a new life. You're young and my God you're beautiful. You can dance again. And there'll be other men.'

'Never!' I cried. 'All other men can only be cheap imitations after you.'

And that's how it's been, Katyusha. And I'm not just talking of the work I had to endure to provide for us in this country – all those businessmen and slobbering adulterers ogling. And as for that good-for-nothing drunk who had the audacity to pretend he was your father, I have nothing more to say.

Anyway, after that I butterfly-kissed your father on the forehead and told him I'd always love him. I also promised him I'd keep our child and – if a girl – use the name Yuri in her patronymic. Oh, my darling... have I ever told you you've got his eyes – blue, cold blue like the Baltic, his chevrons on your cheeks, and that I see him in you every time you laugh?

And oh how proud your father would be of you – a scientist twice published in *Nature* during her twenties!

Back then in Sovetsky Soyuz we didn't have serious environmental activism yet, unlike in the West; the challenges were different; renewable energy wasn't a viable option, and people had to be warmed, society powered. And I'd argue that his work did more for the environment than anyone's if he played even a bit part in preventing a nuclear con-flagration.

I imagine you'll be sceptical, girl. Fortunately, I kept his letter. It's folded in my bible. It's in Cyrillic, of course, but you can find a translator at the club; or google it; but be careful: Russian is a language of nuances. Or post it on social media if you like: no one will believe it.

Sorry for my yawning again; but I'm exhausted. Oh, if I could just hold your hand again; I have a premonition I may not last the night.

But don't cry. My darling… I never wanted to burden you with this heavy load, but I promised your father. And I hope you feel that the telling has brought us closer. It's a good thing. Never let a lack of forgiveness rule you in life or from the grave.

Believe it or not, I did try to start this conversation with you several times over the years. But either you weren't ready to hear it, or I wasn't ready to tell. And actually, a catastrophe of such proportions needs to be seen in perspective, which only time can give. For years I was too busy simply trying to survive. And the wound was too raw.

But I did eventually pluck up the courage to visit Ukraine and face down my demons. I walked the streets of that ghost town Pripyat, now reclaimed by the green, green forest I so loved. I stood on the thistle-cracked paving where your father held my hand and marvelled at the Ferris wheel on the evening this tale began. The other tourists in our group had dispersed to look for keepsakes, perhaps, or take photos, so I had the place all to myself. Amazingly, the bumper cars were still there, in red, green and yellow – my happy colours. And, guess what: I saw the Yavlinsky boy's ghost, I swear I did, teetering on the railing. He looked at me with those brown, believing eyes, and then toppled…

When the tour guide found me, he asked why I was crying. Hay fever, I told him. Because over the years I've learned that people don't want to know about our sorrows unless they've healed. Then I took one last look at the Ferris wheel. The structure had rusted, but the buttercup cars were still dangling, bright and yellow.

Acknowledgements

I would like to thank the following people who helped make this novel possible: my wife Melissa Sutherland for early reader feedback, proofreading, and for all her love, support and encouragement; Margaret Molenaar and Dr Sara Pienaar for reading and commenting on the early manuscript; Dr Irina Filatova, Dzvinka Kachur, Lara Kovalevskaya, the NovaMova Language School in Kyiv and Dr Elina Komarova-Tagar for insights into Ukrainian and Russian history, culture and language; Barbara Erasmus for providing a reader's report and help with the narrative; my editor Gwen Hewett for her professionalism, expertise and unwavering commitment to editing, shaping and structuring the novel; Monique Cleghorn for designing such a beautiful cover and the typesetting; to the team at Protea Distribution including Phil West and Remona Voges for market feedback; and finally my mother, Charmian Sutherland, to whom this book is dedicated, for proofreading the final manuscript and for her constant love and belief in me and my crazy dream to be a novelist.

During my research I read scores of books, articles and reports on the Chernobyl accident, Ukraine, the Soviet Union, the Cold War and other related subjects. This is by no means an exhaustive list, but some of those I found most useful include *Second-Hand Time: The Last of the Soviets and The Chernobyl Prayer: A Chronicle of the Future* (both by Svetlana Alexievich); *The Book of Evidence* (John Banville); *Alone Together: The Story of Elena Bonner and Andrei Sakharov's Internal Exile in the Soviet Union* (Elena Bonner); *A History of Loneliness* (John Boyne); *The Diary of Anatoly Chernyaev* (Anatoly Chernyaev); *Gorbachev: Heretic in the Kremlin* (Dusko Doder and Louise Branson); *The Hidden Thread: Russia and South Africa in the Soviet Era* (Irina Filatova and Apollon Davidson); *Michael Gorbachev: Perestroika* (Michael Gorbachev);

Midnight in Chernobyl (Adam Higginbotham); *The First Socialist Society: A History of the Soviet Union from Within* (Geoffrey Hosking); *Safety Series – INSAG-7 The Chernobyl Accident: Updating of INSAG-1* (A report by the International Nuclear Safety Advisory Group); *Technological Accidents and Vulnerable Communities: Chernobyl Lessons for South Africa* (A paper by Dzvinka Kachur); *Armageddon Averted: The Soviet Collapse 1970–2000* (Stephen Kotkin); *The Chernobyl Reactor: Design Features and Reasons for Accident* (An article by Mikhail V. Malko); *Bolshoi Confidential: Secrets of the Russian Ballet from the Rule of the Tsars to Today* (Simon Morrison); *Alla Osipenko: Biography* (Alla Osipenko); *Maya Plisetskaya* (Maya Plisetskaya); *Chernobyl: History of a Tragedy and The Last Empire: The Final Days of the Soviet Union* (both by Serhii Plokhy); *Pripyat Mon Amour* (Alina Rudya); *Meltdown Inside the Soviet Economy* (Paul Craig Roberts and Karen LaFollette); *Communism in Russia and The Rise and Fall of the Soviet Union* (both by Richard Sakwa); *The Dangers of Thermonuclear War* (Andrei Sakharov); *The Threshold* (Rollan Sergienko); *Ukraine: A Blast from the Past* (An article by Patrick Smith); *The End of the Cold War, 1985–1991* (Robert Service); *The Pripyat Syndrome* (Lyubov Sirota); *The Gulag Archipelago* (Aleksandr Solzhenitsyn); *CIA Target: The USSR* (Nikolai Yakovlev). I am also indebted to the National Chornobyl Museum in Kyiv for the many hours I spent there and the wealth of information I gleaned.

About Ian Sutherland

Ian successfully debuted as a novelist in 2018 with his WW II thriller, *Featherstream* after graduating with an MA in Creative Writing from the University of Cape Town under the supervision of Etienne van Heerden. Ian's latest novel *Catastrophe* is set in the immediate aftermath of the 1986 Chernobyl Nuclear Power Disaster in Ukraine, USSR. His fascination with the event was sparked by a real-time case study in his Mechanical Engineering degree and led to several years of intensive research. Ian has an MBA from Columbia University and has worked in strategy consulting and finance in New York, Sydney and Cape Town, where he currently resides. Passionate about history and travel, Ian enjoys intense, immersive research including language studies.

Made in the USA
Monee, IL
23 November 2022